John Masters was born in Calcutta in 1914. Educated at Wellington and Sandhurst, he returned to India in 1934 to join the 4th Prince of Wales's Own Gurkha Rifles. In 1944 he commanded a brigade of General Wingate's Chindits in Burma, and later fought with the 19th Indian Division at the capture of Mandalay.

Masters retired from the army in 1948 as a lieutenant colonel with the DSO and OBE. He went to America and turned to writing. Several short stories were succeeded by *Nightrunners of Bengal*, the first of an outstanding series of novels set in British India. His most recent books are *Now, God Be Thanked*, *Heart of War*, and *By the Green of the Spring*, which formed his highly acclaimed trilogy of the Great War, *Loss of Eden*, also available in Sphere Books. John Masters died in 1983 in New Mexico.

Man of War

JOHN MASTERS

SPHERE BOOKS LIMITED
London and Sydney

First published in Great Britain by
Michael Joseph Ltd 1983
Copyright © 1983 by Bengal-Rockland Inc
Published by Sphere Books Ltd 1984
30–32 Gray's Inn Road, London WC1X 8JL

Set in 9/11 Compugraphic Plantin

Printed and bound in Great Britain by
Collins, Glasgow

Foreword

Man of War is wholly a work of fiction, and no reference is intended in it to any real person, living or dead, except that a few historical characters are mentioned. The events of the later chapters are loosely based on the Dunkirk campaign of 1940, but I have changed many events, dates, times and places, and invented others, for my purpose has been to show the flowering of Bill Miller as a field commander, not to write a history of that campaign. The events I describe *could* have taken place, and that has been enough for my purposes.

J.M.

Man of War

1

September 1935: India

Captain Bill Miller leaned back in his chair and tried to stifle a yawn. It was a hot, muggy day in September 1935. He had been general staff officer (grade 3) of the Chattarganj Military District for nearly fourteen months, and married for three. The monsoon was barely over, the air heavy and damp. Half the district staff were still up in the cool hills, others on leave. The Chattarganj garrison contained a battalion of British infantry, but half of that was also up in the hills, and would be for another month, together with nearly all the families. The district commander, Major General Sam Langton, known behind his back to most of the Indian Army as Slippery Sam, had just returned from leave, and was not in a good temper.

He was sitting now behind the big desk in his office, his staff officers grouped in a semi-circle facing him – his administrative staff officer, the A/Q, a lieutenant colonel; a lieutenant colonel from the Royal Indian Army Service Corps, which had a big depot in Chattarganj; a major from the Indian Army Ordnance Corps, which had an arsenal at Nawabshah, twenty-five miles upriver; majors from the Indian Medical Service and the Military Engineering Service; one or two others; and Bill, representing the General Staff.

The conference had been going on for an hour and a half. At last the hours of drawing *bhoosa* for unit mules were settled; the malarial precautions reviewed and updated; and the official date for termination of the hot weather decided upon. General Langton, who had been stifling some yawns himself, turned to the A/Q. 'Is that all from your side, Bingo?'

'Yes, sir.'

The general looked at Bill. 'Bill, you told me that you had a report to make. Let's have it.'

Bill opened his folder, cleared his throat and began. 'From various sources it looks as though we're going to be faced with a stepped-up level of anti-government activity in the district. Gupta went to Allahabad for that big Congress conference and the Congress high

1

command are not letting him come back – he's too soft, they think . . . or, as we think, too reasonable . . . for their new plans. They've given him an administrative job at Congress headquarters, and made Chaudhri the boss here. Chaudhri is younger, more capable, and much more ambitious. He means to turn Chattarganj into a hot spot of the civil disobedience campaign, and so make more of a name for himself.'

'Where does this information come from?' the general asked.

'Police intelligence bulletin, sir.'

The general grunted, and said, 'Go on.'

'That's about all the definite information we have. But I think it has to be decided, sir, whether headquarters should issue a policy statement about how to treat satyagraha – civil disobedience and non-cooperation . . . what precautions should be taken, for instance, by the hospital, the arsenal, the RIASC depot, and so on. There's not much the Congress-wallahs can do to the infantry battalion, especially as it's British, but they can disrupt the operations of the services quite easily. The police bulletin also warned that there is a plan being developed to subvert Indian sepoys from their loyalty.'

The service corps colonel snorted and muttered, 'If any of the buggers come near my place, they'll get a rough reception . . . and if anyone tries to stop our convoys by lying down in the road in front of the lorries, we'll just run over them. That's the only sort of thing these swine understand.'

There was a murmur of agreement round the room. Bill was about to say something when another man spoke first, the deputy assistant director of medical services, a major of the Indian Medical Service, and himself an Indian – a Parsee called Engineer. He said now, 'The Congress has found what is from their point of view a very useful weapon to use against the government – that is, non-violent non-cooperation. But we are supposed to be a civilized power. It's one thing to have the police or troops shoot men who are attacking them with spears, crowbars, axes or rocks. It's another to shoot or otherwise kill a man or woman lying unarmed in the road at your feet. We shall get a very bad world press if we do anything like that. At the same time Gandhi, Nehru, Patel and the Congress Party in general will receive worldwide publicity and sympathy. I think we have to counter non-violence with non-violence, in so far as we can.'

The doctor ended and Bill said, 'I agree with Major Engineer, sir. I also think that the more violence we use against the Congress supporters, the more likely they – or some of their more unruly members – are to resort to violence.'

'Good thing,' the RIASC colonel muttered. 'Then we could shoot them. The doc's just said it would be all right then.'

Bill said, 'I'm afraid we wouldn't get many face-to-face confrontations of that sort, sir. What we'd probably get would be derailing of trains, murders of British women travelling alone, perhaps attacks on isolated police *thanas*. If that sort of action became widespread, it would put a heavy strain on our available manpower.'

'. . . which is supposed to be training for a real war,' the general said, 'not wasting their time on Congress barnshoots. You put me up a paper, Bill, with our proposed policy on internal security measures, with special reference to this civil disobedience campaign, or whatever you want to call it. Find out what the DC and the police are going to do – what *their* policy is – before you put pen to paper. The army must not be following one course while the civil are following another. That's all, gentlemen . . .'

Bill sat in his little study at the side of the bungalow, trying to concentrate on what the *munshi* was saying. The *munshi* – teacher – was an old gentleman with a flowing white beard, a scholar of Sanskrit, Persian, Hindi and Urdu. He was sitting bare-footed and cross-legged on the sofa, his wire-rimmed glasses on the end of his nose. His voice droned on.

The lesson had already lasted three quarters of an hour and Bill's brain was tiring. He had studied Urdu when he first came out to India, years ago, and now he was also moderately fluent in Hindi. Normally he loved to hear the old man's dissertations – always in Hindi – about his people's legends and fairy tales, but . . . it had been a hard week, trying to decide just what should be done about civil disobedience, and Lesley had not been well. He had tried to get her to go up to Naini, but she had refused, just as Pauline had so many years ago, but for how different a reason. Pauline had acted the Early Christian Martyr to punish him and make him feel guilty; Lesley knew that he really needed her.

Bill interrupted the old munshi, speaking in Hindi. '*Munshi*-sahib, tell me, what do you think about us – the British – ruling your country?'

3

The old man fell silent, stroking his beard. At length he said, 'When the Moguls came, they were foreigners. It is said that even the Brahmins were not the first to rule here – that they too came from over the mountains. That is the meaning of the Ramayana, some say. It is not for me to judge, but to accept. I am a teacher.'

Bill tried again. 'But, sahib, we do not own land here, we are like birds of passage. We come for a few years, then we retire and go back to Vilayet. So what should be our policy towards the people of India. Do you expect us to stay for ever? Or should we announce a date for our going? Or announce that we will go when certain definite things have been achieved? Such as a working, democratically elected government? What?'

The old *munshi* said, 'The tiger does not announce when he will leave his kill, *huzoor*. When he is no longer hungry, he leaves. Or when he is driven away by a bigger beast.'

'Ah . . . I suppose the Congress would welcome, say, the Russians, as bigger beasts.'

'I know nothing of the Congress, *huzoor*. I am a teacher.'

Bill sighed and said, 'Well, I've had enough for today, *munshi* – sahib. Same time Tuesday.'

The old man rose, eased out of the room, slipped his feet into his slippers which he'd left outside the door and shuffled off.

Bill sat back, pushing the textbooks away from him. What to do now? Have a drink, perhaps? Go and sit with Lesley, and do nothing, relaxing? But it must be three months since he had written to Israel Steinberg, whose last letter had been all about Hitler and the terrible situation developing for German Jews. But Izzy was safe in Austria . . . He hadn't written to Morgan and Cicely Lloyd for a couple of months, either . . . Six months since he'd written to Jim Brock, now a Labour MP . . . And he'd only written once to Bogey Harris since Bogey had been appointed a company quartermaster sergeant in the 1st Battalion and had gone Home early last year. That correspondence must not be allowed to lapse. He and Bogey must remain friends and fellow Moonrakers, whatever the difference in their ranks.

One felt so isolated here. It was easier to let it all go, sink back, float with the stream of petty details . . . No, by God no! He drew some writing paper towards him, glanced at his watch, and began to write: 'Dear Israel . . .'

'I think I understand the peasant pretty well,' Bill said, 'but we've got to find out more of what the educated Indian thinks – what he wants of us. I've met a dozen or so, through you, but none of them will talk about politics – not to me.'

His wife Lesley, working at a tilted sketching board in a far corner of the garden, said, 'The only thing *they* want to know is when we're going to get out. Didn't someone say ages ago – a century at least – that England was only in India to teach the Indians how to govern themselves? Surely that point has been reached, with people like Patel and Nehru and others obviously capable of running the country?'

'I don't know whether they could make it work,' Bill said, 'and then the peasants would suffer.'

'Perhaps not, but it isn't our business, once we've established a government that can be changed by the will of the people.'

'The trouble is that it's very hard to believe that the Indian politician does or can represent other Indians . . . that he thinks the same as the ordinary Indian, or even *knows* what the ordinary Indian thinks. They're as different as chalk from cheese: the peasants – polite, hard-working, frugal, peaceful; and the politicians – demagogues, dishonest, corrupt, treasonable . . .'

She said, 'We've talked about this for three months now, and we've been going round in circles . . . Look, I'll try again to arrange for you to meet Chaudhri at a tea party somewhere. He won't come here . . . What did Roger have to say?'

The mail had arrived later than usual, but there had been a letter from Roger, Bill's son, now near the end of his last summer holidays before going to Cheltenham Senior, in Hazelwell House. Bill had read it, but left it on his desk before going out to join Lesley in the late afternoon stillness of the garden. He said, 'He was just back from spending two weeks in France with another boy and his family. The other boy has a sister, and that seemed to be the attraction.'

Lesley laughed. 'A bit young, isn't he? At thirteen most boys think girls are awful, useless lumps, which a good many of them are. Where are you going? It's not a *munshi* day.'

'To put in an hour's work on *The British Way in Warfare*. A new edition's out, with quite a lot of revisions.'

'I think it's very interesting, but sometimes not very practical.'

'You've been reading it?'

'Yes. I decided a few days ago that I don't want to be shut out from that part of your life, just because I'm a woman. I shall never command an army, but I must understand what faces you, when you do . . . understand technically, not just emotionally.'

Bill said, 'I'll be lucky if I ever command as much as a brigade. Merton really cooked my goose at the Staff College. He would have been happiest if I hadn't got a p.s.c. at all, but he achieved the next best thing, that I was posted here, to the worst staff job in India, except perhaps SSO, Mari Indus.'

Lesley put down her pencil and turned towards him, a frown shadowing her handsome boyish face. She said, 'Bill, you must really exorcize the ghost of Richard Merton from your conscience. Whatever the root of the relationship between you – and I wish you'd tell me – you mustn't let him haunt you, your work, your outlook. Your – our – future lies in *your* hands, not Merton's.'

Bill said at last, 'I know.'

The telephone rang in Bill's office and he reached out for it. 'Chattarganj District Headquarters – G3 speaking.'

'Bill? Rusty Challoner here. That protest meeting of Chaudhri's which we talked about a couple of days ago is under way. It's getting a lot bigger than we thought it would. A hell of a lot of people are heading for the Maidan.'

'How many?'

'It's hard to estimate yet. About five thousand.'

Bill whistled silently. That was a lot of people to get out in the heat of a weekday noon. Challoner was the district superintendent of police of Chattarganj Civil District, and Bill now asked, 'Do you expect any trouble now? You didn't when we talked last.'

'We still don't. And if it comes, we can handle it, unless something quite unforeseen happens.'

'All right. I'll check that the company of the Essex is standing by in barracks, but let's hope they won't be needed. Where will you be?'

'Outside the Bank of India building at the corner of the Maidan.

I'll be there in fifteen minutes.'

'I'll join you.'

After telephoning the adjutant of the Essex, Bill took his solar topi off its hook on the hatstand and went out, tidy and neat in his starched and ironed khaki shorts and thin cotton shirt, the sleeves turned up and ironed, the thick pale blue whistle lanyard round his left shoulder, the black metal stars of his rank and the letters QOWR on his shoulders.

The Maidan, or Plain, a large flat space in the centre of Chattarganj city, was a hard ten minutes' walk from district headquarters. It would have been simple, and less tiring, to take his bicycle; but he wanted to be free to move about once he got there, observing what went on, and the bicycle would have hindered him.

As he approached the Maidan, the crowd moving inward grew thicker; but they did not seem hostile, nor were they mostly young, or political-seeming types. They were just city people, small shop-keepers, labourers, artisans . . . with their women, and some children. A good many, too, were obviously coming in from the nearer countryside and villages within two or three miles of the city. That was interesting – he made a note in his small notepad: Chaudhri had succeeded in getting the attention of what Bill, and most other British always thought of as the 'real' Indian, meaning the rural peasant, as opposed to the urban population. Such people had never before shown any interest in the Congress Party's marches or protests.

Challoner was standing on the ornate steps of the Bank of India, thwacking a swagger cane against his black-putteed leg, two consta-bles and a havildar of police standing off to one side, leaning on their long brass-tipped staves called *lathis*. In the middle of the Maidan a makeshift platform had been erected and now Chaudhri was climb-ing up onto it, followed by another man. Already on the platform three Sikhs in blue overalls were connecting up a microphone to a loudspeaker system. Chaudhri made *namasti* to the crowd, joining his hands in front of his chest, palms together. The nearer people in the crowd cheered. From all corners men and women were still flowing in. Chaudhri waited. Bill and Challoner waited. Round the corner, out of sight at the side of the bank, thirty police armed with shotguns loaded with buckshot waited.

Bill said, 'At least there are plenty of exits here. We won't have another Jallianwallah Bagh, whatever happens.'

'You can't tell what a crowd will do,' Challoner said, 'particularly an Indian crowd. I don't think there'll be any firing, not today.'

Chaudhri seemed to estimate that enough people had arrived to make it worthwhile his starting. He stepped up to the microphone and began to speak, a mixture of Hindi and Urdu. The two languages are closely related, and the peoples who used them had lived intermingled for so long that everyone in the crowd could readily understand both, or either – but, by speaking in this mélange of the two, Chaudhri proved to both Hindus and Muslims that he was one of them.

Bill listened. Chaudhri talked about the Indian people's struggle for freedom from foreign oppression. It was interesting that he did not mention the Congress Party. Congress had a bad name among non-political Indians, and Chaudhri was keeping his distance from that reputation, even though he was the local head of the party, and this protest had been organized under its auspices. Now he was pointing out the iniquity of the salt tax and the land tax, of all taxes, on honest hard-working men. How then to deal with this tyranny? Not by violence, though it would be perfectly justified. Violence was not the Indian way. No, the British must be made to feel that they were not welcome. They must be treated as outcasts, so that of their own accord they would go back whence they came. Let no one help the government, in any way. Refuse all services. Pay no taxes. Support all those who were taking an active part in the struggle to rid India of these foreigners. Why, in a few hours, tomorrow, a band of martyrs would lie down and block the road outside the *bhoosa* depot and would let nothing pass, from nine o'clock to six. Let as many as could come to the *bhoosa* depot and support their brothers and sisters . . . but on no account use violence. That was what the British wanted, for Indians to use violence, so that they could respond with their guns and pistols. Use prayer, but block the road . . . let none pass!

Chaudhir moved on to other themes – the army, the police, the government in general. Service to the Sirkar in any shape was treason to India. The poor young men who had been inveigled into such service must be shown the error of what they had done. It had been

8

understandable enough – there had then been no organized movement to drive the British out, and they needed jobs, money, food. But now there was such a movement, and wise patriotic men to guide it, such as Mahatmaji . . . Let anyone who had a relative in the service of the Sirkar urge that relative to do what he could to throw sand into the engine of government. Let him not say, I refuse to obey the order, for that would bring punishment; but let him say, yes, sahib, I will obey – but do nothing.

'Getting pretty close to sedition,' Challoner said.

Bill nodded. 'Let them talk.'

Chaudhri began to speak about the unity of India. 'We are all brothers and sisters,' he shouted, 'Hindu, Muslim, Sikh, we are all equally oppressed by the British. It is they who sow the seeds of dissension and hate among us. Divide and rule is their motto.'

'It doesn't have to be,' Challoner muttered. 'They divide themselves . . . He's losing the crowd, because they don't want to hear that they're all brothers. The Hindus believe in caste, the Muslims despise the Hindus as idolaters, the Sikhs think all the others are lazy, superstitious and cowardly. Chaudhri should stick to berating us.'

'I don't think anything's going to happen here,' Bill said, 'but I'll go to the *bhoosa* depot tomorrow, in case that turns nasty.'

'Don't bother,' Challoner said. 'I'll be there, with fifty police . . . and our agents are spreading the word that, if there's any interference with the *bhoosa* distribution convoys, government won't buy any more in the Chattarganj area. So the farmers and peasants will try to prevent any interference. Of course Chaudhri and the Congress may ignore them, but I don't think they will – yet. That will come when Congress has real power. Then they can start bullying the farmers, who are essentially conservative, while the Congress is essentially socialistic.'

'But what's going to happen next?' Bill asked. 'Where do we go from here? Just face increasing unrest, bring out the police more and more? Then the army? Is there no way of turning all this . . . dissatisfaction is the least you can call it . . . into cooperation?'

Challoner looked at him quizzically. 'You, a soldier, want to calm things down? Most of the military I meet want the situation to develop so that we can start shooting . . . If there is a solution, it's

9

not here in Chattarganj. It's in London, or Delhi, or Wardha – and it's political . . . and it's an impossibility, for now. The Congress want us out of India altogether, now. We intend to stay. That doesn't leave any room for negotiation.'

Bill was at home in his bungalow, trying to read by the wavering electric light. The local power station was having trouble with its workers and its coal supply, and the current being generated was not steady. The overhead fans worked, creaking and squeaking round and round, but at varying speeds. Bill was reading the latest volume of the *Royal United Services Institute Journal,* trying to digest a long and highly technical article about methods of anti-aircraft defence of large headquarters. It was still hot and muggy. Sweat dripped from his nose and the shirt clung damply to his back . . . It was hard to believe that the kind of war he was reading about would ever come to pass, or that if it did he would take any part in it except as a junior staff officer in India or perhaps Africa, worrying about local politicians, civil unrest, protection of the railways against sabotage, assassinations of officials and police. If it wasn't for Merton, he'd have a better job in England perhaps, and . . . there he went again. Lesley was right. He must get Merton out of his mind. But it was hard, when for so many years the fellow seemed to represent and embody all Bill's difficulties in the regiment and the army.

Back to the subject . . . his job. Once an anti-government campaign such as this one of the Congress Party's was launched, there was no real controlling it. For one thing there'd always be people who for various reasons, personal or ideological, would deliberately sabotage the plan. He had a suspicion that his own general would welcome an opportunity to put down a Congress demonstration with such force that his name would long be associated with stern measures. Just let them give him a chance! And of course there were men inside Congress who also wanted just such a result, to increase the general antagonism towards the British Government. Pressures crowded in on everyone. Small politicians demanded strong action, not for action's sake, but to force their superiors' hands, and to gain fame. British businessmen pressed for law and order at all costs, because the civil disturbance, if allowed to drag on, was bad for business and trade. Insurance premiums went up, losses rose, labour stayed away from work, the market became unsettled, buyers stayed at home, or – worse – joined in boycotts.

He returned to the *Journal*. From over his shoulder, Lesley said, 'What do you think of General Groves's latest book?'

Bill put down the *Journal* and swung round to face her. '*Behind the Smoke Screen*?'

She said, 'You know, it isn't hard to understand the military technicalities, if you concentrate. What is hard is to understand the military attitude, its mind, without revulsion. They all talk or write about casualties and damage without seeming to realize that these are human beings – men, women, children – who are going to be blown to pieces. It's their homes, the places where they live and raise their children, that are to be turned to rubble . . . their savings thrown away on guns and tanks and bombs . . .'

'We're aware of all that,' Bill said defensively. 'I mean, aware of it more than civilians are. We've seen it. I've seen good friends die before my eyes, some of them very painfully and slowly . . . I've seen not just houses but whole towns destroyed. You have to be aware of all this with one part of you. If you weren't, you'd be inhuman, and you wouldn't understand your own men . . . they wouldn't follow you . . . but you can't let this awareness distort your thinking, your planning, or you'll add one more disaster – defeat – to the other inevitable ones that everyone suffers.'

'I understand that better now,' she said. 'And what's happening in Germany has helped. Do you know what I think? That Adolf Hitler means to conquer the world.'

'That's what Israel Steinberg thinks,' Bill said. 'But Hitler may just be a patriotic German. We've treated the Germans pretty badly since the Armistice, and most of it was on behalf of the French, whom we *really* disliked. I can tell you that by the time the last war ended most British soldiers and officers said that the only future war they'd volunteer for would be one against the French.'

She said decisively, her American accent strong, 'Perhaps, but you'll have to think differently now, Bill. France is no threat to anyone . . . rather the reverse. It's so corrupt politically that it's liable to be a millstone to its allies. But Hitler's Germany is far worse even than Mussolini's fascism, and that's bad enough. Hitler's anti-semitism is a . . . it's a disgrace to humanity!'

11

'I haven't met many Jews,' Bill said. 'But they seem to be a very clever people and, if Hitler tries to get rid of them, he'll be the one that'll suffer. But we can't choose our enemies by the way they treat their own people, I'm afraid. It's the way they treat us that matters.'

'If England or America ever became allied to Hitler,' Lesley said furiously, 'I'd . . . I'd join the Communist Party and emigrate to Russia.'

'Where you'd find that the Soviets would not hesitate to befriend Hitler, if it suited their policies.'

'I don't believe it,' she stormed. 'There's got to be some principle in the world, some respect for human rights . . .'

Bill held up his hand. 'Darling, I agree. But I'm a regular officer of the British Army, and for some years to come my duty is not to concern myself with politics but to prepare myself and my men to beat whomever our government tell us to . . . Now, what do you think about General Groves, and Jones, and Trenchard, and the whole air business? Personally, I don't think our government *have* an air policy, any more than they have a tank policy. They tell the factories to build an aeroplane, and when it's finished they say, well, now what shall we do with it, instead of planning what they want the air arm to achieve, and then telling the industry to design machines to do it . . .'

The principal commanders and staff officers of the Chattarganj Military District were again gathered round the table in the general's spacious office. It was October and, though there was no snap in the air yet, it was beginning to dry out.

General Langton said, 'Now that we have all our British troops in hand again, I've decided that we should work out an aggressive cold-weather policy to back up the governor's emergency decrees and counter this civil disobedience campaign of the bloody Congress. Banning the local press is a big help, because it will cut down on all the demagoguery and incitement to riot and spreading of lying propaganda, but we also have to do something positive. The core of our plan, of course, will be the Essex. I want every Indian in the district to realize that they are here, that they are armed, and that they are ready to shoot.'

Good logic, Bill thought, even though it might go against the general's own private wish to force a confrontation. Or perhaps he'd had a talking-to from the army commander about the necessity of handling the situation with kid gloves. If black clouds were beginning to loom over Europe, as Izzy Steinberg warned, it wouldn't help to have India in flames.

'I want companies of the Essex – whole companies, at a time, nothing less – to march through different cities of the district, with the regimental band, or at least the fifes and drums. Let the band give a concert in the Maidan or other suitable place . . . march them to and from the station, escorted by the company, with fixed bayonets . . . they are all to carry ball ammunition . . . Dress, review order . . . Make out a schedule with the Essex, Bill, and coordinate it with the police before you bring it to me.'

'Yes, sir.'

'The Jats can do the same thing out of Ghazipur. They have pipes and drums, don't they?'

'Yes, sir. And a *dhol* and *sarnai* band . . . They could take a *kabbadi* team with the bands, too, to play against the local young men.'

'All right. But make sure that we don't send the Jats to any area that's acting badly. Send the Essex to those places, the Jats to the quiet, loyal places . . . And see that all the depots and arsenals and military factories in the district do something, in whatever way they can, to show the flag – show the people that the army's here, and is ready to do its job. Any questions?'

The A/Q said, 'One thing, sir. It'll cost a bit to move the Essex and the Jats about by train . . . even by bus. Where is the money to come from?'

'Contingency fund,' the general said briefly. 'Make out an estimate of costs as soon as I have approved the plan. I'll go to the army commander if necessary. That's all, gentlemen . . . Bill, stay behind, please.'

The others left, saluting. Bill waited, on his feet. The general said, 'The DC tells me that you have been meeting Chaudhri, the Congress-wallah.'

'Yes, sir,' Bill said. 'It's been a couple of times, at Milkwallah's house – the Parsee Lawyer. Milkwallah's wife and Lesley have become quite friends.'

'Milkwallah is a member of the Congress Party?'

'I don't think so, sir. There have been plenty of politicians there,

13

though – Congress, Muslim League, Hindu Sabha . . . once a Bengali lady who was apparently a communist.'

'Why do you go to the Milkwallahs'?' the general asked, leaning back and playing with the pencil held between his fingers.

Bill hesitated before speaking slowly. 'I went first because Lesley wanted us to. I found Milkwallah a very interesting man, though I can't say we've become friends, as Lesley and Perrin Milkwallah have. Then I found that we were meeting Indian politicians, and the talk was always political – what is so and so going to do next – how can the Congress and the Muslim League get together to stop communal bickering – the iniquities of the 'reserved seats' system – whether Muslims will demand a separate state, now that this man Jinnah has taken over the Muslim League . . . I found it very interesting, as these are the sort of people we have to deal with.'

'So, in a way, you've been consorting with the enemy,' the general said smiling – but rather thinly, Bill thought.

He said, 'I suppose so, sir. But they're not really enemy. They're fellow subjects. I believe we have to know how they think, what they want, and how they propose to set about getting it, if we're to deal with them at all, either by negotiation or . . .'

'We soldiers are not going to do any negotiating,' the general said. 'I don't propose to order you to stop going to the Milkwallahs' . . . but . . . walk carefully. And report anything of military interest that you hear, whether it was spoken in confidence or not. If you are to keep your hands clean, you must make your position absolutely clear: you are a British officer and your loyalty lies entirely to the King, Emperor of India, through the normal military chain of command . . . which, for you, begins with me. That's all.'

Milkwallah's large house stood on the boundary, unmarked but well recognized, between the city and the civil lines. It was furnished in the European style, its French provincial furniture seeming not so out of place in November as it had during the hot weather when the fans swished ceaselessly overhead and the air was like breathable soup, thick and hot. A serving table in the centre of the drawing room was covered with glasses and jugs of various fruit juices, for many of the guests were teetotallers. In order to avoid any contretemps, whisky and sodas were being served from the kitchen, by the Milkwallahs' *khitmatgar*. Bill, a small whisky and long soda in hand, stood in a corner of the crowded room talking to Chaudhri, the Hindu lawyer and local Congress leader. Lesley was across the room, in animated talk with Perrin Milkwallah, her hostess, and a tall thin young man whom Bill recognized as Ghazi Khan, a fiery Muslim politician and poet, the latter in Persian.

Chaudhri said, 'Our campaign seems to be working just as well without our newspapers as it did with them . . . just as well from our point of view, I mean – the opposite from yours.'

Bill said, 'I'm all for satyagraha, or anything else, if it will produce a long-term policy that can be agreed on between the government and the Congress . . . and the Muslim League.'

'I don't believe you, of course,' Chaudhri said. 'And now that that dirty dog Jinnah has taken over the Muslim League, there is no hope of any such agreement with them, at least. Jinnah must be got rid of. Then there will be a full reconciliation between Hindu and Muslim – and Sikh, of course. You British create dissension for your own purpose.'

'That's what every politically minded Indian says,' Bill said with some heat, 'but look at the Indian Army. They have battalions composed of Sikhs, Muslims and Hindus all working together. We'd like the politicians to be the same, working together towards a common goal. Then we could work with them.'

An educated voice behind him, speaking flawless upper-class English, said shortly, 'That's impossible. There are differences of opinion in England, huge differences, as to goals, between the Conservatives and Labour. Why should it be any different here, where we have so much more diversity than there is in England?'

Bill turned to look into a pair of sharp brown eyes under a white Gandhi cap, a long aquiline handsome face and greying hair, a man wearing a white knee-length tunic and tight Rajput-type trousers. It was a face he had seen a hundred times in the newspapers and magazines: Jawaharlal Nehru. Chaudhri made *namasti* with joined palms, and said, 'Good evening, Panditji. I am so glad you could come, after all.'

Bill said, 'I'm Captain Miller . . . G3 at district headquarters here.' He held out his hand.

'British Service or Indian Army?' Nehru asked sharply, taking the hand.

15

Bill said, 'British . . . Queen's Own Wessex Rifles.' He realized that he was faced with a unique opportunity, one such as came to very few junior officers. He quickly collected his thoughts and said, 'Mr Nehru, if the Governor lifts the emergency decree, what would the Congress do?'

Nehru looked at Bill suspiciously, 'Are you offering to negotiate? What are your credentials?'

'No,' Bill said, 'I'm not. I don't have any political position at all. But I'm responsible for making the plans to keep our district peaceful and that's nearly half the province. We were having riots and demonstrations and non-cooperation before the emergency decrees were promulgated, and we're still having them. So what can we do, on the government side, to restore calm?'

Nehru said patiently, 'Young man, England can't preach the virtues of liberty, free speech, parliamentary democracy, representative government, Magna Carta, the Bill of Rights and all the rest, and not expect the young Indians to whom they are teaching all this to say, yes, we agree – when is it going to be applied to us? . . . As an immediate step, I think the first thing that must be done is lift the ban on the vernacular press. Beyond that' – he shrugged – 'you can't force people to work for you. You have to make it worth their while. For our part, non-violent non-cooperation will continue.'

'What about demonstrations, though?' Bill said. 'Those are what we fear the most – fear in the sense that any little spark, any little mistake, on our part or yours, can cause a disaster. There are people who want such a disaster.'

'On both sides,' Nehru said quickly.

'Yes . . . Would you agree not to organize any demonstrations? Street processions?'

'We must have our meetings,' Nehru said.

'They can be limited. Inside halls, perhaps.'

'We could think about it. I could talk about it with Chaudhri here, and our own high command, of course. But I can promise nothing . . . And you?'

'Nor can I. But . . . we've got to get out of this face-to-face confrontation on everything. There are so many things that need doing, and for now can only be done by British and Indian together. I'll speak to my general tomorrow, though any action will have to come

16

from the Governor.'

Nehru said, 'You have a better appreciation of the problem than most soldiers do, Captain Miller. I hope you go far in your profession. Meantime, write to me any time, if you wish. Chaudhri here has my address.'

A month later, in the general's office, the general said shortly to Bill, 'Well, you're going to have your way. The Governor will lift the emergency decrees tomorrow . . . though of course it's nothing to do with you or me really. The truth is that we've got the upper hand of the buggers now, and can afford to ease up a bit.' He nodded in dismissal.

Bill remembered the conversation the next day, when the announcement of the lifting of the decrees was made, and simultaneously the three local newspapers, on their first new day of publication, came out with vitriolic attacks on the government, the British and the decrees; but there was no call for mass demonstrations, and the language, though strong, was general. No specific action, such as suborning the loyalty of government servants, was preached.

Lesley said, 'Have you read the vernacular papers? Are they as rabid as the *Clarion*?'

Bill said, 'Yes, as far as I can make out . . . I can only read the Hindi one, but that's about the same.'

'You couldn't really expect anything else. I think it's going to work out.'

'I hope so,' Bill said; and kept hoping as the days and weeks passed, talking every few days with Challoner or the deputy commissioner, carefully reading newspapers and intelligence reports, going out through the district, listening, watching, feeling its pulse for any sign of the irregularities that would signal trouble. But when it at last came there had been no sign.

2

December 1936: India

It was Lesley who awakened him, nudging him in bed beside her under the big mosquito net. 'Someone's knocking, Bill.'

He sat up sleepily, calling, 'Who is it?'

'Sher Khan, sahib. *Gora* coming from *daftar*.' Sher Khan was his body servant; *gora* was a British soldier; the *daftar* was the office. He struggled out of bed, calling, 'Take him to my study, Sher Khan. I'll be there in a minute.'

'*Bahut achcha*, sahib,' came back through the door. By now Bill was out of the mosquito net and Lesley had switched on the bedside light. 'Heaven knows what it is,' she said, 'but perhaps this will persuade them that the G3 needs a telephone in his bungalow.'

He was in his khaki drill trousers now, tucking in the tails of his shirt. He didn't know what the message or summons might be, but if he was needed, he had better be in uniform. He said, 'I'll let you know,' and went out.

The light was on in his study and the door open. Inside, a soldier was waiting and he recognized Corporal Grant, one of the head-quarters clerks. Grant saluted and said, 'Message for you from the duty officer, sir.'

Bill read the message handed to him, written on an army signal form:

G3 – following message received by telegram 0134 hrs today 7 December from Bhilpur begins mob riot here yesterday evening following motor accident small police station burned down mid-night with four constables inside military assistance urgently needed in addition to extra police requested from Lucknow signed Affleck Graves Deputy Commissioner Bhilpur message ends. Orders please. Duty Officer.

'What action has the duty officer taken on this?' Bill said. 'Who is he?'

'Mr Liddell, sir. I don't think he's done anything, except tell me to bring it to you as fast as I could.'

Bill glanced at his watch. It was a quarter past two in the morning.

Liddell was an inexperienced and nervous young man. He sat down at his desk and quickly wrote out a message to OC 2 Essex:

Prepare your standby company to move to Bhilpur for internal security duties immediately. Transport vide this HQ. IS plan para 9 will report to you at 0400 hrs. Signed, W. Miller, Captain, GSO3.

He gave the original to the corporal and said, 'Take that to the Essex orderly room, and see that it is delivered to their duty officer. He sleeps on a bed outside their orderly room at night.'

The corporal said, 'Yes, sir,' and hurried out. Bill took the carbon copy and folded it away in his pocket. He hurried back to the bedroom and put on his socks, shoes, Sam Browne belt, pistol holster and ammunition pouch. While he dressed, he told Lesley what had happened, ending, 'I'm going to Flagstaff House now, and then to the office. God knows when I'll be back.'

'All right,' she said. 'Be careful. Give me a kiss before you go.' He ducked under the mosquito net and kissed her, then hurried out into the cool December night, found his bicycle, and pedalled fast through the darkness to Flagstaff House, which was in the centre of the civil lines, a mile from his own bungalow. As he pedalled, he was thinking, have to get a message to the Service Corps in a hurry, to send the 3-tonners to the Essex by four o'clock . . . It was 143 miles by road to Bhilpur, on the banks of the Ganges – some manufacturing, leather products, smelled dreadful from the tanneries . . .

The Flagstaff House *chowkidar* was standing on the top step, under the porte-cochère, as Bill pedalled up. Bill said, 'Switch on the lights, *chowkidar*. I have to see the general-sahib.'

The *chowkidar* was an old man armed with an unconvincing *lathi*. He saluted without a word, opened the big front door behind him, and switched on the lights inside. It was a two-storey house, and the bedrooms, as Bill knew, were upstairs. 'Come up,' he said. 'Show me which is the general-sahib's.'

They went up the stairs together and the *chowkidar* pointed silently at a door. 'General-sahib and memsahib,' he whispered.

Bill braced himself a moment, then knocked. After a wait he knocked again, louder. General Langton's voice called, 'Who is it?'

'Captain Miller, G3, sir. There's been a serious riot at Bhilpur and the DC has asked for military assistance.'

He heard a muttering and a scuffling, then another call. 'I'll come right out.'

He waited, the *chowkidar* beside him, till Bill turned and said in Urdu, 'You'd better get back to your post.' The old man made salaam and crept back down the stairs and out of the house.

The general appeared, in pyjamas and a light dressing gown, his reading glasses perched on his nose. Bill gave him the two messages, saying, 'This was from the duty officer, sir. This is what I sent at once to the Essex.'

The general read, standing outside his door under the bright electric lights of the passage. After a time he said, 'Do you think a company will be enough?'

'There'll be extra police as well, sir,' Bill said. 'And if the Essex have to open fire, even a platoon would be enough. But a company is easier to administer, and it can provide reliefs, and so stay on the job longer.'

'All right. Have you warned the RIASC?'

'Not yet, sir. I'd like to use your phone here to call them, before I go on to the office.'

'Of course . . . And find out which Essex company is on standby, and speak to the company commander before he goes. Tell him, from me, that he is not to allow himself to be cajoled or persuaded into doing any police work . . . he is *not* to get involved at close quarters . . . and if the DC hands over the situation to him, to act decisively, but not excessively.'

'Very good, sir.'

'I'll go back to bed now. See that I get a full report on my breakfast table here at eight . . . and I'll be at the office at ten as usual.'

Bill saluted, went downstairs to the general's private office, made his telephone call to the Service Corps about the lorries, and then bicycled on to district headquarters and his office. The duty officer met him in a state of high excitement, gabbling, 'The telephone line's down to Bhilpur, and . . .'

The intelligence officer of the Essex arrived at the same time, and said, 'We're sending B company. Captain Greenway's the company commander. The colonel wants to know what the . . .'

'Will B be ready to move, equipped in all respects, by the time the lorries come?'

'Yes, but they'll only have one day's emergency rations. There'll have to be some sort of ration *bandobast* before evening . . . malarial protection . . . shelter . . .'

That would mean telegrams to Bhilpur, for the civil authorities to commandeer some suitable building, if the telegraph lines weren't down, too. Even if they were, he could probably get through via the railway telegraph system . . . the CQMS of the Essex company would be arranging to collect the men's bedding rolls . . . the CSM would have all the ready-typed Riot Act forms, the megaphones . . . He had met Affleck Graves, the deputy commissioner at Bhilpur, once – a tall, courtly man, one of the older DCs of the province . . . Indian Civil Service, of course, also an old Etonian. He hadn't met the Bhilpur policeman, but knew his name – it was on his list: Jameson . . . It was three o'clock.

At seven o'clock in the morning, Bill was sitting at his desk sipping a cup of tea one of the G clerks had just brought in. A wad would be nice, too, as he was feeling hungry, but the clerk hadn't been able to get one. He looked at the sheet of paper on which he had been noting the times of events and telephone calls during the early hours. A telegram from Bhilpur arrived at 0256 to the effect that the mob had tried to attack the DC's house but had been beaten off by a *lathi* charge of the rest of the police.

0309 – a telegram from Bill to Bhilpur, telling them that one coy of 2 Essex, strength 108 all ranks, was leaving Chattarganj by lorry at 0415, due to reach Bhilpur at approx 1815 hrs. Please arrange guide provide accommodation and up-to-date information.

0317 – another telegram from Bhilpur, that must have crossed his – thirty police from Lucknow were due to arrive before 1000 a.m. by bus AAA when was military help coming, by what means, in what strength . . .?

And so on through the hours, while gradually the darkness faded, the cocks began to crow in the city, and in the civil lines the water cart was out sprinkling the roads and the *malis* were watering the lawns and the flags were floating up to the mastheads at the quarter guard and outside Flagstaff House.

Bill finished the tea. What else could he do? The Essex company should be nearly there. But what sort of situation would they find?

Greenway could deal with riots, but could he oversee the administrative arrangements and liaise with the civil? Suppose new situations arose . . . Greenway had no staff training. Could he speak for the Chattarganj Military District? Was it fair to put that responsibility on him?

The answers were: no. He glanced up at the clock on the wall. Was the general up yet? Yes. Had he read the special report that Bill had prepared and sent to him just after seven? Perhaps. He looked at the telephone . . . damn it, make up your mind what ought to be done, check again that you're right, then do it. He picked up the phone and said, 'The GOC's residence, please.'

The general's wife answered. 'Mrs Langton speaking.'

'This is Captain Miller, the G3, Mrs Langton. May I speak to the general, please?'

'Wait a minute . . . here he is.'

The voice at the other end changed. 'General Langton. What is it?'

'I think someone from the staff ought to go to Bhilpur to coordinate with the civil, sir. Also to get an estimate, or make one, as to how long the company will be there . . . and make sure that everything's as good as it can be as regards food, medical, accommodation, water, and so on.'

There was silence on the other end of the line while Bill waited. Then the general said, 'Greenway ought to be capable of all that.'

Bill said, 'He has no staff training, sir. And he's only been out here six months. He doesn't have much Hindustani.'

More silence, then: 'I suppose you think you ought to go?'

'I think someone ought to, sir, and I'm quite willing to go, if you agree.'

More silence, then: 'All right . . . The telephone's still down to Bhilpur, isn't it?'

'Yes, sir.'

'Then report to me by telegram. And take a cipher book in case you need to send secret information.'

'Yes, sir. I'll start out as soon as I can.'

He hung up. Transport? A car? There were damned few and the owners or entitled users would yell bloody murder. Bike? Ridiculous . . . Ah, what about a motorcycle? 'Netty' Flowers of the Essex had one, and he was a bright young man . . . he'd probably want to come along, too. No, by God, he was in B Company, so he had already gone, and his bike would be at his quarters, in the charge of his bearer. It'd be a very dirty, dusty ride . . . Now what to take? The cipher book, as the general had said . . . he was already armed . . . message forms and carbons, pencils, knife to sharpen them, shaving gear and minimum toiletries, perhaps a change of shirt, waterbottle, money to buy petrol and food in one of the little towns he'd be going through. Warn Lesley – well, he'd have to go back to the bungalow for his toilet stuff and shirt and money. He'd get Netty's bike first and drive home on that . . . He felt alert and happy. It was a tragedy about the four policemen being burned alive, but the blood was running more freely in his arteries. He was going to get out of this bloody office, out into the country, with troops, real troops . . . and *do* something.

The telephone rang. 'General Langton. Bill? Listen, I want to make it clear that you are going to Bhilpur to coordinate matters with the civil and report to me on the situation and future possibilities. You are *not* there to command B Company of the Essex. Don't interfere in that.'

'I understand, sir.'

It was near nine before Bill finally got away, after dealing with a number of small problems at headquarters, putting the other branches of the staff into the picture, and making administrative arrangements with the A/Q for the troops in Bhilpur. The journey itself was, as he had known it would be, very dusty and thirst-making. The roads were mostly simple macadam or simpler earth, though he was able to enjoy forty miles on smooth tarmac on the final stretch into Bhilpur. And as he had hoped, he found a small teahouse en route, which served him rice, curried vegetables, dal and tea.

He rode into Bhilpur to a smell of burning drifting down on the dry wind, soon after one o'clock, and found his way to the civil lines by instinct, for he had never been here before. The lines consisted of four big bungalows, and the DC's was the biggest; also it was guarded by a constable leaning on his *lathi* outside the main gate. The garden was a mess, the flowerbeds trampled down and the hedge in disarray. In the house several windows had been broken, and black marks up

23

one wall showed where a fire had been started. The DC's wife told Bill, 'George is down at the Kotwali, Captain – Miller, you said?' and explained how to get there. Bill climbed back onto the Norton, and headed towards the city. He found the DC and the deputy superintendent of police inside the Kotwali, the former in khaki shorts and a white shirt, the latter in uniform, with his pistol in its holster. The DC said, 'Ah, Miller, we had a telegram that you were coming. Your soldiers are at the moment waiting in a big old house about a hundred yards from here. Captain Greenway just went off to see how they are. He's been with us since they arrived.'

'What's the situation?'

'The police are discouraged. They were very upset by the burning of that police station – it was a small, subsidiary one – and the deaths of their comrades. They didn't believe anything like that could happen under the Raj. They would have liked to go out and burn down the city – would have done them a lot of good, too – but of course we couldn't let them do that . . . The extra fellows from Lucknow have arrived, and we have quite a force, but . . .'

A police constable came in, sweating and breathing hard, and spoke rapidly in Hindustani. Bill caught the gist of it: the crowd in the centre of the city was beginning to loot the houses and shops in that area; repeated police charges had not moved them.

The DC stood up. 'Can't have that. We'd better get down there, and we'll take some of the soldiers with us. About thirty, perhaps?'

'A platoon,' Bill said. 'I think the company commander had better go with them.'

The DC nodded. 'We'll go by their billets now, and they can come on with us.'

The police officer said, 'I'll bring all the Lucknow men and twenty of ours . . . leaving the rest here in reserve.'

Bill said, 'May I come along?'

'Certainly. I hoped you would. It might save time later if . . .' The DC didn't finish the sentence.

The city smelled to heaven, and Bill learned that the municipal sweepers had been on strike for two weeks. The stench was of rotting food, decaying garbage, dead animals – sickly sweet, penetrating, permeating. As they moved on through deserted streets, the DC's party in the lead, followed by the platoon of the Essex, and then by the large contingent of police, a dull roar from ahead grew louder.

The street opened out into a wide square, with a Muslim mosque on the east side and an ornately garish Hindu temple on the west, facing each other across sere grass and beaten earth, here and there paved. The square was half full of people, about three thousand in all, most of whom seemed to be listening to someone speaking from a bullock cart in the middle. Round the sides of the square, groups of men were breaking open barred doors with clubs and crowbars, and dragging out sacks of grain and heavy wooden crates and boxes.

The DC turned to the DSP and said, 'Break up the looting, Frank. Leave the crowd in the middle alone.'

The police officer gave a sharp order and half the police broke into a run and surged round one side of the square, using their *lathis* on the heads of anyone carrying loot. Bill, standing to one side as the DC and the policeman, watched the action, heard a voice beside him: 'Captain Miller . . .'

He turned to see Chaudhri, the Congress leader, beside him. He said, 'What are you doing here, Mr Chaudhri?'

'Bhilpur is in my area, what do you call it, my constituency . . . This is a bad business.'

Bill said, 'You must have known this would happen, somewhere, some time, the way you have been acting and preaching against the government.'

'That is our right,' Chaudhri said. 'But this was an accident. A government lorry was coming into the town . . . it belonged to the Public Works department, and was taking a load of stone somewhere – its steering broke down and it pinned half a dozen people against a wall, killing some of them. They were our supporters, coming to listen to me make a speech . . . not in the open, but in a hall, as we agreed with the Governor.'

'Someone obviously took advantage of the emotion to start the riot last night . . . and I imagine the same people are egging this crowd on, too. Who are they?'

'Bad men,' Chaudhri said. 'They pretend to be of the Congress, but work against us in secret. Men like Bose . . .' He sounded upset and distrait. '*We* don't want this terrible violence. Oh, why don't you British go away, quickly, and leave us . . . then there would be no bloodshed.'

'You think not?' Bill said grimly. 'The people who organized the burning last night think differently. And you will be the victims.'

'Communists, anarchists,' Chaudhri muttered. 'Violent men.'

'What's that fellow on the bullock cart saying? He's speaking too fast for me.'

'He's telling the people to take no notice of the police *lathis* – see how few they are, how many we are . . . but to take the city into their own hands, release the prisoners from the jail . . . burn down the DC's house and the courthouse . . .'

'Get him out of there, then,' Bill said. 'Take his place, man! Preach moderation. Don't you have anyone here who can help you?'

'A dozen. They are . . .'

'Then *act*! Calm them down. Take control of the crowd, or things will get much worse. The soldiers are here, and ready.'

'Oh, my God,' Chaudhri cried, and hurried off.

The DC came up. 'That was Chaudhri, wasn't it?'

'Yes. I told him to pull that fellow off the cart and take control of the crowd.'

'Good man. I hope they'll listen to him.'

Captain Greenway came up, followed by a bugler and a sergeant, saluted the DC and said, 'Second Lieutenant de Mestre is on leave, so Sergeant Henty here is commanding the platoon. Do you think it will be needed?'

The DC said, 'It's hard to tell yet. Look – there's looting all round the square. The crowd in the centre is being treasonably harangued, told to attack us. And they could roll over us like a steamroller, in a couple of minutes, if they decided to act . . . Have your bugler ready to blow – make a loud noise. I will then order the crowd to disperse, and warn them that if they don't they are liable to be fired on. I will then declare that the situation is beyond civil control and sign your card – you have it?' Greenway nodded, pulling the card from the pocket of his khaki drill shorts and showing it.

The DC continued, 'Then you act as you think fit, to disperse the crowd and the looters. As soon as you believe that you can safely hand control back to the civil power, tell me so, and we will move in with the police to make arrests and clean up.'

Greenway said, 'Very well, sir. I'll explain it all to the men.' He moved back to where the platoon waited, standing in line in two ranks. The DC turned to his police superintendent and Bill went a little aside so that he could better concentrate on what was happening. There was a scuffle going on round the ox cart. He recognized Chaudhri's Gandhi cap. After a few seconds of fierce struggle, the man who had been speaking was dragged down from the cart and Chaudhri pushed up in his place. The crowd growled angrily, and surged inward. A sizable mob broke away from the outskirts and ran to help the looters in hand-to-hand struggle with the police. The police reeled back, several with blood streaming from pike or axe cuts. Chaudhri was speaking – yelling – but so were others. The crowd was beginning to coalesce away from the ox cart. There was a strong organization there, Bill thought. The troublemakers had lost control of the ox cart, so they had contrived to focus the attention of the crowd away from it . . . towards the little band of English officials and the soldiers.

The DC had seen, too, and spoke to Greenway. The Essex bugler blew a loud ragged G. Greenway pointed out ringleaders to Sergeant Henty. Six soldiers loaded single rounds into the chambers of their rifles. The crowd was falling silent, as the bugle blared again. Now Bill could hear Chaudhri: 'Brother Indians,' he bellowed, 'Hindus, Muslims, Jains, Sikhs! Men, women, all, listen to me!'

An outcry arose, drowning his voice. Some of the crowd were listening, but a part, perhaps five hundred, were edging towards the DC, shouting and waving their motley weapons.

'I am the Congress leader in this part of the province,' Chaudhri screamed, 'I am the messenger . . .'

The bugler blew again. Everyone heard Chaudhri's next words '. . . of the Mahatma. He weeps now because of what you have done here . . . killed our Indian brothers of the police . . . smashed, burned, looted . . . look round you, see what is being done, to our brothers, the banians of the city . . .'

At the same time, the DC was reading the Riot Act in a loud clear voice. Bill thought, very few of the crowd can have heard him. The DC finished speaking, signed Greenway's card and handed it back to him. Bill heard Sergeant Henty say, 'Private Smithers, on my order, shoot the man I have just pointed out to you.'

Still the large menacing group of the crowd kept creeping forward. Chaudhri had sensed that 'Mahatma' was the name that had caught their attention, and used it again and again. The noise lessened, and Chaudhri's voice was clearly heard.

Bill ran the few steps towards Greenway and said, 'Hold your fire! Chaudhri's got them. They'll disperse . . .'

Greenway said, 'But . . . are you taking over command from me, Miller?'

'Yes! No! I'm just telling you to wait a bit.'

He ran to the DC. 'Sir – Chaudhri's almost got them back. They're ashamed of themselves. They're not listening to the agitators any more . . . I think they'll break up if the police can move forward now, slowly . . . Have the bugler blow another G, then tell them to disperse.'

The DC rubbed his chin, staring at the crowd. He said, 'I've handed over control. You'll have to persuade Captain Greenway.'

Bill ran back to Greenway. 'Have the bugler blow another couple of Gs . . . Go on, man, there's no time to waste!'

Greenway waved a hand and the bugler, at his elbow, stepped forward and blew. As the sound died away, the DC stepped forward, calling, 'Please be quiet a moment, Mr Chaudhri . . . All of you, go to your homes as Mr Chaudhri has asked. Go, now, before worse befalls . . . the police will advance . . . disperse! Disperse!'

A wall of khaki police moved forward, *lathis* held horizontally across their chests; but the crowd was moving. The looters, who had been working behind the cover of the mass of humanity in the middle of the square, realizing they were being uncovered, dropped whatever they were doing, and ran, pursued now by the police and some members of the crowd itself.

The main line of the police kept advancing, chanting, 'Go home . . . brother, sister, go home . . . go home . . .'

At last the square was all but empty, and the DC turned to Greenway. 'Thank you. If you agree, I suggest you can hand back to us now.'

'All right.' Greenway said. He looked at Bill. 'You were right. We didn't have to shoot after all. But if you hadn't been there we would have fired, I can tell you. I didn't see any other way to get that crowd under control, and stop the looting – and prevent ourselves being overrun.'

Chaudhri appeared, pale and excited, but controlling himself with an effort. He walked up to the DC and said, 'Thank you, Mr Affleck Graves. I was afraid you were going to open fire. And though, with the looting going on, you would have been justified, some innocent people would certainly have been killed, too.'

The DC said, 'Thank Captain Miller here. He sensed before any of the rest of us that you were going to be able to control the crowd.'

Chaudhri held out his hand to Bill. 'Thank you then, Bill. I have called you Captain Miller before, at the Milkwallahs', not wanting to get too close to a British officer, but now, if I may . . .'

'Of course,' Bill said, laughing.

'And I shall see that Panditji and Mahatmaji come to know of your action. We have so many reasons to hate the British that when something happens to make us respect and thank an Englishman we must cherish it.'

Bill stood before the general's desk, the lieutenant colonel A/Q standing a little behind and to one side of him. It was January 1937, a month after the affair at Bhilpur. A military court of inquiry had been held to investigate everyone's actions. The army had injured no civilians and damaged no property during its stay in Bhilpur, so there had been no demand from the civil side for an inquiry, but the general wanted to know who had done what, and why, down to the smallest detail. The inquiry had taken four days, back in Bhilpur, starting a week after the incident. Now the general held an official copy of its report in his hand as he looked up at Bill.

'Do you deny that you gave Captain Greenway an order, Captain Miller?'

Bill hesitated a moment, then said, 'I said, "Wait." '

'That's an order, just as much as "Shoot",' the general said coldly. 'Did you also say "Hold your fire"?'

'Yes, sir, because . . .'

'I understand your reasons. Did you tell Captain Greenway to have his bugler blow another G – after the deputy commissioner had handed over control of the situation to the military, in the person of Captain Greenway?'

'Yes, sir,' Bill continued. 'I am two years senior to Captain Greenway, by date of rank. So I was the senior military officer present. I could not avoid that responsibility. I was also your representative, as an officer of your General Staff.'

The general said, 'So that's your excuse, or reason, for acting as you did? That you were the senior military officer present?'

'The reason is that it was not necessary to open fire,' Bill said. 'It would have killed some innocent people, and made our problems in India worse than they now are. I hope Captain Greenway would have held his fire even if I'd been junior to him.'

'That may be,' the general said. 'But he could hardly refuse to obey an order or suggestion coming from my staff officer, and, as he would have reason to believe, my representative.'

'No, sir.'

'And to avoid such a situation, I specifically told you on the telephone before you went to Bhilpur not to take command of the troops.'

'I felt I had to, sir, to ensure that the right thing was done for everyone's sakes, including Captain Greenway's and the many innocent Indians' who would have been killed.'

The general leaned back. 'That's all. You may go.'

A week later Bill came back early from the office, bicycling slowly to the bungalow through a heavy cold-weather shower. Lesley met him at the outer door. 'What brings you back so early? . . . Has the general spoken?'

Bill said, 'Yes. I've been sacked.'

She said, 'Go and have a bath, and change. I'll pour you a drink. I'm not sure whether this is an occasion for mourning or celebration, but a drink will serve, anyway.'

She was waiting for him when he came back twenty minutes later, in dry clothes. She handed him a tall glass of beer and indicated the seat beside her on the sofa. 'Now?' she said.

Bill drank deep, put down the glass, and said, 'He said that I do not have a sense of loyalty to my superior and am therefore unfit for work on the staff. He has recommended I be returned to regimental duty. As I've done more than my due time overseas, that means I will be sent back to England as soon as a replacement can be found and sent here.'

'*We* will,' she said. 'Well, that's not so bad, is it? Chattarganj has its points and I'll be sorry to lose the Milkwallahs, but . . . that's about all. I prefer England.'

Bill burst out, 'Damn it, Lesley, it's the end of my career, as a career! That bastard Slippery Sam has ensured that I shall never go beyond regimental soldiering, after all the study and thought and work I've put in to prepare myself for higher command! He was so smooth, though curt. He never raised his voice. I could kill him! I want to strangle someone!'

'Not me, please. Sit down again, darling.'

Bill slumped down on the sofa and drank deeply. After a time he said, 'I wonder if I was a damned fool in Bhilpur, that's the truth. I could have let matters take their course. The DC had handed over. Damn it, even Chaudhri said we would have been fully justified in opening fire. And I butted in.'

'Because there was actually no need to fire. And you saw it, and you had to do what was right.'

'At the cost of my future,' he said, drinking again. 'I don't think I can stand ten more years of barrack soldiering in Aldershot, Strensall, Tidworth . . . kit inspections, church parades, pay parades, cookhouse inspections, CCMA's inspections . . . I don't know what to do.'

She said, 'Why don't you call Morgan Lloyd in Delhi? You could get through to him from the office.'

After a while Bill said, 'Good idea . . . I'm furious, Lesley! They've finally got me, but I'm not going to knuckle under and go quietly. I'm going to fight, to show them that I *am* a good soldier . . . but how can I do it when all I'll be allowed to do is inspect men's feet, stand at the firing point supervising musketry . . .?'

'Talk to Morgan,' she said. 'He knows you well . . . better than I do.'

From his study Bill could hear the murmuring voices of Lesley and Cicely Lloyd from the drawing room. He shut them out of his consciousness – he must concentrate on what Morgan was saying. All Morgan had said on the telephone yesterday was: 'Cicely and I will be down on the overnight train. Meet us at six forty at the station.' And now they'd had breakfast together and separated, the men to the study, the women to the drawing room.

Morgan said, 'Do you still want to be a general . . . a good one?'

Bill said, 'I do . . . more than ever, in a way. Before, I sometimes felt that I was carrying out your wishes for me, but now, by God, it's me . . . *I* want to do it, for my own sake, and I want to *show* them, but *how*?'

'Go to Spain,' Morgan said. 'The first modern war is being fought there and we need to learn from their mistakes and their successes. We need to learn on the spot, now!'

Bill said, puzzled, 'But there was an ACI threatening any officer with dismissal from the service who volunteered to fight in Spain.'

Morgan said, 'Yes. Resign your commission first, now.' He raised a hand, 'You're looking horrified. But think, Bill! We both know the value of the regiment, the regimental tradition and spirit, but for years you've also been looking wider, deeper. Now they're not going to let you. There'll be nothing but the same old job, the same old jokes. And when you reach the rank of lieutenant colonel – or before – you'll be out . . . But there's a war coming in Europe. Germany means to have it. This business in Spain is just the overture . . . tuning up the instruments, bringing the score up to date. I can't promise you that you'll be taken back into the army when you return from Spain, but I'll stake my reputation on it. The army will need you.'

'I'm not so sure,' Bill muttered. 'But what's the alternative?'

Morgan Lloyd said nothing. Bill said, 'Lesley will be happy. She's been talking about how great the International Brigades are ever since they were formed.'

Morgan said carefully, 'You must fight on Franco's side, Bill.' He leaned forward. 'We have dozens, scores – even hundreds – of people fighting in Spain on the Republican side. A lot of them are communists, but that doesn't matter for the moment. The point is they're learning, and the lessons will be available to us. We have only three – no, four – men of officer rank on the Nationalist side. I can't give you an order to go – no one can, and they couldn't put it in writing or back it up if they did, not even the CIGS, but believe me, I know that that's what they want in the War Office. The men and machines Hitler's sent to Franco are good. They'll change that war . . . and the next one . . . ours.'

Bill said, 'God, what a choice. I don't like communists any more than I like Nazis or fascists . . . Lesley will kill me, but I think you're right. Can you help me get out of the army and back to England quickly, Morgan? I don't want to hang around here and I know Slippery Sam will be glad to see the last of me . . . especially if he thinks that he's really got rid of me.'

It was the next day, and Bill and Lesley were alone in their bungalow, for the Lloyds had returned to Delhi in the morning. It was late, but they were both in the drawing room, fully dressed, Bill seated, Lesley walking up and down like a caged tigress.

'Now,' she said, 'out with it. What really happened yesterday between you and Morgan?'

He said, 'First, we briefly discussed my accepting a permanent return to regimental duty. But I hardly considered it. For years I've been training myself to be a commander and I'm not going to give up that goal, that ambition . . . for my own sake, and, I hope, for England's.'

'That cuts out my hope,' Lesley said, 'that you would resign your commission and come to the States with me. I have connections who could get you a good job and, whatever it was, I know you'd do it well. You'll like America and Americans will like you. We could make America our home.'

'Thanks, but it's not for me,' Bill said. 'What Morgan and I did decide, after a lot of discussion, was that I must resign my commission and go to Spain to fight in the Spanish Civil War.'

Lesley stopped pacing. 'Oh, Bill! That *is* exciting! That's a wonderful idea! I'll come with you. There's a sort of Red Cross working with the International Brigades and I know I could get into that.'

Bill said, 'It's Franco's side that Morgan . . . and I . . . agree that I must volunteer for.'

Lesley seemed to freeze where she stood. Her eyes turned to ice, her hands clenched fiercely. 'You . . . want . . . to fight . . . for . . . Franco?' She spat out each word.

'No,' Bill said. 'Look, there was a left-wing government in Spain from 1931 to 1936 – sort of democratic. A military uprising overthrew it. The Civil War followed. Various countries have seen two main chances for themselves in Spain's agony: first, to influence future Spanish policy; and second, to practise in actual battle new

33

theories and weapons. The British Government's policy is not at all clear. Nor is the American's. But the British Army's duty is very clear. It must learn as much as it can of modern war. Morgan told me that we already have hundreds of volunteers on the Republican side, many of them officers. They are working with the Russians, and they are learning. At the end of the war we shall be able to reap that harvest and use it for our own preservation.'

'Preservation from what?' Lesley snapped.

'Hitler's Germany,' Bill said. 'You've talked about it yourself. Churchill's speaking out about the menace, too, but a lot of people are laughing at him for a warmonger. But Izzy Steinberg's warnings are getting more urgent every time he writes, and he is thoroughly mixed up in politics in Austria and Germany. In his last letter he made it clear that Hitler's mind is now made up and he only awaits the opportunity. Meantime, he's training, and Spain is the field of manoeuvre. He has sent the Condor Legion out there – a whole lot of tanks and aircraft under German control. We *must* have competent men on the spot, to see what is being done, what succeeds, what fails.'

'And in the process destroy the Republic?' Lesley said bitterly.

'If that happens,' Bill said, 'my contribution will hardly be noticeable . . . Darling, I am a trained staff officer. I can see, and learn, and bring back the lessons we in Britain must learn. That's going to be my duty, however unpleasant it may be for me and unpalatable for you.'

'Look,' she said, changing her tone, 'supposing that, instead of fawning on the dictators and learning what they have to teach us about aggressive war, suppose that we combine to overthrow them, Franco and Hitler alike. Then there won't be a big war.'

'It's too late for that now,' Bill said. 'I must go to Spain. I shall travel through England to get the necessary papers. I shall serve as long as I can learn something, or until they kick me out. Then I shall return to England. Will you be there?'

She said, 'I shall go to New York, and do everything I can, from there, to help the Republic . . . and paint, if I can.'

'I have your address,' he said. 'But for God's sake, when it's over, come back to me, darling, come back, because I don't *want* to go. I *must*.'

34

'God knows,' she said miserably. 'God knows. We'll be different people.'

'Not altogether,' he said. 'I'll still be in love with you.'

The *Viceroy of India* butted her blade-like bows into a gathering Atlantic storm, sending surges of water to burst like bombs into the grey air. Bill, huddled in a corner of the promenade deck below the bridge, watched the heave and fall of the rollers, the sweep and plunge of the ship, his mind elsewhere. It was two weeks since Lesley had left him in Chattarganj, eight days since he had sailed from Bombay. His mind was still as unsettled as was the Atlantic around him. He had taken one of the most important decisions in his life, that was clear. Where would it lead? Looking back, as now he glanced towards the stern and its boiling wake, what had brought him here? Running away from home to join the army in the Great War, when he was no more than sixteen years old? Meeting and marrying Pauline ... so obviously a mistake now, but it hadn't seemed so then? Applying for a regular commission? Staying on in the army when Pauline's family were ready to give him a start, and support him in other occupations? Falling afoul of Richard Merton? Listening to Morgan Lloyd, and trying to make himself a good leader, not just a good fellow, 'an officer and a gentleman'? What chain of events, really, had brought him to this place, this ship, thinking these thoughts?

3

June 1919: England

The day Bill first met Morgan Lloyd wasn't his twentieth birthday,
it was the day after – 2 June 1919 – and it was in a train from
Waterloo to Salisbury. Both men were in plain clothes and it had
taken Bill some time to realize that the tall, stooped, gangly figure
with the drooping moustache was the famous Morgan Lloyd, DSO,
MC, of his own regiment, who'd made his name and won temporary
lieutenant colonelcy with the 7th Battalion on the Somme. Now he
was back to his regular rank of lieutenant, and a student at the Staff
College, Camberley. He was going to Salisbury to spend a couple of
days straightening out his service records at the depot. Second Lieutenant Bill Miller was returning from service with the 2nd Battalion
in the British Army of Occupation in Germany. Within a few weeks
he would be released, a civilian again . . . Again? He'd never been
one, really, only a boy.

They talked on the journey, Lloyd asking many questions, Bill
answering as best he could. He wanted to ask questions, too – would
Lloyd tell him how he won his DSO? What was the Staff College
like? What did one *do* there? But in the main he held his tongue, and
spoke only when spoken to.

The carriage wheels began to squeal on a sharply canted curve and
the train entered a tunnel. The lights came on and Lloyd stood up to
retrieve his Gladstone bag from the rack. 'Nearly there,' he said.

A few moments later, the wheels still screeching, the carriage
ground out into the open, wreathed in drifting, grey, sulphurous
smoke. Bill pulled down the window and peered out. The platform
approached slowly, hissing steam from the engine half obscuring the
view. Salisbury . . . capital of Wiltshire, his county. When he was a
boy, he and his Dad would sometimes bicycle here on Sundays –
twenty-two miles each way from Pennel Crecy, it was, but they'd
pass Stonehenge on the way and that was worth the sweat, just to see
those great grey stones standing out there alone on the Plain.

The train stopped and he stood aside, to let Lloyd precede him onto the platform. A lance corporal of the regiment was standing directly opposite the door, stiffening now in salute. Why, it was old Bogey Harris!

Lloyd said, 'Morning, corporal. Have you come to meet us?'

'Mr Lloyd? Yes, sir.' The corporal's hand came down. 'The colonel sent me.' He darted into the carriage and pulled down Bill's two suitcases. 'Anything else, sir?'

Lloyd said, 'Nothing for me, except this Gladstone.'

Bill said, 'My bike's in the guard's van.'

Corporal Harris hurried to the back of the train, returning in a few minutes wheeling Bill's bicycle. Lloyd had his back to them, so for a moment the two younger men stood facing each other, half smiling. Both had Wiltshire accents, though the corporal's was much broader than the second lieutenant's, for Bill had been working at burying his under a standard British upper-class accent for two years now, since he became an officer of the Queen's Own Wessex Rifles.

Harris said, 'Don't know how we're going to get your bike into the taxi, sir.'

Bill said, 'Oh, it's not far to the depot. I'll ride it. You take Mr Lloyd and my suitcases up in the taxi.'

The lance corporal said, 'I'll ride the bike, sir. You go with Mr Lloyd.'

Bill hesitated; but Bogey Harris was a stickler for the proper forms – especially with him, since they had grown up together as boys in the Pennels not so long ago. He mustn't let it appear that Harris was taking advantage of their old closeness. 'All right,' he said. 'The brakes aren't too good, so be careful.'

Then they were outside the station, and a tall old taxi puffed up; Lloyd got in, then he followed, and Bogey handed in his suitcases and stood back, saluting again, holding the bike in his other hand. 'Quebec Barracks,' Lloyd said to the driver, and they were off, puttering through the narrow curved streets of Salisbury, and at last up the slight rise to the blackened brick walls of the Victorian dungeon called Quebec Barracks, depot of the Queen's Own Wessex Rifles. When the taxi stopped outside the officers' mess, Lloyd said, 'Well, good luck to you, Miller, whatever you do. What *will* you do, anyway?'

'I don't know,' Bill said.

*   *   *

37

An hour later Bill was facing Colonel Canby, commanding officer of the depot, across a wide, uncluttered table. All the formalities had been dealt with and he was standing at ease, while Canby leaned back in his chair, twisting a pencil in his fingers. He said, 'I'm making you musketry officer, Miller – that means grenades, too, of course. You know how much stock we put in shooting, being a rifle regiment. We usually win the King's Cup at Bisley one year out of three, on the average. We have half a dozen Bisley candidates here, but you'll have nothing to do with them – they're on their own under Captain Pudney. Your job is to handle the recruits – musketry training in the indoor range, with .22s, and on the open range with .303s.'

'Yes, sir,' Bill said. The Canbys were important County people, and had a big house quite close, in Damerham. The colonel was a baronet, and had white hair and a white moustache.

'That's about all,' Canby said. 'The adjutant will give you a copy of the training programme and then it'll be up to you to fix the musketry timetables with the commanders of the recruit platoons . . . and be careful to watch your expenditures. We can't fire off ammunition the way we could in France . . . You've been shown your quarters? Good. Oh, you come from the Pennels, don't you? You'd better take a few days off to tell them you're home from Germany. But be back on Saturday. We're having a big dance at Damerham Court and we'd like you to come. All the subalterns have been invited.'

'Thank you very much, sir . . . uniform or plain clothes?'

'Do you have mess kit? Of course not . . . well, wear service dress. The war's over but peace hasn't really set in yet, has it . . . certainly not in Ireland.'

He nodded in dismissal. Bill hesitated, then said, 'Sir, do you have any idea how long it will be before I shall be demobbed? My parents will be wanting to know.'

The colonel pulled a document towards him. He looked up. 'Three months, probably, Miller. We're very busy processing the men returning from battalions that have been overseas. When you are demobbed, what will you be doing? You were too young to have had a job or profession when you joined up, weren't you?'

'Yes, sir . . . I don't know, sir . . . I don't know at all.' Bill saluted, wheeled about and marched out.

* * *

Next day, Bill arrived at his parents' home before eleven, having pedalled across the Plain and then up the valley of the Avon. After dinner his mother said, 'Now off with you, Billy, and go and see all your old friends . . . Mary Agnew knows you're back in England.'

'How did she find that out?' Bill asked, wondering.

''Cause Bob Harris came in on the last train last night, and told them in the Grapes that he'd met you at Salisbury station earlier – then of course everyone knew in no time.'

Bill grunted. So Bogey was here, was he? It would be good to talk to him as friend to friend, not officer to soldier. To his mother he said, 'Sure I can't help Dad?'

'Get away with you, lad,' she said, 'You're an officer. You can't be seen behind the counter of a draper's shop.'

'I'm not ashamed of Dad's work,' he said defiantly. He'd taken a lot of ragging about that, some of it good-tempered, most just snobbery, but he'd stood to his guns. If they didn't want a draper's son as an officer of the Wessex, they should have said so before they put the black stars on his shoulders back in '17.

But his mother said, 'Now, Billy, you listen to me. My Dad was a roadmender, a navvy, and well you know it. And I spoke broader than anyone here, broader even than Joe Collins . . . and I put myself up in the world, by working, by listening, reading, learning whatever anyone could teach me, so that your father wasn't ashamed to marry me even though he was a grammar-school man . . . and now you're an officer, you have the commission from His Majesty the King, and we're that proud of you because one day perhaps *your* son will be Sir William Miller, and a knight and all. You go and see Mary Agnew . . . but don't do anything foolish, mind. There are lots of nice girls in the world, you know.'

'I know, Mum,' he said, 'Some of them are even German.'

'Huns!' she said viciously. 'Run along now.' He put on his tweed cap and went out. It was nice wearing plain clothes after over three years in uniform, first during the war and then occupying Germany, so that the Jerries would know you were not just tourists but the winners, to be treated with respect. Before the war, old soldiers told him, officers wore uniform only for morning parades. In the afternoons, what did they do? Go foxhunting? Exercise their polo ponies? Shoot pheasants? Take the train to London and spend the evening with fancy women . . .?

Mrs Agnew was delighted to see him at the door of their little cottage. Mary was in, ironing with a big flat-iron in a corner of the kitchen. She looked up when he went in, following her mother, dropped the iron and ran into his arms. They'd been good friends before the war – but he was just sixteen when he went off, and she was seventeen . . . old enough, he supposed, but it hadn't happened: some kissing behind hedges, trying it out to see what it was like, walking hand in hand . . . a sort of tacit acknowledgement among the boys that she was his, because although they all liked her, especially Jumper Collins, none of them kept hanging round her after she'd shown that she liked Bill best. They cuddled now, her head against his chest, while Mrs Agnew picked up the iron and took up the ironing where Mary had stopped. 'Run along now,' she said. 'Walk up to the canal – it's a beautiful day.' Bill noticed that she didn't urge him to be careful, as his own mother had. She would like him for a son-in-law, especially now that he was an officer.

In the lane, Mary took his hand and they walked slowly up the gradual rise. Ahead of them, Crecy hill was low and flat-topped, crowned with a copse of elms silhouetted against Marlborough down beyond. Short of that, curving hawthorn hedges showed the line of the Kennet and Avon canal, built in the 1830s, now abandoned to weeds, carp, bream, tench, pike – and now and then a punt or a canoe. At the humpbacked old brick bridges where the cart tracks crossed, oval iron notices proclaimed that the canal was the property of the Great Western Railway.

She said shyly, 'You look different than when I last saw 'ee, Bill . . . older, more of a man, loike.'

'I am,' he said. 'I was twenty a couple of days ago. And I've been an officer since 17 August 1917.'

He felt a pompous ass saying it, but she said quickly, 'I *know*, Bill. We're all so proud of you . . . 'Twas Bob Harris brought the news you were back. He's staying in the army, bean't he?'

Bill nodded, 'Yes. He's a lance corporal now . . . Jumper's been home a couple of months, hasn't he?'

'Jumper?'

'Joe, I mean – Joe Collins. In the army every Collins is called "Jumper". All Harrises are "Bogey" . . . and all Millers are "Dusty".'

40

'But they don't call you Dusty no more, do they?'

'Some of the officers do, wartime officers, like me. The others call me Miller. The men don't use any nickname – to my face. Behind my back I'm sure they call me Dusty, if not something like Old Fishface, Moonraker Bill – not many of our officers come from Wiltshire, you know. The gentry from here seem to go into the 60th or the Rifle Brigade or the cavalry . . . though we've got some, like Colonel Canby.'

'Canby of Damerham Court,' she said with almost religious awe. 'My Mum was in service there a few years afore she got married.' She squeezed his hand. 'It's lovely to have you back,' she whispered. He looked down at her, five foot three beside his five foot nine, her hair brown, her eyes deep blue, her bosom deep and wide. Then: 'What are you going to do now, Bill?'

He felt a momentary irritation. His father had asked him; his mother had asked; Colonel Canby had asked; his CO in Cologne had asked; and now Mary. Couldn't they just accept the fact that he was back? He needed time. What was the hurry?

As he had not answered, she said, 'Are you going to stay in the army?'

He said soberly, 'I don't know. It's not up to me. They decide whom they would like to stay on as regular officers, and then ask them if they want to. They haven't asked me.'

'But do *you* want to? Would you say yes if they did?'

He was about to snap at her, but realized that it was an important question which had been in the back of his own mind, if he was honest with himself, for months now. When the war was on, the army was not only a career, it was a place, a home, time and space combined – there was nothing beyond it. Then the war ended and suddenly there were other dimensions, visions – a home, wife, children. But what did one *do*, in this new world?

He said, 'I'm not trained for anything else but to be a soldier. I have never thought of being anything else, because . . .'

'Your father would like you to take over the shop,' she said.

He said, 'I ran away from home and joined up to avoid that, in 1915 . . . I don't feel any different now.'

He sensed the disappointment in her. She would like him to come back, get out of uniform, get behind the counter in the shop. She'd

41

know who he was then; as an officer, he was a stranger, beyond her reach even to understand.

He said, 'I thought I'd want to get out as soon as I could . . . everyone was talking like that after the Armistice, but then . . . there's nothing like war . . . or soldiers . . . they're so hard . . . and soft . . . they'll steal and kill . . . and give their legs, their lives . . . they'll take . . . and share . . . and break, and make . . . I don't know what else will ever satisfy me. But then, will I ever be a *good* soldier?'

'You've done very well,' she cried indignantly, 'being mentioned in dispatches and made an officer.'

'I could have done better,' he said. 'I was learning, and I don't learn very quickly . . . Whatever I do, I want to do well – very well. In the army that's not easy, but it's important. It's what wins . . . and saves men's lives, men who are your friends, like Bogey and Jumper.'

She squeezed his hand again and, pausing, turned him round. 'Kiss!' she pleaded.

He bent and kissed her on her upturned lips. Her soft body pressed and moulded against his. Her arms twined around his neck. She wanted him to ask her to marry him. Perhaps he should, soon. It would be nice to get that settled, and not have to lust after German whores, or London tarts, or romantic girls who fell for your uniform. But not now. He dared not commit himself yet, when he was unsure of so much.

He gradually untangled himself, and they walked slowly on up the rise, over the canal, up Crecy hill, to sit there in the long June grass and talk of nothing, and everything: she telling him with her tone, her eyes, the curves of her body that she loved him, and would make him a good and faithful wife; and he, cautious, avoiding the words that would commit his honour to her, but being drawn closer, recognizing her love from infancy through childhood, through the pains of puberty, at last to manhood and womanhood.

The next day, towards evening, Bill walked with Lance Corporal Bogey Harris along the towpath of the canal. He said, 'Mary told me that you were going to stay in the army.'

'I don't know,' Harris said, 'I thought of it . . . but I might go to Swindon. It's not far.'

'Swindon?' Bill asked, wondering. 'You want to work in the Great Western shops? I thought it was mostly skilled mechanical labour there.'

'It is,' Harris said. 'I'm thinking of the football team, Swindon Town.'

'Ah, you were good at soccer when we were boys.'

'I got better,' Harris said, 'Swindon would give me a tryout, a chance.'

'You're good enough,' Bill said. 'But it's not a long career, you know. Ten years at the most, then . . .' He waved his hand.

'Yes, but then ten years would be a lot better than ten years in Doolalli and those other Indian stations that we heard so much about from the old sweats . . . What are *you* going to do, Dusty?'

'You, too?' Bill said. He was silent, walking on, chewing a blade of grass. 'I don't know.'

'What about Mary Agnew?'

'I don't know that, either.'

Harris said, 'Excuse me, Dusty . . . and if I do stay in the army this'll be the last time I'll ever call you that, I swear . . . excuse me, but the two things are tied up. Jumper Collins looks like a ghost – lost twenty pounds moping since he was demobbed, waiting for Mary to get tired of waiting for you. He loves her . . . more than loves her, he worships her, always has . . . but you've always been in the light.'

'I am very fond of Mary,' Bill said a little stiffly.

'Ah, don't come the officer over me now,' Harris beseeched. 'Listen, Mary's a good girl. She can cook and sew and make clothes and milk cows and grow cabbages and tomatoes and drench sheep and feed chickens. *If* you're going to stay on, and be a regular officer, you can't marry her. It isn't that she'll let you down – though she will, couldn't help it – it's that she'd be miserable the rest of her life. *If* you're going to come back and work in your Dad's until you take over, then she'll be a good wife. It's not a farm, but there's that big plot you have at the back, room for chickens, vegetables and rabbits, and everyone she knows will be her friends from the farms all round . . . you see?'

'I see,' Bill said at last; and then: 'Thanks for telling me straight, Bogey.'

43

They walked on along the towpath, heads bent, silent now.

Bill had bicycled down to Damerham for the ball. One or two of the other subalterns had cars, and three had motorbikes, but none had offered to give him a ride. Perhaps they didn't know yet that he was in the depot; perhaps they meant to show him that the Queen's Own Wessex Rifles didn't take kindly to officers with Wiltshire accents – not in peacetime.

Damerham Court blazed with lights, lights sparkling out of the tall French windows along the ground floor, lights strung from tree to tree of the copper beeches lining the lawn that swept down to the stream, here artificially dammed. The stream marked the limit of the Damerham Court property. Across the little lake the land still belonged to Colonel Canby, but was let out to a tenant farmer. Couples strolled on the lawn, some men in white tie and tails, most in uniform – naval blue, some RAF in their rather alarming bright pale blue, the rest in plain old khaki service dress. The dance band was installed in a corner of the great hall, playing a jerky foxtrot. The place was full of women and the scent of women – a lot of young girls in white or pale blue or green; some dashing widows in black and scarlet . . . plenty of widows these days.

What should he do now? He had introduced himself to the Colonel and Lady Canby, and she'd given him a dance programme with its little pencil tied to it, and turned away to another new arrival. What was he supposed to do next? Go up to some girl and demand a dance? Fill his card for the whole evening, all with strangers? The battalion had thrown a couple of big dances in Cologne, but they'd been rather different – more regimented, thoroughly planned; and of course there'd been nothing like so many women – just the wives and daughters of the British Occupation troops. This ball here at Damerham Court was being given by the colonel, but it was a civilian affair; the Gentry, At Home – where he had never been.

A voice beside him said, 'You look as if you'd like to know where the bathrooms are,' followed by a giggle.

He looked round and saw a young woman of about his own age, with a cat face, turned-up nose, thick fair hair across a low forehead, wide-set blue eyes, a fairly full figure. She giggled again. He found himself blushing. That was a rather daring thing for a respectable

44

young lady to say to a man, and he wasn't used to it. He stammered, 'N-not really . . . I'm just wondering who I should ask to dance. I d-don't know anybody here . . . except a few of the men . . .'

'And you don't want to dance with them, do you? Why not ask me?'

Bill said, 'I'd love to, Miss . . .'

'Canby,' she said. 'Pauline. I have two younger sisters here, at the ball, though one of them's only fifteen and shouldn't really be allowed down. Can you foxtrot?'

'A bit,' he said, smiling now, for she was so animated, her speech made energetic by movements of her hands, her eyes darting to his face, then across the room, back, her lips curling in a smile, fading.

He began to write her name in his programme, but she took his arm with a brusque gesture. 'Come on, let's dance. You only have to write it down when you book dances ahead.'

She led him onto the floor. He started diffidently, then gradually took command, for he'd learned that dancing didn't work if the couple had different ideas about what they were going to do. As he led, she followed, her body moulding more closely to his. As they danced, they talked.

'Why haven't I seen you before?' she asked. 'Daddy is always having the subalterns down, for tennis, croquet, dances . . .'

'I've just arrived from the 2nd Battalion in Cologne,' he said.

'Escaped just in time. They're going to India next trooping season,' she cried, in mock horror. India! What a fate! You dance very well, but not *too* well . . . Daddy says, "Don't trust young fellows who dance like bloody gigolos," . . . but I'd trust you.' She giggled.

She was using a faint flowery perfume, almost as simple as rose water, but not quite. There was something heavier, more exotic in it, something oriental. Sandalwood, that was it. She was really very pretty . . . more than pretty, so alive – her body fairly throbbed against him.

He said, 'You are . . . beautiful, Miss Canby.'

'Speak up.' She put her head closer to his. 'I can't hear you over the band.'

'You are beautiful,' he said. Her head was very close and with a tiny movement she kissed him on the ear. Bill looked round nervously to see if anyone had noticed, especially her father or mother. But apparently not.

'Thank you,' he said, smiling into her eyes.

'Thank *you*,' she said, then: 'My next two dances are booked, but after that – I have two free. Here, write them in.' The music ended and she said, 'I'll be there, in front of the fireplace.' Then she was gone, merged into the crowd, now all moving towards the lawn.

Bill walked slowly out into the open, thinking. Pauline Canby. Eldest daughter of Colonel Sir Roger Canby, Baronet, Commander of the Order of St Michael and St George. Hadn't there been a son, killed with the 5th Battalion at Gallipoli? Now just the three girls . . . she was not only beautiful, but so full of life . . .

A man strolled up beside him under the strung lights by the croquet lawn, and said, 'You have made the acquaintance of our Pauline, I see.'

Bill said, 'Yes. She saw that I didn't know anybody, and introduced herself.'

The man was Richard Merton, another subaltern of the regiment, but four years older than Bill, and a regular, having passed out of Sandhurst just in time to join the 1st Battalion at Mons in 1914. The Mertons were landed gentry, and their property at Manningford Bohun was close to Pennel Crecy. Bill had known Richard all his life, in the sense of having seen him at flower shows and fêtes, or riding on small cobs, hunting with the Tedworth on the rare occasions when hounds met in the Vale . . . then Merton had been Bill's platoon commander when Bill first reached France, as No. 74938861 Rifleman Miller, W.

Merton said, 'I heard you were here. But you'll be demobbed soon.'

'Three months,' Bill said.

'Then . . . back to Pennel Crecy and the drapery? A bit different from this' – he waved his hand nonchalantly at the great house, the lights, the lawn, the lake, the gliding ladies and gentlemen – 'but you'll get used to it again.'

He moved off. Richard Laurence de Houssaye Merton, MC . . . and DS, for Damned Snob, Bill thought. Good God, it was barely a year since that night at the edge of the French wood, when . . . Better try to forget that. But Merton hadn't. Merton never would.

He headed back towards the house. Mustn't miss his dances with Miss Canby.

When his turn came, it was a waltz; and as soon as they were out on the dance floor, moving somewhat cautiously on the uneven boards of the great hall, she said, 'You're a Wiltshire man, aren't you?'

He stiffened, 'Yes,' he said. 'My father has a draper's shop in Pennel Crecy, and I was born there.'

'Oh,' she said. 'Close to Richard Merton's place. I've been there a lot . . . I was quite keen on Richard, as a matter of fact, but he's so GS. He won't marry anyone till he's thirty. I can't wait that long.' She giggled. 'I don't mind your accent a bit. The war blew away all that silly snobbery, didn't it? How can anyone look down on people like you, after what you've done? We ought to look up to you, and I do . . . though you're not so terribly tall, are you?' She giggled again. Then she squeezed his hand and said, 'You have a strong face . . . but such gentle hands.'

He felt a surge of affection for her; admiration for her outspokenness; awe of her beauty: the three emotions merged. Now the hall, the house, the lawn also gradually became one, a place that only existed and took shape from the fact that it enfolded them, the place that they were the centre of. Their dancing together became more fluid, as he led by instinct and she followed not through physical guidance but by intuition. After the dances he had with her, when the music began again they moved automatically onto the floor, and he took her, ready to sweep her out in the slow foxtrot, when a curt voice at his shoulder said, 'My dance, I believe, Miller.' It was Merton.

He let go of Pauline in mid-step, feeling dazed. Pauline mumbled, 'Richard? Oh, is it really?' She peered at the programme that had been dangling from her wrist as she danced. 'So it is.' Then, as Merton took her into the dance, she threw a long look at Bill over his shoulder and mouthed silently, 'Next dance, outside,' inclining her head towards the open doors to the lawn.

Bill was waiting for her, smoking a cigarette, when she eventually hurried out. She peered about, saw him under the nearest copper beech, and came quickly to him. She took both his hands in hers and whispered, 'Bill . . . Bill . . .' She moved close and muttered, 'I've never felt like this before . . . and I've only known you three hours.' She moved round the tree, so that its thick trunk hid them from the doors and the lawn, peopled with strolling couples.

He muttered, 'What will people think, us going behind the . . .?'

'What does it matter what people think?' she said, and moved her face closer. He bent a little and kissed her. Her lips parted. Slowly at first, and then in a flash, he realized that he was in love, head over the heels, helplessly, overwhelmed by love. They stayed locked a long time; at last broke away; returned to the dance floor; and danced again. and again.

Later, she said, 'Tomorrow's Sunday. Come down and play tennis and have tea.'

'Better make it croquet,' he said. 'I've never held a tennis racquet in my life. Or we could swim. I'm a good swimmer.'

'All right. Be here by three o'clock. Now, there are only a few dances left and they're booked. So – see you tomorrow. We're going to dance a lot more together – because . . . I love you.'

'I love you,' he said seriously; serious, for he had never made that declaration before. Then he said his goodbyes and thankyous and bicycled back to Salisbury, thinking, I was wondering in Pennel the other day, why I didn't ask Mary Agnew to marry me. Now I know.

Colonel Sir Roger Canby sat upright in his swivel chair; and Bill, opposite, though he was technically 'standing at ease' did not feel at all at ease; for the colonel's voice was noticeably harder than when he'd greeted Bill on his arrival at the depot. He was saying now, 'You first met my daughter Pauline at the ball we had at Damerham Court early in June, I believe?'

'Yes, sir.'

'And you danced most of the evening with her, I am told – I saw you several times myself.'

'Yes, sir . . . We danced well together.'

'Quite.' Canby's voice softened a bit. 'Look, Miller, I wouldn't normally talk to you about a matter like this in the orderly room, but in your case . . . in *this* case, I think it is the right place, because the army comes into it.'

'How, sir?' Bill asked, mystified.

Canby said, 'In the three weeks since that ball, you have been down to the Court three or four times a week, in the afternoons, playing croquet, learning to play tennis, I believe . . . swimming, bicycling all over the countryside, always with Pauline. You have taken her to tea in Salisbury several times. You attended four other country-house dances, to which Pauline obtained invitations for you.'

He was silent, staring at Bill. Bill said in a low voice, 'Yes, sir.'

The colonel leaned back. 'I have to ask you, what are your intentions towards my daughter?'

Bill hesitated; then, thinking, the only thing to do is tell the truth, he said, 'I love Pauline, sir. I haven't asked her to marry me, because, well, she's your daughter . . . I have no money and no prospects . . . she'll inherit Damerham . . . my father's a draper. But I do love her. I don't know what to do. I'm just happy being with her.'

The colonel said, more kindly, 'And she's obviously happy to be with you. But the situation can't be allowed to drag on like this, can it? It's bad for her reputation, and a stalemate won't do you any good, either . . . You don't have any commitments at home?'

Bill said firmly, 'No, sir.' Mary Agnew loved him, and would marry him, but now he did not love her. He loved Pauline.

The colonel said, 'Now I didn't call you in here on my own initiative. This meeting is Pauline's doing. Over a week ago she told us – her mother and me – that she wanted to marry you. To be honest, we have done all we can to dissuade her, using much the same reasoning that you yourself used just now. We know of several eminently suitable young men who are or have been very much taken with her. But the war has had its effect, even on those who did not take part in it. Young people don't want to wait – because for too long they have known that tomorrow may not come. They don't want to listen, to be careful . . . because caution and patience were not the qualities we needed of them these past four years. Frankly, I think you're both much too young. Also, I must tell you, as her father, that some of Pauline's enthusiasms do not last very long. But she has made up her mind. She wants to marry you, as soon as possible.'

Bill's heart leaped, and he stammered, 'That's . . . wonderful, sir! May I ask her, then?'

'Not so fast, young man. I told you the army came into this. You are at present due to be demobbed in a little over two months' time. What are you going to do then? Join your father in the draper's shop in Pennel Crecy?'

'No, sir,' Bill said without hesitation. 'I ran away to join up to avoid that.'

49

'Farm? You could become a tenant farmer . . . but do you have the skill?'

'No, sir. Nor the desire.'

'You're not university educated. You have no special aptitude for business, that I have heard of. Or connections who would get you good employment. You see, we don't want Pauline to live out her life as . . . well, a nobody. She was raised at Damerham Court, with all that that implies. She has had all the money she could need, in reason. She will still have an ample allowance from me after she marries, if she marries suitably. And believe me, Miller, she will not be a happy wife, or woman, if her husband does not give her a proper position in society. Her mother and I know her a great deal better than you do, even though we are old fogeys by your standards; and there are perhaps some things you have not learned about Pauline . . . you have not had the time. I am not being disloyal to her, but simply stating a fact, when I say that she is not a very constant young woman. She is not happy for long in one situation and seems to like change for the sake of change . . . then, when the change has occurred, she wishes it had not, or that it had been in some other direction. You are both very young; but service in the trenches – command of men in battle – has given *you* a certain maturity beyond your actual years. The same has not happened to Pauline – nor to many other young women left in England. Rather the reverse, for the world they lived in for four years precluded planning. How can a girl make plans when at any moment a healthy and handsome fiancé may suddenly return as a paralysed cripple? You will have a lot to put up with . . . Pauline has a temper, too . . . She is a wilful filly with an inconstant mind of her own, and an iron mouth . . . yet you must be gentle. Brutality won't bring love or happiness. Can you do it, however much you and she may now claim to love each other?'

'I think so, sir,' Bill said obstinately. Of course I can, he thought to himself; Pauline was not the problem; his future career was. He braced himself. There was a way: he held the King's Commission, and he had earned that privilege in battle. What Pauline had said was right – his accent didn't matter; and what he told Mary Agnew up by the canal was right, too. In his heart he was a soldier, and could never be anything else; that was what had made every other possible career seem so unpleasant, or unworthy, or both. He looked the colonel in the eye and said, 'I want to be a regular officer of the regiment, sir. I've commanded our men in battle and that's all I really want to do.'

Colonel Canby got up quickly from his chair and strode round the desk, his hand out. 'Thank God *you* said it. I swore to myself I wouldn't ask you to apply for a regular commission, because I didn't want you to do it just to get my blessing to marry Pauline. It had to come from you. You do want to be an officer, a good one! And of course there's no question of our refusing our daughter permission to marry a regular officer of my own regiment. When shall we have the wedding?'

'I'd better ask Pauline first, sir,' Bill said, smiling at last, feeling his forehead damp with the sweat he had shed during the interview.

Canby said, 'We'll make it 14 September, the day after Quebec Day. The colonel-in-chief usually comes down for that and perhaps we can persuade him to stay over for your wedding.'

'That would be great, sir,' Bill said, thinking, our colonel-in-chief is the Prince of Wales. Phew! What a wedding! Now he'd have to tell Mary Agnew. She'd be miserable, but soon she'd marry Jumper Collins, and Jumper would be the happiest man alive. It seemed that not everyone could be happy in this world. And he'd committed himself to becoming a regular . . . phew again! He braced himself once more. He might not be the cleverest officer in the army, but he was a hard worker and he didn't like to give up, or fail. He knew the men as well as anyone else. And he was committed to them . . . and to the spirit of his boyhood hero, Nelson; which meant, when he was called upon – victory. The only trouble was, he had only known the regiment and the army in war. What would they be like, for him, in peace?

51

4

October 1921: England

Peacetime soldiering . . . he could close his eyes and see it, hear it, feel it, as though it were present, instead of so many years past. The reality of it was fixed in his memory because it was like something ingrained by endless repetition. There must have been little daily differences, but in memory every day was the same: Monday, Tuesday, Wednesday, Thursday, Friday, Saturday, a little hiccup of change on Sunday – but every Sunday was the same as every other . . . on again, Monday, Tuesday, Wednesday . . .

Outside the barrack buildings the rain fell in heavy, straight lines out of a dark, low sky. Puddles covered the uneven gravel surface of the parade ground behind the cookhouses, and the regimental flag clung limp and sodden to its pole outside the quarter guard. Inside Aldershot barrack building H-29 Bill, now a lieutenant, was inspecting the building, the men of his platoon who occupied it, and their clothing and equipment. His platoon sergeant, Dreen, followed at his heels, notebook and pencil at the ready.

Bill stopped at the tenth man, as he had stopped at the first nine, and looked first at the stripped bed, to see that its general shape conformed to regulations and regimental standing orders: blankets folded just so, pillow set there; below that the webbing equipment spread out as though on an invisible soldier's back; waterbottle, corked – he lifted it and shook – full; bayonet in its leather scabbard, the scabbard heelball-polished, shining; pouch studs all closed, the pouches themselves properly puffed out with cardboard and paper to look as they would if they each contained two clips of .303 ball ammunition . . . pack, haversack . . . The pack was open, its official contents spread out below – housewife, groundsheet, boot brush – no button stick for this was a rifle regiment and all buttons were black bone and could not be polished . . . cap with badge, a Maltese Cross surrounded by a laurel wreath and over that the word QUEBEC, all in silver . . . black leather chinstrap gleaming . . . one pair of

52

boots on the stone floor at the foot of the bed, the other on the soldier's feet . . .

He looked the soldier up and down – 74953702 Rifleman Nesbitt; about five foot five, a coal miner before he enlisted soon after the war. Tunic buttoned up, shoulder titles and collar badges in position, boots polished, leather laces tied tight, puttees neat – Bill counted the folds: correct. As he moved on, Rifleman Nesbitt 'stood to his front' and the man by the next bed sprang to attention – Lance Corporal Robert Harris, Bogey Harris. Bill suddenly had a memory of a time when he and Bogey had jumped out of a hedge to frighten some girls walking home from school.

That was a long time ago. They were in the army now. Harris stared straight ahead, shoulders back. He was a good soldier, and a good NCO. He'd get his second stripe as soon as there was a vacancy . . . blankets folded just so, pillow set there, below that the equipment spread out as though on an invisible soldier's back; waterbottle corked – he lifted and shook it – full; bayonet in its scabbard. He pulled it out and looked at it and said, 'Too much oil left on the surface, Harris.'

'Sir!'

'No, don't take his name, sergeant. Just see that he keeps it bright-clean and only slightly oiled – like his rifle.'

'Sir!'

Bill moved on, stifling a yawn. These inspections were important. Soldiering was not and never could be all drill parades, or route marches, or field training, let alone real battle. The men had to be taught to keep their clothing and everything else the government gave them just so, in exactly such and such a place, so that when they needed it it would be there, ready for use. But no one could call barrack-room inspection an exciting occupation, except perhaps some of those fellows who relished the chance to find things wrong and put men on charges or extra drills.

He moved on to the next bed. Harris 'stood to his front', the next soldier jumped to attention . . . blankets folded just so, pillow set there, below that the equipment spread out . . . He shook his head, to concentrate. You got to a point where you did not see what you were looking at. The job deserved more than a robot – the men deserved more. He lifted the man's waterbottle, uncorked it, and sniffed. 'This is beer,' he said. 'Flat, of course. Take his name.'

'Sir!'

He moved on.

The morning's work done, he bicycled slowly home through the rain, his Burberry buttoned up, water dripping down inside his collar from the back of his SD cap. Their house was not a military married quarter, for, having married so young, he was not entitled to one. Still, with the allowance Pauline had from her father, they had been able to rent a nice small house about two miles from the battalion's barracks. He let himself in and stood in the hall, carefully taking off the Burberry and hanging it in the downstairs bathroom to drip off. 'I'm home, darling,' he called.

For a time there was no response, then he heard a door opening upstairs, and Pauline came heavily downstairs. She was very pregnant. He kissed her and she said, 'Mrs Baxter didn't come this morning, heaven knows why. And I haven't had time to cook a thing. Let's go out to lunch.'

'Or have bread and cheese here,' he said, 'I'm always happy with that.'

She gestured a little impatiently. '*I'm* hungry, darling. I'm used to a proper lunch every day, and I need it now.'

'Of course,' he said, 'We'll have to get a taxi. It's pretty awful out there. Where shall we go?'

'Oh, anywhere. The Royal has good lunches.'

Bill picked up the telephone from its hook beyond the hat and umbrella stand, and called Gamble's garage, taxi service. Perhaps they ought to get a car of their own. They could afford one, if they were careful and didn't buy too expensive a model. They needed one, really, if only for when the baby was born. Apparently babies always came at two in the morning, and it wasn't easy to get a taxi at that hour.

He helped Pauline into her coat and soon the taxi came. They hurried out and bundled into the back seat. Then Pauline said, 'Let's get a car, Bill.'

'I've just been thinking we should. What make?'

'Oh . . . a nice one. A Daimler, or a Rolls Royce, everyone knows they're the best . . . perhaps a Sunbeam or a big Vauxhall. It'll have to be big, whatever we get, because there'll be five of us when we go out on picnics or trips.'

'Five?'

'Well, you know we're going to have two children, and we'll have a nanny, who'll always come with us. A picnic's no fun for me if I'm carrying one baby and holding onto the other all the time.'

'All right,' he said, 'but we really must find out about prices, and decide how much we can afford.'

'We can afford what we want,' she said impatiently. 'Daddy'll buy it for us.'

Bill was inspecting cookhouses, as orderly officer, followed by the regimental quartermaster sergeant. The cooking stoves were coal-fired, and now damped down for the inspection. The walls were hung with pots, for each cookhouse had to feed a whole company, officially a hundred and thirty men, but usually less than a hundred in battalions of the Home Establishment. Recruiting chronically fell short of goals, except in very hard times; and the battalions, overseas, guarding the Empire, had to be kept up to full strength; so battalions doing their time at home suffered.

Bill peered into a pot and drew his finger round the bottom . . . dry and clean; nothing came off on his finger. He jumped up and drew his finger along the top of a high shelf. When he brought his hand down the finger was dark with dust. He held it out to the RQMS, and said, 'Filthy.' The RQMS turned on the company cook corporal and bellowed, 'Look at Mr Miller's finger, corporal! I'll be back an hour after inspection's over, to see that all shelves are clean.'

The cooks were wearing off-white tunics over their khaki trousers. The tunics were clean enough, but the fabric was no longer pure white. He'd discuss it with the RQMS. Perhaps they could afford new tunics. But if they did buy new ones, how long would they remain pure white?

'Let's see the menus for the week,' he said. The cook corporal took a notice off the wall and handed it to him . . . mutton and cabbage for dinner today, sausages and mash for supper . . . scrambled eggs and bacon for breakfast tomorrow, Irish stew for dinner, Scotch eggs for supper. He turned to the cook. 'Eggs twice in the day? Is that necessary?'

The corporal answered, 'We got more eggs in the ration this week than we usually do at this time of year, sir. Had to do something with them, so . . .'

The RQMS cut in, 'The men always like eggs, sir. They'd eat 'em three times a day if we let them.'

He's right, Bill thought; but he wished it wasn't so. Eggs produced truly sulphurous farts, and the atmosphere in the barrack rooms when they were doing indoor parades, and even route marches, was sometimes barely breathable.

He moved on to the next cookhouse.

It wasn't raining this day and he had a pleasant ride home in the wintry sun, his Burberry rolled on the carrier of the bike, for it was balmy out, almost warm. If it went on like this much longer, the trees would start coming into bud; and here it was just into the New Year . . . why couldn't a crisis blow up somewhere and the battalion be sent off to deal with it? But where? Ireland had become a Free State and anyway that would be a beastly sort of fighting, like a civil war . . . The Germans were as quiet as mice . . . India now, there was always something going on there; but India already had a large garrison, capable of dealing with any trouble short of a second Indian Mutiny; and the 2nd Battalion was out there, so the 1st would not go overseas until the 2nd came home – that was the Cardwell system . . . He might apply for transfer to the 2nd. There'd be plenty of officers eager to change places with him, as not many liked service in India . . . nor would Pauline.

He reached the house, put his bicycle in the woodshed where it lived, and went in. At once he heard the sound of weeping from upstairs, and called up, 'What's the matter? Can I help?'

Pauline came down and he stooped to kiss her, but she leaned away, saying, 'That girl's pregnant!'

'Who?' Bill gasped, 'Edna?' Edna was the housemaid.

'Who else? It's by some soldier in the battalion, and he says he won't marry her, because he says she's a slut and has been going out with other men.'

'Has she?'

'How should I know? Probably. What are you going to do about it?'

Bill hung up his cap, went into the drawing room and poured himself a glass of sherry. He said, 'This happens pretty often, you know. There's an established procedure for it. I'll have to talk to Edna and find out whom she says is the father. Then I tell his

56

company commander, and the man's had up and asked whether he accepts responsibility, and if he's willing to marry the girl. If he is, the company commander fixes it as soon as possible. If he isn't – we can't make him. The company commander tells the girl, or her parents, to sue through the civil courts for paternity payments.'

Pauline helped herself to sherry and said crossly, 'So now we'll have to find another housemaid, and that's not as easy as it was in my mother's time, I can tell you. Girls don't want to do any sort of domestic service these days. They want to go to the cinema, and have days and half-days off, and work with men in factories and have a good time. Thank goodness Mummy's got a good nanny ready to come up when I have the baby.'

Bill said lightly, 'Cheer up. We'll be getting the car next week.'

'That's right,' she said. She brightened, and said, 'I almost forgot. And this afternoon you can take me out to tea to the Cadena.'

He said, 'Not today, darling. I've promised to play football with my platoon. They're having a friendly against 7 Platoon in B Company.'

'I want you to take me out to tea,' she said crossly. 'You promised you would, whenever I wanted to, if you didn't have an afternoon parade.'

'I know,' he said, 'but this is just as important as a parade.'

'You don't care about me,' she said, bursting into tears. He took her in his arms, she at first sulky, then weeping more copiously but holding him tight. 'It's this baby,' she mumbled. 'He kicks and kicks and weighs a ton . . . You will take me out to tea?'

And he comforted her, but he did not take her out to tea. He played football as left half for No. 2 Platoon, A Company, which beat No. 7 Platoon, B Company by a score of 4 to 2. His captain, Lance Corporal Harris, congratulated him on his performance and Bill went home well pleased; but bracing himself unhappily against the sulkiness which he knew would greet him.

Captain Wainwright, A Company commander, sat at a big table at the far end of the barrack room, facing the doorway. An army blanket had been spread on the table, and on that rested a good deal of money, mostly in shillings and half-crowns, with some ten-shilling and even pound notes. Bill Miller sat on Wainwright's left and

Captain Morgan Lloyd on his right. Bill held in his hand the company payroll, giving every man's name in alphabetical order, with the total amount due to him, deductions, family allotments and fines if any, and the net amount now to be paid to him. The men were formed up in a dense square at the far end of the barrack room, where the beds had been pushed against the wall and piled on top of each other to make room. Outside, it was raining, or the pay parade would have been held in the open.

The company sergeant major marched up, saluted, and said, 'Pay parade ready, sir!'

Wainwright said, 'Go ahead, Miller.'

Bill called, 'Austin, Rifleman.' A soldier detached himself from the others, marched forward, halted in front of the table and saluted. Bill said, 'Twenty-five shillings pay, two and six deductions ... Twenty-two and sixpence.'

Wainwright took a pound note and a half-crown and pushed them across the blanket. Lloyd watched to see that the amount was correct. The soldier took the money, saluted, turned about and marched out of the room.

'Avery, 04, Rifleman ... twenty-five shillings pay, two and six deductions, twenty-two and sixpence ... Avery 98, Rifleman ... Badham, Corporal ... Ballantine, Rifleman ...' Bill smothered a yawn. He must concentrate. Money was involved; there could be a terrible mix-up if he read out the wrong figures ... 'Callaghan, Rifleman ... Carney, Sergeant ... Darling, Rifleman ... Dearden, Rifleman ... Dombey, Rifleman ... Dunn, Lance Corporal ... Eddy, Rifleman ...'

The parade dragged remorselessly on, until every man present had received his week's pay. The company sergeant major reported that all men on the company's roll had received pay except two in hospital and one on compassionate leave. He named them. Captain Wainwright said, 'Take the money to the men in hospital yourself, sar'nt major, and make them sign for it. Keep Thomson's until next pay parade.' He stood up. The other officers followed suit, saluting. Wainwright walked away. The parade was over.

Bill fell in beside Morgan Lloyd as the latter headed for the officers' mess. Lloyd was second-in-command of the company, having just returned to the battalion from a tour of duty on the staff in Germany. Two rows of medal ribbons glittered on his left breast. He said now, 'You looked pretty bored back there, Miller.'

Bill said, 'I was . . . I am, most of the time. I know the jobs have to be done, but they *are* boring, aren't they?'

Lloyd said, 'Nothing bores me that relates to winning the next war.'

Miller stared at him in astonishment. 'The next war? How can a pay parade affect that?'

'Because an army fights with morale as well as tanks and guns. Pay affects morale. It must be paid regularly, properly, and without any corruption or carelessness. And it has to be enough. I am wondering now about how much those men can buy – they and their wives – with what they have received . . . I wish it wasn't such a slow process, but we mustn't lose the personal contact it gives us. Everyone in the company knows – and *feels* – that Peter Wainwright is his company commander, because Peter actually pays him, from his own hand.'

They turned into the mess, took off their Sam Browne belts and caps and hung them up. It was half past eleven, and four or five officers were already in the anteroom, drinking sherry and reading *The Times*, the *Morning Post*, or *Punch*. Lloyd rang a bell and a mess waiter appeared. Bill and Lloyd both ordered dry sherries, and sat down. Lloyd leaned back. 'You fought in France for some time. Did you ever go over the top, or beat off a Jerry attack, without artillery support?' Bill shook his head. 'All right. What's the range of an 18-pounder? How many rounds of HE, smoke and shrapnel does each gun carry in its own limbers, and how many rounds of each are carried in the battery ammunition column?'

Bill's brow wrinkled, as the waiter arrived, bearing their drinks on a large silver salver. 'The gun's range is about ten thousand yards,' he said. 'But the rest . . . I don't know.'

Lloyd said, 'But you ought to know. A platoon commander has to inspect his men's socks and taste their food, and see that they get paid, yes. But if he's going to be any good, he must realize that there's more to it than that. Some time, somewhere, in the future, there'll be war, and we exist to win that war. It won't be enough just to wave your stick and lead the men over the top. It wasn't in 1914–18 and it certainly won't be next time. You have to prepare yourself, rank by rank, so that when the time comes you can make the best possible plans, using all the weapons available to you, to achieve your object, with the least possible loss. *Then*, when the best plans have been made, you lead – and they'll follow – and win.'

Bill sipped his sherry. Everyone knew that Morgan Lloyd would go far in the army; but many among his brother officers also thought he was a bit of a fanatic, and that his absorption in every aspect of his profession was not quite the thing for an officer of the Queen's Own Wessex Rifles. All that was needed was good blood, and guts, then victory came of itself, to be preserved in the flags and trophies hung round this room – the faded French Royal Colour captured on the Heights of Abraham in 1759, the curved *tulwar* taken from Tippoo Sahib at Seringapatam, the Russian Colour, on the opposite wall, taken at Inkermann, the silver gleaming everywhere – presented on appointment, on promotion, on retirement . . . No, the regiment was proud of Morgan Lloyd as a man with a magnificent war record; but they wished he wouldn't keep *thinking* about war. Foxhunting, cricket, Bisley, the drill competition, the army soccer cup: these were enough to occupy an officer's time in a more proper manner. But of course Lloyd was Welsh.

Lloyd said, 'I don't know why I'm lecturing *you* like this. I used to preach the gospel to all and sundry, but it usually went in one ear and out of the other. With you, I think – I hope – it's different. I believe you want to be a good officer and commander in battle.'

'Yes,' Bill said at once. 'I think I owe it to the men.'

'And yourself,' Lloyd said. 'You weren't born into the upper class, so you've got to show those who were – *and* the men – that you can be a good officer . . . in time, a good general . . . You must not let the army bore you, as you have been. Attack it! Learn, learn, learn! If you have any questions about where to get the right books, what to study, come to me.' He got up. 'I'm going home. Cicely'll be expecting me. One other thing – prepare yourself for the next war, not the last one.'

'But how . . .?' Bill began in despair.

'Think,' Lloyd said. 'Think of what has changed in the world, is changing, will change . . . what effect those changes will have – on tactics, strategy, movement, communication, supply . . . everywhere.' He went out of the room.

60

Bill leaned back. His glass was empty. Might as well have another before he set off home; but he wouldn't think too well with two sherries in him. Nor was the mess anteroom the right place to think about military matters. He'd have to do it at home, in the little room he had made his study. Pauline would be upset that he didn't sit with her in the drawing room all the time, or take her out to the cinema, but Morgan Lloyd was right: to be a good officer, he had to learn, and to think – to think about change . . . but what sort of change did Lloyd mean? Industrial? New inventions? Faster, bigger aircraft? Better wireless? Or new ways of thinking and seeing – Einstein? That mad Spanish painter who saw both sides of a woman's head at once? Communism? He found himself clutching his empty glass almost in desperation. Lloyd meant all change, where it affected any part of mankind anywhere; for he was thinking of war, which affected all mankind, everywhere; and was in its turn affected by all mankind. My God, he thought, how does one cope? How does one prevent oneself from going mad with a sense of inadequacy? He glanced around the room at his brother officers. They answered his question: they were pretending that nothing changed.

'Stand to your front! Wessex . . . *Rifles!*' Behind Bill, A Company sprang to attention. Bill jerked the sword in his right hand to a vertical position. The battalion was in line, in two ranks. Barely a dozen officers were present, for this was an adjutant's parade. Only officers junior to the adjutant, Lieutenant Richard Merton, attended, together with all the other ranks, from the regimental sergeant major to the newest joined rifleman.

Merton yelled, 'The battalion will fix swords – *Fix!*' At the command, every soldier armed with a rifle pushed the muzzle out with his right hand, snapped his head right to look at the right marker, and with his left hand grasped the handle of his bayonet – which, in rifle regiments, was always called a sword. The right marker waited for the next command: '. . . swords!' Then he pulled his own bayonet from its scabbard and, flashing it high, brought it down and onto the bayonet boss. Every man armed with a rifle did the same, at the same instant. When the right marker saw that all bayonets were on, he jerked his rifle back to his side, turned, marched back twelve paces to his position, and turned again.

This is a waste of time, Bill thought. Rifle regiments never fixed swords for ceremonial purposes, as Red infantry did, so all the men needed to know was how to fix them in a trench or when lying on their bellies on a battlefield. But Merton wanted it done, and after unfixing, fixed and unfixed again, before ordering, 'Present arms.'

The rifles were jerked up in two motions, and the right feet snapped back diagonally behind the left. In the same rhythm Bill and the other officers lifted the hilts of their swords to their lips, then swung the swords down beside their right thighs, the blades pointed forward and downward.

'Order – arms!' In two motions the battalion returned to its previous posture.

Merton, leaning forward on his chestnut charger, his field boots and spurs gleaming black and silver, shouted, 'Mr Miller, your sword drill is very idle . . . Battalion, right *dress*! . . . Eyes – *front*!'

Merton rode slowly down the front rank, four paces distant on his charger. 'Dirty chinstrap . . . What the hell's that man doing without a cap badge, Mr Miller? Didn't you inspect them before they came on parade?'

'Yes, sir,' Bill said. Beasley had had a cap badge at his inspection. It must have fallen out. Merton passed on, his voice becoming fainter as his horse walked towards the left end of the line; then he came back, between the ranks. 'Boots filthy, there . . . That man hasn't shaved properly . . . haircut . . . haircut . . . Are these your men, Mr Miller? They're a disgrace to the regiment. They look more like refugees from the RAF . . . Why isn't that man wearing gloves? They were ordered for the parade. Take his name . . . Stand up straight, man . . . Sergeant, your rifle's safety catch is off. If you want to keep your stripes, don't let that happen again . . .'

After the inspection, Merton put them through manoeuvres of close-order drill, more arms drill, and finally, before dismissing the officers, said, 'Mr Miller, please stay behind . . . Officers . . . dismiss! Mr Johnstone, march the parade off.' The RSM saluted and came forward, his sword still in its scabbard. Being a warrant officer class I, he wore a Sam Browne belt and carried a sword, but he never drew it. Tucked under his left arm he carried the real badge of his position, more real than the royal coat-of-arms embroidered on his sleeve – the brass-tipped pace stick with which he measured the exact thirty-inch pace on such parades as this, marching at the right of the leading company, 'walking' the pace stick beside him, twirling it with his fingers, his pouter-pigeon chest puffed up . . . As the RSM bellowed the commands that would send the companies back to their barracks under their sergeant majors, Merton, now dismounted, his horse being led away by his groom, said, 'Miller, I hear you're studying military theory.'

Bill said, 'Yes, sir.'

'There's nothing wrong with that.' Merton said. 'I'm studying for the Staff College myself, but in this regiment we don't like officers to spend time on their own advancement which they owe to the men . . . to the regiment, if you like.'

Bill said, 'I haven't, that I know of.'

Merton said, 'Your sword drill is slovenly. Practise that, instead of worrying about how the sappers are organized. Some of your men haven't shaved properly . . . or had their hair cut short enough. That's your responsibility.'

Bill said nothing. Merton said, 'Look, you're not going to the Staff College for a long time, if ever. What the CO expects you to be is a good platoon commander. What the regiment expects of you is that you be a gentleman, which is a great deal more important. You have the right stuff in you, I suppose, or old Colonel Canby would never have accepted you as a regular officer or let you marry Pauline. But you don't know instinctively which knife and fork to use at a big dinner, or what wineglass is for what wine. We do – we learned all that when we were small boys . . . and how to treat servants and soldiers . . . and generals and earls, for that matter. Try to make that sort of knowledge a part of you now, instead of learning the War Establishment of an 18-pounder battery. Make the other subalterns your model, not old Morgan. He's got a bee in his bonnet. That's all.' He nodded and walked away. Bill headed for his bicycle, propped in the rack outside the mess.

'What about my taking some leave, and going down to Damerham,' Bill said that evening.

Pauline said, 'Well, the baby's due in three weeks now. Come down with me then – a week before he's due . . . and stay as long as you can.'

'All right,' Bill said equably. They were sitting on opposite sides of the coal fire in the drawing room, the housemaid gone out for the evening. This one – Violet – was the fourth they'd had since coming to Aldershot to join the 1st Battalion after their honeymoon.

Pauline shifted her weight uncomfortably. She was very heavy now, her complexion sallow. She said, 'How much longer have we got in Aldershot? The place is driving me mad . . . Army, army, army, nothing but army. The GOC acts like a little tin god.'

'There aren't any lords or ladies to give him competition here,' Bill said, smiling. 'Anyway, I hear we're due for Dover in July. It'll be easy to take day or weekend trips over to Calais, for a change of air and food.'

'Calais is not France,' Pauline said. 'They all speak English and serve English food and beer. Dover will be just like Aldershot, for us.'

She returned to her reading, a romantic novel. Bill leaned back in his chair and closed his eyes. The wireless was playing classical music. He shut it out of his mind . . . The main problem that had occupied him since Lloyd's talk to him in the mess was coordination of all arms. But to coordinate different arms you had to know what each was capable of; how each was at present organized; and then, perhaps, how each should be organized. What exactly *was* a tank, for instance? In France, when tanks first appeared, everyone thought of them as wire crushers. Mud and barbed wire, in aprons a hundred yards deep, had been the great obstacles to advance on the Western Front. When he first went out, the artillery were trying to break the wire down by tremendous bombardments, lasting longer and longer, using more and more and heavier and heavier guns. Still, time and again, the infantry found that the bombardment had forewarned the enemy without destroying the wire, and turned good ground into impassable mud; so they became hung up, exposed and held on the wire, to be slaughtered by German machine-guns. Then the tanks came. They crushed the wire and the infantry, following behind in the shelter of the steel toads, could jump straight down into the enemy's front-line trench almost unscathed. But the other obstacle to movement – mud – had stopped the tanks, too, when it was bad enough, as it had been at Passchendaele. Good heavens, he had seen a tank near Tynecot that had absolutely sunk in the mud, only a bit of steel showing, its crew finally suffocated.

And the Germans had taken to plastering the advancing tanks with high-explosive and shrapnel fire, not to damage the tanks, though they did sometimes blow off a tread or jam a gun . . . but to 'scrape off' the following infantry, leaving the tanks alone . . . and alone they were very vulnerable to special anti-tank high-velocity guns, and to storm troops specially trained for the job of destroying them, often with flame throwers.

But now there was talk of tanks that would do twenty and more miles an hour, with infantry following in lorries, and guns towed by other lorries. That sort of tank wasn't a wire crusher . . . A mobile gun, itself, then? He really ought to find out what was going on in the design room of Vickers, or whoever made tanks. And at the War Office – what specifications or purposes had they laid down for tanks, since the Armistice? Who had done it? In consultation with whom?

Pauline said, 'We never decided what to call him.'

Bill returned to the room with a start. 'I like Roger best, after your father . . . if it's a boy.'

'That'll be nice . . . he will be a boy. And as soon as he's born, you must put him down for Cheltenham. That was Daddy's school, and they have a Junior, so we won't have to spend weeks looking for a prep school.'

Bill said, 'Fine.' He had known since they were married that any sons they had would go to a public school. As he didn't know anything about such schools himself, he was happy to let Pauline and her family decide.

She said, 'I want to have some people in to dinner next week, Bill . . . the Curries, the Lentons, Meg Howth, that nice girl from Farnborough . . . Richard Merton . . .'

'Not Merton,' Bill said automatically.

'Why not?' she snapped. 'I like Richard. So does everyone else. What have you got against him?'

'Something,' Bill said; but added at once, 'I think he doesn't like me.'

'You think he has a down on you? That's silly. That's an inferiority complex, because of what your father is, and your accent, though that's much better.'

Bill said, 'I don't like him, and I have some reason. But invite him. I'll behave myself.'

He remembered Colonel Canby's warning about Pauline . . . her enthusiasms didn't always stand up to much testing. Was that becoming true about her enthusiasm and love for him? He loved her still . . . but did he, really? If he did, why did he feel trapped, with an ominous certainty that things would get worse between them, not better? The truth was that she couldn't stand army routine in peacetime any more than he could. So they must escape . . . but where, how? And was he going to give up *his* enthusiasm, to be a good officer, that he had sworn to before Lloyd, after so little testing?

He wrenched his mind away from that distant past. England lay before the ship's bows now and, soon, Spain.

5

March 1938: Spain

The shells burst steadily every twenty seconds in the predawn darkness, sending up invisible columns of earth and dust. They're using a lot of mortars, and high-angle howitzer fire, Bill thought, to search us out here on the reverse side of the hill. The flat-trajectoried field guns were doing less damage, their shells grazing the top of the hill, where there were a few trenches, or missing and whining on to burst harmlessly three or four miles to the rear. He peered at the luminous dial of his watch . . . four thirty in the morning, some day in March, just about a year since he'd arrived in Spain. He didn't know what day – it didn't matter. It mattered that he had not heard from Lesley, but Morgan had told him, in a letter, that she was in London now, not New York; so perhaps she had not totally rejected him. And the shelling did matter. That was steadily quartering the rows of trenches in which the men of his *bandera* were lying, trying to rest, but waiting for an assault. This was the 31st Bandera of the Spanish Foreign Legion; Bill, with the rank of captain, had been its second-in-command until yesterday. Now he was its commander, for Major Almarraz had been killed by a bomb falling from a Russian plane at about ten o'clock in the morning.

They were twenty-five miles north of Teruel, in the Sierra de Villalba. The town of Villalba itself was visible on its eminence four miles ahead. It was occupied by the enemy, the Republican Army, the Reds, as everyone in the legion called them: and they were holding it fiercely; even, if this bombardment meant anything, preparing a counterattack or offensive.

A shell burst close by, followed at once by a terrible scream, coming from more than one throat. A direct hit on a trench, he thought. His men were veterans, but the continuous methodical shelling, following yesterday's four Russian air raids, was getting on their nerves. He'd better make a round of the positions.

He made sure that his cap was firmly on his head, checked that his pistol was loaded and the ammunition pouch full, and said to his soldier runner, '*Ven.*' He had learned enough Spanish to get by with the legion, most of whom were in fact Spanish. In case of need, his runner, Tomas Vereda, helped him out. Vereda had been a merchant seaman before enlisting in the legion, and spoke a smattering of English, as well as German, French and Italian.

Bill set off forward, walking in a half-crouch. It wasn't much protection, but at least it made a smaller target to the shells than if he walked upright. For any reasonable safety he should be crawling, but at that rate it would take him hours to get round all the *bandera's* positions.

He came to a trench and lay down, peering in – '*Que tal?*' he asked. 'How is it?' There were four men in the trench, their faces turned up to him, a pale blur.

'The Reds have all the artillery ammunition in the world, captain,' one said, in Spanish.

A hundred yards to the right, one of the voices that had been screaming faded into silence, with a choking rattle. Another continued, but now in rhythmic bursts. A soldier in the trench said, 'Why can't our gunners destroy theirs?'

'They're doing their best,' Bill said. 'Listen . . . some of those whining shells up there are ours going the other way . . . Courage, man!'

He moved on, and soon found another trench by almost falling into it.

'Who the devil . . .?' a voice spluttered.

'Captain Miller . . . *que tal?*'

'*Regular, mi capitan.* Are they going to attack?'

'I think so . . . Don't waste any ammunition when they come . . . understood?'

Vereda cut in, 'The captain means, don't shoot till you know you will kill.'

Bill moved right. There'd be some light in another half an hour, and then . . . in the past the Reds had always put in a final hour of artillery bombardment starting at first light, when they could see the targets, then attacked. If they did the same now, the *bandera* holding the north slope, the forward slope, would have a rough time, under observed fire from a lot of guns, with, as the legionary back there had said, apparently unlimited ammunition.

'Halt, who goes there?' The challenge was spat out in a strong Andalusian accent.

'Captain Miller, the commanding officer,' Bill said.

'*Pase, mi capitan.*' It was a machine-gun-post position facing east across the rearward slope of the hill. The whole *bandera* was in a large olive grove. This pair of machine-guns and another pair forty yards further forward were on the edge of the wood. Bill slid down into the trench, where the gun teams were crouching or sitting, backs to the earth walls. The guns were set up on an earth platform cut out of the front wall so that the muzzles peered out three inches above ground level.

Bill said, '*Que tal?*'

The gunner said, 'I hope they come soon. Then we'll show them. Then we'll give them lead for breakfast.' He patted the barrel of a gun.

Bill said, haltingly, 'When there's light, make sure you can still cover the other guns, in front there. Understood? There may be piles of earth thrown up by the shelling obstructing your fire.'

A corporal said, 'I understand, captain. We weren't born yesterday in this company.'

Bill went on, half running, to the forward machine-gun post and gave them the same message – to make sure they could cover the front of the rear guns. Then back towards the left flank of the position – first to the place where the screaming had come from. All was silent there now, but for the remorseless flash and crump and whine of the bursting shells, and the smell of lyddite, and the choking clouds of dust that floated down on the slight night breeze.

He crouched by a small trench system. '*Que tal?*'

'This shelling,' a man's voice muttered. 'It's unbearable. It's . . .'

'Courage, man,' Bill said. 'You're alive, you're not hurt . . . and how long have they been shelling us now? Three hours, at least.'

Another voice spoke, 'You should have seen the men hit just now, captain . . . I went over to help, when they screamed . . . tripped up in a fellow's entrails . . . it was Lamasona, the fellow from Granada, who had a guitar . . . and two others, blood six inches deep in the trench, I swear it, captain, and . . .'

Bill interrupted him. 'Don't think about it. Think about the Reds, and what you are going to do to them. And lie low until they come.'

He returned to his command post, Vereda at his heels, just as the first light spread a thin greenish glow under the olives. He plumped down in the trench, and searched automatically for a cigarette . . . then swore, remembering he'd given up smoking two days ago, because the craving had become so strong in times of stress, but the availability of cigarettes had grown correspondingly less. A craving for nicotine that couldn't be satisfied was one stress he did not need during this bloody and brutal campaign.

Vereda had seen the motion, and said, 'I have a cigarette, captain . . .'

Bill waved him off. 'No, thanks.' He sat up, detecting a change in the sounds surrounding him. 'Listen!' A few enemy shells were still coming low over the top of the rise in front, to whine and shriek on southwards. But the shelling on the olive grove had stopped . . . and shelling on the forward face of the rise had begun. He leaned back, saying, 'The 17th will get it for the next hour or so. *Nosotros, tranquilos.*'

Vereda moved a few feet away along the trench towards the *bandera* signallers, and started to make a little fire on the parapet. He had it going in a couple of minutes, and then took his bayonet and toasted thick slices of bread on the end of it. Then he opened a shirt pocket and extracted three cloves of garlic. A signaller came along to watch, and without looking up Vereda said, 'Bring a little oil, Jesus.' The other scrambled off, returning in a few moments. By then, Vereda had crushed the garlic between two stones, spread it on slices of toast, sprinkled salt from another little pouch and, taking the oil jar from the other man, spread olive oil thinly over all. He handed the slices to Bill with a small bow. '*Desayuno, mi capitan.*'

Bill took it and ate hungrily, listening to the sound of the artillery on the forward slope of the hill and the fierce crunching of the toasted bread between his jaws. 'All that we need now,' he said, 'is coffee.'

'Coming, captain,' Vereda said. 'And then . . .' He held out his waterbottle towards Bill. 'Anise, captain. The best – anise del Mono . . . took it off a Red sergeant two days ago. He was full of maggots, but the bottle was well corked.'

Bill took the proffered mug of coffee, then a mouthful of anise, and finished the oiled garlic toast. It was not a typical British breakfast, but then this wasn't a typical British war.

He looked around, standing in his trench. The light was strong now, and the men were astir, the fears of the night driven away by the light and by the fact that someone else was getting the shelling now. They were good men, Bill thought, quite different from British troops in many ways, very like them in others. The discipline was savage. Any form of disobedience was punished with death, administered on the spot. Lesser crimes received brutal duties and drills, half-rations and worse. The legionaries took it all with an ironic humour and, in general, little outward show of emotion. It was the Italians he had met who gesticulated and danced up and down in excitement – not the Spanish.

He cocked his head, listening. The shelling out front had stopped. The only shells flying over now were his own side's. The Red attack must have begun. He wished he could get up on the crest of the hill and watch, see exactly what was happening; but he dared not leave his position until the enemy had fully revealed his intentions.

'I hear tanks, captain,' Vereda said.

'Italians? Fiats? . . . German?'

'No, captain. Russian . . . north-west . . . and a lot of machine-gun fire.'

Bill could hear it all himself now, brought over the crest of the low hill on the morning wind, the sounds of battle on the forward slope, about half a mile from him ... rattle of machine-guns, in long bursts, hiccup of grenades, and – farther west – the grumble of tank engines. So the Reds were attacking on the Nationalist left front, at least the tanks were ... they might launch more troops at the right front ... His own *bandera* was right rear, so he would get involved in the battle, if it developed that way.

Five men passed close, walking fast against the slope through the trees. One was a Spanish major of artillery whom he knew slightly; three were artillery soldiers, carrying survey equipment, telephone wire and field telephones; and the fifth was Colonel Stefan von Krug, the chief German representative of the Condor Legion on this front. Bill had seen a lot of him in the last few months, since this campaign began on the Teruel front. He was a short, spare Prussian with duelling scars, a monocle and cropped hair, but his head was long and thin, not bullet-shaped. He spoke good English and had twice visited Bill's *bandera* to spend an evening discussing the philosophy of war with him. His German nickname, Bill had found out, was '*der Henker*', the Hangman.

Bill called out, 'What's the news, colonel?'

Von Krug paused a moment. 'The Reds are attacking. I think they're feinting with tanks on the left. The main attack will come later on your flank.' He added, as if sensing the question in Bill's mind, 'That's the way Daroca's mind works ... Hold fast today, and they'll spend themselves. Tomorrow we'll finish them off.'

He turned and hurried after the others, soon catching up with them. Bill thought, he's going to watch the battle from the top of the hill. That's where our general ought to be, but he's no good. Von Krug was an artillery officer, and from up there he'd have a wonderful observation post from which to control the Nationalist artillery. Von Krug worshipped artillery.

Vereda said, 'The Red tanks are almost level with the hill now, captain, from what I hear.' He pointed westwards. 'But they're not engaged with our people. They're too far away.'

A runner passed through, shambling fast towards the rear. Bill called, 'What's the message?'

'To the general, captain, from us – 17th Bandera – asking for

71

reinforcements. There are scores of Red tanks on our front, and none of ours . . . and we only have four anti-tank guns.'

He ran on. Bill thought, they won't have any luck. Von Krug had obviously decided that the main enemy attack would come in on the right. 17th Bandera would get no help unless the general, with von Krug not at his side, gave in to their pleading.

Vereda suddenly grabbed his rifle, propped it against the side of an olive tree and fired. 'Here they come, captain,' he called. Bill looked in the direction Vereda had fired. Men were coming across the open heathland outside the grove, moving slowly in scattered groups among clumps of gorse and heather and low thorn bushes. The nearest were about four hundred yards away, heading slightly across his front, as though to strike at the junction between his *bandera* and the 17th. He raised his binoculars to his eyes and looked more carefully. There were an awful lot of them coming on through the scrub – at least three hundred . . . as many more behind. And after the recent fighting his *bandera* was down to just about the same – three hundred.

The machine-guns that he had placed on the edge of the grove opened fire, and Bill saw several enemy stumble and fall. Then they all seemed to go to ground. After twenty minutes the enemy began to advance again. Again his machine-guns opened fire. Again the enemy went to ground; but almost at once a multiple whining scream preceded the simultaneous bursts of four mortar bombs all round the forward machine-gun position. Now they would wipe them out, and then continue their advance. More mortar bombs burst round the forward guns. The rearward gun teams jumped out of their trench carrying their guns and ammunition, and ran back to disappear into another trench.

Good, Bill thought, for by now the forward post had been obliterated, the guns smashed and the crews dead. The enemy apparently had not seen the other team change position and mortar bombs started to rain down on their old position. After ten minutes of this, the enemy advance continued. The machine-guns opened fire and simultaneously a heavy artillery bombardment struck the advancing Reds. Good, again, Bill thought. That's von Krug's work; he can see it all from up there.

The enemy's reaction to the shelling was to break into a run. Faint on the breeze Bill heard the ragged calls to charge. Bayonets flashed in the low sun, bullets clacked more insistently through the olives, so that leaves and twigs and olives just ripe for the picking fell to the ground below.

Out in the ploughed field between the olive grove and the heathland there were some ragged rows of barbed wire, which Bill had had put up late yesterday evening, just after dark. It was not much but it served now to channel the attacking Republicans into the beaten zones of Bill's machine-guns, and of another two guns positioned inside the defensive area of the next *bandera* to the south-east.

The Republican attack faltered and stopped. We've got them, Bill thought, his jaw setting in determination. They would not pass, in spite of their numbers. Von Krug on top of the hill must have seen some greater danger on the other flank, for the Nationalist artillery, which had been blasting big gaps among the attacking infantry, now turned to other targets. At the same time the Republican guns increased their fire on Bill's olive grove and the trenches half hidden in it.

Firing broke out suddenly from behind Bill's right shoulder, while he was still staring forward through his binoculars. Behind him, he heard the loud crack of Vereda's rifle, and his call: 'Reds coming up from behind us, captain!' Bill whirled round, pistol raised. There they were, barely a hundred yards away, about fifty men, coming fast, firing from the hip, here and there falling, jerking in the dust, dying, others coming on, three jumping down into a trench, bayonets out-thrust. Where the hell had these come from? They were going through Campoamor's section like a hot knife through butter. Campoamor was a young second lieutenant of noble family, brave enough but too careless, too much of a playboy to be a really good officer. Bill leaped out of his trench and shouted to Lieutenant Aguirre, commanding the reserve of thirty men he had kept close to his headquarters. 'Follow me, Aguirre! Charge!' They came out at once, appearing from holes in the ground, Aguirre at their head, a pair of sergeants yelling and threatening with their bayonets any who were slow in moving.

The Republicans who had infiltrated through Campoamor's position were moving across Bill's front now, and his charge hit them in the flank, from close range. The firing became frenzied as the soldiers on both sides fired rifles and pistols point-blank before going in with the bayonet. A huge black-avised figure with rifle pointed and blood dripping from his bayonet appeared in front of Bill, looming up gigantic out of the dust. Bill fired at once into the man's body, and he sagged, but the rifle still came up towards Bill's chest, the finger on the trigger. Then Vereda fired into the man's face, and the rifle clattered down, jerked away in the sudden spasm. Now Bill saw the backs of two Republicans, running away, and fired at both of them. 'They're on the run,' he exulted, and yelled in Spanish, 'On! Out with them!' and fired again. Then suddenly he was at the rearmost edge of the grove, and there were no more enemy.

He grasped the trunk of an olive tree for support and for a moment stood bowed, panting, dust-caked, gasping for air, sweat black on his shirt. Aguirre was at his side. 'Well done, *mi capitan*. We've got rid of that lot, at least.'

'Yes, but how did they get right in among us?' Bill said. 'Any casualties?'

'Three or four, I think.'

'Where's Campoamor? They came right through his section.'

'Dead, captain . . . We'd better get under cover. The Reds seem to have set up a couple of machine-guns to fire through the grove.'

Bill stooped, and hurried back to his command post. The battle had changed pattern. The Reds weren't still coming across the plough in large numbers – there were very few to be seen, except the dead and wounded lying out there under the climbing sun. But from the heath beyond the plough they were firing with machine-guns, mortars, and . . . ah, here it came, observed artillery. The Nationalist guns were silent, and he could no longer hear the sound of tank engines.

Vereda said, 'They're going to try to eat us in many little bites, captain, now that they've failed to do it in one big one.'

Bill nodded. Vereda was probably right. So now they must grit their teeth, keep the trenches in good repair as far as could be done under continuous artillery fire, see that the men had food and water, keep communications open, go round the positions regularly to keep up morale, and . . . what else?

He started. Counterattack! He had forgotten the cardinal principle of defence: attack. The troops holding the hill would probably not themselves be able to counterattack, but others could, passing through them, perhaps, or round the flanks of the hill. At any event, there should be a counterattack, and it was his job to look for opportunities to make it.

Vereda was right. The forward *banderas* of the legion settled down to a long day of cat-and-mouse warfare in and around the hill, the olive grove on its southern side, and the surrounding fields and heathland. The Republicans pushed forward patrols down the dry arroyos that wound through the heath. Snipers in well-concealed positions began to take a steady toll of the legionaries in the grove – until Bill told Aguirre to sweep the front under the protection of mortar and machine-gun fire and take out the snipers. This operation lasted an hour, and Aguirre lost four more men, but they had killed seven snipers and sent another running for his life.

No big concerted attack, such as the Republicans had launched an hour after dawn, was mounted by either side; but gun fire would suddenly increase on a small portion of a *bandera*'s front, smoke shells would blind it and the supporting units on its flanks, then a small determined band of Republicans would burst out of the smoke right on top of the Nationalist trenches. Sometimes a *bandera* lost a forward post, sometimes the post held. Always, afterwards, there were more dead lying on the pale earth.

For Bill the worst problem became water. The men had enough food and in most cases were not hungry; but the conditions of close combat, dust and danger produced great and lasting thirst, which could not be satisfied, for the water point was half a mile to the rear and the donkey water cart with its two barrels could not come up to the *bandera*, nor could the men, pinned down by fire and constantly engaged in action, go back. Bill's own tongue was swollen and thick in his mouth, half choking him, and once a man from his left forward company, in the western edge of the grove, jumped out of his trench, threw away his rifle and ran to the rear, mouthing, '*Agua, agua!*' He got only twenty yards before the sergeant of his section shot him in the back; but soon afterwards the company commander came running to Bill's command post, jumped down and cried, 'We must get water soon, *mi capitan*, or' – he spread his hands energetically – 'the men will disappear, to find it.'

Bill thought a moment and said, 'Vereda, do we still have the telephone to the artillery?'

'Yes, captain.'

Bill turned to the company commander. 'Send a good sergeant and three or four men, no more, back to the water point. Bring up the donkey cart and the barrels, filled. When they get up as far as that farmhouse – you can see it from here – one of them is to come up to me, at the double. I'll have arranged for the gunners to fire smoke on the ground between here and the farmhouse . . . as soon as the smoke shells start to land, the sergeant is to bring the water cart up as fast as he can. Set the barrels up in a trench and I'll arrange for men to go back and refill their bottles by sections.'

'Very good, *mi capitan*.' The officer saluted and crawled away. That was three o'clock in the afternoon. The water came up at five, but only one barrel; the other was demolished by a shell splinter while still set up in the donkey cart. Still, the sun was sinking, and as soon as it was dark the cart could make regular trips . . . then, he'd have to inspect the trenches again, get casualty reports, talk to the company and section commanders to make sure that they were standing up to the strain . . . and try to get more rest himself. God, he was tired . . . What would the Reds do next? Would they rest during the night and come on again in the morning? Would they try a night attack? The *bandera* had suffered some casualties during the long day, he knew, but he did not think it was very many. They were tired, that was the main problem – tired, still thirsty and not exactly downhearted, but grim, for, whatever was happening in the war as a whole, they were not winning this particular battle, here in front of Villalba. The Republicans were, with their remorseless, grinding attacks and varied, subtle tactics.

It was dark soon after seven at night, and Bill started a careful check of his whole position. More water was brought up, and he arranged for more rations to be delivered before daylight, for now the men were beginning to eat their bread and sausage, which they had not touched during the hours of heat and battle. He switched two companies, for one had suffered disproportionately, while the other had had an almost restful day. He spoke to all his officers, checked ammunition supplies with the headquarters sergeant, and marked on his maps the positions of all units and sub-units as they had been

76

reported to him from his companies or sent to him in messages from the General Staff and flanking *banderas*. In most places the Reds had advanced about half a mile from their positions of this time yesterday evening; they had a small foothold on the forward slope of the hill; but not in his olive grove.

At nine o'clock the Republicans started a series of small infiltration attacks direct at Bill's *bandera*. Movement in the grove became almost impossible, for the only way to combat the infiltration was to sit tight and shoot at anything that moved. For four hours, Bill stayed tense in his trench, occasionally shouting to other officers, and receiving muffled shouts in reply. Twice he engaged in fire fights with small bands of Republicans moving between the trench systems. Soon after one o'clock, firing started in the south and soon he heard shouts of 'Hold fire, Thirty-one! The legions's coming!'

Two hundred men of a reserve *bandera* swept slowly through the grove, wiping out three or four remaining pockets of Republicans. Later, the commander of the cleaning-up force found Bill and said, 'Ah, it is the Englishman, Miller . . . I'm taking my men back now. Are you all right?'

'Yes,' Bill said. 'Just tired. I could sleep for a week now, I think.'

The German-accented voice of Colonel von Krug spoke out of the darkness nearby. 'But you won't, Captain Miller. You will attack the enemy instead.'

'Now?' Bill gasped.

'No, soon after dawn. Where is your command post? Here? Good. Come and sit down with me . . . Do you have any water, by chance?'

Bill said, 'A little. Vereda, give the colonel some water.'

He saw von Krug drink in the starlight, and hand the *bota* back to Vereda. Then he said, 'Since ten o'clock we have been having a conference at the general's headquarters. You were sent for but the messengers could not get through to you, so when the conference was over, I brought your orders, escorted by these fellows who have just cleaned up the olive grove for you.'

Bill said, 'If the Reds attack at dawn, we'll have a hard time holding them. My men are dead tired.'

Von Krug's voice was acid. 'The Reds will not attack, captain. We will. You will, you and your *bandera* . . . You remember, before

Teruel, we spent a couple of days practising cooperation between tanks and infantry? Your *bandera* provided the infantry, and I want them to support my tanks tomorrow. They don't know much, but they know something.'

'But they're absolutely exhausted,' Bill cried. 'Can't you use a *bandera* from general reserve?'

'We will, later,' von Krug said, 'but not with our tanks, our German tanks . . . Listen. Our aircraft will attack the enemy reserve positions an hour after dawn. That will be followed by an hour's intense artillery bombardment of their forward positions. During the bombardment our tanks will move up to the rear of this grove. Previously you will have heard them, or some of them, during the latter part of the night, moving round the western flank of this hill . . .'

'Towards where the Russian tanks were yesterday?' Bill asked.

'Yes. But the Russians never came close. As I thought, they were a feint, to draw our attention to the west while most of the Red effort went in on the east, against you . . . and our own tank movements to that flank will also be a feint. Our real tank attack, supported by your *bandera*, will be on the east. I'll show you your first and second objectives on the map soon. When it's light, you'll be able to see them on the ground. You will be under my command, and after the second objective, I will decide how far to go.'

Bill said doubtfully, 'I saw the ground to the north of the hill, between us and Villalba, when we were moving up, and the west flank looked much better for tanks. The east is split up by some quite deep arroyos and there's a fair amount of broken ground.'

'Correct, captain,' von Krug said, 'and there are also two small hills . . .'

'I noticed them . . . rather like the little hills at Salamanca, where Wellington won his battle.'

'Los Arapiles,' von Krug said. 'Yes, they do resemble Los Arapiles . . . and they give wonderful artillery observation over the whole of that flank. There is no place which gives good observation on the western side. The enemy expect tanks on the west, because the terrain is better for them. Therefore . . .'

'. . . we go east,' Bill said. 'But . . .'

'Not "therefore",' von Krug said. 'The reason we go east is the

78

artillery observation. The tank cannot win alone, captain. It must have infantry in close support, not sheltering behind the tanks but going out and wiping out anti-tank guns, marking minefields, just as the tanks will wipe out machine-gun nests for the infantry . . . and over all there are the guns. Neither tanks nor infantry can do their work without artillery support . . . Since our tank radios have not yet been made reliable enough, the artillery commander will observe the advance and direct fire, first from this hill, where I was yesterday, and then from Los Arapiles, as we shall call them. The Reds have an observation post on them now, but they'll run as soon as we get close.'

Bill said, 'We'll do our best, colonel, but the men really are out on their feet. I don't know whether I can get them to move.'

Von Krug didn't speak for a moment, then said, 'I heard you let the Reds infiltrate your position here yesterday afternoon.'

'They came up a fold in the ground through a young second lieutenant's position. He hadn't noticed the fold and wasn't covering it.'

'And why didn't *you* notice it?'

'It was late, and I was too busy . . .' Bill began.

'A commander can delegate much – he must,' the Hangman said, 'but he cannot delegate study of the ground, in defence, or attack.'

'You're right, colonel,' Bill said at last. 'It was my fault. Campoamor was killed.'

'That was not your fault,' von Krug said. 'That was war . . . About the attack, I shall have thirty tanks.'

'But that's all you have!'

'Quite. The other *banderas* are screaming that they must have tanks too. The general wanted to agree.'

'It seems only fair.'

Von Krug said harshly, 'Tanks *must* be used in the largest masses that the ground will allow. The 31st Bandera must get *all* the tanks, I told the general, or no one will get any. I am responsible to the Führer for these tanks and their crews. The general finally came round. He had to . . . As to getting your *bandera* to move . . . either you use firing squads, or the general will . . . The time now is . . . 2.14 a.m. Zero hour for us to move out of this grove is 8.05 a.m. *Heil Hitler!*' He saluted with outflung arm, the motion barely seen in the dark, and vanished.

Bill sat down, collecting his thoughts. Von Krug was doing his *bandera* an honour in selecting it for this attack with his entire tank force, but, after a day and a night of continuous fighting, and two days and nights' marching before that ... He grimaced wryly, thinking of days in India when he had prayed for something, anything, to *do*. To Vereda he said, 'I want to see all officers and sergeants there, at once.'

'*A sus ordenes*,' Vereda said.

They were gathered in front of him in the dark, Bill knew, but he could not make out anything more exact than the blurred paleness of their faces, here and there a wink of light as a bayonet or pistol barrel caught the starlight. He was speaking slowly in Spanish. 'Tomorrow, at 8.05 a.m., we will attack. The time now is 2.56. Set your watches ... We are to attack with the whole of the German tank force in this area – thirty tanks. I will give out detailed orders after Colonel von Krug has brought up the tanks, about first light. But I want to make this clear – every man will advance, even if he is asleep, or has to crawl forward on all fours. Officers will use their pistols at the first sign of any hesitation or delay in obeying orders. No complaints about fatigue or exhaustion will be heard. The enemy is just as tired as we are, *but our will is stronger*. That's all.'

It was another long day and afterwards Bill did not know how he had got through it. He was inclined to believe that, for at least part of the time, he had been sleepwalking, moving and giving orders from some deep subconscious level. At first the attack went exactly as planned. The German tanks rumbled about to his left late in the night, and in the dawn came close up behind his positions. Later he heard distant rumbling of tanks on the wind, and Vereda said, 'The Russians again, captain ... moving back over to that western side.'

So von Krug's feint had worked, and now the Republican tanks, if they moved from the positions they had taken up to halt a German attack on that flank, would be vulnerable to the Nationalist aircraft. These were busy from soon after dawn, the Italians strafing ground targets, the Germans putting in the heavy bombardment an hour later. Then the guns began ... pounding the Republican troops close to the edge of the grove; and at 8.05 a.m. to the second, the 31st Bandera, two companies up, each company allotted to a squadron of fifteen tanks, moved out into the open, followed by the tanks, they in turn followed by the other rifle company. The machine-gun company was split among the three rifle companies. Bill, with his small headquarters group, kept as close to von Krug's tank as he could. From the beginning, events proved that von Krug had been right to insist on massive artillery support, and on using all his tanks together. The *bandera*'s forward companies soon ran into dug-in machine-guns protected by infantry platoons; but within five minutes, artillery fire was raining down on them, and the tanks moving forward through the foot soldiers had engaged and destroyed what remained of the nests and their crews. Then the infantry moved on again, and the tanks fell back. His men were moving faster now, Bill thought, encouraged by the clockwork precision of the little action against the machine-guns.

Then anti-tank guns opened up from the left, immediately setting one German tank on fire. Von Krug leaned out of his turret and shouted down, 'Wipe them out, fast, captain.' Then his head disappeared, the tank swung round, and, followed by the rest, retreated a hundred yards to dead ground, where only the turrets of a few of them showed. Once more the artillery began to send over heavy concentrations of high explosive and smoke. Bill's forward companies, edging left, encircled and wiped out the anti-tank guns. The German tanks rumbled out of cover and on again, moving fast until they were level with the leading troops . . . so they went, for a mile, two miles. Villalba on its hill loomed closer. The ground was covered with huge craters and dead bodies, both the results of the earlier air raids. They were through the enemy front and into his reserve.

Suddenly the Republican artillery, which had been very quiet, burst into life with a furious bombardment of the tank group and the infantry scattered round them. The legionaries dived for the ground. But, a little to his right, Bill saw three men break and run to the rear, throwing away their rifles for extra speed. Vereda's rifle was up beside him, ready to shoot. Bill hesitated. Now he had to live up to his fierce exhortation of the night . . . use his pistol. But these were his men. In the end, he was a British officer, not a legionary. He knocked Vereda's rifle up and said, 'No, man! Let others kill them, if it must be.'

He moved on, but von Krug was over him, shouting, 'You English are too soft on your men . . . Get them moving forward now, captain. We are not going to stay here and be shelled to bits. Forward, forward!'

He disappeared inside his turret, and his tank started to grind forward, soon followed by the others, spread out in three arrowhead groups of ten tanks each. Bill, glancing round, saw columns of dust to the west. Stopping to put up his binoculars, he looked again, and saw the shape of tanks under and in the dust . . . the distinctive bulbous shape of the Russians. He ran forward and hammered against the side of von Krug's tank with his pistol. Von Krug looked out.

Bill shouted, 'Tanks, Red tanks, attacking, there!' He pointed.

As he spoke, the Nationalist artillery, controlled by the observers who had moved up from the original hill to the Arapiles, switched all available guns onto the new threat, shelling the Russian tanks as furiously as the Republican guns had just been shelling von Krug's.

Von Krug cupped his hands and called down, 'Get your men back a bit. Have your machine-guns in position to scrape off any infantry who are accompanying their tanks . . . but I don't think there are any. They're coming too fast.' His tank accelerated away, followed by the others, heading for a steep-sided little bank two hundred yards to the right flank which would give them hull-down positions to engage the Russians. Bill's own men, in response to his hand signals, and messages sent by runners, fell back by companies until they were well behind the tanks, disposed to engage any enemy infantry accompanying the tanks.

The Russians came on and Bill thought, it's a pity that von Krug didn't bring his towed anti-tank guns right up with him . . . but they couldn't have crossed a couple of the arroyos without long delay. The Russians closed to within two hundred yards, firing fast but without much effect at the heavily armoured turrets of the German tanks, the only parts they could see. When they had closed to a hundred yards, the Germans opened fire, aiming at the Russians' vulnerable tank treads and lower chassis. One by one, three Russian tanks wheeled to a stop, their suspension destroyed or treads blown off. One by one, three more burst into flames, the crews tumbling out of them into the machine-gun fire of Bill's guns. Four more tanks were put out of action by the artillery fire. After ten minutes of fierce close-quarter fighting between the two tank forces, the remaining

Russians turned and retreated . . . only twelve out of the original thirty.

Bill thought, von Krug will chase them . . . but he didn't and Bill remembered him saying, 'Be careful not to let an enemy draw your tanks onto concealed anti-tank guns or mines.' Von Krug was not going to be taken in now.

Bill moved his *bandera* forward. Von Krug's tank rumbled alongside and the colonel called, 'Well, there's Villalba, and you could take it without much trouble now. But we've broken clear through, and every Red forward of us will start running for his life any moment, if he hasn't already done so. We'll get astride their line of retreat, and cut them to pieces. See those low cliffs and ploughed fields there? You occupy them, facing south. We'll be behind you, turrets down. Get moving!'

The *bandera* plunged on through the rising dust, Bill stumbling light-headed in his tracks now. God, he thought, what would I not give to be drinking a pint of beer in the mess in Aldershot now, or in the Lord Nelson bar in Dover, morning parades done with and nothing whatever to do or think about until inspection tomorrow.

6

October 1924: Dover

Actually, what he remembered most about those years of 1924 and '25 with the 1st Battalion in Dover was the rain – the Union Jack clinging sodden to its staff over the tower of Dover Castle; the regimental flag hanging limp outside the quarterguard; far below, a Channel steamer driving through the rain towards the harbour; and, because of the rain, himself inspecting his platoon in barracks instead of on the parade ground. He passed down the row of beds, looking first at the bed, to see whether the overall shape was correct; then at the folded blankets; then the pillow set just there; the webbing equipment spread out as though on a man's back . . . he was twenty-five years of age, his son Roger was two and a half and his daughter Brenda three months. They were both with Pauline and Nanny in Damerham, where Pauline had gone for a fortnight's hunting. The little house down in the town felt very empty without them.

He lifted a man's waterbottle in its webbing sling, removed the cork, sniffed, put the cork back – all right. He half pulled the bayonet from its scabbard and ran his finger down the blade. 'Your sword's too oily, Thompson. I've told you about this before. Give him three extra drills with the defaulters, sergeant.'

'Sir!'

He moved on. Morgan Lloyd was A Company's commander now. He was a captain and Bill still a lieutenant, but promotion was devilish slow in the regiment – there were subalterns approaching sixteen years of service and captains with twenty-two. Bill had already passed his promotion exam for captain, but God knew when there'd be a vacancy. Reading and studying at home helped a lot to combat *le cafard*; but there were still these damned boring jobs to do over and over again . . . counting the ball and blank ammunition in hand; getting pay money from the bank in small coins and notes, counting it, recounting, paying it out; keeping the imprest account; recording and checking all the family allotments. But it wasn't all dull. Next week he'd be running a course in map reading for junior NCOs – that was Morgan's idea; and the week after that Morgan himself was giving the NCOs two hours a day minor tactics out on the downland north of the castle.

At the next bed he said, 'Boots filthy.'

'I had to run to the latrines just before inspection began, sir,' the soldier said, 'It's muddy out there.'

'All right. Clean them after parade and show them to Sergeant Dreen.'

'Sir!'

Why couldn't the battalion go overseas . . . but where? He'd been thinking like this practically ever since coming back from Germany in 1919, and it always led to the same dead end. So, why did he allow himself to get so bored? Some of the chaps had boats and went sailing;

two had made friends with naval officers and took cruises in destroyers; others went up to London – but Pauline had taken the Vauxhall so Bill was tied to his bike; some went pub crawling round eastern Kent; some played golf. The point was that they were not bored; each found a way to keep himself content, even if that way was largely a waste of time.

The inspection was over. 'No. 3 . . . *platoon*!' Sergeant Dreen barked: the soldiers came to attention. Bill walked out, touching his swagger cane to the peak of his cap. Behind him Dreen bellowed, 'Stand to your front! Stand easy! Now listen to me . . .'

Bill entered the saloon bar of the Lord Nelson soon after half past six, and ordered a half-pint of bitter. Perry Hillman wasn't here yet – you'd know at once if he was. He sat down in a corner nursing his beer and looked round. It was a nice old pub in one of the narrow streets below the castle, though not much frequented by the soldiers. Bill liked pubs. Pauline didn't, though she had come in here with him once or twice. 'What's the attraction?' she asked. 'You can drink beer at home . . . there's an awful fug in there, and shove ha'penny doesn't look very exciting.' Oh, but it is, he had thought, when you're playing with other pub regulars, sharing that mysterious indefinable something, the inner life of an English pub.

The door burst open a voice cried, 'What bloody ho, one and all!' Perry Hillman swept in with a gust of cold wind from the street. He was a tall man of about forty with a mop of reddish hair, untidy clothes, down-at-heel shoes, and an unrolled umbrella flapping in one hand. To the barmaid he called, 'The usual, Glad'; then, as his eyes swept the room he cried, 'Evening, Tom . . . Peter . . . Greene, your health, sir . . . Mary . . .' He saw Bill and stiffened in an exaggerated salute: 'General!'

He went to the bar, picked up his pint of foaming beer, and joined Bill in the corner. As he sat down he said, 'Got another poem back from the bloody editor today.' He drank deep. 'I'll show 'em though, one day. One day they'll come crawling to my door, on hands and knees . . . How's the army? How's your beautiful lady?'

'In Wiltshire with the kids,' Bill said. 'I'm a bachelor for a couple of weeks.'

'Fat lot of good it will do you in Dover,' Hillman said. 'The virginities here are made of cast iron – like the drawers.' He jumped up, went to the bar and got another pint. Bill waited for him to come back. He'd met Hillman here, nearly two years ago, and soon learned that he was a poet. But as he apparently never sold any poems it was a mystery what he lived on. Some thought his women had private means – there were two of them who came occasionally to the Lord Nelson with him, never together: both strait-laced, stern-faced, strictly dressed ladies of about his age; but as different from him as governesses from a ballet dancer.

Hillman fascinated Bill. His was another world, and another mind. It was the opportunity of hearing him talk or spout his own poetry that brought Bill to this pub rather than some other. He was off now, speculating on the education of apes, waving his tankard in the air, his eyes gleaming, his mane of hair flying. His mind was like a jungle, you never knew what to expect next . . . his ways of thought were as erratic as a dragonfly's flight . . . darting here, there, side-ways. There was no logic in him, until suddenly, as though looking at an object from a different angle, or a face taking shape in a cliff, the sense was clear and undeniable. He talked about anything and every-thing: the handling of small boats in Channel tide rips; the Cubists' theory of light; Gladstone and the Irish Question; the guilt or inno-cence of Richard III in the murder of the babes in the Tower – he would take either side of that argument with equal enthusiasm; the military mind in the Victorian era; female underclothes in the Middle Ages . . . anything. All the time he drank too much, and was not perhaps altogether sane. But he was different. Bill had never met anyone like him. The army did not, could not, contain anyone like him. Being in the Lord Nelson with him was to be transported on a magic carpet away from the routine, the boredom, the uniformity, the uniform. Pauline had met him and thought he was impossible. 'How he can get any woman to live with him is a mystery to me,' she had said. 'Let alone two.' Bill had thought that those particular women might have had a hard time finding anyone else, for they were not beauties; but he had said nothing.

Time passed. Hillman declaimed poetry at the bar. He was a part of the Lord Nelson and everyone had their own way of fitting him into their lives. Some shut him out, in friendly enough ways, by not hearing or really seeing him. Others came close and listened, some

86

just to the music, others – you could tell by their wrinkling brows – trying to make sense of the coruscating words.

Half past seven. Bill got up to go. Hillman stopped in mid-flow and said, 'One day you'll have a drap of whisky with each of those three half-pints, and then God help all women!'

Bill raised a hand, grinning, 'Good night, Perry.'

'Good night, general. And take my advice – while your wife's away, do something she won't let you do when she's at home . . . smoke some opium . . . piss out of an upstairs window . . . wear one of her dresses down to breakfast . . . It'll be good for you – prevents ankylosis of the outlook. And that's a very prevalent disease among the military.'

An important soccer game was played the next day in steady rain, ending at five o'clock in near darkness. The teams were both from A Company, for the game was a trial to help Corporal Harris, the company's football captain, to choose the company team for the battalion championships. Bill had refereed, and Morgan Lloyd had watched with his wife. As Bill walked off the muddy field, putting away his whistle, the Lloyds came up to him. Lloyd said, 'Thanks, Bill. You did a good job – especially the way you handled that near fight . . . You're soaked, and alone. Come back and have tea with us – high tea . . . not fashionable but very nice sometimes.'

'I'd love to,' Bill said, 'I'll have a bath and change first, though.'

'Of course. You don't have the car, do you? I'll pick you up at your house in half an hour.'

Half an hour later, the Lloyds' little Citroen rolled up to Bill's door, and he followed Morgan out into the slackening rain. Already he felt warm and dry, but after a few minutes at the Lloyds' the glow had spread all through him, for he held a whisky and splash in his hand, and from the back of the house he could smell cooking sausages and bacon and the sharper tang of frying tomatoes. Morgan caught him appreciatively sniffing the air, and said, 'And after that, scones, Devonshire cream, and home-made strawberry jam!'

Bill leaned back, closing his eyes. He knew the Lloyds well by now. Morgan was a much looser company commander than Wainwright had been, and his attention was focused differently. He held close-order drill and arms-drill parades, and insisted on a high standard, but it was in the field that he really drove them, officers, NCOs and men alike. He didn't notice, or care, whether a steel helmet was at exactly the right angle or a respirator worn just so, but he had whole platoons on extra running practice at dawn if any man in them fell out on the cross-country marches, and runs under full field-service marching-order loads; and the musketry . . . A Company, from ranking fourth in the battalion was now first, by a large margin, though it did not contain any of the battalion's Bisley team. 'I don't want to produce a handful of expert snipers at the cost of time that ought to be spent on raising the general level of the company,' he'd said. 'The Bisley boys will be doled out to us as snipers when war comes, anyway.'

Soon now, they joined Cicely Lloyd in the kitchen and ate on the plain well-scrubbed table there; and when they had finished, returned to the drawing room with a big pot of tea, and milk and sugar and their teacups. Morgan said, 'Your platoon sergeant, Dreen, is going to the depot as a CSM. That'll be his last job before he's retired.'

Bill said, 'What? But . . .'

Morgan said, 'We can't stand in the way of his promotion, Bill. You're getting Riddle from the 2nd Battalion – he was sent home on compassionate grounds a month ago – wife ran away with a Wapping bargee – he's getting a divorce.'

'He'll be in a pretty bad mood,' Bill said.

'Probably, but he has good reports, and it'll be up to you to provide a shoulder he can cry on. Officers lean on their sergeants often enough, God knows. Now's your chance to turn the tables . . . How's your reading coming along?'

'I've been reading Slessor on air power and cooperation with the army, but mainly now I'm reading General Fuller. He really makes you think.'

'He's got two more books on the stocks now,' Morgan said drily. 'One's about transportation, and he tells me he's going to call it *Pegasus, or Problems of Transportation*. The other is to be called *Yoga: A Study of the Mystical Philosophy of the Brahmins and Buddhists*.'

'Well, I won't have to read that, at least.'

'I would if I were you,' Morgan said seriously. 'General Fuller has the best military mind in or out of the army, and it's an education to see how it works . . . and to work out logically why and how you disagree with him, when you do. Have you read his pieces in the *RUSI Journal*?'

'Some.'

'Well, don't miss his Gold Medal Essay of 1919 about the application of recent developments to future war. It was published in May 1920. I have it here, if you want to borrow it.'

Cicely Lloyd came in. 'I've washed up – the maid's got flu or ringworm or something . . . more probably, a boyfriend. Are you two talking shop?'

'We were,' Morgan said.

'Give it a rest . . . and talk to Bill about what we were discussing yesterday.'

Morgan turned to Bill. 'I have a hobby, you know. Oh, some people think I do nothing but read military theses – or write them . . . but I do have a hobby, a healthy, outdoor sport.'

'Someone told me,' Bill said. 'Rock climbing, isn't it? But you haven't had much opportunity for that here, have you?'

'I found an almost perfect place for it,' Morgan said. 'It's an outcrop of limestone near Elham. The Dover cliffs are chalk and quite useless – worse than useless, they're a bloody menace. At Elham there are faces almost a hundred foot high with firm honest rock. There are pitches of almost every grade of difficulty . . . though most difficult ones are very short. Do you have a hobby?'

Bill thought. He liked soccer, but wasn't good enough at it to make the company team, let alone anything higher. He liked shooting, but only rifle shooting, not shotgun shooting after gamebirds, which was the socially correct hobby or avocation for an officer and gentleman in England, where there was no big game. He had gone sailing, but didn't really take to it. Cricket – a bit. Golf – he'd thought of it, but surely it was an old man's sport.

Morgan said, 'You have a good eye and good balance. I've watched you on the obstacle course. Rock climbing is a sport which teaches you what risks are acceptable, and what are not . . .'

'That, only once,' Bill said, smiling.

'Not necessarily – and that's true in war, too . . . It teaches you where your limits are . . . limits of physical strength and skill, limits of moral strength and endurance. It teaches you that you must expand those limits, push them higher, farther . . . It teaches you to keep your head, keep cool. Panic will kill you, rock climbing . . . as it will in war. It teaches you to look after and check your equipment, over and over again . . . to find what is best for your purpose, see that you get it, learn how to use it, and maintain it . . . as in war, you have to use men and machines. But, unlike war, it's done on clean, hard rock that responds in perfect honesty to you. There is no deception, no filth, no treachery. Would you like to try it?'

Bill thought some more . . . sounded bloody dangerous; but Morgan wore thick glasses, and certainly didn't look athletic – and *he'd* survived. Obviously, there were risks; but what sport was worthwhile without some element of danger?

'I would,' he said. 'If you'll teach me . . . Does Cicely climb too?'

Cicely said, 'No. I come out with a good book, an umbrella and a pair of binoculars, and watch birds . . . I never took it up because I thought I'd be tied down at home looking after babies – and now we've been married nine years and no luck. But I'm very happy watching Morgan and the birds. There are always birds at cliffs.'

'This Saturday, after parade then,' Morgan said. 'I'll pick you up at noon, and Cicely will make up a picnic lunch for the three of us.'

'Oh damn!' Bill said. 'Merton's going up to town for the weekend and I said I'd take his turn as orderly officer from noon on.'

'Richard's courting,' Morgan said. 'But he's being very cautious about it. I'll call Tanner and get him to stand in for Merton. He's broke and will welcome an enforced weekend in barracks.'

By half past twelve on Saturday the three of them were squeezing out of the Citroen at the base of the irregular line of the Elham cliffs. Ten minutes later, the first lesson began – rather informally, Bill thought, with Morgan walking up a steepish slope and himself following. He had expected something much more exciting, and had geared himself up for it. So, at first, he had felt let down; but now, three and a half hours later, with the wintry dusk settling in fast, he had had enough. It hadn't been particularly physical, nor at all dangerous – not even the small amount of rope work – but he'd had to concentrate as he'd never done before, nor for so long.

Cicely Lloyd was sitting at the foot of the slope on her stool, looking up at them. Morgan shouted down, 'We're stopping now, darling.'

'About time. The Barley Mow will be open in ten minutes.'

The two men walked towards her. Morgan said, 'Think you'll like it?'

'I'm sure,' Bill said. 'There's a wonderful discipline in it. I haven't really been a very self-disciplined person, I suppose, but rock climbing demands it. And concentration! Even on the places that look the easiest you have to keep up your concentration. I think that's what I like best: the being forced to concentrate. Though it's made me more tired than a twenty-five-mile route march, and we didn't do anything very energetic.'

'Quite. The Barley Mow has some excellent home-brewed ale, and also serves a very good country dinner – Cornish pasties are their speciality, in spite of being in Kent. Come on!'

They were sitting in the saloon bar of the Barley Mow, in Elham. Bill and Morgan had tankards of beer in front of them and Cicely a glass of sherry. Outside it was a clear night, stars bright in the early evening. Morgan drank, put down his tankard, and said, 'Tomorrow I become a field officer. The CO called me just before we left and told me I'd got a brevet majority. He didn't sound very pleased about it.'

'Oh, congratulations, sir,' Bill said. He put out his hand eagerly, then wished he hadn't as Morgan squeezed it where he had grazed it on a rock.

'Well, it's nice to put up the crowns comparatively young,' Morgan said. 'But brevets always create some friction: I stay junior to those captains I'm now junior to, as long as it's a regimental matter; but, if it's an army matter – a court martial, for instance, or the directing of staff manoeuvres – I become senior to them, as a major . . . I'm glad you liked your first experience on the rocks.'

'Can we come back tomorrow?' Bill asked.

Morgan looked at his wife. 'Why not?' she said. 'I'll be quite happy, unless it rains all day.'

'Then we shall,' Morgan said. 'We'll really work on handling the rope . . . looking for belays . . . making running loops for belaying down . . . we might start on simple rappels . . .'

'Chimneying,' Bill said. 'I've heard about that but never seen it done. I suppose you go up a wide crack, one leg on each side.'

'Sometimes,' Morgan answered. 'More often, you brace your back against one side, and your feet against the other, and then walk up, a bit at a time . . . I've been climbing for a good many years and I don't pretend to know everything, even in theory, let alone be able to tackle any given pitch in practice. So you've got a lot of learning to do. I think you'll be good, though, because you have an inquisitive mind. You ask questions. That's why you find regimental soldiering in peacetime so boring. Have you ever thought of applying for a secondment – to the King's African Rifles, for instance? They're always having little scraps against marauding Somalis or Abyssinians.'

Cicely broke in. 'I don't think they'd have him. He's quite junior, but married and with children.'

'Of course, I wasn't thinking . . . You could do a tour with the 2nd Battalion in India. There's always a chance of action on the North-west Frontier.'

Bill said, 'I've thought of applying for language study. If you choose Chinese, they send you out there for two years. That would be a change, and very interesting.'

'And when war comes they'll snaffle you and you'll spend your war translating Chinese documents and papers in some cubbyhole in the War Office. No, you're a soldier's soldier, Bill. Don't get turned aside from that. I don't mean that you must not go on the staff, as some of our brother officers would think. On the contrary, you *must* go on the staff, if you're to learn where your platoon or company or battalion fits into the whole effort. The heart of the matter is: what do you want to do, to achieve, in your life? I remember the first time we met, in that train going down to Salisbury in 1919. You seemed so young, and sort of lost. Your time in France had matured you in some ways, but – now it was peace, and you didn't know quite who you were, or where you were, or where you were going . . .'

Bill said slowly, 'You were right. I didn't . . . I ran away from home when I was sixteen because Dad wanted me to join him in the draper's shop and Mum wanted me to go to university and be a professor or schoolmaster or something, and I didn't want to do either. I didn't enlist because I wanted to, but to avoid the other things. I didn't go to Officers' School in France because I really wanted to be an officer, but because they sent me. I didn't become a regular officer afterwards because that had always been my ambition, but because I didn't know what else to do . . . I soon persuaded myself that my heart was in soldiering . . . but it wasn't really true, until you taught me to start working at it.'

Cicely said, 'Did you like fighting, Bill? Can you remember your first time under fire? How did you feel then, that first time?'

'I remember very well,' Bill said. 'The Germans made a big raid on our trenches the night I arrived from the depot, after recruit training. The row was terrible – shooting, screaming, grenades bursting, everything . . . I was just struck dumb at first, then I realized that I was feeling very strong, the rifle was no more than a toy in my hands. I was up on the parapet, on sentry, but I jumped down into the trench and bayonetted two Jerries right off, then shot two more . . . I was trembling later, when it was all over, but not then . . . No, honestly, I loved it. I had never felt better.'

'That's what I hoped there was in you,' Morgan said. 'Great leaders have to love battle. Nelson did –'

'He's my hero,' Bill said.

'Some people's faculties slow down and go numb when they are faced with battle,' Morgan said. 'Others' sharpen and quicken. You are one of those. They are rare.'

7

May 1926: England

Bill remembered a day early in May 1926. He was eating in the mess, because Pauline was having a hen lunch and bridge party at home. Round the long mahogany table, groaning with silver, the voices sounded outraged: 'They've *all* gone on strike, every damned one of them!'

'Not all the labourers in the country, Harry, only those in trade unions.'

'Not even all of those,' Bill said, 'Only those in unions affiliated to the Trades Union Congress.'

'Bloody swine! They should all be shot!'

'There's been a call for volunteers, and Churchill's putting out a government newspaper, the *British Gazette*, because none of the real newspapers can be published – printers on strike.'

'They'll starve the country, if the dockers are striking.'

'They are.'

'They don't have the right to strike! It's worse than Bolshevism!'

A sour voice from halfway down one side of the table growled, 'This sounds like a political discussion to me. Shut up, and wait for orders . . . if any.' Major Turnbull took a hefty swig from his wineglass before returning to address his roast pork.

The adjutant came in and said to Turnbull, the senior officer present, 'Excuse me, sir – message from the CO.' He took up the little bell that stood on the sideboard and rang it. The officers fell silent, the hovering mess waiters paused, listening. The adjutant raised his voice, 'We have been ordered to send two companies to the London docks to guard against sabotage. A and C Companies will go tomorrow, in MT, under Major Prentiss. Orders in the CO's office at four pip emma. Company and platoon commanders concerned, also CSMs and CQMSs will attend.' He hurried out.

There'd have to be a pee stop about halfway up to London, Bill thought; and Rifleman Glennie would be sick, but they couldn't stop for that – his comrades in the platoon would push him to the back of the lorry and see that he threw up over the tailgate. The countryside looked at its very best – Kent, the Garden of England, in May, the fruit trees in blossom casting a pink glow over the column of military trucks, painted dark green, grinding up to London. Inside each, twenty men sat on filled sandbags, their packs and greatcoats stacked down the middle. They were wearing steel helmets and their pouches were full of ball ammunition.

Bill leaned back. He felt sleepy but it was too beautiful a morning to close your eyes . . . little columns of smoke rose from old brick chimneys, the hooded cowls of the oast houses looked like the heads of huge monks gathered in the valley . . . a train drew a plume of white across the green, heading for Folkestone and the sea . . . He wondered what the strike was all about. Should he have known that it was coming, or likely to be? Here were millions of his fellow country-men doing their best to paralyse the country, but in the regiment it had come like a bombshell. And the strikers were men who would form a large part of a national army in any war to come, as they had been in the last one, only eight years ago. Morgan Lloyd would have known, he thought, because he was fond of saying that the army was a part of the whole body politic. If that got sick, or feverish, so did the army. But Morgan was in Egypt, on the staff in Cairo. Merton, newly a captain, was commanding A Company now.

An hour later, the road now walled by houses and shops, the convoy came to a halt. From ahead Bill heard the bugle call 'Offi-cers'. He jumped down and ran forward. He found the other officers already at the front of the column where Major Prentiss was talking to a superintendent of Metropolitan Police. After a time Prentiss turned to the gathered officers and said, 'The superintendent tells me there are a hundred or so strikers up the road, near the dock gates, with brickbats, pickhandles and crowbars. They may try to stop us going in. I want an armed man on the step on each side of each lorry cab, from here on, with orders to shoot to kill if they make any attack on us.'

Bill looked round. The other officers, ten altogether, were non-chalant. Well why not? Half of them had fought in France. But these were Englishmen whom Major Prentiss was proposing to fire on. He said, 'Sir, is there any way that they – the strikers – can be told it's us coming, the army, and not volunteer strikebreakers, or more police?'

'Perhaps you'd like us to have borrowed some heavy-infantry colours, Miller, to show what we are?' Prentiss asked sarcastically.

'No, sir, but if I could debus my platoon and march them up the road ahead of the lorries, we can tell the strikers who's coming.'

'Not a bad idea, sir,' the superintendent said.

Prentiss hesitated; then said, 'Very well. Start off at once . . . but don't *you* get mobbed or, above all, disarmed.'

Bill ran back to the trucks holding his men and shouted, 'No. 3 Platoon, debus! . . . Fall in . . . Rifles only. Leave your packs and greatcoats in the lorries.'

The men tumbled out, stretching and stamping their booted feet. Bill turned to his sergeant, Riddle. 'Once we pass the front of the convoy we'll march at ease, and sing. When we get close to the strikers, I'll halt. You see that the men keep on their toes while I'm talking, but don't let anyone fire unless a full-scale riot develops and they're trying to kill us, or grab our arms.'

'Very good, sir. They won't do that.'

'I don't think so . . . All right.' He raised his voice, 'No. 3 Platoon. Quick – march!'

The little column of men moved up the convoy and passed the head of it, where Richard Merton was standing with a small scowl on his face. Well, to hell with him. He was angry because he hadn't thought of the idea himself; or perhaps because it would prevent him getting the chance to have half a dozen strikers shot down. Merton despised the British working class – and that included his own soldiers.

Bill turned round as he marched and shouted, 'Sing, men! Corporal Harris, start up something. Or Evans – you're always singing about Wales. Sing now.'

'That's in the barrack room, sir,' the Welshman answered. 'Well, what about the old favourite?'

He began to sing:

'We are Fred Karno's Army
No bloody good are we . . .'

The rest of the platoon took up the doleful dirge, to the tune of 'The Church's One Foundation' with gloomy enthusiasm. Sergeant Riddle, running up beside Bill, said anxiously, 'That isn't the sort of song

96

they ought to be singing, is it, sir? Shall I stop them?'

Bill said, 'No, it's all right. Plenty of the strikers will know it. It's only eight years since 1918, remember . . . And there they are – our welcoming committee.'

They were drawn up across the road in a dense mass, a hundred men in dark working clothes, mostly capless. Many of them were leaning on cudgels or pickhandles. Beside them the pavement was piled with stacks of half-bricks – ammunition. Another hundred women and old men stood to either side. Fifty yards short of them, Bill raised his hand and bellowed, 'Stop singing! . . . Halt! Stand easy . . . No smoking.' He walked forward, swinging his ashplant. Half a dozen men were standing in front of the other strikers, and now one of these came forward.

Bill said, 'I have come to tell you that the army's coming – two companies, in lorries, just back down the road. We have to get through to the docks.'

'What regiment?' the man said curtly. 'Oh, rifles, I see.'

'Queen's Own Wessex,' Bill said, 'from Dover. Were you rifles?'

'Rifle Brigade,' the man said, '2nd Battalion. We were all cockneys. There's plenty of old Greenjackets here –' He nodded towards the men behind him.

A woman from the crowd shouted, 'Don't let 'em through, Jim!'

The man said, 'Shut your trap, Mary Jane. I'm speaking for you all now . . . I'm Jim Brock, Mr Lieutenant. What are you going to do, when you get into the docks?'

'Protect them – and the ships – against sabotage.'

'You'll be loading and unloading the ships . . . blacklegging,' Brock said angrily.

'I don't know. Perhaps. But I don't think so. We'll probably protect whoever does. I believe there are a lot of volunteers coming soon from all over the country – university students, even schoolboys.'

'From the upper class,' Brock said. 'The class that does no work – except blackleg work.'

They stood staring at each other. Brock was five or six years older than Bill, of about the same height and build, but Brock's face and jaw were set in anger, Bill's in anxious concern, only partly hidden by a feigned nonchalance.

Bill said, 'We have our orders, you know, Mr Brock. You've been a soldier. You understand. Just stand back and let us through. Anything else, and there'll just be bad blood . . . and real blood spilled, perhaps . . . but we'll still go through.'

Brock stood, glowering. At last he turned, calling, 'Stand back, everyone. Let the soldiers through.' Behind him Bill heard the grinding of gears as the convoy began to move forward between the dingy houses. He put out his hand to Brock: 'Thanks.'

Brock didn't take the hand but said shortly, 'We'll not let the volunteer blacklegs through so easy . . . But we're loyal Englishmen and you're the King's men. A lot of us were too, once – most of us. Just remember that when you read about us being traitors and all.'

Bill said, 'I will.' He faced his platoon. 'Stand to your front! Our lorries will stop here – get into the same ones you were in before.'

The leading trucks passed, the guards standing on the running boards, rifles in one hand, holding on with the other. Bill waved to the crowd, and shouted, 'Thanks. And good luck.' Then his platoon's lorries came.

Major Prentiss was holding a conference in one of the big warehouses on No. 1 Dock. The shadow of an Elder Fyffe's banana ship fell across the warehouse. Outside, a string of goods wagons was being shunted under a travelling crane by a small humpbacked steam engine. Prentiss said, 'The police have asked me to send troops out to escort the volunteer workers into the docks. They had trouble getting in yesterday.'

Bill knew that. The lorries that brought the workers in from collecting points near the big West End termini were not army vehicles but civilian ones, hired from many sources, most with the names and addresses of their owners emblazoned on them. Some were flatbeds, and the volunteers riding on these had had a particularly dangerous passage back and forth; for bricks were thrown at them from both sides of the road, and from windows of the buildings, as the lorries came in in the morning, and went back, late in the afternoon, running the gauntlet both ways.

'I'd like to do it,' Prentiss said. 'Damn it, the volunteers are saving the country from these striking swine . . . but I can't spare the men unless we go four hours on and four hours off for guards. Do you think the men will be happy doing that?'

'No,' Captain Merton said, 'But they'll obey orders.'

Bill thought, Prentiss is passing the baby. The decision was his, inside the frame of reference of his orders.

'Does everyone agree?' Prentiss asked.

Bill said, 'I don't think the men would mind doing four and four if they thought the cause was worthy . . . but these strikers come from the same background as they do. For all we know they have brothers and sisters out there, picketing.'

'And throwing bricks,' Merton said.

'Yes, but we're here to defend the docks, I believe, not the men who come to work here. Let the police do that, so that we can keep in the background.'

Merton said angrily, 'When I say something, I won't be contradicted by one of my platoon commanders, Miller.'

'Major Prentiss asked for our opinions, sir,' Bill said.

Prentiss made up his mind. 'We'll go four and four, effective six pip emma tonight,' he said. 'Let me know at once how many men that will release. Captain Merton – you will be responsible for organizing the escort service for the volunteer workers. They'll have to go out in their own lorry to meet the volunteer convoy in the mornings, and do the same in reverse in the evenings.'

'Yes, sir.' Merton turned to Bill. 'You'll be doing it tomorrow . . . and the next day . . . and the next day, so make a plan, once the CSM has worked out the numbers available.'

'Yes, sir,' Bill said. He wished he could be in another company, away from Merton's permanent hostility, but there was no hope of that. He'd just have to grin and bear it. And Merton was probably in a bad temper at being separated so suddenly from his new bride, the Honourable Penelope. They'd been married in April and had got back from their honeymoon the day before the strike began. And the Hon. looked, and was rumoured to be, a very hot piece. Ah well, you couldn't expect every day to be sunny, and that went for both Merton and himself.

It was midnight, the fourth day of the strike. The soldiers were sleeping in warehouses. Temporary latrines had been set up behind them. Double sentries guarded the dock gates and single sentries the gangway from each docked ship. At night a picquet of four men under a NCO patrolled the whole dock area with fixed bayonets. The men not on guard or sentry duty slept fully dressed, their equipment beside them, their arms piled at the end of the room, ready to be called out in case of emergency.

Bill was orderly officer, and had been awakened half an hour ago, at the time he had set for himself to inspect guards, patrols and pickets. He left the warehouse where he slept, at the other end from his platoon, followed by Rifleman Virgil, his batman and platoon runner. Flashlight in hand, but not switched on, for the moonlight was strong, Bill walked to the main gate – the sentries there were alert and wide awake, having been posted only a quarter of an hour earlier – then slowly along the dockside, water gleaming oil-sheened in the moonlight beside him. Six freighters were moored in the dock. Lights burned in the stern cabins of one of them, the others were all dark, the Wessex sentry at the foot of each gangway moving back and forth, a balaclava cap on his head under his steel helmet to keep out the night chill. Beyond the last ship Bill paused. So far he had not passed the picket. Its orders were to check at the main gate; and to inspect the whole length of the outer dock wall from inside. That's what they must be doing now.

Bill set off past the warehouses for the wall, and came to it a couple of hundred yards west of the main gate. It was sixteen foot high, made of Victorian brick, and topped for all its snaky length by a frieze of broken glass. Bill turned left, Virgil at his heels, and walked carefully along the narrow space, littered with paper and broken bottles and trash of all kinds, between the wall and the nearest warehouses. After five minutes, when they were nearing the western end of the dock area, and the wall was beginning to curve down to the ship passage which led to the Thames and the sea, Virgil touched his arm and whispered, 'Something moved ahead, sir.'

They stopped, both peering. Suddenly Bill made out a wavering line, whitish, down the wall, and a lump against the sky above, at the top. Then he understood and whispered, 'It's a rope . . . and a man coming over the top.'

'He's halfway down now, sir.'

'Anyone else following him, that you can see?'

'No, sir.'

Bill walked forward, drawing his revolver. At the foot of the rope he peered upward and said, 'Come down quietly, and stand still, unless you want to be shot.'

The figure on the rope dropped the last six feet, landing heavily beside Bill, then staggering back against the wall. Virgil was on him at once, his bayonet point thrust close to the man's throat, whispering furiously, 'Now stand still, you dirty bugger!'

Bill switched on his flashlight. The bull's eye revealed a square face, dark clothes, a cap, dark intense eyes, thick brows. The man hadn't shaved for a couple of days. It was Jim Brock who now suddenly whistled twice, not loudly. The rope between them twitched, jerked up and vanished over the wall.

Bill returned his revolver to its holster and said, 'You're lucky you didn't get shot, Brock. If that fellow over the wall is planning to come over, you'd better tell him to stay where he is. And any others.'

'No one's coming,' Brock said shortly.

'Then what on earth were you planning to do, alone?'

Brock said nothing. Rifleman Virgil said, 'There's the picquet, sir. Coming this way.'

Bill thought a moment, then said, 'Tell them I'm investigating a suspicious occurrence, and to go back the way they came. And the corporal is to bring them all to Warehouse No. 2, main doors, at half past one.'

'Very good, sir.' Virgil hurried off, stumbling over the uneven ground.

Bill pulled out his cigarette case and offered it to Brock. Brock took one and, when Bill felt for his matches, Brock beat him to it, drawing a match across the seat of his trousers and into flame. 'Now,' Bill said, 'one good turn deserves another. You let us get through your people without violence the other day, and I'll let you go now, if you can get back over the wall. But – you have to tell me what you were planning to do. I must know, or I will just have to hand you over for interrogation by the police.'

Brock seemed to be thinking, while he drew on his cigarette. Then he said, as though to himself, 'They'd know as soon as they saw the tools.' He patted his side pockets which, as Bill could just make out, were bulging. 'Tools,' Brock said succinctly, 'to short-circuit the crane motors as soon as anyone tries to start them up. I'm a travelling crane operator – the best – and I know the wiring inside out, which is more than some of our blokes do.'

Bill said, 'Sabotage. You might have killed someone, too.'

Brock said, 'Not a chance, unless they were sticking their hands into the motor when it was switched on. I suppose one of your public-school volunteers might be daft enough to do that, but then he'd deserve what he got, wouldn't he?'

'I still think it's a dirty trick,' Bill said, 'to ruin the machinery we're trying to feed the people of the country with.'

'*We* think it's a dirty trick to use the army and police in a trade dispute between the owners and the workers.'

'If you had the country on your side, the government wouldn't be able to use the army, and this mass of volunteers wouldn't have come forward.'

Brock said, 'The bourgeoisie doesn't understand what we're fighting for: decent wages, decent working conditions, security in a job you've made, security in your old age, by right . . . I wish I could get to the soldiers, and make them understand, too. Then they wouldn't be so keen to break the strike. They'd know that we're striking for them, as well as for ourselves.'

Bill said, 'I've got to move on. I'd like to continue this discussion. Where do you live? Perhaps I could get in touch with you when this is over.'

'42 Gideon Lane, Wapping,' Brock said. 'But I'm not there much. If you want to find me, ask at the Dead Man's Chest, in Wapping, any evening. I may be there, may be not, but they'll tell you where to find me, that day or the next . . . Now, is it safe for me to whistle?'

Bill said, 'Yes – not too loud.' He had been wondering how Brock had planned to get back over the wall after his sabotage of the cranes, and now learned. Brock whistled twice, then said, 'Stand back a bit.' A moment later, a half-brick came over the wall, the end of the rope tied round it. Brock said, 'Well, thanks . . . what's your name?'

'Miller . . . Bill Miller. Dusty Miller, when I was in the ranks.'

'Oh, a ranker, eh? I wondered where you'd lost that potato all officers carry in their mouths.' He grasped the rope and shinnied up, as agile as a monkey. In a moment he was over the top, where Bill could make out that a thick piece of blanketing had been spread over the broken glass. A few seconds later the rope twitched, and was drawn up and over. Inside, all was silent, except for the crunch of

Rifleman Virgil's boots, as he came along from the direction of the main gate.

Bill did not accompany his escort troops every time they went out – the small squads were usually under the command of a corporal or sergeant; but the day after his midnight meeting with Brock under the wall he did go, sitting in the front of the leading lorry, next to the driver, Virgil squeezed in outside him. The convoy of four lorries, carrying now only the drivers, the eight men of the escort and Bill, wound out of the gate and along a narrow street, its left side bordered by the dock wall. Beyond, the funnels and masts of the docked ships seemed to lean far out over the wall, over the dingy slate roofs of the houses, a few people walking in the light spring rain, women watching them from behind half-drawn curtains.

'Pretty peaceful, so far,' Bill said.

'It'll be different when we come back,' the Army Service Corps driver said gloomily, 'but even then they seem to try not to throw their bricks at us – just at the blacklegs in the back.'

Bill said nothing; but thought, if this goes on much longer we ought to put up some sort of covering over the backs of the lorries, to protect the men inside . . . chicken wire, perhaps, like they'd used in some of the trench forward-observation bays to keep out hurled grenades. He huddled back in the seat, trying to keep out of the drifting rain . . . lucky this General Strike hadn't taken place in midwinter, he thought; if the three of them had been wearing great-coats, they'd hardly have fitted into the front seat . . . the strikers would have been very badly off, too, with no money to buy coal or warm clothes. God, someone ought to see that it was settled very soon, before it created more bitterness, just by dragging on; or before some unfortunate incident caused a flare-up of emotions and hatred that might never die.

The convoy reached the railway station which was the rendezvous and started loading the volunteer workers, who had been waiting under the station's wooden awning, huddled together for protection – over a hundred of them. Bill watched, slapping his swagger cane against his leg, as his corporal loaded them. From their accents and dress he guessed that about half of them were upper class, mostly from the universities and even some public schools – that fellow didn't look a day more than sixteen . . . the rest the usual mixture of retired men – retired chemists, retired petty officers, retired anything – and men who had been unemployed before the strike and would be again as soon as it ended.

The corporal reported all volunteers loaded, and Bill gave the signal to start on the journey to the docks. Trouble began at once, not a hundred yards from the station, with a bottle flying through the air to bounce off the canvas covering of the second lorry and shatter in the road.

'Don't usually waste their time with bottles,' the driver muttered. 'They ain't heavy enough to break through the canvas.'

'They use 'em on the trains though,' Rifleman Virgil said. 'Did ye see the train windows, sir, what the volunteers came down in? More'n half of them broken . . . it's a wonder most of them blokes weren't cut to pieces.'

A rock arched through the air, crashing through the old and worn canvas of the leading lorry, followed by a sharp exclamation from the back of the lorry. Bill called back, 'Anyone hurt?'

An upper-class voice answered, 'Knocked one out . . . but he's breathing . . . I don't think his skull's cracked.'

A half-brick whirled through the windscreen just between Bill and the driver, shattering the glass. It was quickly followed by three more. The glass was splinterproof, but the third brick struck Bill a glancing blow across his right cheekbone just under the rim of his steel helmet. The lorry was grinding to a stop. The driver cried, 'They've blocked the road, sir! Look!'

Rifleman Virgil jumped down, followed by Bill, his cheek bleeding. The road was blocked by some sofas, chairs and railway sleepers, piled two or three high – a flimsy enough obstacle, but impassable as it stood. Bill called back, 'Get the volunteers out and up here, all of them! Corporal and escort, to me!'

The volunteers scrambled out of the lorries and ran forward. The escort took position, rifles at the high port. Two score men in working clothes had appeared out of houses and alleys, all armed with half-bricks. The bricks began to fly and one of the volunteers fell, hit square on the left temple.

Bill turned to the corporal of the escort – it was Bogey Harris – and said, 'Corporal, load!' The men loaded a round into the chamber with a jerk and slam of the right hand, and waited.

Bill bellowed at the workers, 'Get away before someone is hurt!'

A brickbat just missed his head and another struck his right shoulder. He shouted to the volunteers, 'Clear this barricade out of the way!'

'Make the soldiers fire,' one of the volunteers yelled at him, 'or they'll kill us with those damned bricks.'

Bill pointed at the workers, and shouted, 'If you don't get out of the way, I'll fire.' He turned to the volunteers, 'Before we remove this stuff, remove those men . . . Charge!'

He waved his arm. The volunteers, suddenly realizing that they heavily outnumbered the strikers, charged forward, yelling obscenities. For a moment there was confused scuffling on the barricade; then the strikers broke and fled, vanishing in a moment. The volunteer set up a ragged cheer.

'Get it out of the way. Hurry!' Bill commanded.

In a few minutes it was done. Four men were carrying away the volunteer who'd been hit, and he seemed to have regained consciousness, for he was groaning.

'Into the lorries!' Bill yelled.

Then they were on the move, and soon again inside the docks.

Captain Merton was in a rage. 'Three of your men – *my* men – were hit by brickbats . . . fortunately none seriously, but they were wounded, while standing with their rifles in their hands, while the enemy threw bricks at them from ten yards' range! Why the hell didn't you open fire? You would've scattered that bloody rabble with the first shot . . . and taught the swine a lesson that would be understood all over the country.'

Bill said, 'General Dyer was found guilty of using excessive force, sir, when he said he meant to teach Indians a lesson. My orders weren't to teach anyone a lesson, but to escort the volunteers to work here. I didn't need to open fire to do that.'

'How much longer would you have let your men stand there, being wounded?' Merton snarled. 'Till they were all lying dead or unconscious in the street, in pools of their own blood – while the strikers ran off with their rifles and ammunition?'

'I didn't think it was necessary to open fire, sir,' Bill repeated obstinately, 'and we got through.'

105

Merton snapped, 'You are too indecisive, Miller, I shall say so in your next confidential report.'

Bill saluted, turned, and marched out.

After nine days the strike was declared illegal by the Attorney General, and the strikers, law-abiding Britons, went back to work. The detachment of the Queen's Own Wessex Rifles guarding the docks was under orders to return to Dover; meantime, a football match had been played with the ex-strikers on a nearby ground; and, on this evening before the return to Dover, Bill Miller was drinking beer in the Dead Man's Chest, a Wapping pub by the river, with Jim Brock and a tall lantern-jawed man called Lefty. Bill had not been told his surname.

Brock said, 'You did all right that day some of the blokes attacked the volunteers, though Lefty here was hoping you'd open fire.'

Lefty said, 'I was. Hate, that's what you got to have, to win. That's why we're going to win. We hate you.'

'The army?' Bill asked.

Lefty said, 'No, the bosses, the university twits, everyone who's never done a day's hard work in his life. When the revolution comes, we'll look at everyone's hands, and if they got no calluses –' He made a gesture of jerking a rope taut round his neck.

Bill said, 'Someone's got to think, others have got to *do* . . . someone's got to lead, someone's got to follow. But no one has to *hate*. We have to understand. I'm trying to understand you.'

'I know,' Brock said. 'You are. Not many of your class do. It's in the past, a lot of it. Everyone knows what it was like fifty or sixty years ago – starving women, children begging in the snow, men dying of hunger outside the rich man's mansion, barefoot kids working sixteen hours a day for sixpence . . . you *know* all that, but you've pushed it back, down, so that it doesn't really exist any more for you. We haven't. For us it's still here, and now. It could happen again, if we don't make ourselves strong.'

Bill began, 'I understand that, but . . .'

The talk continued, round and slowly round in circles, as it had been doing for three quarters of an hour. Gradually, hazily, Bill came to understand something of what drove these men and others like them; and through that knowledge, something more of his own men, the soldiers he commanded, and, in the end, of his country.

They stopped talking at last, exhausted. Brock ordered another round of beers. Then, before he began to drink, he pointed a finger at Bill. 'Bill, you're a good officer. You'll be a general one day.' Bill waved a hand in disclaimer. 'Oh yes, I think you will. I just hope it won't be a civil war you'll be a general in, the rich against the poor here in England.'

'It won't,' Bill said firmly.

'Or against the Russians,' Brock said. 'Christ, would the upper class here like to push that revolution back down the Russian people's throats – but we working folk won't have it, see? . . . I want to tell you that if you're going to be a good general you have to make everyone, *all* the soldiers, believe in what you're doing, believe in the war. If they think they're fighting people like themselves, who are just trying to make a better place for their kids, they won't fight well, not even the old regulars. And in a big war they won't be regulars, will they, they'll be us.'

'The army is part of the nation,' Bill murmured.

'Eh? Right. And don't forget it.'

Bill said, 'I won't. All I want to be is a good soldier, to earn my pay, and protect the things I believe in . . . which have nothing to do with wages and pensions, and working conditions, I'm afraid. I'm not a socialist, or a Liberal, or a Conservative. I'm an Englishman, a Wiltshireman, and a professional soldier. I'll learn whatever I can, wherever I can, so that I'm ready, when the time comes.'

He thought, I'm a little drunk. Drunk with two strike leaders in a working men's pub. Merton wouldn't like it; but Morgan Lloyd would understand. Even if no one understood, Bill knew, in himself, that this was where he should be, at this time.

Two nights later, in their house in Dover, Bill faced Pauline in the little drawing room. He said, 'Sorry I'm home late, but we were all held for a CO's conference . . . The battalion's going to Plymouth in August.'

'Oh, what a bore!' Pauline cried. 'Plymouth's the wettest station in England. Daddy says it's always raining there. The battalion was there right after the Boer War, I think.'

'It may not be too bad,' Bill said placatingly, 'Dartmoor's near, and . . .'

107

'That's all very well for you, but *I* don't like rock climbing. And on Dartmoor it rains even more than it does in Plymouth. And prisoners are always escaping from the gaol . . .'

Bill said, 'There's a lot of social life in Plymouth, with the navy there.'

'I'll have to get some new clothes.'

'Of course.' Bill steeled himself. He went on, 'Before we leave Plymouth – it's supposed to be a four-year tour – I'm going to apply for transfer to the 2nd Battalion in India.'

'Then we'll be abroad for . . . heaven knows how long,' Pauline wailed. 'What on earth do you want to do that for?'

'There's no chance of active service anywhere except in India.'

'The children . . .' Pauline began. 'They'll have a black nanny! They won't learn anything!'

'They'll be just the same as thousands of other British children in India,' Bill said. 'There are twelve married officers with the 2nd Battalion now, with their wives, and most of those have small children with them, too.'

'But India's such a dreadful place,' she wailed. 'Full of disease and heatstroke and . . .' She stopped, breathless.

Bill said, 'If you really don't want to come to India, go back to Damerham with the children. Bring them out for a cold weather each year, or every other year.'

'Of course not,' she said petulantly. 'If you go to India, I'll come too . . . but I won't enjoy it.'

8

June 1939: England

Brigadier Morgan Lloyd's office looked out on Great Scotland Yard, and the sun seldom reached it, but there were flowers on a corner of his desk, and the open windows let in the scent of petrol fumes and the grumble of traffic. Morgan was sitting behind the desk, hunched forward, making notes on a big yellow pad. He looked up. 'You weren't wounded?'

'Twice, both in the last year,' Bill said. 'Neither was serious.'

'And you finished up as a major?'

Bill said, 'Yes, sir. General Millan Astray said they'd make me a full colonel, but they never did, and then the war ended. I think they didn't want a foreigner in that high rank, where he'd be bound to see a lot of confidential information.'

'You think you learned a lot . . . enough to make the two years worthwhile, in spite of everything?'

'I'm sure of it, myself,' Bill said. 'I learned particularly from von Krug, who was the Condor Legion's chief tank man under von Thoma. The main lesson is . . .'

Morgan held up a hand. 'Later, Bill. There are half a dozen fellows back in England from the Republican side – Mason, Hadfield, McGowan, others. Mason was a colonel and worked a lot with the Russians. The chief has told me to arrange a study committee consisting of these people, representatives from the various branches of our staff, and you.'

'Very good, sir, though perhaps you'd better have some military police present, too, in case the Reds and the Blues from Spain try to get at each others' throats . . . May I get back in uniform, now? My mother's been looking after it all the time . . . My father died soon after I got to Spain in '37.'

Morgan said, 'Not just yet, Bill. There is some paperwork to be done, and a couple more people to be persuaded, but it shouldn't take long. Meanwhile, come to the committee meetings in mufti . . . Now, I have some news for you. Lesley's living in a little flat in Soho, off Gerrard Street. She's been in England for a long time.'

'She never wrote,' Bill said. 'Does she want to see me?'

'I don't know, but otherwise why should she come back to England?'

'But she hasn't said so?'

'No. She telephoned me here a day or two after she was settled in this flat. She didn't say I was to tell you where she was, but what other interpretation could anyone put on it?'

Bill stood up. 'I hope I'll be able to get a few days' rest before the committee work begins. I'll let you know where I am, by tomorrow evening.'

Morgan stood up in his turn, his hand out. 'I can't promise much rest just yet,' he said. 'We're now absolutely certain that Hitler means to start a war soon. The only question is, when, and just where. We have to prepare for it, and we have to do it fast . . . Good luck.'

Bill shook hands, then stepped back, saluted, and went out. He knew that Morgan was not wishing him luck in the war that seemed inevitable, but with Lesley.

She answered the doorbell herself, wearing a paint-spattered smock, her hair swept back from her forehead and tied with a ribbon at the back of her head. He waited on the doorstep, looking into her eyes. Behind him two women with heavy grocery baskets gossiped in Spanish. He understood most of what they were saying, and their talk of children's ailments, the price of bananas, the quality of meat, was like a drumbeat in the silence of his mind, as he waited.

At last she said, 'Come in.'

She led him up a flight of stairs into a large studio, with northern skylights, a couple of dishevelled couches, a chair, a table with some fruit in bowls on it, an easel and its canvas. Lesley was in the middle of painting a still life of the fruit. Her palette rested on one of the sofas. She stood back, close to the easel and said, 'Well?'

Bill said, 'I love you. I didn't know whether you still knew, so I thought I'd come and tell you.'

'You're not sorry for what you did? You haven't come to tell me that?'

Bill shook his head. 'No. It was necessary that we had a competent observer on Franco's side, and I learned lessons which we in this country – the military here, and the government – must absorb and benefit from, because war with Hitler's coming.'

'We all know that,' she said, 'and now we won't have Spain on our side. Spain will fight for Hitler.'

'Not if Franco can help it,' Bill said. 'The country's been bled white . . . It's in ruins – its agriculture, shipping, economy, roads, transportation, banking – everything. It'll take twenty years to recover. And just because the Germans helped the Nationalists, don't think that Franco or anyone else loves them any more than the Republicans did. Franco's top general, Yagüe, called the Germans and Italians beasts of prey.'

She suddenly broke down, falling back on a sofa, weeping, covering her face with her hands. 'How could you wear that uniform when you knew about Guernica . . . about prisoners being shot . . . women and children massacred . . . democracy murdered . . . all to set up a fascist state under this monstrous Franco?'

Bill said heatedly, 'Prisoners were shot on both sides, often . . . *always* if they were foreigners . . . Guernica wasn't the only city bombed nor the Germans the only bombers . . . and by the early part of 1938 it was quite clear that the Republicans in Spain were under the control of the communists. The only thing that could have prevented a communist takeover was massive intervention by Britain, France and America. They didn't do anything. They didn't want to get involved!'

He realized that he was shouting at her, his nerves still taut from the endless months of slaughter, of suppressed fear, of raw emotions, shame, pride, disgust, all at the highest intensity.

He dropped to his knees beside her and said, 'I'm sorry, darling. I'm overwrought. Look, let's not talk about it, but remember that we love each other. I'll be back in British uniform soon and all this will be a bad dream. I was so lonely and miserable without you . . .'

'No Spanish señoritas to provide home comforts?' she said, mopping her eyes.

He took her in his arms, murmuring, 'Not a chance . . . there, there . . .'

Slowly she relaxed on the couch, stretching out, holding out her arms to him, whispering in his ear, 'Oh, Bill, Bill . . . I've missed you, I ache for you . . . I love you . . .'

They met in the door of the War Office conference room, Bill coming from one direction with Morgan Lloyd, in the opposite direction five men in plain clothes, guided by a lieutenant colonel of the General Staff. Morgan said, 'Mr Mason, this is Mr Miller, who served with the Spanish Foreign Legion, and has much experience to share, as do you and your friends.'

Bill put out his hand but Mason snapped, 'I don't shake hands with fascists.'

Bill said, 'Just as you please.'

Morgan led through the door and said, 'You gentlemen sit on that side of the table, and our staff officers will sit opposite. Please try to bury whatever feelings you developed in Spain. We are all British, and these meetings are for the benefit of our country, not of any faction in Spain or anywhere else.'

Half a dozen officers filed in, all with briefcases or clipboards, and sat down facing the civilians. Morgan took the head of the table, and a young captain the foot.

Morgan said, 'The purpose of this committee is to bring out the lessons to be learned, for Britain, from the recent civil war in Spain. We are interested in all lessons, whether tactical, strategical, organizational . . . whether they relate to supply, use of air, or anything else.'

'What about political?' Mason said. 'We had a good system of commissars to see that none of our men got any fascist or bourgeois ideas.'

'I don't think that we will change our views on politics in the fighting services here, whatever might have been done in Spain,' Morgan Lloyd said coldly. He went on, 'Captain Grey there will be our secretary and record the gist of what has been suggested, and the details of what has been decided. Now, I think we should each stand up and say who we are. In the case of the staff officers, state what position you hold and what your responsibilities are here in the War Office. Let's begin with you, Mr Mason.'

One by one they stood up round the table, and gave the details Morgan had asked for. When that was done Morgan said, 'Now, where shall we begin? We have a large field to cover.'

'Air support and transport,' Mason said promptly.

'Armoured strategy and tactics,' Bill said.

'Guerilla warfare,' another civilian said.

Morgan held up his hand. 'I think we'd better start with organization, so that we are all speaking the same language when we use such words as battalion, company, etc. Let's start with infantry, at the battalion level, of five hundred to seven hundred men. Bill . . . how was the legion organized in this respect? No, stay seated, it's easier for you, and we can all hear . . .'

Bill explained the organization of the legion into battalions called *banderas*, they into companies, and they into sections. The other civilians followed suit for the battalions of the Republican International Brigades, and of the various corps of militia.

When all had spoken, Morgan said, 'That gives us a start. And now I suggest we talk about methods of communication, particularly at the brigade level, and with supporting artillery and aircraft. How was it done? Did it work? How could it be improved? I'm handing over to Colonel Egan here, one of my G1s, as I have other matters to attend to, unfortunately. Take over, Tom.'

He left the room and the conference continued. It soon became obvious to Bill that Mason and his followers meant to ensure that their view prevailed, that the future British Army would much more closely resemble the International Brigades and their command structure than it would the Spanish Foreign Legion or the regulars. Egan's attempts to start discussions in a contrary sense were almost shouted down and whenever Bill spoke he was rudely interrupted and cut off.

At a few minutes to twelve Colonel Egan adjourned till 9.00 a.m. the following day, and the conference broke up. Walking along the passage, Bill thought, this won't do. We must cooperate, for England's sake. He hurried to catch up with Mason and the other men walking down the long corridor with him, and said, 'Mr Mason, listen to me, please . . .'

Mason walked on. Bill caught his elbow and pulled him round. 'Listen, you bastard,' he snarled. 'I think you're a communist and I know damned well that your lot murdered and raped in Spain, just as ours did. But I also think you're a loyal Englishman. If you think I'm

113

not, I suggest we go outside and take off our coats.'

Mason seemed taken aback. 'You, knock my block off?' he said. 'Pick on someone your own size.' Mason was over six feet and burly in proportion, with huge meaty hands.

Bill said, 'We must work together. I'm willing to bury the hatchet. Are you?'

Mason snapped, 'No. We'll never have truck with fascists, and that's final.'

Bill said, 'We won some battles. Our organization was proved superior to yours, particularly in the later campaigns and in the handling of all arms together. These are military, professional facts, not ideological questions. You can't call one sort of artillery communication Red and another fascist in its nature.'

'We think you can. That's why we have commissars all the way up and down.'

'That will never happen in the British Army and you know it,' Bill said heatedly. 'Let's just be professional, for the good of England, and work together.'

'Not bloody likely,' Mason said and stalked on along the corridor with his supporters.

Where the winding road ended, a mile past the farmhouse, at the foot of the head wall of the valley, Bill stopped the car and the four of them squeezed out – Lesley, himself and Bill's two children by his first marriage, Roger and Brenda. Roger, seventeen, was nearly the same build and size as Joe Mason. He would soon be a young giant, and had been in his school's rugby XV for three years. Brenda, fifteen, too, was no waif, busty and almost fully developed. When she had lost some of her present puppy fat, she would be a good-looking, rather large, young woman.

Lesley looked up at the rock wall and said, 'Not for me today, Bill. I'll sketch and read.'

Bill turned to his children. 'Do you remember anything of rock climbing?'

'Not really, Daddy,' the girl said. 'We were awfully small, and we haven't done any since.'

'Well, all right, let's begin at the beginning. I want you both to walk up that slope . . . it's a little steeper than it looks from here . . .

114

not to the top – that's too far – to the grassy step about a quarter of the way up . . . you go that side, Brenda, and you go that side, Roger. When you're up, I'll signal, and you come back down towards me.'

The young people set off. They were both fit, Bill noted approvingly – Brenda was in her school's hockey XI – and they climbed fast, but making just the sort of mistakes he had made that first day on the Elham cliffs with Morgan and Cicely. He watched them come down and gave them the same lecture Morgan had given him; then, as Morgan had done, he made them follow him up a different route, putting their feet exactly where he put his. 'But, Dad,' Roger said, 'Your legs are shorter than mine. I'll want to take longer steps.'

'Later, when you know where to put your feet down, you can,' Bill said. 'For now, put them just where I put mine.'

So an hour passed, and Bill noted that Lesley had wandered off back down the valley towards the farmhouse. This was the first time he'd been alone with his children for a long, long time. He looked at them with sudden love and, as they came down from a traverse of the steep hillside, following behind him, he held out his arms and hugged them both. 'God, I love you!' he exclaimed. 'And what a miserable father I've been.'

Roger, acutely embarrassed, mumbled, 'No, you haven't . . . you've been great . . . when you could.'

'It ought to have been more, though.'

It was late July, the first day of their summer holidays. Pauline had sent them up to Wales yesterday, and this was Bill's first full day with them. 'It was good of you to write to me in Spain,' he said. 'I don't know whether I got all your letters, but I got some, and they made a big difference to me, I can tell you.'

'Lesley didn't write, did she?' Brenda said.

Bill said, 'No. She was very upset because I was fighting for Franco.'

'I think Franco's all right,' Brenda said. 'Better than those Bolshies in France anyway.'

Bill said, 'Well, let's not waste precious time talking politics. How's Mummy?'

The children looked at each other and Roger mumbled, 'Oh, all right.'

Bill said, 'Good. I'm glad to . . .'

Brenda broke in, 'No, she's not all right, Daddy. She drinks too

115

much, and Paul's beastly to her and has other women. He doesn't love her . . . never did, if you ask me.'

Bill sat silent on the rock, thinking. At last he said, 'Is there anything I can do, do you think?'

Brenda said, 'I don't know, Daddy. But I think it would make Mummy feel better if you'd see her. She has no one to talk to now, and you know how much she used to like parties and seeing people.'

'I'll call her and see if she'll meet me. Whatever happens, she was my wife . . . and she is your mother . . . All right, let's run through the rope drill . . . This is a climbing rope. It is made of finest three-strand manila hemp and it's eighty foot long – that's about the right length for a cordee of three. It weighs one pound per twenty feet, so the whole rope here weighs four pounds. The leader and the last man tie themselves onto the rope with . . .'

Pauline didn't look much different, at first; but as he got used to the dim light in the big South Kensington flat where she lived with her new husband and Roger and Brenda, Bill saw that she was using make-up to hide the dissolution of her beauty. She was developing baggy pouches under the eyes, the fine line of her jaw had gone puffy, and her hands trembled unless she kept them folded in her lap.

They had been talking for ten minutes, mostly about the children and their futures. Now there was an uncomfortable pause, because both wanted to speak more personally, but did not know how to begin. It was Pauline who spoke first. 'They hate him . . . Paul. He's not good with them. At first I thought it was just jealousy, of the time I spent with them, but it's changed. He really dislikes them.'

'Perhaps they remind him of me,' Bill said. 'Though I must say that neither of them looks much like me, and they're both a couple of sizes bigger than I am or ever was . . .'

She said, 'I meant to write to you in Spain, but never got round to it. Morgan told us where you were and how to write to you. The children wrote, didn't they?'

Bill nodded, then said bluntly, 'Are you happy, Pauline?'

She took out her handkerchief, blew her nose, and started crying. 'No, Bill. I'm miserable. Paul's really a beast . . . beastly to me. Now he's off in Paris, business he said, but he's with another woman, a terrible tart . . . I heard that Lesley was angry with you for going to Franco's side.'

'I told the kids that, when I saw them on my way to Spain,' he said.

'For the last year I've been hoping she wouldn't have you back, and . . .'

'I'd come back to you?' he said. He reached out and took her hands. 'I'm sorry, Pauline, there's no chance of that. We're not suited, you and I, while Lesley and I are, even if we have disagreements . . . I want to help you, as a friend . . . as the father of your children. Is there anything I can do?'

She sobbed unhappily. 'You can't change Paul . . . I could divorce him. I have plenty of money, now that Mummy and Daddy are dead. That was all Paul was after, really . . . But I'd be so lonely. I can't stand being alone . . . Have a drink?'

Bill thought, it's a bit early, but what the hell? He couldn't change her, he could only try to help her. He said, 'Yes . . . whisky and splash . . . Look, Pauline, call and talk to me occasionally, let's take the kids out together, when they're home from school . . .'

She said, 'All right. Oh, you're a darling, Bill. You always were. What a damned idiot I was to leave you, just because I didn't like India . . . and a bit because, from the beginning, Richard Merton was always hinting that you weren't good enough for me . . . He's divorced Penelope, by the way – adultery with a lot of men . . . Poor Richard.'

Poor Richard, Bill echoed mentally. He never thought he'd be saying those words about Merton, but obviously there'd been pains other than himself in Merton's life.

General Lloyd said, 'I've been reading all the minutes of your committee meetings and, as you know, I've been able to attend some of them myself. You don't seem to be getting much help from the Republicans. Whatever you say is just left to lie there, while they go on riding their own hobby horses.'

Bill said, 'Mason told me they'd never cooperate with me, weeks ago. So what's developed is a struggle for power and influence here in the War Office.'

'They're not acting purely from ideological spite,' Morgan said. 'They have their own ideas about the right lessons to be learned. But don't feel you're on your own. You have plenty of allies on your side. Though they don't talk as much as Mason, they have more influence.' He winked solemnly.

'And Mason doesn't like me personally,' Bill said, 'so there's a sort of personal hate going on, as well. First it was Merton, now Mason. What do I do to deserve this?'

Morgan laughed. 'Be Bill Miller . . . Have you finished that paper I asked for about your suggested organization for an armoured division?'

'Yes,' Bill said. 'I'll bring it in tomorrow. But I can tell you now that its main thrust is that there must be a balance between armoured fighting vehicles – tanks – and everything that goes with them – infantry, artillery, engineers *and* a supply column. None can function without the other. They must all be able to keep up with each other and all must have some cross-country performance. My outline war establishments are aimed at achieving that. The biggest gap is that we don't have a cross-country vehicle for the infantry.'

'The Germans have half-tracks,' Morgan said.

'I know . . . Sir, is there any word as to when I will get my commission back? It's been nearly two months since I came home from Spain.'

Morgan looked unhappy as he answered. 'We're still dealing with some very cautious people, on the permanent under-secretary's side. He wants to be sure that there's no political backlash over it.'

'Over re-commissioning one middle-aged officer with a DSO?' Bill said bitterly.

Morgan said, 'I'm doing my best to speed things up . . . Bill, don't get downhearted. If the worst comes to the very worst and they finally balk, I'll bet we're at war before the New Year, and then we won't have to ask anyone. We'll just commission you, in any rank we choose, in exercise of our wartime powers . . . Would you and Lesley like to come round for drinks this evening at about seven? Nothing formal, but Cicely wants to see you both again, and there's a chance that we can all get up to the Lake District for some climbing.'

'When?' Bill asked quickly.

'Towards the end of this month, August,' Morgan said. 'The chief has practically ordered me to take a week off then.'

'That would be great,' Bill said. 'But I'm afraid we can't come over this evening. We have some guests for dinner – Jim Brock, the Labour leader, and his wife . . . Izzy and Mrs Steinberg – you remember them from Lucknow in, God, 1928 – they're refugees from Hitler now, and live in Golders Green . . . and an Indian politician, Chaudhri. He's a bachelor, or at any rate doesn't have a wife here in England. I met him in Chattarganj in '36 when I was G3 there. I don't know what he's doing in England.'

'On a mission from Congress,' Morgan said, 'to get to know our Labour and socialist leaders and make them aware of what the Congress Party wants from the British Government, and what they might promise in return.'

'I hope the evening doesn't get too political,' Bill said. 'Jim Brock and Izzy Steinberg are good fellows, and I liked Chaudhri, but personally I'd rather get to know them and the wives better as people rather than delve deep into their ideals and policies . . . but with Lesley in charge, we'll probably end up making blueprints for a new heaven and a new earth.'

'Tanks use a great deal of petrol,' Bill said, 'and everything that supports them also uses fuel. A tank immobilized because it has run out of fuel is a sitting duck for anything that comes along that *can* move, including ordinary infantry or guerillas armed with Molotov cocktails. A formation of tanks that has to stop because its fuel supplies can't keep up with it will ruin an entire operation. We had to do that twice on the Teruel Front, and once, later, on the Ebro. Von Krug swore that when he got back to Germany he'd devote his energies to seeing that a proper supply system was organized to go with armoured forces.'

Morgan Lloyd was attending this meeting of the committee and now cut in drily, 'I think the people in Germany became aware of that some time ago,' he said. 'We have information that Guderian's all-armoured advance that took over Vienna in the spring of '38 was a disaster, due to the breakdown of the fuel supplies.'

After a few moments of silence Joe Mason spoke up. 'We want to talk about air support, general. We want to know what's being done about it, because it worked in Spain, both for us and for the fascists – I mean air support of tanks, when they get beyond the range of their own artillery.'

119

'That was never allowed to happen by von Thoma or von Krug,' Bill said. 'They both believe fanatically that tanks must have artillery in close support all the time.'

'I wasn't talking to you.' Mason snapped. He turned again to Morgan Lloyd. 'We think that tanks can go almost alone . . . a lot of them together, of course, with some infantry going with them in vehicles like bigger carriers . . . but why do tanks need artillery to support them when they can have a big gun themselves?'

Morgan said, 'Our tanks carry only a 2-pounder, Mr Mason. The German Mark IV has a 75 mm gun, it's true, but no one knows how well it will work, or whether it can carry enough ammunition to carry out a real bombardment with its gun. A round of 75 mm fixed ammunition is pretty big. Not many of them will fit inside a tank if you remember everything else that's got to fit in too.'

'We think a tank is a mobile armoured gun,' Mason said obstinately. 'If we had an armoured division consisting of a brigade of tanks like the Mark IV, with a big gun, and a brigade of tanks with high velocity 2-pounders, and a brigade of infantry in these big carriers, we'd have a division that could move fast, off roads, sweep behind the enemy and cut up his supply routes and headquarters. When they met real opposition they'd call up bombers on their radios. The bombers would be their heavy artillery.'

'It must have field artillery and anti-tank artillery, too,' Bill said, 'preferably fully tracked. The weather's too unreliable for such a division to rely always on bombers for heavy support.'

Mason said, 'We don't agree.' He turned to Morgan. 'Well, general, what are we going to *do*? We've been talking for weeks now and everyone's said everything he has to say. It's time we made up our minds.'

General Lloyd leaned back in his chair at the head of the table. 'First, we get our own tank and artillery and supply people to comment on the proposals made in this committee – they've had their representatives here all along, of course, but now that we're nearly done, they have to put the pieces together and look at them from their own points of view. Then we shall have meetings at the highest level here in the War Office . . .'

'. . . including representatives of Vickers and the people who are going to make these tanks and radios and big carriers,' Bill cut in.

'Of course . . . And then we shall ask for designs . . . Let's see, what are the main items we have concluded we are going to need? . . . Better two-way radio sets, suitable for use in tanks and aircraft; aircraft that can both fight other aircraft and support ground troops; vehicles, probably half-tracks, that can form supply columns for armoured forces; compact, lightweight mobile bridging equipment; a tank with a gun of about 75 mm size; fully tracked armoured personnel carriers of largish size . . . phew, it's quite a list. And finally, we have to get money for all this out of the Treasury, while at the same time the navy is demanding more aircraft carriers, the RAF more fighters, more anti-submarine patrol craft . . .'

'Great!' Mason exclaimed, standing up. 'And meanwhile, the Nazis take over France, bomb our airfields till we don't have any fighters left, then walk over the Channel and install a Gauleiter in Buckingham Palace, and put von Thoma where you're sitting now . . . We've said all we have to say. You know our views. We're not coming back.'

Morgan stood up too, and said, 'Thanks for all the help and information you have given us, all of you.'

The room quickly emptied, until only Bill and Morgan were left. Morgan sat down, lighting a cigarette, and offered the pack to Bill. Bill shook his head and Morgan said, 'You did well, fighting the good fight against the Red Brigades. But what we need now is luck. Remember what Napoleon said about generals: "Don't tell me if he's good, only if he's lucky." *We'd* better be lucky . . . By the way, tomorrow you will be commissioned as a major in the Queen's Own Wessex Rifles. Congratulations!'

Lesley, looking at Bill across the small dining table, said, 'Pauline rang up again. She's had to cancel the dinner date she had with you for tomorrow. Some old aunt's died and she has to take the kids to the funeral . . . You know, I think you should have her here, rather than take her out.'

'I don't know whether that would be a good idea,' Bill said dubiously.

'It might not, but it might. I don't have anything against her,' Lesley said. 'She made a mistake in marrying you, another in leaving you, and a third in marrying this Paul fellow. She's miserable and it might make her feel better to have another woman to talk to. Mind, I don't want to become a bosom pal, or visitor of the sick, but if she comes here, with the children sometimes, there's much that we can talk about, and do, that will take her mind off her troubles. Speak to her about it next time you see her.'

'Don't know when that will be,' Bill said, 'now that our dinner's cancelled . . . and next week we're going up to the Lake District, and . . .'

Lesley said, 'We'll be very lucky if *that* comes off.'

'You think the balloon will go up first?'

'I don't like the way the Russians are dragging their feet in these Anglo-Soviet negotiations. There should have been agreement on a common front against Hitler long ago, but there's been nothing, and I don't like it.'

'You're being very pessimistic,' Bill said. 'The Russians will make common cause with us, never fear. *You've* always sworn they will . . . rather, that we'll have to make common cause with them, against fascism.'

'I have an awful feeling about that, in the pit of my stomach,' she said. 'But maybe the delay is only in drawing up the proceedings of the meetings, when they have to type out our admiral's name a few dozen times. Only the British would send a negotiating team to Soviet Russia headed by an admiral with three titles, three Christian names, four surnames, and half the alphabet after that: Admiral the Honourable Sir Robert Reginald Ranfurly Plunkett-Ernle-Erle-Drax GCB etc., etc., etc. . . .'

'We'll keep our fingers crossed,' Bill said.

'And our powder dry, if it isn't already too damp, and in a hopelessly small quantity . . . You know, when Pauline was speaking to me on the phone today, she asked me how I had liked India. I said I had loved it, especially Quetta.'

Bill said, 'She feels that if she'd stuck it out with me in India when we went out together, we'd still be together. She's wrong, but . . .'

'What was it like? You've never talked much about it . . .'

9

March 1928: England

It was early 1928 and the battalion was stationed in Plymouth. The Jack flapped damply over the barracks, the regimental flag clung sodden to its post in front of the quarterguard, and Bill was inspecting his platoon in barracks, for it was raining.

It's always raining in Plymouth, he thought angrily. It isn't raining in Cornwall, or on Dartmoor, it isn't raining out to sea beyond the Hoe – only on Plymouth, and especially on the barracks. The battalion was due for another two years here, and no one liked the idea, except the amateur sailors.

In the barracks the row of beds, the blankets folded on them, the equipment set out on each, as though on invisible corpses, had become hostile. Studying the theory of war was all very well, but how could you keep your enthusiasm, your interest, when it actually boiled down to this? When your only opportunities to command came in reprimanding soldiers for failing to clean the hobnails under their ammunition boots? Damn it, here was Rifleman Hunt's cap badge, with dried Silvo left in the crevices. He'd been forgetting to brush the stuff off since he'd joined the platoon, and he had five years' service by now. He must be doing it on purpose, to assert his individuality. 'Give him three extra drills with the defaulters, sergeant.'

'Sir!'

He moved on. How much longer could he find any desire, in himself, to do his job well? It had been possible when Morgan Lloyd had the company, but Morgan was in India now, Merton was still the company commander, and his open hostility had not abated. But there was hope, for Merton had won a place on the next Staff College course, by competitive examination, so would be leaving the battalion in a few months. And the children were growing up strong and healthy and he loved them deeply, but wondered whether they knew it, for he could not easily express or show his love. Pauline had become bosom friends with the Hon. Penelope, Merton's sexy wife . . . but that friendship would soon be broken up, when the Mertons went to the Staff College and . . . Damn it, why was he waiting for Merton to go? If he didn't like it here, why didn't *he* go, as he'd been talking about for the last two years? Because Pauline cried, and sobbed that he didn't love her, and life at home was hell every time he even alluded to the subject. But today, now, this instant of awarding punishment to Rifleman Hunt, something had snapped. He *would* act, as soon as he got home after parades. The afternoon was free. He'd take her up onto the edge of the moor, and have it out.

After lunch they put on their mackintoshes and scarves; Pauline covered her head with another scarf, well tied down against the wind, Bill covered his with a tweed cap. Then Bill took his ashplant, which he carried on route marches now that swords were no longer worn on such occasions, and they drove off in the Vauxhall onto the moor. As they started walking, the wind blew sharp from the south-west, at their backs, and a hunting kestrel hovered against it, wings fluttering.

Bill said, 'You remember I told you in Dover, when we heard that we were being sent here, that before our tour was up I'd apply for transfer to the 2nd Battalion in India. I'm going to do it now – tomorrow . . .'

She said, 'I've been thinking, Bill. I know how miserable you are doing the same things over and over again. I've talked about it with Daddy, several times . . . the last time, when I was home for Christmas. It's a pity you couldn't have come up for a couple of days.'

'Someone has to stay with the men over Christmas,' Bill said, a little shortly. They had had this argument before.

Pauline said, 'Well, don't let's fight about that. The point is that Daddy agrees with you.'

'He does?' Bill said, wonderingly. His father-in-law had retired back in 1922, but he was still regimental from his toes to the carefully brushed ends of his grey moustache. Bill always thought that he slept in pyjamas striped in Rifle green and pale blue, the regimental colours.

'Oh yes,' Pauline said. 'He thinks there ought to be more fighting, and he can quite see how you would get bored, with no small wars going to make a change. But going to India would only be jumping out of the frying pan into the fire – certainly for me, and perhaps for you, too. You'd still have inspections and parades, and in awful places where there are no shops, cinemas, golf links, foxhunting . . . just natives and desert for hundreds of miles, and the temperature a hundred and twenty in the shade all the time. The battalion would usually be alone in the station, so you couldn't get away from someone you didn't like. You'd get on each other's nerves, and as for us, the women . . . what sort of a life would we have?'

'It's not as bad as that,' Bill said.

'Nanny won't come to India. She went with Mummy and Daddy before the war, and hated it. So we'll have black ayahs, full of fleas. And it's nearly time that Roger went to prep school. He's down for 1930, which is only two years off.'

Bill said nothing, but set his jaw obstinately. Pauline continued, 'Listen to me, Bill. Daddy suggested that you leave the army altogether, and go into politics. There's a safe seat in Sarum North, and he'd back you . . . and finance you.'

'As a Conservative, presumably?'

'What else could anyone be, after what happened to Ramsay MacDonald's socialist government, in 1924, wasn't it?'

'I don't think I'm a Conservative,' Bill said.

'What does it matter? As long as you're not a socialist, they're really all the same, Liberals, Independents, the lot.'

Bill did not speak for a long time, turning the idea over in his mind, as the wind tugged at the skirts of his mackintosh and bit at his exposed ears. At last he said, 'I suppose you're right. But I'm not a politician. I don't want to go into Parliament.'

She said, 'You're just as good as half the people who are there now – nincompoops and liars, Daddy calls them.'

'Yes, but I don't want to be a politician. Or even a statesman. I . . .'

She interrupted. 'Very well. Daddy didn't think you'd take to the idea, but I had to bring it up, as it is a possibility, and it would make such an interesting life for all of us – a flat in town, a place in the constituency – or we could just take a wing of Damerham Court. Daddy would be happy if we did, and . . .'

'I don't want to be a politician,' Bill repeated. 'I'm *not* a politician, I . . .'

She cut in again, 'Daddy had another idea. Commander Braintree wants to retire soon.'

'Braintree? Oh, the secretary of the Golf Club.'

'Yes. And Daddy is sure that you could get the job. It doesn't pay much, but we could live at Damerham. You have to like and play golf, of course, and know all about it, but the important thing is to be able to see that everything works smoothly.'

Bill said, 'I'm not a golf-club secretary, Pauline, just as I'm not a politician. It isn't exactly that I don't *want* to be any of those things, but that I *do* want to be something else – a soldier, a commander. I don't want to leave the army, but to go somewhere in it that is more exciting, and useful for the future, than inspecting haircuts and barrack rooms. I think the best solution for me is a spell with the 2nd Battalion. Morgan Lloyd's going there next month, remember.'

'It might be best for you,' Pauline cried, 'but not for me!'

Captain Richard Merton leaned back in his chair behind his desk in the little A Company office, and said, 'So you want to transfer to the 2nd Battalion, so that you can earn glory and a few medals on the North-west Frontier . . . You know how they describe India? A first-rate country for second-rate people.'

Bill said nothing. Merton swung forward. 'All right. You are probably doing the wise thing, though Penelope will miss Pauline. India's the place for you, Miller. Eventually, you should probably transfer to the Indian Army. You've never really fitted in here, though you've tried, I suppose. I'll forward your application, with my recommendation.'

Bill said, 'Thank you, sir.'

It was June 1929, and outside the long barrack building the sun beat almost vertically down out of a leaden sky. The super-heated air hung in quivering mirages over the gravel surface of the parade ground behind the cookhouses, and the regimental flag hung limp, crushed by the heat, to its pole outside the quarterguard. Inside barrack building No. 14 of the British infantry lines in Lucknow, India, Lieutenant Bill Miller was inspecting the men of No. 6 Platoon, B Company, 2nd Battalion Queen's Own Wessex Rifles, who occupied it, with their clothing and equipment. At his heels his platoon sergeant, Denton, followed, notebook and pencil at the ready.

126

Bill stopped at the tenth man, as he had stopped at the first nine. His Wolseley pith helmet felt heavy on his head and its sweatband was already soaked. An hour ago his khaki shirt had been smooth and clean, his knee-length khaki drill shorts ironed to knife creases, but now the shorts were crumpling and black patches of sweat were spreading across his back. He felt as though he were in a trance of eternity, and this was the same Plymouth barrack room in which he had punished Rifleman Hunt and in that moment decided to come to India; and the same Aldershot barrack room in which he had inspected his platoon immediately after he had been given his regular commission; and even before that, the German barracks the battalion had occupied in Cologne had felt the same, looked the same, though smelling subtly different. There was a different smell here, too, the scent of India: burning cowdung, a long way off but brought down here by the languid stirring of the heated air; water from the stone floor, which was always washed down soon after reveille – most of it had dried up, but Sergeant Denton saw to it that there were always some damp patches left to prove that the floor had indeed been washed down, as per standing orders. Another strange smell in here was rifle oil; it came from the clamps at each end of the barrack, where the men's rifles were stored, protected by sliding steel bars and padlocked chains. The natives were supposed to be constantly on the lookout to steal a rifle, yet in India British soldiers always had to have their weapons close at hand – for example, they took them to church with them, each man with ten rounds of ball ammunition in his pouches . . . because the Indian Mutiny had broken out on a Sunday in May 1857, and the British battalions had been in church, without their rifles, or ammunition, so . . .

He heard a sharp movement behind him and looked round. Sergeant Denton was motioning energetically at an Indian in white *achchkan* and pyjamas standing just outside the barrack-room door, a bicycle leaning against one of the verandah pillars behind him. The sergeant said, 'It's your bearer, sir. Shall I go and see what he wants?'

Bill shook his head and beckoned. The bearer, his personal valet, came forward looking nervous, for the only Indians allowed into the barrack rooms were the sweepers, and those who provided services, such as the *napi*, who shaved the men while they were still abed; and the *char*-wallah, who sold tea and buns. 'What is it, Sher Khan?' Bill asked. 'It had better be important.'

'*Chota*-sahib bitten by *pagal* dog, *huzoor*,' the servant said. 'Memsahib say, bring sahib running jumping . . . Memsahib crying, *huzoor*.'

Bill hesitated briefly. He was less than halfway through the inspection. Damn the bloody inspection! He said, 'Carry on, sergeant,' and left the barrack room followed by the bearer. Bill's own bicycle was parked in the rack outside B Company's office. He jumped on and pedalled across the parade ground and out of the gates at a fast pace, the sweat now pouring down his face and neck, his shirt quite black. It took him ten minutes to reach the comfortable bungalow he had rented just outside the civil lines. Now that he was past thirty he was at last entitled to a government married quarter, but there was none available.

He found Pauline in the children's bedroom, with ayah rocking on her heels and wailing in the corner, Roger sitting on the edge of his bed, a handkerchief wound loosely round his left forearm, and Brenda standing by the window, looking frightened. Bill took the handkerchief off his son's arm, revealing a gash about three inches long that had been bleeding profusely and started to do so again when the handkerchief was removed.

'Where's the dog?' he asked.

'It ran away,' Pauline said. 'I didn't see it at all, that's what ayah says.'

Bill turned to the ayah. '*Chup raho!*' he snarled. 'What happened? *Kya logya?*'

Ayah began to explain, in the servants' pidgin English – Urdu . . . The *chota*-sahib had been running across the lawn, chasing a ball . . . she had been telling stories to Miss Sahiba under the peepul tree in the corner. A white dog ran in, through the open gate from the road, snapping at the air as it went, bounding along. It passed close by the *chota*-sahib and bit him as it passed . . . then it ran on through the hedge. She'd never seen it before. It was just a dog, not a sahib's dog, no collar . . .

'Bloody pie dog,' Bill growled. 'How long ago did this happen?'

'Half an hour,' Pauline said. 'What are we going to do?' Oh, he'll get rabies . . . he'll die . . .'

128

'Shut up,' Bill said. He took his son's hand. 'Can you ride your bike?'

'Oh yes, Daddy.'

'Well, we'll go to the hospital right away . . . Keep everyone calm, Pauline. Pasteur discovered the serum for this years ago.'

Over forty years ago, in fact; still rabies was a terrifying disease, he thought, as he watched the doctor examine Roger's arm, clean the wound, and bandage it. The doctor looked up and said in a strong Irish brogue, 'This will prevent any ordinary infection, but unless you can find the dog, have it killed, and bring it here for us to test the brains within forty-eight hours, the boy will have to go tò Kasauli.'

'I know,' Bill said. Kasauli was in the Simla Hills, the seat of the Pasteur Institute of India. It was the only place in India where anti-rabies serum was available, for the serum could not safely be shipped any distance without risk of spoilage. He didn't know how long the journey would take – about twenty-four hours, probably, with at least two changes of train; and he was due to sit on a court martial tomorrow. Pauline would have to go with Roger. To the doctor, a major of the Indian Medical Service, he said, 'Will you arrange the Kasauli end, sir? My wife will take him up.'

'Sure, me bhoy, and don't worry . . . He has a week yet before there's any danger.' He took Bill aside. 'You know what the bite treatment is?' Bill shook his head. 'Fourteen days at 10 cc a day, in the belly, alternate sides. The poor little fellow's going to be very sore, and bored . . . just as long as he's not frightened, too. There's no need for that. It's a sure preventive.'

Bill walked, out, holding Roger's hand. What a trip poor Pauline and Roger would have, in the hottest of the hot weather. It was near noon now, about the same temperature as it had been yesterday – 1·14 in the shade.

Two weeks later Bill was sitting in the drawing room of Morgan Lloyd's big bungalow in the civil lines, about a mile from his own. Morgan was second-in-command of the battalion, having joined just before Bill's own arrival from England. Bill thought, it's nice to be having a cool drink in the early twilight with Morgan, but I ought to be getting home. Pauline would be waiting and she'd have problems. She always did. She and Roger had been back ten days from Kasauli now, and it had been a terrible journey, worse even than he had imagined: a breakdown of the electric fans in their railway carriage; a dust storm en route that had filled the compartment with choking dust and set Roger to coughing all the rest of the way; the poor boy frightened and waking up screaming four or five times in the night – this was probably Pauline's fault, she was terrified of the needle herself, and even more of rabies, and she had obviously passed on her terror to Roger.

Morgan interrupted his train of thought. 'Have you had a chance to digest *On Future Warfare* yet?'

'Not really,' Bill said, a little uncomfortably. In truth, he had hardly glanced at it.

Morgan leaned forward, stabbing the air with his cigarette. 'Well, do it soon. You must get a firm grasp of Fuller's ideas, and contrast them with other people's, especially Liddell Hart's of some years back. Take tanks . . . Fuller is advocating a heavy division of over three hundred tanks, each with three crews, that can act as infantry when needed, and a light division, with no infantry or artillery, which would act like cavalry, and a third division whose job is really cleaning up the battlefield after victory . . .'

Bill gathered his thoughts, and said, 'While Liddell Hart wants us to have divisions that are completely mechanized, and that can be made into separate combat teams of different sizes.'

'Yes,' Morgan said eagerly. 'But each of them's thinking and projecting from his own viewpoint, his own stance, if you like . . . Fuller is recreating the force that was the most advanced that he thought could be accepted in 1919, but this is 1929 . . . Liddell Hart's going for efficiency and cooperation in units larger than a platoon, and also for much more flexibility. What do you think?'

Bill said, 'I incline towards Liddell Hart in the organization area . . . Fuller's light division is not going to be any use at all without some artillery – even the old cavalry division of 1914 had several batteries of 13-pounders in its establishment. And the clean-up division is a waste of manpower, if that's all it's going to do.'

'I agree,' Morgan said. 'But the nub of the matter is the air. There's got to be an air component. These new divisions have to be linked to an air force both for action – fire support, reconnaissance, and so on – and for supply . . . Did you see that Fuller's advocating the use of gas?'

'But that's against the Geneva Convention.'

'There could be a new convention if the powers decide that gas is more humane than other weapons . . . or cheaper . . . or more useful. Apart from military technical matters, what we must really get our teeth into is Fuller's analysis of the general European situation. Europe's obviously a mess. There ought to be a United States of Europe, or at least Confederated States – but there's nothing. And as long as that's true, Fuller believes that war is inevitable. In that case we in Britain must do one of two things . . . maintain a really strong friendship with America, or rearm Germany, which the French are trying to starve out of existence. But what we *have* done is guarantee the frontiers of France, which is comparatively strong. It makes no sense. Fuller thinks our best bet is to go back to the old-time professional army, relatively small . . . modernized, organized, trained, and led by intelligent, able men, men who understand their business, and have the will and the knowledge to act independently. You see, Fuller always comes back to the Man, and to the aim of war, which is peace or better conditions than before. That's why the sort of destructive war that some people envisage – particularly the air-power advocates – makes no sense at all . . . You aren't listening, Bill.'

'I am, I was,' Bill said, 'but it's so damnably hot. I find it hard to concentrate.'

Morgan took off his heavy horn-rimmed glasses, wiped them carefully, and looked at Bill across the coffee table. 'You are sinking in a swamp of routine, Bill – military and domestic. Why aren't Pauline and the children up in Naini?'

'She doesn't want to go,' Bill said. 'She thinks that if I have to stay down here, she should.'

'Stuff and nonsense!' a woman's voice said from behind him. Bill rose as Cicely Lloyd walked into the room. She pecked Bill's cheek while Morgan poured her a glass of lemonade from a side table.

Cicely said, 'Will it be any good me speaking to her? She really ought to go up now . . . and you'll be going up for a month later, won't you?'

Bill said unhappily, 'Well, try if you like, but I'm afraid . . .' He gestured helplessly. 'I've done my best, but she seems determined.'

Cicely said gently, 'Determined to make herself an Early Christian

Martyr, Bill. That's the truth. I'm an old married woman, my dear. You have to try to find out what makes her want to do that. Then everything else will fall into place.'

Bill said, 'I think I know. It's me . . . I don't play polo or want to. I don't really enjoy parties, unless it's just a few people I like, who can do more than gossip or talk petty shop. I work too hard, think too much about the army, study at home . . .'

She patted his hand, 'Just like Morgan. Try and soften up a bit, if you can . . . Talking about gossip, I had a letter from Judy Whitehorn – her husband's at Camberley on Richard Merton's course. She says that the Hon. Penelope is having a passionate affair with an RAF officer, and everyone knows about it – including Richard . . . Poor Richard.'

Serves the bugger right, Bill thought, but said nothing. After a time he said, 'I must be getting home, sir. Thanks very much for having me in . . . thanks, Cicely.'

Morgan accompanied him to the front door and out onto the drive. He said, 'Before you go – I've succeeded in getting your friend Harris out of Merton's clutches. He'll be coming out with his wife and kids, on the first trooper of the trooping season, to join us as a sergeant. I don't know whether he'll be going to you, as platoon sergeant – probably not. But he might well come to B Company . . . In your private life perhaps you should soften, relax a bit, as Cicely said. But militarily you must learn to concentrate on the job you have put your mind to, whatever the distractions – hot weather, crying children, rabies scares, barrack inspections. It's harder still in battle, and it needs practice. Good night.'

'Good night, sir. Any idea when we might be sent to the frontier, sir?'

''Fraid not, but I'm pulling every string I can to have us sent up next year or the year after.'

Bill was climbing a steep rock surface, smooth except for a long almost vertical fissure, into which he was managing to jam one nailed boot, or three fingers of a hand, at a time. It was July and the monsoon was in full flood, but here in the Himalayan foothills between Kathgodam and Naini Tal it was not raining, though the air was heavy with moisture, and the surface of the rock humid to the touch. Tommy Bateman, Indian Civil Service, the Governor's young private secretary, had suggested the expedition a week earlier, and Bill had had no difficulty getting weekend leave. Pauline had refused to join him, and after a fruitless quarter of an hour arguing with her Bill had given up.

But when he reached the railway station on Friday afternoon he had been surprised to find a third person waiting for him, besides Tommy and his bearer. It was Dr Israel Steinberg, a Viennese doctor in the new, strange science of psychiatry, having studied under Dr Jung. He was spending a year in Lucknow on a project to do with the analysis of the behaviour patterns of rural people with non-European non-Christian backgrounds. He was about forty, quite tall, his dark hair streaked with grey, long-faced with a high curved nose and large dark eyes. Bill and Pauline had met him several times at social or official functions. His manner was not much different from an upper-echelon Indian Congress politician, say Nehru.

Tommy said, 'You know Dr Steinberg, of course . . . We met by chance in the bazaar this morning, and when it came out that we were going rock climbing, he . . .'

'I invited myself, on my knees,' the doctor said, smiling, in his Austrian accent. 'I hope you don't mind a stranger intruding on your weekend, but oh, I miss my climbing so much . . .'

Then there was nothing for it but to accept him with a good grace, and in fact he had made the train journey pass very pleasantly with his talk, his comments on the India that he was studying, and on its British overlords – these last delivered with sly good humour and an infallible eye for hidden pomposities. By the time they reached the end of the line at Kathgodam, Bill was calling him 'Izzy'.

Now, early on Saturday morning, Izzy was above him on the rope, and had a good belay. Already Bill trusted him as much as he had any other person with whom he had climbed: he had a good technique and a great rhythm, climbing in short, sure phases, each complete in itself, from one firm hold or footing to another; then a pause, while the next phase was studied and the course of action decided on, and then, execution, with no waste of time or effort, and no hesitation.

Bill paused, staring up. How the hell had Izzy got up this stretch, where the crack all but petered out and there seemed to be nothing but the smooth steep rock on either side, sliding up to where Izzy waited on a ledge, the rope well belayed?

Izzy called down, 'Look to your right, Bill. See, there is a small protuberance in the rock, about a foot above your eye level. If you can get a foot on that, you can come on up by friction if you don't linger.'

Bill peered up and saw the protuberance – he should have noticed it before, but the light was falling full on it, casting no shadow . . . no excuse, Izzy had seen it. Now, how to get up to it . . . couldn't possibly swing his foot up that high and even if he could he'd be in an impossible position to start on up the slope . . . ah, above him there was a small rock wedged in the crack – get a hand behind that and pull up? No, no, he could hear Morgan's voice in his ear, 'Never pull with your hands if you can possibly help it, push down and in. Hundreds of chocks will come out if pulled but are perfectly safe if pushed.' This looked like one such – but how to get up to it? The crack was not quite dead. He could use it to gain another four feet, and then . . . hands on the chock stone, press down, and lift one foot – which? – left – onto it, then reach out with the right foot onto the rock protuberance, press firmly and start up, perhaps four strides and he'd be there, helped a touch by the rope, which Izzy was holding firm and straight between them . . . Ready? Go! He braced himself and pressed down and in with his boot into the crack, forcing his thigh and calf muscles to push him up . . . going up . . . here was the chock stone, his shoulders were well above it, the rope just right, not jerking or dragging but firm . . . elbows bent, close to his sides, hands on the chock stone, down, slowly firmly straighten the elbows; up up . . . now the left boot onto the chock stone . . . keep moving, straighten the left knee slowly, steadily, that leg was anchored, reach out with the right to the protuberance, momentarily palpate the surface of the rock with the boot nails, selecting, feeling, this was good – straighten the knee, slide on up in the same motion, launching his whole body onto the slope, up up up, the rope shortening to him . . . the rope was tight to the belay and he stepped onto the ledge beside Izzy.

'Sorry to keep you waiting,' he said.

Steinberg said nothing, but nodded and called down to Tommy Bateman, waiting at the same resting place where Bill had been, 'Ready, Tommy?'

Tommy called up, 'I can't see the stance where Bill stepped out of the crack and started up towards you.'

'You will when you get to the top of the crack. Wait till Bill gets his belay here . . . all right, ready here!'

'Climbing!'

Tommy came up as Bill had done, and so for another half-hour they climbed rhythmically and well, reached the grassy alp above, and lay down, smoking cigarettes and discussing what to do next.

Izzy said, 'It's going to rain. Shall we go back down?'

Bill said, 'We haven't passed anything that would be much more difficult in rain so far, have we?'

'Don't think so,' Tommy said.

'Then let's go on . . . along a bit and up that section, there. It'll take a bit of reconnaissance but it looks interesting.'

' "Interesting" is a very British understatement,' Dr Steinberg said laughing. 'It looks perilous . . . or, in English, "bloody dangerous".'

'Who'll lead?' Tommy said. 'Not me, I'm not good enough.'

Izzy said, 'I would prefer Bill to lead . . . I have a better technique than his because I have more experience, but . . . I have sensed something in our Lieutenant Miller . . . he gets better the more "bloody dangerous" things look. Let's go and examine this monster thoroughly before we tackle it . . . in the rain, which is now falling.'

They turned up the collars of their tweed climbing jackets, loose-fitting, with all the pockets on the inside, pulled down their tweed caps, and set off along the grassy alp to the base of the cliffs a few hundred yards to the east.

Bill in the lead, both the others standing beside him on the narrow resting place, they surveyed the pitch above. The rain was driving hard into his face, but it was not cold here at barely five thousand feet above sea level. This would be a miserable climb at ten thousand feet . . . but he wouldn't be trying it at ten thousand . . . or would he? Why was he here now? Determined to show them that he could force the cliff? Show who? Tommy and Izzy? Would he do the same in command of a division, fifteen thousand men, putting their lives at risk just to prove himself? He shook the raindrops off his cap by shaking his head from side to side and looked up again. Concentrate!

135

There was the route . . . traverse here, friction hold, to the crevice twenty feet right . . . get into it . . . start chimneying, sideways position . . . have to start that at once, because the only resting place was in the crevice, so he'd have to go up and make room for the others . . . then they'd all three chimney up for about forty feet . . . to there . . . out, and traverse back left to this side of the snout of the ridge . . . next resting place on the dark outcrop . . .

He said, 'Ready, Tommy? Izzy? Climbing!' and set off across the steep sideways-sloping rock, moving steadily and fast, to reach the crevice in a few seconds, Tommy keeping the rope firm. Bill wedged his back firmly, put up one boot against the opposite wall, then the other, and started up . . . like a leech, he thought . . . plenty of leeches in the Himalayas at these altitudes. He went up fifteen feet, searched for a belay, found it and called, 'Belay set! Ready!'

Tommy called, 'Climbing!' and came on across the rock. At his third step his nailed boot grated on the rock, did not hold, and slid down, pulling his body over and outwards. Bill, peering into the rain from the partial shelter of the crevice, had the lead rope tight before any weight came on it; and Izzy, belayed behind, had the trailing rope taut at the same time. A second later Tommy, brought up short against the rock, and acting instinctively, pushed his upper body away from the face and raised his legs. 'Pull!' he yelled to Bill. Bill pulled, Izzy paid out rope behind, and in the middle, on the steep rock, Tommy, leaning far out over the hundred-foot fall held by the two ropes, fore and aft, walked sideways three steps to the crevice.

He slipped in, wedged himself and hung for a moment, head lowered. Bill called, 'All right, Tommy?'

'I think so . . . Thanks.' He raised his voice. 'Thanks, Izzy . . . Sorry about that slip, Bill. The traverse is perfectly safe. It was just my carelessness.'

Perhaps, Bill thought, perhaps it was my vaingloriousness. Anyway no one had been hurt and they'd better get ready for Izzy. 'Chimney up close to me,' he called down, and Tommy began to move.

A moment later a torrent of muddy water poured down the crevice and over Bill, then drained off onto Tommy below him. Bill couldn't look up, but hunched over as best he could. Small and not so small stones clattered down on his head together with mud down his neck.

One big rock would finish off this climb, he thought, and probably himself into the bargain.

The flood did not stop, but abated to a steady stream of water, mud and small stones. 'This damned crevice is a drainpipe, too,' Bill shouted down.

'I don't think it'll get any worse,' Tommy said. 'Are you coming over, Izzy? This flood's not going to stop.'

'As soon as you're ready.'

'Belay set! Ready here.'

'Climbing!'

An hour and a half later, in driving rain, Bill led up and across the final pitch, his clothes sodden, the wind now lashing rain into his face. He moved fast, subtly changing his balance, using his hands only here and there . . . not much hope for him if he fell on this pitch, because it was long, and an insupportable strain would be put on the rope when the jerk came . . . So, *must* not fall, even slip or slide . . . At last, force up, body over, down with his arms, leg up, out – on top!

Five minutes later, Tommy joined him, and five minutes later again, Izzy. For a moment they lay side by side in the warm rain, looking up into the dark clouds racing across the low sky. At last Izzy Steinberg said, 'I was right to suggest that you lead, Bill. You weren't very sure of yourself at the beginning, but as conditions became worse – the weather, the rock, everything – you became better. That's the mark of a great climber.'

'I'll never be a great climber,' Bill said. 'I don't have the time. I just want to be a great soldier.'

'It's the mark of a great soldier, too,' Izzy said. 'You grow in stature on the mountain, Bill . . . and in life . . . But what will you do if there's no war?'

Early on Monday morning, at Kathgodam, they transferred their gear from the rickety old bus to the narrow-gauge train and spread themselves comfortably in a four-berth compartment for the tedious journey back to Lucknow.

'That was a good weekend,' Tommy said. 'The rain on Saturday and early this morning was a bore, but' – he shrugged – 'it's July.'

Bill said, 'We have to be able to climb on wet rock as well as on

137

dry. You can never tell, on a mountain, when it's going to rain or snow . . .'

'I am most grateful to you both for letting me join you,' Izzy said. 'I trust I was not too much of a nuisance . . . and did not talk too much. That is we Europeans' chief fault, in the eyes of you strong, silent English, eh?'

Bill laughed. 'You didn't talk enough for me, Izzy. If we hadn't been getting up at four this morning, I would have liked to continue our talk all night. I still had so many questions to ask . . .'

The doctor stretched and lit a small thin cigar. When it was drawing well he said, 'Why not continue it now, then? Tommy can always go to sleep' – he indicated one of the upper berths – 'and we shall talk in low voices.'

Tommy said, 'I'm interested, too. Bali Ram managed to get us plenty of beer and some sodas. That bottle of whisky is less then half empty. We have a cold chicken. So . . .' He leaned back on one of the lower bunks, crossing his arms behind his head. 'What are we waiting for?'

Bill said, 'Well, when we went to bed last night, we had just begun talking about extroversion and introversion. You say that these types can be recognized in analysis, and often even in ordinary behaviour, by laymen – people like Tommy and me.'

Israel nodded, 'Yes, you can often tell, if the person tends towards the extreme of his type. The extreme extrovert is in flight from the self – so he acts out his feelings in society. The extreme introvert lives within the self, replacing outward reality with inner fantasies. We all have something of both extrovert and introvert in us, as we all have both male and female characteristics, but in most people one dominates. We can tell which it is by observing the behaviour pattern. If a stranger rushes into a bar and starts shooting, the introvert says afterwards, "I was terrified"; the extrovert says, "He wounded two women." '

It was raining again, and the green fields of Oudh were half hidden by low drifting clouds. They had had to close the windows against the rain, so it was hot and humid in the carriage, and all three men were perspiring steadily, even though the fans were whirling round at full speed. Smoke from the little engine lay like a black carpet between the clouds and the fields.

'All right,' Bill said, 'suppose I cannot observe a person at close hand, or analyse him, as you described. Suppose I can only observe his actions at a distance, would I be able to tell what type he was?'

Israel looked at him quizzically. 'What are you thinking of, Lieutenant Miller? Of an opposing general, by chance?'

Bill flushed. 'As a matter of fact, I was . . . I mean, we can't observe an enemy general close up, or analyse him, but we can usually find out a lot about his background, his upbringing, his boyhood . . .'

'The collective consciousness,' Izzy said, 'and, don't forget also collective training and thinking. You will find that most German General Staff officers think of problems, they attack problems, if you like, in just the same way – because they have been trained to, and have spent years living together discussing these methods.'

Bill said, 'We know what an enemy general does, because we see its effects. I wonder whether it would be possible to develop a system to work out what he *will* do.'

'Not what he certainly will, but what he probably will, at the most,' Izzy said. 'It has not been isolated as a field of study, but . . .' He became more animated, his expressive hands now spreading, now closing, his eyes fixed on Bill's when he was speaking to him. The train chugged and whistled on. The rain continued to fall. Bill thought, it is not enough that Izzy's and my paths should cross so briefly. We must keep in touch. He has much to teach me.

It was late in August. The monsoon was still in full blast. On a Thursday afternoon Bill came home from playing soccer in the rain with his platoon – every Thursday was a holiday for all troops in India – to be met by Pauline in the entrance hall. As he handed his wet mackintosh to the bearer, she said, 'Lunch will be half an hour late. And Brenda's got ringworm.'

'Ringworm?' Bill gasped. 'That's impossible!'

'It's not impossible! She got it from ayah or ayah's nephews or nieces, or some other filthy native child in the bazaar or the park. You can't escape from disease in this country . . . disease of heat or rabies or mould . . . all my shoes are green with mould, from the rain rain rain . . . bedbugs – fleas. I found I had fleas this morning, just after you left, twenty or thirty of them. I've sacked ayah . . . Your breath smells of booze.'

'I had a pink gin with the Lloyds on the way home. Morgan was watching the soccer . . . Has the doctor seen Brenda?'

'Yes. He's given me some stuff to put on. She's to be kept away from Roger, or he'll get it, too.'

Bill's frayed composure broke. He snapped, 'All this has happened because you won't go up to Naini. You say it's your duty to stay down here with me in the plains, but the truth is you want to make an Early Christian Martyr out of yourself. In the process, you're martyring the kids, and me . . . all suffering because you're determined to show what a bloody place India is. Really, it's not that bad at all. There are lots of interesting things to do, interesting people to meet, talk to. And Naini's *beautiful* – fresh cool mountain air, sailing, riding, dancing, walking – the kids would love it, there are hundreds of other children their age up there, and . . .'

'*I* don't want to be ogled and pinched by hungry bachelors and dirty old majors. They have mad dogs in Naini just as much as they do here . . . and filthy natives with ringworm and fleas . . . *I* don't think there are any interesting people about. *I* didn't find anything interesting in that Jew doctor you're so keen on, whom you invited for dinner one night. He's as boring as that drunken poet you became so friendly with in Dover. Those aren't *my* kind of people – and nor is anyone else I've met in India. That's why I'm going Home, and I'm taking Roger and Brenda with me. I sent a cable to Cox & King's at ten o'clock this morning and I expect a reply tomorrow. At this time of year the boats will be empty, and we won't have to wait for a passage.'

She turned and stalked away. Bill stood a moment, undecided. What a mess. What a bloody day. He needed another drink. No, he didn't, he needed to concentrate; secure his base; find out whether Pauline was serious, and if so make plans to dine in mess, get rid of this bungalow, and take a bachelor quarter; and all the time, think of war, of organization for war, of command and administration in battle.

He cleared his mind and walked through to the back of the bungalow to talk to the children. They'd been having a hard time, too; and they were not masters of their fates.

10

May 1932: India

Bill waited beside the dusty track, leaning on his ashplant. It was noon of a day in May 1932, in Waziristan, North-west Frontier of India. The Kari Khel tribe had been creating trouble for months – shooting up militia posts, kidnapping girls from the settled areas, ambushing and robbing supply convoys. The army had been sent in to bring the tribe to heel. So the Indus Brigade, of which Bill's battalion formed part, was now advancing through mountainous country towards the Kari Khel stronghold of Dalzai. The sun beat down from a coppery sky with intense heat, and there was no refuge from it other than the thin shade of the holly oak that covered the otherwise barren mountainsides. No water ran in the bottom of the shallow creek up which the column was moving, and all the men and animals were parched with thirst and exhausted with the day's advance.

Ahead, shells from the 3.7-inch screw guns of the mountain artillery were bursting along the crest of a ridge a mile and a half forward and four hundred feet higher up. By using the binoculars slung round his neck, Bill could occasionally pick up the khaki spots that were Indian soldiers advancing through the holly oak up the slope. It was the Dogras, for they had been leading the column since ten o'clock. Now they had apparently met opposition. Behind the Dogras followed a battalion of Gurkhas, which would be passed through the Dogras as soon as the enemy had been driven off these ridges. Behind them came the Wessex, the only British battalion in force: and, as rearguard today, a battalion of Frontier Force, always known as Piffers, from their old title of Punjab Irregular Frontier Force. The brigade also contained some Madras Sappers and Miners in tall khaki cylindrical hats, relics of eighteenth-century shakos, three batteries of Mountain Artillery, and a squadron of Bengal Lancers, together with such auxiliaries as transport companies of camels and mules, and a field ambulance, its equipment carried by pack animals.

Up there on the ridge, the shelling stopped, and a moment later little khaki figures appeared on the crest, here and there a bayonet catching the sun. Now, for the first time, Bill heard the snap and crackle of small-arms fire. The Wazirs must have been firing at the attacking Dogras, but he hadn't heard it till now: the first time he'd heard shots fired in anger in fourteen years. He looked round at his B Company sprawled along the bank behind him, attempting to find shade where there was none. For how many of these men would this be their baptism of fire? Easier to work out for how many it would not: the CSM and CQMS; Bogey Harris and all the other sergeants except Filton; three corporals; two old sweats trying to get long-service medals; that was all. And the company was at full strength, 121 men.

C Company, ahead, began to move again, and Bill signalled to B to advance. The CSM shouted, 'On your feet! Get cracking!' The men fell in in ragged fours, slung their rifles, and advanced. The platoon mules, carrying the Lewis guns, were led on in their places at the back of each platoon.

Ahead, Bill saw a runner, a man of the regiment, coming back at a jog trot, stopping to say a few words to C Company commander, then on. He reached Bill and said, 'The CO's been taken ill, sir. Don't know what it is, but Colonel Lloyd thinks it's a heart attack. He's taken over command.' He tapped his rifle sling in salute and ran on.

Hm, Bill thought – that's rough luck on old Kellerman-Browne, who'd now be riding in a fiendishly uncomfortable *khajawa* on one side of a jolting camel, but it might be a good thing for the battalion. K-B was a nice enough old fellow, but he should have been pensioned off years ago. He liked bridge and port, and the society columns of the papers, when they reached the battalion from England weeks late. He was personally brave enough but knew little about tactics or training his men for war. Morgan, who'd been a brevet lieutenant colonel since mid-1930, would tighten all the loose nuts a great deal – he and the Wazirs between them.

The column struggled on and, after an hour, halted. No word came back about the reason for the halt. The sun beat down hotter than ever in the stifling afternoon. The CSM came up and asked if the men could use their waterbottles. 'No,' Bill said shortly. 'Not till we come across more drinkable water. You know the orders.'

'Yes, sir, but some of them's in a bad way.'

'Tell them to suck pebbles. God knows there are plenty of those

142

about . . . even if most of them are covered with mule shit by now.'

Bill tried to relax. Hurry up and wait. The army all over. Never tell anyone anything until it's too late. It was just as important to put that right as to study tactics, the organization of armour and cooperation with artillery. In the last resort, wars were fought by men, and . . .

Another runner came down the column, stopping beside Bill. 'CO's compliments, sir – report to battalion headquarters, at once.'

Bill turned to his CSM. 'Sarn't major, tell Mr Joinville that I've been called forward, and he's in command.'

Then, with his batman behind him, he broke into a fast walk. In ten minutes he reached battalion headquarters, recognizable by the mules carrying the office *yakdans*, more mules with reserve ammunition and water *pakhals*, and the presence of the RSM and the adjutant. Morgan Lloyd was standing to one side, studying a map folded in his map case.

Bill reported to his back, 'Captain Miller here, sir.'

Lloyd turned. 'Ah, Bill. Good. Here's the situation . . . The Gurkhas are passing through the Dogra pickets now. Their objective is the next ridge – there! Dalzai is the other side of that ridge. As soon as the Gurkhas are in position, we are passing through them with the field company of sappers under command, to take and picket all ground dominating Dalzai from the north – the Gurkha pickets will protect this south side. We drop off the sappers in Dalzai itself to start preparing to blow up the towers, while the rest of the brigade follows and settles in. All our pickets will probably be taken over before nightfall by the Piffers, but that's not certain yet. We may have to stay out on the ridges all night . . . Now, I'm going forward to reconnoitre, and I've brought you up so that you can learn something. The other company commanders never will learn – because they don't want to. Come on, you fellows –'He waved at the artillery major and engineer captain standing nearby, and at once the little party moved forward. Bill thought, this is the R or Reconnaissance Group that Morgan's always talking about as one of the essential elements of good battle drills. He would already have told the adjutant to call forward the O or Orders Group, consisting of the other company commanders and the machine-gun officer, after a certain time. And already orders would be going down for the battalion to do whatever needed to be done to prepare for action – which, at this moment, might well mean no more than checking ammunition and having a smoke.

Morgan turned to the artilleryman. 'I know I have all three batteries in support, unless the Pathans attack somewhere else, but how many of them actually have their trails down?'

'Two, sir. One is on the move.'

'Good. Tell me as soon as it has its trails down, too.'

He turned to the engineer. 'Charlie, I'll probably move your men and equipment up behind by reserve company. I'm not going to use you in the attack.'

'The men would like it if you did, sir,' the engineer officer said.

'I know,' Morgan said. 'They're real fire eaters – but they're too valuable as sappers. And in any case, I want to use you to protect one flank or the other – we'll see which as soon as we've had a look at the ground.'

They rounded a corner in the rocky pass and came upon a group of men, horses and mules, the men wearing the wide-brimmed Gurkha hat. Morgan went up to the Gurkha colonel and, after greeting him, the latter said, 'We're nearly there now, Morgan, two companies up. Look!'

'It won't take long,' Morgan said. 'The wily Wazir won't stand and fight today.'

'But it'll be a different kettle of fish when we come back out the day after tomorrow, eh?'

'Exactly . . . Do you mind if I bring my battalion up pretty close? I want to pass through as soon as you've got the ridge . . . hit them again before they're ready.'

'Certainly.'

Morgan beckoned to one of his two runners, scribbled on his message pad, tore out the sheet, and sent the runner back with it. Then his party found a place to rest, and watch the final phase of the Gurkha attack.

Ten minutes later, the Gurkha colonel called over, 'You can go forward now. We've got the ridge. Our vanguard's about half a mile up the path. I wouldn't recommend going past them except in strength. For reconnaissance, you can see pretty well from the saddle where they are.'

Morgan said, 'Up, you fellows. Let's go forward and have a look at our objective . . . and don't stand about by prominent rocks from here forward. The wily Wazir will have ranged in on them days ago.'

The little party hurried forward, more spread out now, passing under the ridge just occupied by the Gurkhas. Ten minutes later, a new vista opened up ahead, blocked by a single lion-like ridge running across the front about a mile and a half away, and, nestled under it, the towers and mud houses of Dalzai.

Morgan Lloyd moved out into the open and stopped, his binoculars raised. A Gurkha soldier lying behind a rock a few yards off called back, '*Khabbardar*, sahib!' Be careful, Bill thought; quite right, for here came a bullet, quite close, and ten seconds later, another – closer. He dropped to his stomach behind Morgan with the rest of the group and cried, 'They're sniping at us, sir.'

Morgan said nothing, but continued to stare through his glasses, methodically quartering the ground ahead and to the flanks. After more shots had passed close, he retreated behind a cliff face: 'Couldn't see properly lying down . . . It's clear to go straight at them. The Gurkhas can cover with machine-guns from up there beside us . . . Let's see now, where shall we have the artillery support, though I want the companies to be able to call for it as opposition shows itself, too. We don't want a lot of guns committed to tasks where there may turn out to be no enemy.' He turned to the gunner major, and they began to discuss where hidden Wazirs might be lying up, and how companies could best call for fire through the limited number of artillery observers available. The artillery signaller unfurled his flags and began wigwagging in morse to the rear. Some more bullets flew by, but they were all safe in defilade.

Morgan said to Bill, 'You've seen the country – how are we going to pull out of Dalzai? Back down this valley?'

Bill said, 'I don't know . . . I hadn't thought . . .'

'Well, think,' Morgan said curtly. 'We're going up now, but we know we're coming back after we've blown up the towers. Is there any other way back to base? Practically, no. Therefore we are being given the inestimable advantage of seeing the enemy's side of the hill. The ridges which we've attacked up from the south over the last six days will be the ones that the Wazirs will try to ambush us on on our way back. I've been marking my map with every likely gully and *tangi*. You should have been, too . . . Now, the O Group will be here in ten minutes. Until then, let's take a good look at this Gurkha ridge, from what will be the enemy's side when we come back.'

The taking of Dalzai and the lion ridge beyond went without incident, only two men being wounded by distant sniping. In near darkness turbaned Piffers struggled up the big ridge to relieve the Wessex picquets, and the British soldiers ran back down into Dalzai, to start another longer and more indecisive battle, against the myriads of fleas. Next day the towers were blown up at ten in the morning, and then, under the protection of Gurkhas and Piffers on the ridges to south and north, the Dogras began a thorough search for hidden or buried weapons, while the Wessex rested, but ready for action in any direction, one company and one Mountain Battery being at five minutes' notice. At eleven, when Bill's B Company had just rotated down from five to thirty minutes' notice, he was sent for by Colonel Morgan Lloyd.

Bill found the CO sitting alone on a primitive bench in the main room of the big house which was being used as the Wessex officers' mess. Bill came in, saluted and waited. Morgan said abruptly, 'How's your company? What shape is it in?'

'Not bad, sir,' Bill said. 'They're pretty tired, but they're all right.'

'Unfit,' Morgan said. 'It's not your fault, Old K-B wouldn't allow really hard training, for the sake of the men's health, he said! And he certainly didn't insist on physical fitness, so he didn't get it. We'll alter that as soon as we get back to Pindi . . . The Wazirs think they know exactly what we're going to do, now that we've blown up their towers. They think we're going to start back tomorrow, the way we came. So they've had plenty of time to plan a big ambush somewhere, probably close to Dalzai here, and then harry us all the way back, collecting a good number of rifles off our dead and wounded in the process . . . Well, they're not. I've got permission from the brigadier to lay an ambush for *them*! You're going to do it – your whole company, with some extra Lewis gunners – because, when the ambush is sprung, there'll only be a few seconds before the Wazirs realize what's happening and dive for cover. During those seconds a great deal of execution must be done. Now, come up onto the roof, and I'll show you what I want you to do. But don't point. There are Wazir binoculars, plus very sharp eyes, trained on us. We've got to look as though we're just having pink gins.'

Bill waited, lying still, close to the ground, trying not to feel tense. The company had been here for two hours now, and it was impossible to stay tense that long without stiffening up. Then you'd be unable to move fast when you had to. There were sounds in the darkness, the night breeze in the holly oak, a breathing of the rocky earth, but so far nothing from his men, 130 of them, including four extra Lewis guns and the twelve men of their crews, from A and C Companies. They had moved out of Dalzai an hour after full dark, leaving by the east gate and, once well clear, turning south and heading up onto what had been the Gurkhas' ridge. There was no moon and it had not been easy to find the exact place where Morgan Lloyd wanted him to set the ambush; but he thought he had it right – anyway there was no changing now. The gorge down which the brigade would start its retirement tomorrow was half a mile ahead. The Dogras would come out at first light to secure the heights immediately commanding it, and then the column would start moving back down and through. But Morgan was sure that during this night the Wazirs would plant at least a hundred men among the broken rocks, steep little valleys and eroded hillsides on this side of the gorge. Bill's ambush was placed to catch those men moving into their positions.

Morgan thought that the Wazirs would aim to be ready by about three or four in the morning. It was now two . . . A soldier stifled a sneeze nearby and Bill stiffened. Bloody fool. If the Wazirs were within a quarter of a mile, they'd have heard that . . . Nothing . . . No more sound . . . More waiting. He'd set ambushes in France, but they weren't like this. There, you lay out in a specific place – by a gap in the Jerries' wire, for instance – and waited to catch a patrol coming out or in, or a working party. You were never very far from other troops. Here, it was just the darkness, the barren hillside and . . . not a light from Dalzai down there . . .

He heard light footsteps and sensed rather than saw movement in front of him. It was impossible to judge exactly what it was, but out on that ridge, at that hour, it had to be the Wazir *lashkar* moving to its ambush positions. Now, in what strength were they? Morgan had thought they would send out about a hundred men – it would not be easy to conceal many more than that in the area where he thought that the ambush would be set; nor would it be easy to extricate many more once the ambush had been sprung and the casualties inflicted. So, lying tensed now, counting the seconds, Bill tried to guess . . . about twenty-five men could have passed by now . . . forty . . .

But suppose the Wazirs had more than ambush in mind? Suppose they intended to back up the ambush with an attack on the centre of the column?

Sixty . . . eighty . . .

Thank God the men were holding their fire. A shot now would lead to disaster. The Wazirs had to be taken totally by surprise, cut down by a huge blast of fire that would leave them a broken, reeling mass, leaderless . . .

A hundred . . . and twenty . . . but he might be wrong by as much as fifty per cent, either way . . . and forty . . . and seventy . . . ninety . . . two hundred . . . and twenty . . . silence, only the wind in the holly oak.

Bill tapped his company sergeant major beside him on the shoulder and whispered, 'Ready?'

'Yes, sir.'

'Fire!'

The CSM rolled on his back, raised his right arm and fired his already loaded Very pistol in his hand straight up into the air, immediately reloading with another white cartridge. A ghostly white light grew in the night above them, spreading across the ridge, as simultaneously seven Lewis guns and a hundred magazine rifles opened rapid fire. Now Bill could clearly see the dark lumps of the Wazirs in grey and black robes, huddled in masses and lines over the flat crest about a hundred yards away. They were breaking up, dispersing like ants in a disturbed nest, many falling as they ran, to crawl or lie still. The storm of firing increased to a fury; the CSM kept at least one Very light in the air all the time . . . but only fifty seconds had passed since he had fired the first.

Bill yelled in the CSM's ear, 'Red!'

The CSM broke open the pistol, pulled out the white cartridge he had just loaded into it, replaced it with a red, and fired that into the air. The firing stopped as though mechanically turned off, to be followed in the silence by a metallic whirring as the soldiers drew their bayonets from their scabbards and jammed them down onto the bayonet bosses.

Bill was on his feet, running, his revolver drawn. B Company, spread out, ran at his heels, baying and yelling, all charging at the broken mass of the Wazirs. Next moment the fighting changed its character completely. Now it was cut, thrust and stab, butt stroke, kick and kill. The surviving Wazirs had pulled their long knives from their waistbands and met the men of the Wessex with rifle or jezail in one hand and the knife out-thrust in the other, blade up. They were fighting as though on a tussocky plain, but the tussocks were the bodies of dead and wounded Wazirs caught in the first murderous fire of the ambush, and the rocky ground was slippery with their blood and the blood now being shed in the hand-to-hand fighting.

So they fought under the faintest of starlight until suddenly Bill heard a voice near him screaming in Pushtu. Until that moment, after the exhilarated whooping of the charge, there had been nothing but the desperate grunts and groans and gasps of men locked in mortal combat. In a moment another voice echoed the first, also in Pushtu . . . then another . . . and, mysteriously, the Wazirs vanished. Bill fired a last shot at a figure vanishing into the night five paces away, but missed. He called, 'Sarn't major? Sarn't major?'

'Here, sir.' A presence loomed up close beside him.

'Is the bugler with you?'

'Yes, sir.'

'Sound the rally . . . three times . . . get reports from the platoon commanders . . . I'm going to hold the ridge, right here, till dawn.'

'We'll be sitting ducks then, sir.'

'If they're in the mood to start the fight again, we could be, for an hour or so . . . but they're not. Have the dead counted, and see that any wounded Wazirs are disarmed – *not* killed.'

'Very good, sir.'

The bugle blared out the 'rally'. Shapes appeared in the gloom, gathering together, dispersing again under their platoon commanders as Bill ordered them to take up positions along the ridge facing both ways. They would have heard the sound of the firing down in

Dalzai, but would have no idea of what had happened. He was shaking with excitement, and his back was wet with sweat. Well, it was a warm night, for seven thousand feet up, even in May . . . but it wasn't the heat causing the sweat, it was the fight. Thank God the men had kept their heads, and held their fire until the signal.

He heard the CSM's voice: 'Captain Miller?'

'Here.'

'We've had seven killed, sir. Mr Joinville has a bad wound in his belly. Sergeant Harris took over the platoon and did wonders, though he was wounded too, in the chest. Sixteen others wounded, mostly knife cuts . . . only one real bad, with a stab in the chest. He's lying down . . . Seventy-seven Wazir bodies counted, and five more too bad wounded to move.'

Bill whistled softly through his teeth. 'Good shooting,' he said. 'It's so bloody easy to fire high at night . . . Have all those bodies piled in one place, in the middle of our position, here. I don't want them left out where they can be used as stalking horses. Lay out our own dead here, too, in a row. We'll get them down into the gorge for burial at dawn – there's some softer soil there.'

'Very good, sir.'

'Now we just sit tight. It won't be long.'

The brigade returned to its base in Rawalpindi ten days after the Dalzai expedition, without incident, for the ambush on Gurkha ridge had broken the Kari Khel's resistance, and within the week they had surrendered to the political agent's demands. Two days after the return to barracks, Bill was sent for to the orderly room, where Morgan Lloyd had been confirmed in command and given the substantive rank of lieutenant colonel. As soon as the adjutant had left the room, Morgan leaned back and said, 'How long is it since you've seen Pauline and your children?'

Bill thought. 'Three years, sir . . . The kids write regularly.'

'I can't send you back on exchange – you haven't done enough time abroad. But you can have privilege leave at once, now. You'll get a month at home.'

'But, sir, I'm due to take the Staff College exam here from 4 to 7 July.'

'I know. You can apply to take it in Tidworth instead. I'll see that

150

the change is made, by cable. You'll be staying at Damerham Court, I suppose?'

'If I go . . . I'll lose study time, sir.'

'Study on board ship. Shuffleboard and deck tennis aren't that exciting.'

Bill still looked undecided. He had been planning to devote most of his time now to studying. Major Stillford was back from leave, so he was no longer a company commander, and had little to do. And England seemed so far away. Nor did Pauline sound, in her occasional letters, as though she was missing him or particularly wanted to see him.

Morgan Lloyd said, 'Look, Bill, you said just now that you were getting regular letters from your kids. You didn't mention Pauline. Now –' He paused a moment, then went on, 'When we got back to 'Pindi there were several letters waiting for me. One was from an old friend of ours in Salisbury. She is not a gossip, but she mentioned that your wife, Pauline, had been going out a lot in the evenings with other men, one in particular. She's been seen with him in London, too.' He raised a hand as Bill made to interject. 'Wait! I spent a long time worrying over whether I ought to pass on stuff like this. I still don't know whether I'm right to do so. But in any case I decided that whatever difficulties you might have in your marriage will be better managed or solved face to face. And kids grow, you know. And grow away. And change. Will they both be home?'

'Roger will be at prep school till the end of July,' Bill said shortly. 'Brenda's at home, with a governess.'

'Better than not seeing either of them at all . . . Well, do you accept the leave? I'm not going to order you off.'

Bill said, 'I do, sir. Thank you.'

So here he was, in the library at Damerham Court, with Pauline standing beside him interrupting his work and breaking his concentration. She had asked him just what sort of leave he had, and how long he would be staying.

'It's privilege leave,' Bill explained patiently. 'Two months, of which I spent nearly two weeks getting home. I get full pay.'

'But you have to report back to the 2nd battalion within the two months,' Pauline said. 'That'll take another two weeks, and you've been here two, so you only have two left. Are you going to spend your *whole* leave sitting in the library working?'

'The Staff College exam is the most important thing in my military life, so far,' Bill said. 'If I don't pass in by competition, or get a nomination, and eventually p.s.c. after my name, I don't have any chance of going beyond lieutenant colonel. And the exam's next week.'

Outside, his father-in-law, the old colonel, was pottering about in the garden wearing clothes that a scarecrow would be ashamed of. Pauline rambled on. Bill thought, if I'm not going to be allowed to work, I'll take Brenda out riding, rather than sit here listening and arguing. He had been home a fortnight and was already counting the days before he'd set off for London and Dover and the trains across France that would enable him to catch the P & O liner at Marseilles and so save four days. But he was not sure, in his own mind, just what his emotions were when he counted the days. Did he want to get back to the battalion, which had been visibly becoming a taut, exciting entity under Morgan's command . . . or did he want to get away from Pauline?

Pauline was saying, 'Well, as you're taking the exam here, they'll send you to Camberley rather than Quetta, won't they?'

He said, 'They may not. Each Staff College is supposed to have a proportion of both British Service and Indian Army officers. As the battalion I'm with is on the Indian establishment at the moment, it's quite possible they'll send me to Quetta.' He steeled himself, and ended, 'If that is the case, I think you ought to come with me.'

'Ought?' she said, bristling. 'Why should I?'

'Because we are married. I am a captain, and thirty-three, and we'll get a married quarter. Quetta's six thousand feet up, and the climate's good, though cold in winter. I've been finding out about it . . . riding, tennis, a pack of hounds – they hunt jackals, but they give good sport . . . good climbing, Morgan says, on mountains quite close, real mountains, thirteen thousand feet and more.'

She said, 'We can't take Roger out of Cheltenham Junior. Where will he spend his holidays?'

'Here,' he said.

'Mother's not as fit as she was, and Daddy – well, he's not very happy looking after children. And what about Brenda?'

'She can come to Quetta with us. We could take Miss Riggs, too, if she'll come and if we can afford it . . . and if you think it's necessary, which it really isn't. She'll hardly be ten when I finish the course.'

He watched the expressions chase each other across her face: concern over where her duty lay, distaste for India, fear of homesickness . . . She was looking out of the window now at the green lawn sweeping down to the lake, the willows guarding the bank, the wheat field rising beyond, a copse of elms against a pale sky.

She said, 'I don't want to come, Bill. I think the children should stay at home, and I should stay with them.'

He said, 'Is there any other reason why you don't want to come out with me?' He had not yet spoken to her about the rumours Morgan had warned him of. Now he felt that he must, for it seemed to him that there was more at stake than whether Pauline and the children would come to Quetta with him.

'What do you mean?' she asked, but her face was a little paler of a sudden.

'I mean, is there another man? Or are you tired of being my wife, with or without another man?'

She snapped, 'You have no right to ask me that . . . you're accusing me of being no better than a . . . a *whore*!'

'You could have been lonely here,' he said. 'You must have found friends of our age, people you liked. It wouldn't be the first time in history that a lonely wife had had a fling. But if you want to perpetuate it, at the expense of our marriage, that's something else.'

'Why do you talk of our marriage?' she said, but she had turned her back to him. 'Haven't I made love whenever you wanted to?'

'Yes,' he said, thinking, it was true, but it had been as a duty, no longer as an act of love or even passion.

'Well, then?'

He said, 'Then you must realize that, even if you have not been lonely, I have. Very. For a long time. There have been friends – Morgan and Cicely, since they came back, others . . .'

'The Regiment,' she said. 'The Men!'

'Yes, but none of them fills the same place in me as a wife does. As you used to.'

She burst suddenly into tears and rushed out of the room, crying, 'I'm not coming, I'm not coming!'

Bill stood silent, looking at the open door. The telephone in the hall rang and Bill went out and picked up the receiver.

He said, 'Bill Miller, here, speaking from Damerham Court.'

'Captain Miller? General Dabney speaking.'

'Good morning, sir.'

Major General Dabney was the colonel of the regiment, a dear white-moustached old boy who'd commanded the 1st Battalion in South Africa and reached major general's rank at the beginning of the Great War, to be promptly put out to grass. He was widowed and lived in a flat in South Kensington.

'Have you seen the morning paper, my boy?'

'Yes, sir.'

'Ah, the country edition. Well, I have the London edition. You have been awarded the DSO.'

Bill was astounded. What was this for? The old general's voice rambled on: 'Night of 22/23 May 1932, near Dalzai, Waziristan . . .' Ah, the ambush; but he'd just done his job . . . 'Holding his position although heavily outnumbered . . .' So, that was what Morgan has based the recommendation on – the fact that he'd held his fire while the enemy piled up, and not sprung the ambush too soon. 'Moral courage,' Morgan had once said to him, 'is much more important in a commander than physical, though he needs both.'

'Congratulations,' the old general was saying. 'I'm very proud of you and so is the regiment.'

'Thank you, sir . . . Were there any other awards?'

'Two DCMs – Sergeant Harris and Rifleman Badger . . . Three MMs . . .'

Good old Bogey, Bill thought. He was doing well, in his chosen sphere. He hung up. The DSO would help him get a nomination if he failed to win one of the competitive places. But it would be a lonely time, those two years, even if he was sent to Camberley; but he felt in his bones that he would not be. And would it really be better to have Pauline physically present with him but in her heart not present, thinking of dances, parties, hunting, shooting, other men . . . or another man. Better to face the fact, as he would have to in Quetta, that she was several thousand miles away in both body and soul – and not coming back, ever.

He went back into the library, carefully closed the door behind

154

him, returned to the table where he had been working, opened Henderson's *Stonewall Jackson* and began to read chapter 5 for the third time, pausing every now and then to make a note on his yellow pad. When he had finished the chapter, he sat back and set his mind to think of certain specific problems. What, for instance, was the proper military lesson to be learned from Jackson's action or the Federal general's inaction? What could a twentieth-century British general learn from the nineteenth-century American?'

An hour later, he put Stonewall Jackson away and pulled down a sheaf of papers that were in fact last year's Staff College examination in military law. These he began to answer, always giving in the margin his authority from the *Manual of Military Law*, *King's Regulations*, or *Army Council Instructions*, all of which lay on the table at his elbow. And up on the shelves stood the small handbooks of *Field Service Regulations, Vols. I, II and III, Infantry Training*, and a thick red book on *Military Organization and Administration*.

Outside, Brenda was playing croquet with the rector's daughter. Pauline was picking flowers with her father. Bill worked on.

11

August 1939: England

Chaudhri waved an expressive hand, almost knocking over his water glass. 'I have to thank you, dear Bill, for introducing me to Dr Steinberg here. It is only – how many days? – not many, that we met and already I feel that I have known him all my life. Perhaps it was in a previous incarnation, when he too was a Hindu.'

Israel Steinberg raised his glass, which contained a South Tyrolean Sandbichler Rot, and bowed slightly. 'I can return the compliment . . . though I don't know whether Bill is really happy that he has put two dedicated socialists in touch with each other, to the mutual benefit of the party and the policy.'

Bill grinned. 'Quite the opposite. I believe in shooting all the workers – you know that. After all, I'm a soldier, a'n't I?'

The telephone rang in the little hallway outside the dining room and Dr Steinberg, the host, got up with a murmured 'Excuse me,' and left the table.

Lesley turned to Chaudhri. 'How are things in Chattarganj these days?'

'Very well,' Chaudhri said eagerly. 'I am on the national committee, of course, and will not be returning to Chattarganj in the same position I was in before, but I keep in close touch with it, and with all our Congress people there. It was where I got my real start, thanks to Panditji. He was the one who had me appointed when it became clear that Gupta was not even holding the party together there, let alone increasing its strength.'

Steinberg came back into the room. 'It's your son Roger, Bill, calling from your flat. He says your mother's on the phone from Wiltshire and wants to speak with you, so will you call her back.'

Bill got up, leaving his napkin on the table. He said, 'Roger could have just given her your number here . . . but she hates using the phone, so I'll have to call her. Excuse me a moment, please.'

He picked up the phone and called his mother's number in Pennel Crecy through the operator. 'Mummy? Bill here . . . You wanted to speak to me?'

Her voice was tiny but strong, excited and a little breathless. 'Billy, darling, a telegram came for you . . . addressed to you here, so I opened it so that I could telephone it to you, that would be the quickest way . . . and guess who it's from?'

'I can't guess, Mummy,' Bill said patiently, 'Tell me.'

'A funny name . . . Y-a-g-u-e.'

'Yague?' Bill said, 'General Yagüe? Is the telegram from Spain?'

'I think so . . . yes, here it is . . . Madrid.'

'Can you read it? Is it in English or Spanish?'

'Oh, English, Bill . . . otherwise I'd have had to put it into an envelope and post it to you.'

'Well, read it please, Mummy.'

'Wait a minute . . . my specs are fogging up . . . there . . . Now: "The Generalissimo has decided to confer on you the Cross of San

156

Jaime for valour and devotion to the cause. Congratulations. The award will be made to you through the embassy in London . . ." Then there's a funny bit, *"Arriba España"* and then "Y-a-g-u-e", what a funny name, like "vague", isn't it?'

'General Yagüe is not at all a vague man, Mummy.'

'Well, I'm so proud of you. It's just like getting the VC, isn't it, only it's Spanish. What does it look like, the medal, I mean?'

Bill said, 'I'm not sure, Mummy. How are you? Well, we spoke to each other a couple of days ago and I hope nothing terrible's happened since then.'

'I'm very well, a little cough but I always get a little cough at this time of year, the heat doesn't agree with me, and they're reaping the wheat and barley in all the fields and I'm *sure* that has something to do with it, and . . .'

Five minutes later, Bill returned to the table, sat down and started eating his lentil cakes, for they were having a vegetarian meal in deference to Chaudhri's principles.

As soon as he had swallowed the first mouthful, he said, 'You can all congratulate me. Franco's going to give me a medal . . . the Cross of San Jaime. . . . for valour and devotion to the cause.'

'How's he getting it to you?' Lesley asked quickly.

'Through the embassy, the telegram said. It was from Yagüe, whom the legion served under while I was with it. He's a hell of a good general, and very liberal-thinking for a Nationalist.'

Lesley turned to Steinberg. 'What do you think we should do? Nothing, and hope for the best?'

'I don't think that will be wise,' Steinberg said. 'The Republican faction here is out for blood, especially since they lost the war over there.'

'What are you talking about?' Bill asked, puzzled.

Chaudhri took his hand. 'Dear Bill . . . you have just been reinstated in the British Army, as a major. You are working in the War Office, at the centre of the British military establishment. And now your name and the details of your exploits for Franco will be spread over the newspapers, for the opposition to use as ammunition against Chamberlain and the Tories. The country doesn't like communists, but since Hitler rose to power, and Mussolini tweaked the lion's tail in the Spanish affair, they dislike fascists even more. We've got to try to scotch this medal-giving . . . You don't *want* it, do you?'

Bill hesitated. Damn it, he had earned it, and what else did a soldier have to show for his work and wounds? No money certainly, only those bits of coloured ribbon. He said, 'I don't suppose I'll be allowed to wear it, so . . . no, it doesn't matter.'

Lesley said, 'We must try to have the award just quietly cancelled. If we fail in that, we must see that there is absolutely no publicity about it anywhere.'

Steinberg said, 'I have contacts in the Spanish Embassy, not very important ones, but people in humble positions can sometimes work very effectively, just because they *are* in humble positions. This medal will probably be sent by diplomatic courier, and will arrive any day, if it hasn't already done so. I think my contacts can arrange to get it lost, together with the covering letter.'

Lesley said, 'The letter may go separately, or it may be a cable.'

'That's possible, even probable; and then our task will be more difficult . . . but the loss of the actual medal will cause some delay . . . I think that Bill should go to the ambassador and say that he does not want to accept any award for his service in Spain. He could threaten to throw the medal into the Thames, publicly, because he has come to disagree with Franco's policies. They wouldn't want to risk that sort of publicity.'

'That's a good idea,' Chaudhri said, 'Are you willing to do that, Bill?'

'No,' Bill said, 'I shall tell the ambassador that I don't want to accept the medal because I was in fact committed not to Franco's cause but to learning as much as I could on behalf of the British Army.'

Lesley said ruefully, 'It's no good arguing with him any more. He's not going to lie.'

The ambassador was tall, thin, grey, and a duke. He received Bill standing, but with great courtesy. Bill came to the point at once. 'Your Excellency, I have had a cable from General Yagüe telling me that General Franco has awarded me the Cross of San Jaime.'

'I have had a cable from the Caudillo's office to the same effect,' the ambassador said, speaking perfect English, which was not strange, for he was descended from an English king and claimed an

English dukedom as well as his Spanish one. He went on, 'The medal and ribbon were apparently sent by courier a week ago and should have arrived long since, but we do not seem to have them yet.'

'I wish to decline the honour the Generalissimo has done me,' Bill said.

The ambassador raised his eyebrows. 'It is a considerable honour, Major Miller, as you know if you served with the legion.'

'I know, sir, but . . . I went to Spain only to learn what I could for the benefit of my country. I didn't kill Spaniards for the sake of General Franco, and I don't think I should get a medal for killing them so that a foreign country could benefit, however remotely, from their deaths.'

The ambassador said, 'I appreciate your delicacy of feeling, but from our point of view it will improve our position in English eyes for it to be known that there were good, honest Englishmen who fought for us. The world believes that only the Republic received any disinterested aid.'

'My help wasn't disinterested, sir,' Bill repeated. 'It was for England.'

The ambassador said, 'I shall see what I can do, but it is not easy to change the Caudillo's mind, major. I can promise nothing.'

In the flat the phone rang close to midnight. Bill reached out for the bedside table where it stood, and picked it up. 'Bill Miller,' he said.

'Morgan here . . . I've just had a visit from Joe Mason. He's learned that Franco's going to award a Major Miller one of his decorations, and wanted me to confirm that this Major Miller was you.'

'I told you about the decoration yesterday, sir.'

'I know. You were going to see the ambassador.'

'He wouldn't promise anything. He said it would be good publicity for Franco.'

'Well, it's very bad publicity for us. Mason was hostile to you all the time he was working on that committee of ours, and now he's going to see that the medal gets maximum publicity. He's determined to ruin anyone who fought or worked for Franco.'

'What can we do, sir?'

'To prevent publication? Nothing. It's already in the hands of the

Daily Herald, and will be on the front page in the morning. I have to tell the chief, and he will probably want to tell the minister, so that he will be forewarned, if not forearmed. If they choose to make a major case of it, we don't have a leg to stand on.'

Bill grew angry. 'I don't see what we have to defend ourselves against, sir,' he said forcefully. 'I went to Spain to learn something for England. I have done so, and am now in a position, back in the British Army, where I can begin to put those lessons to use.'

Morgan's voice was weary, 'Politics, Bill. Franco's a friend of Hitler. Hitler's not a friend of ours, and war is coming very soon. If there's an outcry, someone will be sacrificed to those plain facts of political life.'

'I'll go,' Bill snapped, 'I'll resign my commission again, and start again in the ranks.'

'No, you won't,' Morgan said, 'I shall put *my* head on the block. They won't call on me to resign my commission. They'll just get me out of the public eye, post me to India probably, in my present rank, after I've made some sort of apology, through the minister, for knowingly employing such a fascist beast as you. I'll do my very best to protect you . . . No, no, don't argue, please, Bill. Just tell Lesley and go back to sleep.'

The *Herald* was on the breakfast table between them, with the sedate *Times* and *Telegraph*: FASCIST MAJOR IN WAR OFFICE . . . FRANCO GIVES MEDAL TO BRITISH OFFICER . . . The phone had rung twice already and it was barely half past seven in the morning. One call had been from Chaudhri: 'Bill, have you seen the *Daily Herald*?'

'Yes.'

'How did the news get out?'

'Joe Mason . . . a fellow who fought for the Republic while I was in the legion. He must have contacts in the Spanish Embassy, too.'

'I've been thinking ever since I read it . . . This will lead to questions in the House of Commons, you know.'

'I suppose so.'

'I am sure of it. I am going to see Mr Bevin. He has been kind to me . . .'

'He's been buttering you up, Chaudhri, because he thinks you'll be the next prime minister of India after Nehru.'

'After independence,' Chaudhri said. 'But when is *that* coming? My God, Bill, when . . . ? Well, that's what I shall do, try to get Mr Bevin to understand what a jolly good fellow you really are, and not a fascist at all.'

'Thanks, Chaudhri – and good luck to all of us. It looks as though we'll need it.' He hung up.

Next it had been Morgan again: 'I've spoken to the chief and he's warned the minister. A question will be asked; we don't know just when, perhaps by Attlee himself, otherwise by Bevin. They're out for blood. I told the minister to say he'd sacked me, and posted you out of the War Office. He said that was probably the best thing to do, but he might be forced to withdraw your commission again.'

'Thanks, sir.'

Now the phone rang again, and a strange voice said, 'Major Miller? This is Lord Tregellan speaking. I've been reading the disgraceful attack on you in the *Daily Herald* . . . I don't normally take that Bolshie rag, I can assure you, but a friend phoned me and told me to get the paper today . . . I would like to do anything I can to help you defend yourself against this scandalous attack. I have a good many friends in high places, besides of course being a member of the House of Lords. I would be honoured if you would have lunch with me in my London house, 27 Park Lane, today.'

Bill said, 'Well, thank you. That's very kind of you.'

'About half past twelve then. Good. Good.'

Bill returned to his wife at the breakfast table. 'Lord Tregellan offering to help me. I'm having lunch with him today.'

'Hm . . . multi-millionaire industrialist, used to be undersecretary of something in one of Baldwin's governments. What is he, about sixty?'

'About. His horse won the Derby a year or two after Tom Wall's did. I won quite a bit of money on that.'

'Well, be careful. Eat with a long spoon. You are so innocent.'

A footman met Bill at the door of the big Park Lane house, and led him up two flights of stairs to a large drawing room hung with paintings in gold frames. He wished Lesley was with him to tell him more about them, for they would be good, or at least important.

Lord Tregellan came forward with outstretched hand. 'Major

Miller, so glad you could come.'

'Sorry to be in uniform,' Bill said, 'but . . .'

'Don't apologize, my dear fellow. There's nothing to be ashamed of in the King's uniform, surely? Just the opposite.'

'Yes,' Bill said, 'but we don't usually wear it except on military duty, and . . .'

'I know, I know . . . Ah, here he is.'

The door behind Bill had opened, and the same footman announced in a deferential tone, 'Sir Oswald Mosley, milord.'

Bill turned. He'd heard a lot about Mosley, of course, and seen his picture countless times in newspapers. As he turned, he was half expecting to see a black shirt, black breeches and field boots, but he was wrong: Mosley was wearing a well-cut suit of navy blue with an Old Harrovian tie.

He came forward, hand outstretched, and shook hands first with his host. As he shook hands with Bill, he caught Bill's eye on his tie and said cheerfully, 'No, I'm not an Old Harrovian, but Churchill is, and it annoys him so much when I wear it . . . Major Miller, the prey of the *Herald*?'

'It looks like it,' Bill said.

The footman brought in a silver tray with a decanter of whisky, a soda siphon and glasses, and poured as the men ordered. Tregellan said, 'I should have told you that Oswald was going to join us at lunch, major, but I wasn't sure that he would be free.'

Mosley swirled the whisky round in his glass, and said abruptly, 'Tell us what you did in Spain, Miller. All the details. Where you fought, who with, wounds . . . personalities . . . tactics . . . everything.'

Bill began; and half an hour later was still at it when Lord Tregellan interrupted smoothly, 'Let's go on with this at lunch, major. We have some really excellent lamb cutlets, followed by fruit sherbet, and, of course, champagne . . . and none of that should be left to get cold . . . or hot.'

They moved to a smaller room next door, where a table had been laid for three. Bill continued talking, answering Mosley's piercing and well-informed questions, Tregellan saying very little, until dessert was served. Then Bill paused, feeling that Mosley had brought out of him a good deal more than he had believed he had in him to say about the legion, peace and war, battle and rest, in Spain.

Finally, as the butler passed round cigars, Mosley pushed back his chair, and said to Tregellan, 'Just the sort we want, don't you think, Harry?'

Tregellan nodded, 'Exactly.'

Mosley turned to Bill. 'I know you're not a member of my British Union of Fascists, and I suspect that you don't agree with what you think are our goals . . . because what the press publishes about us is garbled trash, fit only for the dustbin . . . sewer muck spread by the Jews . . . This' – he tapped the *Daily Herald* that he had brought in and kept beside his plate throughout the meal – 'will probably result in your losing your commission, won't it?'

'That's possible,' Bill said.

'Don't worry. I'll take you. We have plenty of funds, thanks to people like Lord Tregellan here, who see where the real danger to England lies. I can employ you full-time. The communists are getting more sophisticated in their attacks on our meetings, our headquarters and branch offices. I want to develop a tough core of troopers who will take them on at their own game, both at our meetings and at theirs . . . street fighting, Miller, that's our first priority. The cities are the heart of the Jew communist strength . . . the farmers and country people are on our side – they can be organized later. But first we have to break the Reds in the cities.'

Bill said cautiously, 'What if war comes? The government won't allow any meetings or street fighting.'

'I think there'll be some anyway, especially if things go badly for us at first, which they always do . . . but war against Hitler's Germany would be an unmitigated disaster in itself. It's got to be stopped, and one way to do that is to demonstrate against the very idea . . . against the course our so-called leaders are taking us down, which will certainly lead to a clash with Germany very soon. That must not happen.'

'It is not certain that I shall be called upon to resign my commission,' Bill said. 'There are influential people trying to help me.'

'I know, but it's doubtful whether they can succeed. The Jew Reds have smelled blood – yours . . . Relax, Miller, enjoy your cigar . . . Listen! You are an officer and a gentleman.'

'Not by birth,' Bill said firmly.

'I thought not, but you've made yourself one. You must realize by now that most people of our class are very stupid. They don't think! They don't see! They have physical courage but no moral courage! Think of your brother officers in the mess . . . Ah, that made you see some light, didn't it? Well, my organization is taking people who are *not* stupid, who *do* think, who *do* see, and we are training them to defend the ideals of England by wiping out the rats in the cellar . . . nameless, faceless Jews, communists, men without faith in God or country . . . rats nibbling away at the foundations of our society . . .'

He went on, speaking forcefully. Is this the man who was a dedicated young socialist, Bill wondered. What can have happened to him to turn him into an English Hitler? But those words didn't go together. His moustache wasn't as funny as Hitler's, but . . . yes, it was, in the context. It was funny. He started laughing, not uproariously, but quietly. At last he said, 'Sir Oswald, you flatter me, but I do not think there should be any private armies, and I definitely do not want to organize or lead one.'

Lord Tregellan broke in suavely, 'I fear that you will find yourself deserted in your hour of need, major. The people who run this country at the moment have no sense of honour. They will not stand by their servants, even when those servants have been obeying their orders. We will. Although you would in fact be working full-time with Sir Oswald, in the sphere he indicated, on paper you would be a member of Tregellan Industries, with a starting salary roughly three times what you earn at present. And once anyone enters Tregellan Industries, we look after him for life.'

It was tempting, Bill thought. To escape for ever from the backbiting knife-wielding atmosphere of the War Office, to have security of income, a job . . . Even if the army didn't sack him now, what guarantee did he have that they wouldn't let him rot out his time as a major in some godforsaken bywater, and at the end simply not promote him – let him go, as a major, with a minuscule pension?

But how could he face Lesley, wearing comic-opera black shirt and jackboots? How could he learn to throw out his right arm in the fascist salute, first made ridiculous by that fat oaf in Italy, and now made shameful by the evil man in Berlin? He said slowly, 'I believe that you would stand by me, to the end, if I were to join your organization,' he said, addressing Mosley, 'but I will not. I cannot, because I absolutely disagree with your policies as well as your methods. The *Daily Herald* has called me a fascist, but that does not make me one.' He looked at his wristwatch. 'I am grateful to you for your interest, Lord Tregellan,' he said, 'but now I must go, or I will be late for my work at the War Office.'

With a small bow he left the table, and found his way out of the room, down the two flights of ornate stairs, and out of the house.

Lesley said, 'The question is second on the list, and is being put by Mr Attlee. The Secretary of War will answer, and is planning to surrender, do whatever Attlee wants, because they need the Labour Party's help in many defence-related measures that will be coming up next week, or later this week if the situation gets any worse with Germany and Poland. The least that will happen is that you will be deprived of your commission, and Morgan will be relieved of his job and sent to India.'

'But Morgan's the heart and soul of the modernization movement in the War Office,' Bill wailed. 'It doesn't matter about me, but without Morgan's driving and searching nothing will get done. There's an enormous inertia in the War Office . . . in the British Army as a whole.'

'I know, but that's the situation, unless . . .'

'Wait a minute,' Bill exclaimed. 'Jim Brock's an MP now, and in the shadow cabinet, too, isn't he?'

She nodded and Bill said, 'And he's got some job at TUC headquarters, too. Do you think . . .'

'It's worth trying,' she said. 'Anything is. What's the time?' She glanced at the clock on the mantel. 'He's probably at Transport House.'

Bill went out to the telephone, calling over his shoulder, 'Nothing more from Chaudhri?'

'Nothing,' she called back, 'but from appearances, Bevin's not going to speak to Attlee about you. He has no reason to.'

Bill looked up the Transport House number and dialled. A male voice answered. 'Transport House switchboard,' it said.

'I'm Major Miller, Wessex Rifles. I want to speak to Jim Brock, please. I am an old friend of his.'

165

'I'll put you through.'

A moment later Brock came on, saying bluntly, 'Brock.'

Bill said, 'Bill Miller here, Jim. I'm . . .'

'A bloody fascist, according to the *Herald*,' Brock cut in, ending with a deep chuckle. 'Want some help?'

'If I can get it.'

'Come up. There's a big pot of tea on the gas ring, and a bottle of something stronger in the cupboard. Mind, I can't promise, but come along . . . ages since I've seen you, anyway.'

Brock had gained a lot of polish since the distant days of the General Strike and their meetings by the London docks, but it was only a superficial layer, which he assumed or shed at will, now speaking like a lawyer, now like a true union organizer. He leaned back in his swivel chair behind the cluttered desk, a mug of sweet strong tea in one big hand. 'So in effect this General Lloyd ordered you to go to Spain, on Franco's side?'

'He didn't have the power to order me to do that,' Bill said. 'He saw that, because of what I'd done in Chattarganj, and the way my general took it, I was finished in the army unless I did something drastic and risky. He spoke or cabled to some friends in the War Office – he was in India, too, at the time – and obviously got confirmation of his plan that I should go to Spain, learn what I could on the Franco side, and then I would be reinstated and could . . .'

'These high-up friends he cabled, are they still in the army?'

'Some probably are. I believe the chief, the present chief of the Imperial General Staff, is one of them . . . but Morgan won't bring their names into it. That was understood at the time, just as I understood that I couldn't say that Morgan Lloyd sent me.'

'Hm . . . So the man at the bottom will get the load of codswallop, as usual – you . . . Did you learn anything valuable with the Germans in Spain?'

'Very much so. It was hell, but it was worth it.'

After a time Brock said, 'Do you think you'll make a general, then . . . a good one?'

'I think so,' Bill said.

'God knows, we need them . . . How's your new wife like the army?'

'She doesn't, but she's beginning to understand that we are not parasites, but very necessary parts of the body politic. Hitler's made a lot of people see that.'

'The Russians are going to sign a treaty with the Germans.'

'It's been suspected.'

'I *know*. Probably tomorrow. Then' – he made a small powerful upward gesture with his hands – 'the balloon ascends.'

'How soon?'

'Within a week, probably less. What'll you do then?'

'It's planned for now for me to stay at the War Office in Staff Duties, become a G1 and really be Morgan's right-hand man. But if there is a war I ought to be with troops, not in a headquarters, let alone the War House. And Morgan is liable to be on a boat to Bombay by then. The question about me is being asked in the House tomorrow, and the government's going to give Attlee whosever heads he wants.

Brock sat up suddenly. 'All right. I know you're not a fascist. You're a working-class man, and a friend of the working class, even though you do speak different than what you did back in '26. I'll talk to Clem first thing tomorrow morning. There won't be any new Jerusalem for the working men and women of this country if Hitler gets here first . . . Now, let's open that cupboard, Bill, and have a sniff of the stuff that makes you frisky . . .'

They waited in the big studio room of the flat, glasses in their hands, Lesley and Bill side by side on the big couch where often nude or half-draped models lay, Chaudhri by the north window, Israel Steinberg on a hard stool by the easel, Cicely Lloyd near the door, and Morgan Lloyd, in uniform pacing the floor, which creaked every time he passed close to the easel. A half-finished canvas, of still life, was set up on the easel. Chaudhri's glass was full of milk, the others were drinking whisky and soda. It was five o'clock.

The telephone rang and Cicely, the closest, hurried to pick it up. They all heard her: 'Major Miller's flat . . . Oh, Roger, where are you calling from? Damerham? No, we've heard nothing yet. We'll call you as soon as we do.' She hung up. The phone rang again, and again she picked it up: 'Major Miller's flat . . . Oh, Mrs Miller, we're waiting for a call from the House of Commons.' She covered the speaker with one hand. 'It's your mother, Bill.'

Bill got up reluctantly. He hadn't told his mother anything about the present crisis. She wouldn't understand if he did; time enough to explain things as best he could once the dust had settled.

He took the phone. 'I'm fine, Mother. Listen. We're expecting an important call, so . . . No, it's not about the Spanish medal . . . or perhaps it is, in a way. I'll explain later, but hang up now and I'll call you back as soon as I can . . . Lots of love and kisses to you, Mummy.' He replaced the receiver.

The bell rang again. 'Miller speaking,' Bill said. He stopped, listening, then burst out, 'It's settled. Jim did it!' Back into the mouthpiece he shouted, 'Jim, you've saved my career!'

'And mine,' Morgan called.

Bill hung up and turned to face the room. 'Jim Brock spoke to Mr Attlee this morning and persuaded him to accept a much milder answer from the government. The minister assured Attlee that the government were as eager as the opposition to ensure that no fascists were employed in sensitive positions at the War Office or anywhere else; that the officer referred to in various press stories was not a fascist nor ever had been; and that he, the minister, would welcome any suggestions from the opposition which would ensure that no fascists or communists or other totalitarians received encouragement in any department. In these dangerous times it was imperative that we all stand together as loyal Britons in the face of unknown but great peril.'

'And Attlee accepted that?' Morgan said incredulously.

'On Jim Brock's advice, yes.'

Lesley went out and came back with a tray loaded with glasses and two bottles of Taittinger Brut. 'We have something to celebrate,' she said. 'One of you men, open up the bottles . . . but don't splash the ceiling. It's only just been repainted.'

The champagne corks popped, the wine fizzed and bubbled, and they clinked glasses and laughed, their voices rising.

'We ought to sing "For he's a jolly good fellow",' Chaudhri cried, waving his glass of milk.

'For *they* are jolly good fellows,' Lesley corrected. 'Morgan risked his career, too.'

They all burst into song, stamping on the wooden floor, their song surging out through the open windows over Soho, which through the centuries had heard that and every other song under the sun.

When they had finished, Israel Steinberg stepped forward. 'I want to propose a toast, and make a little speech,' he said, his Viennese accent strong. 'The toast is to General Lloyd and Major Miller – Morgan and Bill – that God keep them in safety and good health in the days to come . . . and that God may give them the wisdom and the strength to lead our people to victory . . . For some of us, victory is the same as survival.' He turned slightly, addressing himself directly to Bill. 'Bill, you have been making yourself a leader of soldiers for twenty years now. As far as I can tell, you have mastered your profession as well as that can be done short of experience in modern battle. You are a professional, of the best. But you always have been more than a military professional. Look at your closest friends, who are gathered in this room with you . . . a Viennese Jewish intellectual socialist and doctor . . . a Hindu patriot, vegetarian, non-violent enemy of the British . . . Morgan, one of the finest brains in the army, and one of its most gallant young men in his youth . . . your wife, an independently minded American aristocrat and artist – and also a socialist at heart. And all these love you, because you are them – you are us become professional. You will have passion in this war now, because you will be fighting for all those who have suffered and will suffer under Hitler – like us. You have made us your friends because of what you are, and we know that you feel for us . . . for the Jews of the world, the untouchables, the liberals, the humble, the intellectuals, writers, artists, professors. You are our only defence and only hope, you and those, like us, whom you will lead.'

An hour later, now alone in the flat, Bill and Lesley looked at each other across the last bottle of champagne, their glasses almost empty. Bill had spoken to his children on the telephone and said a few words to Pauline and his own mother. They had not mentioned Izzy Steinberg's passionate appeal because Bill was too moved to do so, and Lesley recognized that fact.

Lesley said at last, 'Where to, now?'

'War.'

She drained her glass and put it down. 'Is this where it will end? God knows. I pray not. It's been a long journey, with its ups and downs, but if I had to do it over again I wouldn't change anything. Especially where it began . . . that was a magical time for me . . .'

'Quetta,' he said, '1933, six years ago.'

'Do you remember when I wished we had some champagne, after we'd climbed Takht-i-Sulaiman?'

'I remember everything.'

12

February 1933: India

The wind howled over the roof of the big hall, rattling the windows, while snow flurries danced round the chimneys of the main buildings and the plane trees shook their bare limbs. It was February 1933, and a small blizzard was dying away across the Quetta plain. Tonight it would be followed by the *khojak*, the bitter wind that blew in from Afghanistan through the Khojak pass. Inside the hall, the officers attending the Staff College course were wearing serge service-dress uniforms and, over them, greatcoats, British warms or the goatskin coats called *poshteens*, for the hall was Government of India property and the government chose not to heat it adequately. Captain Bill Miller of the Queen's Own Wessex Rifles sat near the middle of the fifth row, watching and listening. As he had expected, the powers had sent him to Quetta, after he had passed the examination. He had not won a competitive vacancy, but his DSO had ensured his nomination; so here he was, a student of the Junior Division – that is, in the first year of the two-year course. And up there on the platform, drawing diagrams on the blackboard, was Captain (Brevet Major), (local Lieutenant Colonel) Richard Merton, of his own regiment, arrived a month ago to join the Directing Staff, or DS, as they were singly and collectively called.

The present lecture was part of the Attack series, in which the students studied the attack from beginning to end, and from every angle. It took over a month, and they were half way through. Before the series began, they had spent two months learning to walk – that is, absorbing some basic military facts and techniques. They had written each other hundreds of messages on army message forms – not to impart information, but to learn and use the correct styles and abbreviations. They knew how to ensure that a signal was sent to some units for action and to others only for information. They had studied the Orders of Battle of infantry and cavalry divisions; and the War Establishments of every unit contained in them; and made out ration returns for such and such a force – noting carefully that on active service *Sweepers – 3* and *First Reinforcements – 57* did *not* accompany an infantry battalion or cavalry regiment. They had done some fairly complex map-reading exercises, both in the halls of study and in the field. More important, according to the assistant commandant, a full colonel of Royal Engineers, they had produced a new master and whippers-in for the Quetta hunt. The kennelmen and other hunt servants were local Baluchis who had been in those services since the end of the Great War.

Up on the wide dais by the blackboard, Merton said, 'I should like the comments now on the order of march that we have proposed here –' He indicated the blackboard with his pointer staff. 'Remember, we are advancing to contact with an enemy whose strength, we believe, is that of a reinforced division . . . Hunnicutt.'

Captain Hunnicutt was a tall thin officer of the Poona Horse. Everyone liked him, but no one regarded him as a deep thinker. He said, 'Well, I don't know, but in Palestine in '18 we'd have had the cavalry farther out ahead than you have there – and probably on a wider front.'

Merton said, 'Millington, do you agree?' Millington, a gunner subaltern said, 'No. They'd be beyond field-artillery-support range if they went any farther out, and we don't have any horse artillery to go with them. Besides, enemy cavalry could get in between them and our main body.'

'Miller?'

Bill rose, cleared his throat, and said, 'I think the squadron of tanks has been put too far forward . . . and it should not be split between the three roads we are advancing on, but kept together.'

Merton leaned on his pointer staff. 'Anyone want to comment on that? Bainbridge.'

Bainbridge was a captain of the Green Howards, with two MCs. He said, 'The tanks are where they ought to be, in my opinion – just about where the enemy would strike if they did push in a raid or counterstroke behind the cavalry. And if that happens, they – the tanks – should be on the spot; they shouldn't have to be sent for.'

Bill, still on his feet, said, 'General Fuller has always said that tanks must be used en masse, with full infantry and artillery support.'

Merton cut in brusquely, 'We aren't discussing the theories of General Fuller, Miller, but the plan suggested by the DS, our collective wisdom, if you like.'

Bill said, 'If the enemy counterstroke includes tanks, they'll be able to destroy ours piecemeal.'

Merton said, 'We've heard your views. Now let's continue with the advance, using the formations and distances on the blackboard . . . B Squadron of Skinners, out here on the right front, is now fired upon from the outskirts of a village – look at the diagram on the other board . . . here. The squadron commander is on the spot himself and he estimates that he is being opposed by a defensive outpost, of about fifty rifles, with several light machine-guns. But they do have artillery support, for his squadron is now being shelled by a battery – eight guns – of field guns, from a range of about nine thousand yards. First, let's briefly discuss what the squadron commander should do, what messages he should send and what action he should take. Then, we'll look at what the CO of Skinners should do, as the vanguard commander, then what the advanced-guard commander does, and finally the force commander . . .'

Colonel Vernon, the assistant commandant, liked horses and thought that no machine could ever take their place in the British Army; but otherwise he was a shrewd and thoughtful soldier who had done much planning in the latter stages of the Great War in France and Flanders. His wife was American, a rich lady from Virginia hunting country, whose interests were even more fully concentrated on horses than were his. Now, for the last week or two, Bill had occasionally noticed another, younger woman in company with the colonel or his wife. He had himself seen her sketching in the bazaar, bundled up against the *khojak*, and also at the club. He had heard that she was Mrs Colonel's niece, and now, dining at the Vernons' bungalow with five others, the colonel had confirmed it, introducing him. 'Lesley, this is Captain Miller . . . Captain Miller, this is my wife's niece, Lesley Hawthorne. She's an artist.'

'I've seen you sketching,' Bill said, after a brief bow and handshake. They wandered off to a corner of the big drawing room, where a servant brought them a tray of drinks. Bill began the inane conversation that seemed to be required on such occasions, asking her how she liked Quetta.

'I like Quetta all right,' she said, 'but I don't think much of the army.'

She had an American accent, but a drawl rather than a twang. She was tall, as tall or an inch taller than he, seeming more so in her heels, her dark hair bobbed, a cigarette in her hand in a long amber holder, a silver bandanna low round her head, cutting off the hairline in front as sharply as the bobbed bangs did at the sides. She was wearing a very dark red lipstick, but her skin was not rouged. She was about his own age, thirty-four.

Bill said, 'We're a necessary evil. . . . I hope.'

'It seems such a waste of this glorious country here, to sit in stuffy classrooms studying how to kill people and blow up things, when you might be up on Chiltan, or living with some Powindahs.'

'I was, last weekend,' Bill said.

'Living with nomads?' she said incredulously.

'No, rock climbing on Chiltan, Jim Rainsford and I, and we did have a young Baluchi with us. He lives in the nearest village to where we climb and says he wants to learn how . . .'

Then their hostess came, bringing up another couple, and soon the last guests arrived, and after another sherry they all went in to dinner, where the talk was exclusively about the Quetta hunt and its last three outings, as compared with the Peshawar Vale hunt, and the quality of sport each provided. Bill saw that he had been invited as a man for Lesley, and was placed beside her at the table; but it was impossible to carry on a private conversation with everyone else talking about fetlocks and martingales across them, so he said little, but when the gentlemen finally rejoined the ladies in the drawing room, after coffee and brandy, he went to her, sat beside her, and said, 'Can I see your paintings sometime?'

She looked up. 'Oh, the etching ploy!'

Bill was puzzled, and began, 'I don't quite . . .'

She said quickly, 'I see you don't . . . Sorry. They're in my bedroom, which is also my studio – good north light and lots of room. Yes, come along.'

She rose and walked easily out of the room. Bill, after a hesitation, followed her. She didn't seem to care what anyone thought, inviting him to her bedroom like this. Having reached it, she didn't close the door but turned on the lights and said, 'There . . . that's what I'm working on now. Some others I did on my travels before reaching Quetta are stacked against the wall on that side.'

Bill looked carefully. She painted in a style and manner that was not familiar to him. The painting on the easel might have been a distorted man at a strange plough with a jagged blue mountain behind and dark earth below; but again, it might have been a purely abstract construction of light and colour.

'I'm a sort of cubist,' she said. 'You just have to like them or not. It's no good trying to explain them . . . It's a matter of breaking up the light on a subject into its component parts . . .'

Bill found his eyes held by another painting, a small figure, dismembered and violently coloured but definitely a human female nude. 'Oh, that's a Picasso,' she said. 'He did it and gave it to me. I was sort of living with him then . . . for a few months.'

She pulled out some of the work stacked against the wall, and said, 'This is what I've done here . . . that was in a snowstorm outside the railway station . . . this is in the bazaar . . . a girl, probably a whore . . . evening light. That's all. I haven't been here long.'

She headed back for the door and switched out the light. They returned to the drawing room, and Bill said, 'I didn't understand your paintings . . . but could you show me, one day, *how* you break up light? What decided you to form the prisms one way rather than another? Is the choice in the subject or in the light?'

She said, 'Hm. All I can do is let you watch – if you don't ask too many questions. You don't like horses, do you?'

'I'm not mad on them, but I ride sometimes. I'm glad they won't last much longer in war. I don't want to see them mangled and

174

mutilated the way they were in the last war.'

'I was a British VAD for a year . . . New York was boring, when that war was going on. I was nineteen and I went over . . . Now, *I* want to know how to climb cliffs without being afraid. How do you tackle the rock? Or is it yourself you tackle first?'

He smiled and said, 'Come out with Jim and me next time we go. Get some good nailed boots, and mittens in this weather.'

'And breeches or trousers,' she said, 'I often do, anyway . . . the Baluchi women all wear them, so why not?'

He said, 'No reason. Wear anything you like . . . just don't ask too many questions.'

She laughed openly then and said, 'Pax! Get me a drink, will you, please, Captain Miller?'

The Attack series moved outdoors, the weather temporarily abated. The syndicates were spread out across a sloping hillside, facing the wind, looking past Chaman Fort into Afghanistan. The advance to contact had been succeeded by the encounter battle, dealing with a diversion, and now by a full-scale attack to be made against Blue forces holding the frontier line in strength. And the Blue enemy were not Afghans, for they were well equipped with artillery, tanks and aircraft, none of which was true of the Afghan Army . . . but would be true if the Afghans were being supported by their northern neighbour across the Oxus and the Hindu Kush, Soviet Russia.

Merton was the DS of Bill's syndicate. The assistant commandant had asked him once whether he wanted to be put in another syndicate, as Merton was in the same regiment and perhaps there were personal animosities or feelings which should not be allowed to flourish at the Staff College. But Bill had said, 'No, sir, I'm sure that Colonel Merton will be quite fair.' He was not at all sure that he was right, but if Merton became too obvious in his baiting the other DS would notice. One was here for two full years and in that time, under the pressures of the course, on which depended everyone's military future, all truths came out.

Merton said, 'Let's have your appreciation, Miller.'

Bill began, glancing now and then at his notes to refresh himself. 'Our object is to destroy the enemy holding the position in front of us, from Nawakot on the right to Bilid Manza on the left. The first factor affecting the attainment of the object is –'

Merton cut in, 'Is that really the object here? You weren't given that object in the army commander's operation instruction. You were told to clear the valley as far as Spinwam, so that further forces could be passed through towards Kandahar.'

'Yes, but I can't achieve that without destroying the enemy here. That's my immediate object.'

Merton turned to another officer. 'Do you agree, Bingham?'

'No, I think our object is to capture the enemy positions and the ridge to the right, which dominates them.'

'Smythe?'

'I agree with Bingham. The enemy here might retreat northwards, and then, according to Miller's object, we'd have to follow them, to destroy them.'

'And the way would be clear for the army commander to pass a corps through towards Kandahar,' Bill said.

Merton said, 'I think you'd get some rude words from the army commander . . . but go on, let's have your plan.'

Bill continued. The problem they'd just been arguing about was a very real one, and he'd thought about it carefully before deciding what the division's object should be, to meet the general task given to it in the army commander's instruction. The nub of the matter was that taking the defences would be of little value if the enemy now occupying them survived somewhere else, as a force still in being. But Merton was not missing any opportunity to point up differences in opinion or viewpoint between Bill and the Directing Staff, the official Opinion, the Pink Paper, as it was called in its final form. But he knew he was right. Ground didn't matter a damn. What mattered was the enemy's forces. *They* were the obstacles to an advance on Kandahar, not that ridge, or that valley, or that town.

He came to the details of his tactical plan. 'We have two squadrons of Mark I tanks. They will be the spearhead of the attack, which will be on the right, where there is good defilade against anti-tank guns. The deception plan will be to make the enemy think that we are going to attack on the left. Therefore, though there will be patrol activity on the right, to cover mine clearing, 7 Brigade with heavy artillery support will mount a night attack on the left. Until dark the tanks will be located where they can move equally easily to the right or left fronts. After dark, while the artillery bombardment is in full swing on the left – it will drown the sound of their engines – they will move into position five hundred yards behind the front line on the right. The whole two squadrons will pass through the front line ten minutes after first light, closely supported by one battalion of infantry and the whole divisional artillery. The reserve brigades will be prepared to exploit success on either front, on my orders.'

Merton interjected, 'You don't expect the diversionary attack to achieve success, do you, with no tank support at all?'

'It might,' Bill said, 'especially if the enemy doesn't buy our deception plan, and switches his main strength and reserves to the right.'

Then the discussion began. The attacker on the left would have a hard time if the enemy counterattacked with tanks . . . but the attack there was to be at night, and tanks were at a great disadvantage at night . . . that applies to our tanks too . . . quite, but our tanks are attacking by daylight . . . suppose the enemy has massed his anti-tank guns on that flank. Our tanks will be stopped, if not destroyed . . . That's why a full battalion is going with them. If the tanks can fight hull-down, an infantry battalion supported by about eighty guns ought to be able to knock out a dozen anti-tank guns. But with luck, if the deception attack succeeds at all, the enemy will have moved his anti-tank guns and tanks to our left, expecting the next assault to be a breakout from the positions taken in the night battle . . . and so on, and so on, until Merton said, 'All right, that's enough of Miller's plan. Bedloe, let's have yours, and after that we'll break for lunch.'

Jim Rainsford was a tall, thin lieutenant of Gurkhas, and a very good technical climber. Bill watched him now, as he led Lesley up a short pitch of steep bare rock high on the southern face of the mountain Chiltan. The three of them had spent two hours lower down, giving Lesley her preliminary indoctrination into the art. Bill smiled involuntarily, thinking back to his own first lesson, under Morgan Lloyd, all those years ago near Dover; and, last year, his son Roger's first essays on the rocks near Old Sarum, while he was at home on leave studying for the Staff College exam and trying to salvage his marriage. He had succeeded into getting into the Staff College, but the status of his marriage to Pauline had not altered. Then, as now, it appeared to be in a sort of limbo.

He heard Jim call down, 'Put your feet exactly where I did, Lesley, and, as far as you can, move in the same rhythm, take the same time that I did, no more and no less·. . .'

Bill thought that she did not like the looks of a stretch of rock near the middle of the pitch, where Jim had put his right foot and traversed across without hurry, using the friction of the bootnails under the whole surface of the boot's sole and heel to hold him on the steep face. Jim sensed it too, and called, 'It's firm enough . . . ready when you are.'

Then, 'Climbing!' she called and set off up towards him, moving well, up, now to the right, onto the steep rock, foot firmly down, next foot forward, down, on, off, up. She reached Jim's side, and he hitched what had been slack rope round the belay. Then Jim gazed upwards, while Lesley gathered her breath. Jim's hand came out, pointing, and he was talking to her in a low voice, but Bill could not hear what he was saying – planning the route up the next pitch, obviously. Then they worked together to establish a new belay, for, if Jim fell on the pitch, the strain would come from a different angle from that which it would have before. That done, Jim set off upwards, Lesley watching, one hand shading her eyes from the sun.

She would be good, Bill thought. She wasn't unafraid, but she conquered her fear. That was better than dealing with someone who simply did not realize that the mountain was dangerous, to be treated with respect and carefully acquired skill . . .

Now they were both up the final pitch of this climb, and resting. In a few minutes Jim would bring her down, teaching her how to rappel; then all three of them would climb the same cliff by a different route, Lesley in the middle on the rope, and go on to the crest of Chiltan, finding good pitches where they could for practice.

Bill lit a cigarette, and for a moment turned his back on the cliff and the climbers above him and looked out to the south over the mountainous sea of Baluchistan, stretching away in ridge upon ridge of purple-shaded blue-green. The course was going reasonably well. Jim Rainsford was one good friend he'd made here, George Millington the gunner was another, and there were more, men he'd know the rest of his career as they all climbed the ladder together. Lesley was good to be with, on the mountain, or in the bazaar as he stood behind her, watching her paint. He felt content.

Summer was upon them, although, at five and a half thousand feet above sea level and ringed by mountains twice that height, Quetta was never oppressively hot. Bill bicycled slowly up the Hanna valley, his front basket loaded with his swimming trunks and towel. Richard Merton was giving a Sunday picnic at Hanna lake, and had invited Bill; but had warned him that he'd have to find his own way up there, as his car would be full of other guests. Bill would have liked to ask whether Lesley Hawthorne would be one of them, but decided he'd better not. She would probably not be there, he thought; she wasn't much of a socialite. Come to that, he thought, bending his back into the long slope of the rough road, nor was he. For himself, he'd rather have spent the day on Chiltan or Takatu, but the invitation had come before he'd fixed anything for this Sunday, and in any case it would have been churlish to refuse it. Was Richard offering an olive branch in the invitation? Or just doing his duty as a DS? The DS, he'd learned, almost never accepted invitations to married students' bungalows, because all students would feel obliged to invite them, and then the DS would have no time for anything else. Instead, most DS entertained the students in fairly large dinner or other parties, and so could deal with their whole syndicate at one swoop. The assistant commandant entertained everyone twice, once in each year of their course.

It wasn't scorching, but all the same sweat pearled his face and darkened his shirt as he pedalled on. The water would feel good after this, though it was cold as charity, being fed by snow water and underground springs deep in the Panezai mountains to the east, which eventually closed in the valley. Ah, nearly there, at last . . . bright colours gleamed through the few trees lining the road, and he saw that beside the lake they'd set up coloured beach umbrellas of the sort you saw in pictures of the French Riviera. That must be the Hon. Penelope's doing. Richard must have given her a talking-to about keeping her reputation clean, because he'd heard nothing scandalous about her. There'd been plenty of gossip about her in Salisbury and Tidworth when he was at home taking the Staff College exam last year.

He leaned his bicycle against a tree and walked forward, carrying towel and trunks. The Hon. Penelope was lying beside the water in a white maillot that accentuated her every curve and set off her blonde hair. She raised herself on one elbow. 'Ah, here you are . . . a hot ride, I'll bet. You'd better jump in. There's lots of beer on ice in the buckets. The Gents' changing room is behind that bit of canvas strung between those two trees, the Ladies' over there, behind the other canvas . . . and don't pretend you can't tell which is which, when you come back.' She smiled up at him. 'Go on. Look, everyone else is in already.'

Bill said, 'Thanks. All right. I will.' And went behind the screen. A few moments later, his clothes folded on the dusty ground with the others' – must remember to shake them thoroughly for scorpions when he came out – he walked gingerly, barefoot, to the water's edge and plunged in, surfacing at once with a gasp of shock from the bite of the cold. Who else was here? He swam lazily towards a group splashing about near the middle of the lake . . . and recognized Bainbridge, Thompson and Bedloe, with their wives. The men were all in Merton's syndicate until next month, when new syndicates would be formed, and every student would work under a different DS. This was designed to get new views of the students' capabilities, and to teach them to work with different personalities, both as to their superiors and as to their fellows . . . Mrs Bedloe could kindly be described as matronly, but she wasn't – she was fat, much too fat . . . Mrs Bainbridge was a hearty, had played hockey for some huge ladies' public school, and for her county . . . Mrs Thompson drank a lot, but so did Tommy; they were a happy couple, with two small children. Where were all the kids, come to that? At home being looked after by the ayahs, he supposed. Pity they couldn't come up here . . . well, they could, on working days and during normal working hours, with their mothers, but on Sundays the lake was for grown-ups.

Richard Merton greeted him. 'Hullo, Miller . . . We tried to get Lesley Hawthorne for you, but she couldn't come . . . So you're the odd man out.'

'That's all right,' Bill said. So Richard had noticed, or heard, that he was seeing quite a bit of Lesley. He had nothing to be ashamed of – or to keep secret about, even if he'd wanted to. Still, he must be careful. He mustn't risk harming Lesley's reputation. He swam vigorously away, up and down the lake several times, then back to the bank, and headed for the canvas screen. The Hon. Penelope, sitting up now with hands clasped round her knees, called out, 'You don't have to change. You're prefectly decent in those trunks. Come and lie down here . . . and bring two beers.'

He got the beers and glasses, took them to her, and carefully sat down on the other half of her huge beach towel. She raised her glass, drank and said, 'Bung ho! . . . Sorry we couldn't get your Yankee painter for you. How is she these days?'

Bill said shortly, 'She's fine, as far as I know.'

The Hon. Penelope said, 'You're fond of her, aren't you?'

Bill said, 'I like her, yes. I find her a very interesting person.'

'And that's all? She's got a good figure . . . probably swims like an Olympic champion. Most American and Australian girls seem to . . . Bill, this rock climbing of yours – is it a private thing, for just you, Jim Rainsford and Lesley Hawthorne?'

'No, of course not,' he said.

'You aren't a club or anything?'

'No. Jim and I found that we were both enthusiasts as soon as the course began, and later Lesley asked if we would teach her.'

'Well, will you teach me?'

Bill could not help himself blurting out, 'You?' in a tone of great astonishment.

The Hon. Penelope said aggrievedly, 'Why not? Dancing and riding aren't my only sports. I've done some climbing in Switzerland, before I was married. That was with guides, of course, and we didn't do anything difficult. We don't have any children . . . Richard works so hard, so late, every day – this is the first Sunday he's taken off since we came to Quetta . . . I would like a hobby . . . and a challenge.'

Bill had been thinking fast. This was a real surprise, but he couldn't say no to her, not because she was a DS wife, but because she wanted to face the rocks. It would not be in the tradition of mountaineers to refuse her. Later, if she showed that she had no nerve, or no aptitude, they could gently ease her out, but for now . . .

'Of course,' he said.

She seemed to have read his thoughts, for she said, 'I won't fail you. I'll learn, and fast.'

Bill felt a gloomy certainty that she would. He cheered up. All that he knew of her was really hearsay. She might be quite a different person – indeed, her request now showed that she was. Lesley and Jim might like her . . . it wouldn't be too bad.

From the lip of the crest of Takht-i-Sulaiman, Bill and Lesley looked out two hundred miles towards the Indus, the Lion river of ancient legend, crawling wide and silent to the Indian Ocean. 'The Throne of Solomon,' Lesley whispered, flinging herself down on her stomach, cupping her chin in her hands and staring out. Bill, standing beside her, felt deeply moved by something more than the immense grandeur of the scene. Over the months he had shared with her a little of his particular skills: overcoming the challenge of steep rock, and of one's own fears – not in conquest of them, but in partnership with them. Now he felt that in her turn she was sharing something with him, something that she had shared seldom before, except perhaps with Picasso: herself.

He said at last, 'We have a long way to go.'

'A few minutes more,' she said, still staring. 'I want to imprint this on my mind so that I shall never forget it.'

'Will you paint it?'

'Probably. Not just yet.' She rolled over and to her feet with a single easy motion. They started back, at first across bare rock, then picking up the narrow goat trail by which they had climbed: they followed it, as the sun sank lower, its rays falling softer and more golden across the western face of the Throne.

After three hours they reached the place where they had been rock climbing, and where they had left their blankets, food and drink, stowed away in the back of a shallow cave.

They sat down side by side and opened the packet of curry puffs and the thermos of hot coffee. She raised her mug to him. 'Thanks, Bill . . . a perfect day . . . except that I'm bourgeois enough to wish we had some champagne.'

'Next time,' he said, 'we'll hire a couple of men to carry up some real luxuries . . . even a tent, perhaps.'

'No,' she said, 'This is better. No one else . . . How did you manage to prevent the Hon. Penelope from coming with us?'

'I didn't ask her, or really tell her anything about it. Besides, I don't think Richard would approve of her spending two nights out with us.'

'He wouldn't mind,' Lesley said, 'not a bit . . . She's learned very fast . . . faster than I did. She wants to prove something: that she's more than a dumb society sexpot with too much money.'

'But whom does she want to impress?' Bill asked, puzzled.

'You, you dope.'

'I don't believe it!'

She shrugged. 'All right, don't.' She returned to her curry puff.

After a time he said, 'I don't want *anyone* else here. They'd spoil it. But I wish that other people . . . lots of other people . . . could know what this is like . . . the unemployed back at home . . . so many people living in city slums all over the world.'

'What do you know about the slums . . . or the unemployed?' she asked, not harshly, but directly.

'Not much,' he said, 'but I read the papers carefully, and I've been corresponding off and on with the trade union leader Jim Brock since we met – as enemies – during the General Strike. A good officer ought to know what his men's concerns are both inside and outside the army – Morgan Lloyd has always hammered that into me. I wish you could meet him, and Cicely, his wife. He'll be a general soon.'

'If you care about the soldiers, the enlisted men – who, in your army, are all from the working class – why don't you join the Labour Party? That's their party.'

'In some cases,' he said, 'but it isn't always true. And it's less than half true in the peacetime army. All the men are volunteers and they aren't necessarily socialists or Labour Party men. But in a major war we'll be dealing with conscripts – the general mass of the population. There'll be a much more political atmosphere, and we ought to know about it . . . Anyway, I just feel that there'd be less bitterness if more people had the opportunity to see and share this country, any country that's grand, and empty, and noble.'

'You are a romantic,' she said. 'Like practically all the other British officers I've met . . . Have you ever thought of doing social work with the poor? You wouldn't make much money but you'd be working with people, such as soldiers, but with women and children and old people as well . . . You love people. And you wouldn't be thinking of killing.'

He said, 'A country. . . . yours . . . mine . . . contains a lot of things that its people think are worth protecting . . . things that they won't allow anyone else to take away or destroy. That means that the country has to be protected, by force of arms if necessary. There have to be people ready and trained to do that defending. I chose that life a long time ago. I try to make myself better at it, so that when the time comes I won't fail.'

'When!' she cried, 'Ordinary people hope it will *never* come! And if enough people believe that, it never will. Besides, modern war will destroy the very things you would go to war to protect!'

'They can bomb Westminster Abbey,' Bill said obstinately, 'but they can't bomb Magna Carta. Look, Lesley, I don't think the last war was a very good example . . . or the Boer War . . . but there have been necessary wars in history – necessary from the point of view of the country that was threatened – and there will be again . . . What do you think ought to be done if Russia invaded America?'

She laughed scornfully, 'Stuff and nonsense, Bill! You can't frighten me by waving a red flag and talking about the Bolshevik menace. They're ordinary people just like us, and all they want is to live in peace.'

'That's what the people may want, but I don't think it's what Stalin wants . . . and the people have no way of stopping him.'

She passed over the thermos, saying, 'Finish it . . . Have you finished your curry puffs?' Bill nodded. She said, 'There's a full moon and its damnably cold sleeping on sand . . . even on the beach in St Tropez. God knows what it'll be like here. Let's nap for an hour or so, and then go on down back to Ziarat by moonlight. It won't take us more than about five hours, even going slowly. And then, a swim in the pool and a good breakfast in the rondavel. What say?'

'I'm game,' he said, 'but I don't have an alarm.'

'I'll wake you. I can't sleep in this splendour. I'll just rest, staring at God, or whoever's up there watching us.'

She rolled over, wrapped her blanket around her, and lay facing the bright sky. Bill slowly followed suit; but he knew that he would sleep soon. Meantime, he closed his eyes and let the pictures of the day replace the moonlit rocks . . . Lesley working up a long crack above him, early in the morning . . . Lesley, stopping dead as they breasted the final lip of the Throne, and the mountain dropped away

at their feet . . . He thought of her most of the time now. Why? Did
he love her? She made his mind and conscience work. She had long
legs, her body moved gracefully on the rock and in the dance, when
they met at the club . . . How did Pauline dance now? They used to
dance well together. He had not thought of Pauline in some time. Of
Roger and Brenda, but not of her. Why? Because it hurt? No, it
didn't hurt. But when he thought of Lesley, there was joy . . . feeling
. . . worry for her . . . care. He turned over, willing himself to think
of other things . . . he'd go through the full Order of Battle of the 3rd
Indian Infantry Division, unit by unit . . . recite the weights and
ranges of all artillery projectiles . . .

13

June 1934: India

Bill took a last glance at the big situation map and lit a cigarette. The
retreat was proceeding according to plan – so far. His 3rd Brigade,
spread over two roads, was at the front of the retreat – that is, farthest
from the advancing Blue enemy. The rear guard seemed to be secure
on the river line, and as no sign of enemy bridging material had been
reported by extensive and intensive air reconnaissance, it was fairly
safe to say it would hold for several more hours. There'd be a catch
somewhere, of course, for the war game was scheduled to last forty-
eight hours, and as this was part of the Retreat series, the enemy were
obviously going to break the river line and force the British to
continue their rearward movement. The role he had been given was
commander of the 3rd Indian Infantry Brigade; and at any moment
now he would probably be ordered to take up a delaying position, but
meantime . . .

He sat down a few feet away from the wall map, staring through it
rather than at it. He had a letter from Lesley in his pocket. This one

had been written from the farthest reaches of Assam. The flowers were amazing, she wrote, the people nearly as gorgeous in their semi-barbaric costumes, or lack of them. The trees were immensely tall and strong, the mountains steep, full of brilliant birds. The rivers ran fast and deep in steep heavily forested valleys, and teemed with great fish. She had caught a mahseer weighing fifty-eight pounds. She expected to be back in Quetta in two or three weeks; and then she'd have to think of getting back to New York or Paris before she forgot what modern painting was all about.

She'd left Quetta at the end of last year, 1933, and been away six months, seeing India and Ceylon: Madras, Kandy, the Nilgiris, the Hindu cities of the south, the Mogul cities of the north – Agra, Delhi, Lahore, Fatehpur Sikri. She'd travelled all along the northern border, the Himalayas, from Kashmir to Assam; through the Central Provinces' *Jungle Book* country; across the western deserts of Jaipur, Jodhpur, Bikaner, and down to the Rann of Curch; up and down the Indus, over the broad plain they had looked at from the Takht-i-Sulaiman; she had crossed the Ganges and the Brahmaputra, and ridden into tribal territory, as far as they'd let her. She had met with Gandhi and talked with Pandit Nehru, also the viceroy, the commander-in-chief, and the Rawal of the sacred Hindu temple at Badrinath, by the source of the Ganges – all this alone, with her painting gear and the smallest possible amount of baggage. She had reached Badrinath on foot, half her belongings on her own back, the other half carried by a hired Nepali coolie, who walked beside her up the steep path beside the roaring river, teaching her Khaskura.

He'd missed her. By God, he'd missed her. And now, soon, she'd be back. Then what? He was near the end of his senior year at Quetta. Then what?

The DS supervising this brigade headquarters handed the brigade major a message, saying 'Just in by DR.'

A moment later, the brigade major came over to Bill. 'The divisional commander has been killed. You are to take over.'

Bill got up, stubbing out his cigarette. 'Any orders as to who is to replace me?'

'I am.'

'And who's becoming BM?'

'Jenkins.'

Bill nodded. This exercise was not being conducted in syndicates. Every member of the senior division had been appointed to fill all the command and staff positions in the 3rd Indian Infantry Division and its brigades, down to staff captain – except that a few had been appointed to brigades without any definite posting, obviously to fill vacancies later caused by sudden death or promotion. Captain Jenkins of the 8th Cavalry was one of these. The DS were scattered everywhere, directing the exercise under the overall control of the chief instructor, senior division.

The DS in the room said, 'Go over to Birdwood, Miller. As we're advancing all clocks one hour now, exercise time, by the time you get there you could have got to div HQ in the exercise.'

Bill headed for the door and walked across the lawn towards Birdwood Hall. Inside was the headquarters of the 3rd Indian Infantry Division, which he now commanded. The DS were mostly concentrated in there, but some were working out of a study hall nearby – which housed both the control staff of the war game and the headquarters of the enemy Blue force. DS telephones linked the DS together, wherever they were. A separate field telephone and radio net linked various parts of the British force with other parts; but the radio kept going out of action, and the lines were often cut, or sometimes could not be laid as fast as the force was retreating.

Bill walked in, and at once George Cheadle came forward. George, a fellow student, was G1 of the division – the chief of staff. He said, 'While you were on your way here, we had an unconfirmed aircraft report that the enemy has swum a cavalry regiment across the river two miles upstream. A patrol of ours fired on them but couldn't prevent them getting over. There's been increased artillery fire on our left, near here' – he pointed on the map – 'and the enemy air force is very active.'

'All over the front?' Bill asked.

'Yes, but mainly on the right – the north. Two of our reconnaissance planes have been shot down there.'

'Is that all?'

'So far.'

Bill went to the big map and looked at it. Most of the dispositions it showed he already knew, because they had also been marked on his 3rd Brigade map. He said, 'What orders did General Cane give about the cavalry?'

187

'None. He was killed right after we had the information. I told Skinner's to send out a strong flank guard, make contact, and watch them.'

Bill thought, it's fishy having our aircraft shot down just on the right. There must be something there the enemy don't want us to find out about. And the cavalry crossed the river also on the right. It wasn't much of a river but it would need some bridging equipment and perhaps six hours' work to make it passable for lorries, field artillery and tanks.

He said, 'Do I have an air adviser here?'

Richard Merton, wearing the white armband of the control staff, said, 'No.'

'I think I should have,' Bill said.

'Well, you won't get one. You communicate with the RAF by W/T to their airfield which is now at Dost Barat, thirty miles east.'

Bill said to the G1, 'Send the RAF a message in cipher asking them to find out what's going on in this area' – he laid his hand on the enemy left front – 'even if it means escorting the recce plane with fighters . . . I want to speak to the CRA.'

'Here.'

'George, I think the enemy may be sneaking some infantry over the river on our right, and then they and the cavalry regiment, with heavy artillery support, will try to keep us busy while their sappers get to work on putting a bridge across . . . How long is it to dark, exercise time?'

'Three hours,' Merton cut in.

Bill continued to the artillery brigadier, George Millington, 'I'm going to get the CRE to report what is the best place for the enemy to put over a bridge in our right sector. Then be prepared to have all the divisional artillery support an attack in that area, to wipe out any lodgement they've made.'

The G1 came up. 'We may be too late. A heavy artillery bombardment has started on 4 Brigade – our left front.'

'Left!' Bill exclaimed. 'Perhaps we've been had – or nearly.'

He stayed, looking at the map. A road came up to the river on each flank, crossed it on bridges (which had long since been destroyed) and continued eastwards, eventually joining six miles east of 3 Brigade's present position, in reserve. Air reconnaissance had shown that the enemy had no bridging train on his right flank (the British left). The country between the roads on the enemy side of the river was impassable to wheeled vehicles. So, if he also had no bridging train on his left (the British right), he had none at all. That was the area he had asked the RAF to recce. It might take an hour or more to get an answer. And what did the artillery fire on 4 Brigade mean? It might be simple harassing fire, but the lines of communication in this campaign were long and tenuous and both sides were short of artillery ammunition. So . . .

He turned suddenly on the G1. 'Where does this river come from?' The G1 looked puzzled. Bill said urgently, 'Is there any dam reasonably close upstream where the enemy could close the sluice gates?'

He turned to the map and quickly traced the course of the river upstream. There was the dam, twenty miles away, near the edge of the map. No one had mentioned it in the briefing. He had not noticed it before, because it was off in the mountains, a long way from the axis of retreat. Timmy Drayton, on the I Staff, should have, though.

The G2 came up from a desk which represented a radio set, but was in fact one of the DS control tables. 'From brigade – the river level's going down fast.'

Bill thought, they're going to attack in force across the empty riverbed on my left, not my right. The cavalry were a feint, so was the excessive protection against air reconnaissance.

He said to the G1, 'Tell 4 Brigade to hold the position as long as they can without being cut off. I want 3 Brigade to move to 4's right rear, with the tank squadron under command. 5 Brigade to be ready to withdraw into reserve on my orders . . . George, forget what we were talking about, the right front. Can all your guns fire on 4 Brigade's front?'

'Yes.'

'Well, give 4 Brigade all the support you can, though you may have to help 3 Brigade get forward, too. The Blue cavalry regiment's probably going to try to cut the roads, or one of them.'

The G2 returned. 'Enemy tanks seen moving up opposite 4 Brigade . . . two hundred enemy cavalry reported at Fateh Khel, here . . . Twelve enemy aircraft bombing 3 Brigade area, concentrating on tanks . . .'

'Right. No change in the orders. Cancel that message to the RAF and send them another asking them to stand by to give air support to 4 Brigade as soon as the enemy actually forms up to assault the river line. They should see that from 4. According to the map, the ground's higher on our side of the river . . .'

The exercise continued all through the afternoon. By eight o'clock at night, real time, it was dark and moonless outside; in the lighted halls messages and signals kept coming and going. Bill had been commanding the division for eight hours and already felt dog-tired. He must find a way to achieve greater stamina, mental as well as physical. There might be some drug or pill that would help for a time; but it wouldn't do to become dependent on them.

He was making some mistakes now, not so much from his weariness as because the DS were piling on the horrors almost faster than they could happen even in real war, and causing everything that could conceivably go wrong to do so. Orders did not reach their destinations, a cipher was lost to the enemy, the RAF moved their machines back and wireless communication with them went from bad to worse, information about the enemy became increasingly sketchy and unreliable, and the tanks kept breaking down.

Merton was there all the time. Bill thought, he's watching me, making notes every time I do something that's not right, or might turn out to be not right . . . mustn't think like that, mustn't think I'm being persecuted. Merton wasn't the only DS here, and he wasn't running the exercise. As the divisional commander, Bill often had the chief instructor at his elbow.

The mess sent sandwiches and coffee, and the real night of Baluchistan wore on. In Birdwood Hall, on the ground covered by the maps, the war game continued.

He had to get the division extricated before it was cut off by superior forces, Bill thought, staring bleary-eyed at the maps under the electric lights; but he must not let the enemy just push us back. He must instil caution in them, even fear . . . What was that French joke people were always quoting, but had to explain to him because he didn't speak French? Something about 'This animal is wicked. When one attacks it, it defends itself.' . . . Ah, here was an opportunity – a palpable gap between one enemy battalion and the rest of its brigade, on the left. They were pushing too hard. He called the CRA and G1 and quickly issued orders for a limited counterattack by 3 Brigade on that flank. 'With tank support?' the G1 asked.

Bill shook his head. 'No time. And I want to keep the tanks for the next defensive position . . . where I think we'll really be able to stop them. We're supposed to be getting another infantry brigade any time now . . . Is 4 Brigade dug in on the Malozai foothill line?'

'Not finished. The DS say it will take four more hours, exercise time, to complete the position.'

'Another reason to give the enemy a bloody nose . . . Listen, I'm going over to speak to 3 Brigade commander myself. How long will that take?'

Merton said, 'Two hours, exercise time, before you can get back.'

'This counterattack's important. I've got to see that it is properly mounted and supported. Tommy, you take over the division. No more retreat until 4 Brigade is dug in, including all their machine-guns and anti-tank guns. Then start passing 5 back through them to the next position we recced. No other retreat. Just tell everyone who asks to dig in their toes and fight it out till' – he glanced at the clock – 'ten a.m., exercise time.'

'Shall do. Warning order to 3?'

'Yes.'

Merton made a long note. The chief instructor looked at the map, stroking his chin. Bill said, 'Well, what I'd like to do is take a nap, but that wouldn't be right, as I'm supposed to be racing across country on my horse . . . or perhaps on a signals motorbike. I'll take a run round the grounds instead.'

About a week later, on a Friday afternoon, Bill found a letter from Pauline in his pigeonhole, together with one from his mother. He took them back to his room and opened them, the one from his mother first. She was well, but his father was a bit poorly, had a cold he didn't seem to be able to shake off. They sent their love.

He turned to Pauline's letter and read:

Dear Bill,

I am writing to tell you that I want to end our marriage. It has not been a real marriage for a long time, and now I want to marry another man. I do not love you any more, and am sure that I never can again. The man I want to marry is a serving officer of the army, with a great career before him, everyone says. I hope you will act like a gentleman and give me the evidence so that I can divorce you. I shall go and see Mr Prettyman tomorrow, so if you have anything to say please write direct to him, but don't say anything about what you are going to do as I think that's called collusion and would make the divorce difficult.

PS We haven't done anything wrong.

He crunched the letter up angrily. Damned bitch . . . running off with another man while he sweated and slaved in India. No mention of what she proposed to do about Roger and Brenda . . . Poor little devils . . . Well, they hadn't seen much of their father in the past six years, so probably wouldn't notice anything much different. And God damn it, he was supposed to get up at dawn tomorrow to go climbing on Takatu with Jim and the Hon. Penelope. He didn't feel like it at all. So what *was* he proposing to do? Sit in his room all weekend, moping over a short letter he'd read and understood? Do some swatting for the big combined operations exercise? To hell with it. He'd go to Takatu. Penelope was going to take them in the Mertons' car, and they were camping the night out, at a spring near the base of the west flank of the mountain, to do some more rock work on Sunday before returning to Quetta.

The camp fire was of small twigs and herbal shrubs, and burned low, now, the wisps of blue thyme-scented smoke curling away to the north across the face of the mountain. They had eaten and drunk, and the sun had set in a ball of red fire behind the Khojak range forty miles to the west, and now the light was fading over the plain stretching out to the Afghan frontier, lights were beginning to glow in Bostan, and a goods train was labouring up out of the Chapper Rift gorge, belching smoke.

There were only two of them, himself and Penelope Merton. When Penelope came with the car to pick them up, early yesterday morning, Jim Rainsford's bearer had arrived, too, with a note from his master. Jim was sick with a severely upset stomach and was sorry but he'd have to cry off. Penelope said, 'What a shame. Hop in, Bill.'

'But –' he began, and stopped. If she didn't realize that it would look bad, the two of them spending a night and two days alone in the mountains, how could he explain?

'Oh, don't be silly,' she cried, from behind the steering wheel. 'This is 1934 . . . and anyway, you slept out on Takht-i-Sulaiman with Lesley, and nobody made a fuss.'

'She isn't married,' he said.

She said, 'And my husband doesn't mind.'

So Bill had shrugged, and climbed into the big, high old Bentley. And now, after a long day of climbing, first to the peak, then down to some more interesting rocks, he felt full and satisfied, but not tired. The Hon. Penelope – she liked them to call her Penny – was a good sort . . . she'd learned fast and climbed well; she didn't talk a lot; she was always willing and cheerful. Jim liked her, too. He'd actually said she'd make a good Gurkha, if she was a bit shorter and had bigger calves . . . God, he had to tell someone.

He looked at her across the fire in the deepening twilight and said, 'Pauline wants a divorce.'

After a while she said, 'I'm not surprised. Does she say who the man is?' He shook his head. Penelope continued, 'It might be Paul Dillon . . . or Pat Donovan . . . or George Straight . . . probably Paul. He's in the Bays.'

'She says they've done nothing wrong,' he muttered, angry that she should know more about Pauline's doings than he did.

She said, 'I'm sorry, Bill, I can understand how it hurts. But they always say the husband is the last to know, don't they? Of course, she'd say that . . . You know our family place is about halfway between Salisbury and Tidworth . . . and I have a lot of friends in town, too . . . I've had letters. So has Richard. I don't know that it's going to be for the worst, for you, eventually. Pauline's really just not your type. You married very young, didn't you?'

'Yes,' he said, 'We were both just twenty, and fell head over heels in love when I came back from Germany in 1919, ready to be demobbed. Instead, I got engaged and took a regular commission.'

'She's been sleeping with other men, Bill . . . ever since she went back from India, in 1929, wasn't it?'

'Christ!' Bill exclaimed, grinding his teeth.

She stood up, came to him, sat down, put her arm round his waist and laid her head on his shoulder. She murmured, 'Now I'll tell you something. I don't love Richard. He's an ambitious ass . . . and he hates you, God knows why. But I . . . I love you. Richard wants to get rid of me . . . Let him. Let Pauline go, and good riddance. Then we'll marry, you and I, and spend our lives together on the mountains, like this. I've got more money than Pauline has, a lot more. You want to be a general, and my father can help you. People still listen to a viscount in England.'

Her hand slid to the back of his neck and turned his head. 'Kiss me, Bill . . . anything . . . feel my lips . . . me . . . I want you . . . I'm yours.'

Bill struggled with powerful emotions. He was furious against Pauline for betraying him. Here was Penny . . . in her body he could avenge the insult. That would show Pauline! In Penny he could avenge himself for all the humiliations and menaces from Richard Merton . . . He hadn't made love to a woman since he was back in England taking the Staff College exam, nor for years before that . . . Here was a lovely woman, her lips parted, eyes closed, in his arms . . .

He jumped up with clenched teeth, and stumbled away from the fire across the dark mountainside.

Eight days later, on Monday, he received a note by a messenger to report to the commandant's office at noon, after morning classes. When he went in, he found the general sitting behind his desk, the assistant commandant on his right.

Bill saluted and waited. The general said, 'Captain Miller, Colonel Merton has reported to me that his wife admits committing adultery with you. He proposes to sue for divorce, citing you as co-respondent. Is this accusation true?'

Bill answered at once, 'No, sir.'

'You spent the night with Mrs Merton, alone on Takatu, last Saturday week, I believe.'

'Yes, sir. We did not commit adultery.'

But she must have told Merton that they had, he thought. She wanted a divorce, and she wanted him.

'When this goes to court, do you intend to prove it?'

'It's impossible to prove or disprove the accusation, sir. We were alone.'

194

He ought to tell the commandant the whole background, what Penny had said about them being able to get married, how she wanted to, how she had tried to get him to make love to her . . . he couldn't do that.

The commandant said, 'Fortunately the course is nearly over and the case will not reach the courts before we break up. So I shall not send you down, especially as I am bound to accept your denial of guilt until it is proved against you. But you realize what an effect this will have on your career, after the matter has been decided in court?'

'Yes, sir,' Bill said. It was army policy that any officer guiltily involved in a divorce case should be asked why he should not be called upon to resign his commission. That resignation was almost invariably called for if the woman's husband was also an army officer.

'That's all, then.'

Bill saluted and marched out. This needed some thinking over, but he was sure that his first impression was right. Penny wanted to leave Richard. She had lied about their night on Takatu. If he wasn't careful, he'd be trapped into a marriage he didn't want. Climbing with Penny, even dancing with her at the club now and then – these were one thing; marrying her was another.

Bill strode out, Lesley Hawthorne at his side, along the ridge above the Hanna lake. It was Sunday again, and Lesley had come back to Quetta the day before. He'd received an urgent note:

> Gerald has told me everything. Must meet urgently. Let's spend tomorrow out, anywhere. Pick me up here at eight, bikes.

She said, 'Now that I've got my wind back . . . tell me what's going on. The Hon. Penelope is in Karachi, by the way. Richard sent her down there, or she left, I don't know which. If he slept with her now, it would be a reason not to grant him a divorce, once he claims she's committed adultery. It's called condonation.'

'She hasn't committed adultery with *me*.'

'I believe you,' she said.

'There's something else. Pauline wants a divorce.'

Lesley whistled low. 'You poor darling, what a pack of trouble! But you don't love her any more, do you?'

195

'No. I know that. But I don't intend to let her take Roger and Brenda away from me. They're mine, and I mean to have a hand and a say in bringing them up. I'm their father.'

'Hire a private detective. You shouldn't have any difficulty in getting evidence against her, if there's some particular man she's going out with.'

'I can't do that. It would ruin her socially. I shall give her the evidence she needs.'

'What? You, the innocent party, will agree to become the guilty party?'

'It's much worse for a woman to have been divorced than for a man.'

'Hmmm. Pity you didn't make love to the Hon. Penelope that night, then you could kill two birds with one stone.'

'I didn't . . . though how I'm going to prove it, I don't know.'

She said, 'This was on Takatu, wasn't it? Whereabouts?'

'At the Karez spring.'

'That's used quite a bit by picnickers, campers, butterfly hunters, lots of the *sahib log*. Remember we went there the week before I left Quetta . . . with the Holcombes?' He nodded. She continued, 'And I went off behind a rock to pee . . . and realized that a small Baluchi boy was doing a Peeping Tom at me from behind another rock ten yards away . . . I think it's quite likely that the same boy or one of his friends from the village was watching you two at the camp fire, hoping to see some action. The village below there, Karchap, isn't it, is quite close really, and they'd have seen you go through earlier.'

'We left the car in Karchap.'

'Well, I shall go out tomorrow, and see what I can dig up. A few rupees will produce some evidence, I think, and my Pushtu's good enough . . . Take me to the dance on Saturday? Your course is nearly over, isn't it?'

'Yes.'

'Well, we've got to get this mess cleared up before you leave.'

'What are you going to do then? Are you staying on? Brigadier Holcombe has another year here.'

She said shortly, 'I don't know. I haven't made up my mind. And it doesn't all depend on me, either.'

*   *   *

On Wednesday evening Bill received another note from Lesley:

> It took me two days but I have it. A signed witnessed statement
> from Jamal Khan, aged twenty, of Karchap, to the effect that on
> the date concerned he watched a sahib and a memsahib at a camp
> fire by the Karez spring from an hour before sunset till two hours
> after, and there was no copulation, though the couple kissed, and
> then the sahib went away for an hour before coming back and
> then they talked some more before going to sleep under their
> blankets, on opposite sides of the fire. He can identify both
> people if necessary.

On the Saturday evening Lesley was dancing in his arms in the club.
In the sun, on Chiltan, he had not really noticed her tan, but here, in
the artificial light of the ballroom, and against the incongruity of her
long pale blue and silver evening gown, she seemed as dark as an
Indian, the deep tan going up into the roots of her hair, the ends of it
bleached like straws.

'I've been back a week,' she said, 'and I can hardly believe I've
been away. Nothing's changed . . . Gerald, Betty, the bungalow . . .
And meantime I was travelling in the realms of gold . . .' She looked
at him. 'I missed you.'

'I missed you,' Bill said. God, what a damned inane remark. He'd
had plenty of company. Jim and Penny on the rocks, others in the
mess, playing billiards after dinner . . . they were a good crowd, on
the course. But there'd always been an ache for her.

He said, 'Did you do any painting?'

'Some. You must see them . . . More storing of memories, colours, light, people . . . A Naga wanted to marry me . . . I nearly
became a Hindu in an ashram in Pondicherry . . . The Wali of
Swat's brother wanted me to paint his concubines in the nude . . . all
ten of them together . . . Your letters weren't very informative.'

'It was hard to write, not knowing whether it would ever catch up
with you. And what I had to say seemed so boring. I knew you didn't
want to hear about the army or the Staff College.'

She said, 'No. And this dance is a bit of a bore, too. I'll get
Gerald's permission to keep the car and let's change and go out to
Chiltan. Right now! For the night.'

197

'All right,' he said eagerly. It was summer, the evening warm for the height, a half-moon shining down on the lawns outside.

It was the cold hour after dawn, and they were nine thousand feet up, two thousand feet above the plain below, the lights of Quetta still sparkling to the north, the great rock mass of the mountain shining grey above. One climbing rope was looped over Bill's shoulder, and another over Lesley's, racks of carabiners hanging at their waists.

The sun burst over the eastern horizon, rising out of the jagged earth beyond the rim of the high plateau, out of the dark of the valleys. Bill turned and stopped, looking down and across the void of the dying night into the yellow glow of day. He turned back to her and said, 'I missed you, Lesley, because I love you.'

She didn't speak for a long time. Then she said, 'Me, too. I couldn't believe it, when I knew . . . It was in Assam, following a Naga head-hunter down a jungle path . . . I was looking at his bare bottom, and I thought, I love Bill Miller, what the hell am I going to do?'

He stretched out his hands to her and she came forward. The racks of steel carabiners clanked together as they kissed, their mouths melting into one. Her breast heaved and her breathing came shorter. She broke a little away. 'I want you, Bill. That, too. I've been thinking of . . . this . . . how it would happen, for a long time, even before I knew it was love.'

He said, 'I can't make love to you until . . . we're settled, in our own minds. I mustn't make any mistake with you . . . hurt you. I am married, and in spite of what Pauline has asked me to do, I still feel that I am. I must, somehow, learn not to feel like that.'

She said softly, 'Good old Bill . . . "I could not love thee, dear, so much, loved I not honour more." Let's get on with the day, and then tonight, by the fire, we'll talk . . . without any nasty-minded little Baluchi boys spying or eavesdropping.'

He kissed her again, and for a moment laid his hand on her cheek. Then they turned and faced the mountain.

By the fire she passed the thermos of hot coffee laced with rum back to him, saying. 'Finish it . . . So you think that after Pauline gets a divorce, on the evidence of your adultery with some nameless woman, you will be called on to resign your commission?'

Bill said, 'It's possible, even probable.'

198

'And that'll be the end of your career, regardless of your DSO or of how good a report you get from the course here?'

Bill nodded, adding, 'But I won't get a good one. I've disagreed with the DS too often.'

'Then tell Pauline to go to hell. And, as I said, get the evidence to sue her for divorce.'

He said, after a time, 'I was not born a gentleman, Lesley. I have made myself one. I speak almost without my Wiltshire accent. I think like a gentleman. I am a gentleman, an English gentleman . . . I must do it, to maintain myself as what I have worked so hard to be. It's myself that has made this decision, it's myself that will stick to it.'

'Whom are you going to sleep with for the purpose?'

'I don't know,' he said miserably. 'It's not difficult in England to find some slut . . . even quite respectable women do it for a living: provide evidence. They are seen in the same bed by a waiter or chambermaid – that's all. I suppose one does the same in India. I'll find out as soon as the course is over.'

She said, 'So you give her a divorce. You become a free man again, except for your ties to your children, and with luck you'll be out of the army. Then what?'

'Luck?' he said. 'I'm a soldier, Lesley. I don't know what else to do, or be.'

She spoke energetically, gesturing with animation: 'There's no future in the army anyway! It's being cut down in this depression, and a good thing, too. There are much more important things to spend money on than tanks and guns and battleships. There's no threat to peace anywhere, except perhaps from that Nazi Hitler in Germany, but he's mad . . . These little frontier wars don't count. They're not war, but policing. It's just a pity you have to do it with guns, but I've seen the tribesmen, and I understand why it is . . . Forget the army. Think! What do you really want to be, if you were free of everything, all commitments?'

He said, 'I'm hoping to get advice from Morgan and Cicely Lloyd. I wrote to them as soon as I got Pauline's letter, and Morgan wired back – I got it yesterday – that they were coming here to stay with the commandant for a week on their way back to England – Morgan's been posted to Aldershot command – and would talk it all over with me.'

'But what do you *want*? Haven't you had any thoughts, any secret longings?'

'A farm in Wiltshire, perhaps,' he said thoughtfully, 'not a big one . . . I do know something about farming. My father's a draper . . . dry-goods store, I think you call it . . . but the Pennels were so rural that we all grew up on farms, in a way. I'd have to borrow a lot of money from the bank to get started, and they probably wouldn't lend it to me, as I have no collateral . . . Ah, it's a dream. I'm a soldier.'

'But you won't be, after you've spent your night with your professional lady and sent the evidence to Pauline. So, what *else* do you want?'

He said, 'Well, I've been thinking all day and I know what I want to be. I want to be your husband. At the same time, I feel that I am still Pauline's husband. It doesn't make sense.'

'Yes, it does,' she said. 'Now, let's take things step by step. When we get back to Quetta, I want you to give me a written note asking me to marry you, as soon as you are free. Declare in it that you have no intention of marrying anyone else, even if I should refuse you.'

'But what . . . ?'

'I'm going to Karachi with it. It's time that the Hon. Penelope had her pipedream punctured. As soon as I get back, I'll return the note to you, and you can destroy it.'

'I'll have spoken to the Lloyds by then. They're due here on Tuesday,' he said. 'And perhaps I'll feel differently about Pauline. But not about you, ever.'

'I believe you,' she said softly. 'Now, let's sleep.'

Morgan and Cicely were staying at the commandant's house – Morgan had been the general's brigade major late in the big war. Bill did not want to call on them there, so sent a message asking them to come to his room when they could. They were here now, and Morgan was speaking. 'Bill, if you haven't done anything wrong with Penelope Merton – and Miss Hawthorne's document here certainly proves that you didn't on that particular night – there's no earthly need for you to do what Pauline wants. If you were both unhappy, there might be . . .'

'We are. It's over. She discovered it first, that's all. Or at least, she came out in the open first.'

'You'll be getting your report tomorrow, but it's not the last word in your career. You are a man of war. There's a war coming, sooner than you think.'

'Where from?' Bill asked quickly.

'Germany,' Morgan said. 'Some of us who have been studying the matter are convinced of it. The politicians think they can parley with Hitler, persuade him, civilize him . . . but they can't. They'll find that out in time and we can only pray that it *is* in time . . . You have a career in front of you. Don't for God's sake throw it away for the sake of an outdated chivalrous gesture.'

Bill did not speak for a long time. Then he said, 'I wanted to ask you, sir, whether you or Cicely could give me any advice about what I could do in civilian life.'

Morgan said, 'Changing the subject, eh? So your mind's made up?'

Cicely cut in, 'Bill wants to marry Miss Hawthorne, Morgan. Mrs Holcombe's sure of it.'

Morgan said, 'Well, Bill, my advice would be the same in any case, but this makes it the more applicable, I think. Emigrate to America. Miss Hawthorne's second cousin, I think it is, is a senator from Virginia. Get into the US Regular Army, using his influence. They're going to be in the war, too. They don't believe it now, but they are.'

He rose. 'We'll see you again before we leave, Bill. Think over what I've said, even if your mind is made up. You'll do more, and go higher, with us than with the Americans. And there, you'd have to replace Nelson and Wiltshire in your heart with Lincoln and Lee and Virginia. It takes time.'

The commandant said, 'Initial it as seen, Captain Miller. Now, sit down. Do you have any comments?'

Bill sat down in the chair facing the general across the wide desk. He had been reading his Staff College report, set up on a small stand in the corner, a small bright light shining down on the white paper. It had been a yes and no report: on the one hand, he worked hard and had interesting ideas; on the other, he was basically unsound in some of his military thinking; on the one hand, he was popular with other officers, and worked well with them in syndicate; on the other, he was too independent in thought, and sometimes created friction thereby.

Bill said now, 'No, sir.'

'You have a stubborn streak in you,' the general said, 'some call it opinionated . . . To be determined is one thing, to be opinionated is another.'

Yes, Bill thought, but how do you tell the difference? You don't, except by trial, in war.

The general said, 'We were seriously discussing whether you were really suited for the staff and, frankly, I am still not sure whether that is your métier. But the Staff College is much more than a training school for the staff. It is also, we hope, the chrysalis for our future commanders, and there you may find your place . . . in war. If you have great qualities . . . if your stubbornness is indeed determination in a right course, only war will give you the chance to prove it. We were particularly worried by your acts in the Retreat series, when you left your headquarters for two hours, exercise time, and went off to see a brigade commander. It seemed irresponsible.'

Bill said, 'We couldn't retreat any further until positions were prepared in rear. That would take four hours. On the other hand, it was vital that 3 Brigade should counterattack, with all the force and support available. Otherwise our retreat would turn into a rout. You remember, sir, that we weren't retreating just for the exercise, but because an enemy corps of three full divisions was forcing us back. All the rest of my division had to do was dig in and hang on until the counterattack made its effect felt.'

The general said, 'Well, as I've just said, only real war would prove you right or wrong. But it was a very risky action . . . On balance, as you see, we have decided that you have passed satisfactorily. You will get a third-grade staff appointment somewhere . . . heaven knows where. Your future will depend as much on what you do in this first job as on your report, from here . . . And I wish you a happy outcome in your private affairs, if that is possible.'

'I think it is, sir. Thank you.' He saluted and marched out.

They were dancing in the club again, the ballroom half empty now, for the Staff College was a large supporter of the club, and most of the old course had gone their ways, on short leave, prior to posting, and the new course had not arrived. He said, 'How did you do it?'

Lesley said, 'Talked to her as woman to woman. Told her that you liked her, and admired her as a climber, but there wasn't a chance that you'd marry her. Showed her the note . . . She didn't cry. Said she'd lied to Richard because he wanted it, and because she wanted you . . . she knew we were going out a lot together, of course, but not that we were in love. Who did know that? Not I, yet . . . So she wrote a letter to Richard there and then, on a typewriter with a carbon, and gave me a copy – telling him she had lied, that she hadn't committed adultery with you. But she added – I didn't tell her to do this, she did it of her own accord – she added, 'I have committed adultery with other men and will give you a list and produce evidence on demand.' So they're going to get divorced anyway . . . Now, what are we going to do about you? You refuse to divorce Pauline, but you're going to allow her to divorce you. But I refuse to let you sleep with another woman, even a professional Woman Named. You're going to sleep with me, and make love to me. When? Where?'

'Your reputation . . .' he began. 'We can't get married for a long time, perhaps a year, until my divorce is final.'

'*My* reputation is concerned with how well I paint and draw, not with whom I sleep. In a year it'll be the same with you, in your new job. Though I hope to god it isn't with the US Army.'

'Morgan Lloyd said he'd speak with the Military Secretary as soon as he got back to London, and explain some of the background of my case. He thought there'd be quite a chance I'd get away with it, as long as the other woman was not the wife of a serving officer.'

'Well, I'm not anyone's wife, and rather than this unknown female, it shall be me . . . You have two weeks' leave. Listen, on my travels everyone told me how beautiful the Garhwal Himalaya was. Let's trek up into it from Ranikhet. There are some rest houses, other times we sleep out. We can hire coolies and a cook and buy supplies in Ranikhet. Let's go . . . It'll be our last time together before we're married . . . I know you may get a family station, probably will – but I can't hang around until then, seeing you on the side, sneaking in the back door after everyone else has gone home. I'm going back to New York and will stay there till you send for me . . . Now, let's dance . . . and drink . . . and soon we'll be in a log cabin thousands of feet up, with a fire in the hearth and wildflowers all over the place . . . and then you shall tell me why Richard Merton hates and fears you so much. There's something between you that no one else knows, but you both do. As your wife-elect, I have to know, too.'

14

August 1934: Garhwal, India

This day she had asked him again to tell her about the source of the antagonism between himself and Richard Merton; and after their simple supper in the rest house, he began.

It had been 13 August 1918, Bill remembered clearly, because he'd got a slight wound the day before. A shell splinter grazed his left arm, and tore his sleeve, causing some bleeding. The wound stung for several hours, but he'd shrugged it off, for great things were happening. The war on the Western Front was at last freeing itself from the mud. On 8 August the British Army had begun a massive offensive, but this one did not soon grind to a halt, as all the others had done, since Loos in September 1915. Ludendorff called 8 August the Black Day of the German Army, but Bill did not know that at the time. All he knew was that a miracle happened – the Germans broke, and the British advanced, not a few yards, but miles. They took prisoners by the thousands, because the Germans surrendered – that was the first time they ever had unless they were cornered and helpless . . . that day they just gave up. And it was such a short time since March, 21 March, when the Germans attacked the British Army and broke through; and for a week or two it was the British who were demoralized and retreating, and the Germans who were advancing in the open, the trenches left behind, no barbed wire, no torn-up ground. It was then that Haig issued his order about 'backs to the wall', and how everyone must fight on to the end. And now everything had been turned upside down, and it felt very strange. He'd spent nearly two and a half years in France by then, over a year as an officer, and he knew the minutiae of trench warfare by heart – the preparation of trench maps, the organization of trench reliefs, bombing raids, raids to get prisoners, what to do when the Boche started heavy artillery bombardment in obvious preparation for an assault, sanitation in the trenches, wiring fatigues . . . all this, and more, he knew; but he knew and had been taught nothing of open warfare, of coordinated fire and movement by small bodies of men, of how supplies of food and ammunition kept up with a rapidly advancing force. Now he, and all of them, were learning, fast.

That day Merton was acting in command of C Company of the battalion, the 1st Battalion of the Queen's Own Wessex Rifles. Bill was a second lieutenant commanding a platoon in the company, No. 9. Bogey Harris, his boyhood friend, was then a lance corporal in the platoon. The brigade had just been advancing, but they ran into opposition at about eleven in the morning, and a formal attack was set up for two in the afternoon. That was strange, too, because the British Army always attacked at dawn. By so doing, they could move the attacking troops up by night, and under cover of darkness make other preparations, which the enemy air forces couldn't spot. The attack went in as soon as there was light to see by, so that, once the objective had been taken, there was daylight to look around and make defensive preparations against the German counterattack: the Germans *always* counterattacked, in those days. But that 13 August the divisional commander didn't want to give the Germans time to dig in and strengthen their defences, so he ordered the brigade to put in an attack as soon as it could be mounted. The Wessex were hoping for tank support but it never came – the machines broke down farther back, they heard later. So at two pip emma the battalion went over the top; but there was no real 'top' because they weren't in trenches, but in a sunken road. The leading wave was A Company on the right, and D on the left; the second wave was C on the right, behind A, and B on the left behind D. There had been an hour's artillery preparation, and a gunner officer with binoculars and a field telephone was stationed up on the bank of the lane, looking for German machine-gun positions. When he spotted any, he'd call down fire on them; but the men of the Wessex didn't really know where the enemy were, except that they were in front, and that there weren't an awful lot of them, though they had some machine-guns.

The companies moved off behind a rolling barrage, which would keep advancing at a steady rate until the leading company commander fired Very lights as signals to stop the forward movement. All went well for three or four minutes. Bill thought that C Company looked like recruits practising an attack during the last week of their training at Salisbury, doing a scheme out by Old Sarum, all in line, spaced exactly five paces apart, swords fixed, rifles at the high port . . . Then the Germans opened up with several more hidden machine-guns and a lot of artillery fire, mainly from light field guns.

A Company, in front of C, went to ground. A lot of the overs were falling among C Company. Bill saw three men drop, as C Company also went to cover. Bill crept forward to where he could see better, crawling on his belly, and saw that the two left companies, D and B, were continuing to advance, while A and C were pinned down. They lay there for a while, firing at what they could see, which was not much, until a runner came up from battalion to Merton. Bill saw that clearly, for Merton was about two hundred yards to his right. Soon afterwards a company runner crawled out to 9 Platoon and told Bill to follow Merton and company headquarters farther right, under cover of smoke from the artillery, and then to advance again, past the right flank of A, clean up whatever enemy they found and then consolidate.

Bill and his platoon did as ordered, and in about an hour were past A, in oak and chestnut woods. Then Merton called all the platoon commanders together and said that the German machine-gunners who'd been holding up the battalion attack had run away, and they should now consolidate, as ordered. Bill went back to his platoon and the men started digging. By then it was about half past four. The men had no picks or shovels, only their entrenching tools, and the battle seemed to have gone miles away. There was some shelling, and a few bullets flying about, but not close, and no one knew where from or where to. It felt a little eerie, all alone in that wood, only a hundred of them, for during that war, in France, Bill had always felt that he was part of an army – hundreds of thousands, millions and millions. The only time before this when he'd felt so isolated was the fourth day of the March retreat, when roughly the same thing had happened, only in reverse. He and his platoon began the day's retreat as part of a battalion, but when they stopped, they were alone. They'd lost contact . . . and now it had happened again.

The men were in good spirits, talking and even singing, until Merton gave orders for everyone to be quiet and show no light, not even smoking. He was right, because if some larger German force had spotted them, unsupported and all alone, they could have wiped the company out. For the moment the best course was to lie doggo, until contact had been re-established. But the men didn't like it and it emphasized their aloneness out there in what they would have called no-man's land a week earlier, only now it was just France. Bill didn't know whether Merton had sent out patrols to establish contact on the flanks, or with the Germans. If so, they had not come from 9 Platoon. So it became dark and they sat in their shallow trenches, eating cold bully beef and stale biscuits and drinking water without any rum in it, and there was no tea . . . Then one of Bill's sentries muttered loudly, 'Halt! Who goes there?'

'Paddy O'Flynn, battalion runner,' the voice answered out of the darkness a few yards beyond the edge of the wood – Bill was close to the sentry's position and heard everything.

'What battalion?' the sentry asked suspiciously.

'1st Wessex,' the man out there said. 'What push are you?'

The corporal of the sentry post – Bogey Harris – answered, '1st Wessex. I know you. You were in A and played inside left for the company team.'

'That's me. Can I come on now?'

'Advance, and be recognized,' the sentry said, because he'd been taught that was what he was supposed to say.

O'Flynn came into the wood, tripping over some branches, and Harris said, 'Do you have a message, or what?'

'If this is C Company, I have,' O'Flynn said.

'You're in luck. You've found us, and about fucking time, too.'

'Take me to the company commander,' O'Flynn said, and Harris said, 'Follow me, carefully, Paddy bhoy,' and they went cautiously off in the dark, breaking small branches and crunching twigs under their boots. Bill lay back and waited.

About a quarter of an hour later, Harris brought O'Flynn back to the edge of the wood and Bill heard O'Flynn say, 'Now I've got to find my fucking way back to the battalion, and it's black as the inside of a cow . . . Well, ta-ta'; and off he went.

A little later again, Merton sent for all the platoon commanders. When they were gathered round his trench in the middle of the wood, he said, 'We have orders from battalion. The 10th Royal Fusiliers are somewhere on our right. They have been told where we are and they are sending runners out to find us, because at dawn we will advance with them, on their left flank. Our objective is to take the ridge we saw ahead yesterday – it was on a bearing of twenty degrees magnetic and about a mile and a half away.' He pointed out through the wood – there was a little light there, as Merton had an electric torch switched on, but lying flat on its side with a steel helmet covering most of the light; but that was enough for the platoon commanders to see around the little circle and recognize each other.

Then Merton said, 'Further orders will depend on what instructions we get from the Fusiliers. We don't know what opposition we'll meet, if any. We don't know whether the Fusiliers will have tank support. We don't know much, yet,' he ended.

Bill said, 'If the Fusiliers haven't found us yet, and it's nearly eleven o'clock at night, hadn't we better try to find them?'

'No,' Merton said shortly. 'We sit tight, they find us. If we both go wandering about looking for each other in the middle of the night, we'll start a battle and the whole plan for tomorrow will be napooed.'

Bill went back to his platoon and gathered them round him in the dark, except the sentries – and told them what he could. Then the platoon sergeant took over and arranged the night's duties and reliefs, and Bill went to sleep under a tree . . . it was a beautiful warm night, he was tired, and fairly full of bully and biscuits . . . He'd told his sergeant to awaken him at one o'clock, when he intended to take a look round the position, make sure the sentries were awake and knew their orders, and that everyone else was asleep and reasonably comfortable.

The sergeant awakened him at one, as ordered, and he was pulling on his boots – they were the only things he'd taken off – when a man came up in the dark, and said, 'Message from Mr Merton, sir . . . all platoon commanders to his headquarters at once.' Bill shambled off through the trees until he saw the dim light of Merton's torch, and there he was, standing. The others were already there, with the

CSM, and Merton said at once, 'The Fusiliers have made no contact with us. The orders for the advance are cancelled.'

Cancelled, Bill thought? By whom? But Merton said just that, leaving them all free to think that another runner had come from somewhere bringing new orders.

'We'll sit tight, holding this wood,' Merton said, 'until the Fusiliers do make contact . . . Reveille same hour, but stand to till half past five, instead of forming up for the advance. Dismiss!'

They went back to their platoons. Bill noticed that warlike activity in the area had increased while he was asleep. Two or three batteries, German and British, were firing something like harassing fire, searching in the darkness for targets, it seemed, and these were heavier guns than the whizzbangs, 18-pounders and 4.5 hows which had been firing during the day. These were German 5.9s and British 6-inch hows . . . a whistling whine through the dark high overhead, and then boooom, craaash, somewhere a mile away, or a hundred yards. They don't know what they're doing, Bill thought, except use up ammunition. And there were machine-guns firing on fixed lines across their front, from right to left. He thought the guns on the left were German, coming more or less in across the front; and those on the right were British, going diagonally out. Both beaten zones were close to the front edge of the wood, perhaps a hundred yards out. If they advanced they'd have to walk through both of them, he thought. He shivered a bit. There'd be light when they advanced, *if* they advanced. And there were quite a number of those damned machine-guns and howitzers. The thought of being riddled or pulverized at that late stage of the war was very uninspiring. But the company *ought* to advance. He couldn't get back to sleep, thinking about the cancellation of the advance. The Germans were on the run. They weren't totally broken but they were breaking. The company *should* advance, even if its flanks were hanging in the air, even if it had no contact, or for that matter, no orders . . . go, go, go, until it was stopped. He thought of going to Merton and arguing with him, to change his mind . . . but he wouldn't, Bill knew it. He had felt a great tension in Merton when he cancelled the advance. His face was shiny with sweat, and the only reason his hands didn't tremble was that he kept them clasped behind his back.

No. 9 Platoon's sector of the wood faced roughly south. The

209

Fusiliers must be somewhere to the south-east. Bill decided to go and look for them himself. He thought he could safely be away for a couple of hours. He couldn't get far in that time, in the dark, but he didn't believe the Fusiliers were very far away: they'd been there on the right when the attack started at two o'clock the previous afternoon – in full view, about three hundred yards off. So why hadn't their patrols or runners been able to find C Company? He came to the conclusion that the Fusiliers must have been stopped farther back than the Wessex had but thought that everyone was in the same relative positions as when they'd started. So they'd been searching empty ground behind C Company, believing that they would run into Germans if they went any farther out. So Bill, to find them, must head more to the south – say on a bearing of 160 degrees, or south-south-east.

He went to his sentry post, but before he could speak Corporal Harris sat up from where he was lying behind the sentries, and said, 'Mr Miller?'

Bill said, 'Yes. I can't sleep. I'm going out for a bit.'

Harris said, 'Better be careful, sir. God knows how many Jerries are out there.'

'I'm not worried about them,' Bill said. 'But I don't want to be shot coming back in. I won't be more than two hours. Make sure that our sentries know.'

'Right you are, sir,' Harris said. He didn't sound a bit surprised. Officers were all mad was a belief Bill had had himself when he was an other rank; or, he thought, Bogey, knowing him so well, had guessed why he was really going out. So he left the wood, crept far enough – about a hundred paces – so that no one would hear if he stumbled, then took out his compass and headed south-south-east, walking fast. The surface underfoot was good grass, smooth-cropped by fat cows until two days ago, probably. Then he ran into some deserted farm buildings and it took him a little time to work cautiously through them . . . then came some thick hedges which he had to break through by brute strength . . . then a couple of drainage ditches, which took careful crossing . . . then fields again, going gently downhill now – he knew C Company's copse was on a bit of high land – and suddenly a challenge, in cockney. He answered. The sentries were suspicious, but soon an officer was awakened, and he was taken in. They had a hut of some kind and a couple of barns close behind, and that was the headquarters of one of the Royal Fusiliers' companies. They were delighted to see him and the company commander gave him a written message, saying, 'This is a copy of the signal we've been trying to reach you with for hours.'

'All right,' Bill said, 'I'll take it back to my company commander.'

'Don't get yourself shot,' the Fusilier captain said, 'and have a tot of rum to speed you on your way.'

'Thank you, sir,' Bill said, and they gave him a tin mug half full of the stuff, which he swallowed in two gulps.

The Fusilier captain said, 'There's not much in the message – just instructions to conform to our movements and protect our left flank. We'll halt and make a plan of attack if we run into real opposition, and in that case you are to halt too, and just see that no one interferes with us from the left. We have twelve tanks and six field batteries in support. It should be a good party. Now, before you go, show me on this map where you are. We're here.' He put his finger on the map, and after a bit of careful study Bill found what must be C Company's wood – it was called Bois des Loups – and pointed it out to him. The captain said, 'Good. We'll be passing just to the east of you, and you can pick up and tag along on our left.'

Bill set off back, thinking, Merton will be pleased to hear this: but will he? . . . Back across the fields, the ditches, through the farm building, then working his way carefully north-north-west and, when he thought he was in the right place, heading due north for what he hoped was his own platoon's position on the edge of the wood.

Bill's memory was very vivid here, and even as he spoke in the Himalayan evening he could smell the grass in that French field so far away and long ago, and the tang of the farmyard wafting up the slope in the night and now, vaguely seen, the bulk of the wood ahead. He was heading for the wood . . . not absolutely sure that it was *his* wood . . . when he heard a challenge: 'Halt. Who goes there?' He even recognized the voice – a Wiltshire farmboy called Dearden. He was from the northern part of the county, and he'd had a cold for the last few days and his voice was still hoarse. Bill heard Harris say, 'It's . . .' and then, over that, Merton fairly yelling, 'It's a Hun patrol, fire, fire!'

Harris shouted, 'Sir, it's M . . .'

'Fire!' Merton screamed.

211

Bill dropped flat, and two rifles were fired, Dearden and the other sentry on the post – two rounds each. The shots went high over his head. He was sure they had both fired deliberately high. Then he shouted, 'Cease fire . . . It's Mr Miller, friend, friend!'

Dearden cried, 'Oh my God, it's Mr Dusty!'

'Captain Merton,' Bill shouted, 'make sure they don't fire again. Do you hear me?'

After a time Merton answered, out of the darkness, 'Step forward, with your hands raised. Don't try anything. Cover him, men!'

Bill scrambled to his feet and went forward, speaking: 'It's me . . . Miller . . .'

At this, Merton's torch flashed on and shone in his eyes, and he said, 'Miller . . . it sounded like you. What the hell are you doing out there?'

'Finding the Royal Fusiliers,' Bill said. 'And I did.' He fished in his tunic pocket and handed Merton the signal form. 'Those are our orders. The nearest company of the Fusiliers is about five hundred yards south-south-east of here. I can show you on the map.'

'You went out, without telling anyone, in disobedience of my orders?'

'I told my sentry post,' Bill said, getting angry. 'And I heard Corporal Harris trying to tell you it was me, but you still made them fire.'

'You'll hear more of this later,' Merton said. His torch went out. An hour later he gave out orders for the advance. At dawn a lieutenant of Fusiliers came to be liaison officer with the Wessex company, then a gunner observation officer, and soon they all advanced and took their objective without any trouble.

'And that's the whole story,' Bill said.

There was a long silence in the little hut, scented by woodsmoke from the fire, seven thousand feet up under the western face of Trisul. At last Lesley said, 'Merton tried to kill you. Why?'

Bill said, 'It took me some time to work it out. Remember, Merton had been a pretty good officer in battle. He'd won an MC. He'd been in the March retreat and had kept his head. I'd been with him in some nasty spots and he hadn't disgraced himself, though he was always tense and irritable when we were in the line – had a hard time

212

controlling himself. So why should he act so peculiarly now? . . . I think he broke, something snapped, and he felt that he just couldn't continue the advance through the machine-guns and the shelling. That wood, the Bois des Loups, was a perfectly isolated, cosy little haven. No one reached us after the CO's runner, O'Flynn, with the original message. We were alone and could just stay there, doing nothing, safe. I think Merton was praying that the Fusiliers wouldn't find us, and when he thought he'd waited long enough he cancelled the orders to advance. He was the man on the spot and he could always say that there was no contact with the Fusiliers. But I think he sensed that I was unhappy about the cancellation. Because, about twenty minutes after I'd gone, he made a tour of the wood. When he couldn't find me, he awakened my sergeant, then Harris had to tell him I'd gone out . . . and he guessed why. So he waited – they told me he did not move from the sentry post . . . and did his best to get me shot. They wouldn't have gone out to get my body until daylight, and then, even if they found the message in my pocket, it would have been too late to advance with the Fusiliers.'

Lesley said, 'It was quite risky for him, wasn't it, ordering your men to shoot when they had told him you were out?'

'A bit,' Bill said, 'but we were all jittery, from fighting in the open, after so long in the trenches . . . which meant that Germans could pop up anywhere, behind, in front, on either or both flanks, suddenly and without warning, and it was all worse at night.'

Lesley said thoughtfully, 'And he has been afraid you would somehow reveal this . . . let the regiment and the army know that he had tried to murder you because, in effect, you had shown up his cowardice . . . his breakdown, if you like.'

'Partly,' Bill said, 'Remember, he's a snob, and I was not born a member of the officer caste. He never liked my becoming an officer. And all the troubles between us are not his fault. I have rubbed him up the wrong way in the past. If I don't get a good staff posting it won't be entirely because of him, but because I rubbed up the whole Quetta directing staff the wrong way. But there it is, and we both have to live with it . . . he with the knowledge that I know the whole truth about the affair of the Bois des Loups, and I with the knowledge that he'll do almost anything to get rid of me . . . Look at the way he egged on the Hon. Penelope to commit adultery with me . . .

We'll serve together again – bound to, unless one of us leaves the army. But at least, after all these years, we understand each other better, even if we don't like each other any better. That'll help . . . I hope.'

15

August 1939: England

Three of them were on the rope, halfway up the face of the quarry wall, while Brenda sat below on a rock in the late August sun, studying a book on integral calculus. The quarry was outside the village of Claygate, and they were climbing there because Morgan Lloyd had decreed that no one in his branch could go more than an hour's travel distant from the War Office during these final taut days of August 1939. So this Sunday morning Bill had said, 'I've got to get out of London. Let's go to that quarry near Claygate that Morgan told us about . . . and he says there's a good pub for lunch.'

'See if Roger or Brenda want to come,' Lesley said. 'If war's so close, you ought to take every chance you get of seeing them.'

So Bill had called Pauline, and both the children wanted to join the expedition, though Brenda said, 'I want to come, Daddy, but not climb. I don't really like it all that much, and I have some swotting to do for exams.'

'Come along anyway, darling,' Bill said, 'and bring your books.'

It was a limestone quarry, the rock mostly reddish in colour, and broken up into strange shapes and sharp edges by the quarrying, which had been going on for a century or more, latterly using dynamite to blast open new faces. The main face was just over a hundred feet high from the muddy floor of the quarry to the grassy lip above, where a wire fence protected unwary passers-by from walking over the edge. Before starting to climb, the three had sat on rocks at the bottom and made a thorough visual reconnaissance of the cliff, with naked eyes and with binoculars. Then they'd spent half an hour discussing and arguing over the easiest route up.

'Straight up from here,' Roger had said. 'There are lots of holds and belays because the rock has been split, and the corners are not rough.'

Lesley said, 'Some of those edges are sharp enough to cut into the rope. We'll have to watch that in belaying.'

Bill said, 'Another thing – the inner structure of the rock must have been affected by the dynamiting that's been going on for so long. We've got to make absolutely sure that a hold or a stance is really secure, and hasn't been loosened somewhere inside the face by blasting . . . Do you want to lead, Roger? This may be the easiest route, but it's not all *that* easy.'

'I'd rather you led, Dad. I can see the way up, but I know that I'm not very expert with the rope when I'm leading. You set a better pace, and choose better footholds than I do. I'll be number three if Lesley doesn't mind going in the middle.'

'That's my usual place,' she said. 'Suits me today, too . . . All right, let's rope up . . . Once we get up and down this route I think there's something more exciting out near the edge of the face, over there, and on that one, I'll lead.'

'Right you are.'

They roped up, thoroughly tested the knots, checked that boot-laces were tightly tied, turned up coat collars, saw that nothing was liable to fall out of their pockets, and started up the face.

Almost at once Bill found that there were going to be unexpected problems. First, the rock, though split by explosives and picks, thus creating sharp edges and well-defined surfaces for stances, was also liable to break off in small pieces when he put his weight on it. Secondly, those sharp edges grabbed at his clothes. And thirdly, though there were indeed plenty of stances created by the quarrying, they were mostly very small. At his third step up he found that the stance was a ledge about an inch wide, on which he could place no more than the edge of his boot sole . . . might be easier to go up this wearing gym shoes, which more and more people were doing . . . or using pitons . . . but neither were for him. He'd been taught to do it in nailed boots first, and never to destroy the texture of rock by hammering steel spikes into it: and he wasn't going to start now.

He went up smoothly for thirty feet, until he came to the place he had marked as the end of the first pitch, as it was the only place for another thirty feet where there was room for another climber on the stance. He called down, 'Come on up, Lesley!'

'Climbing,' she shouted, and started up. He could see by her face when she looked up to pick out the next hand or footholds that she too was finding it hard, and tricky. A sheen of sweat had begun to form on her upper lip, her face was paler than usual, and her knuckles were white with tension where he could see them when she took a grip above her shoulders.

'Over to your right a bit now,' he said quietly to her, for she was close. He eased up on the belay, leaving her just enough rope to make the sideways step. She stepped out, momentarily lost her footing, then came on up, stepping long with the other foot. Bill tightened the belay, holding her against the rock beside him.

'Slipped a bit there,' she said. 'Those footholds are damned small.'

'I know . . . There's no room for Roger here, I'll go on up . . . Loosen the belay a bit . . . Climbing!'

He went up another thirty feet, made a good belay by chocking a stone into a crack, and called down, 'Roger, are you ready?'

'Ready!'

'Take the first pitch, then.'

Roger came up faster and more gracefully than either Bill or Lesley had. He has a good natural balance, Bill thought with pride; he's strong as well as agile, and at least two sizes bigger than me, so my long stretches are short reaches for him. But he is still young, and inexperienced . . . that last foothold was badly chosen, for it crumbled even as he stepped off it. Now he was up with Lesley. Lesley called, 'Ready above?'

Bill checked his belay, coiled the live rope round his shoulder and chest, ready to pay out, and answered, 'Ready!'

'Climbing!'

He watched Lesley climb carefully, aware from the corner of his eye that Brenda's face was a whitish blur down behind, on the quarry floor. She had put down her book and was watching, too.

Lesley was ten feet below him now, coming straight up a short

216

vertical section of cliff, both hands with good grips at shoulder level, her left knee doubled, foot reaching out . . . The foothold under her right foot crumbled with an audible crack, all her weight came suddenly on her hands, and she fell, on the instant crying, 'Falling!' In the same instant Bill leaned back and tightened his grip on the rope. He had only given her a yard of spare rope while she was climbing, so when she had fallen that yard the jerk came on Bill's shoulder and chest. He was leaning back against the rock, heels dug in . . . for a moment he thought he was going . . . the rope would pay out about twenty feet, then the belay should hold, but he and Lesley would be dangling together close to Roger on the first stance . . . but how much damage would they sustain in falling?

The rope held. Bill's stance held. Lesley was pressed against the face fifteen feet below him, almost motionless. He called down, 'Any damage done, Lesley?'

'Wrist hurts a bit . . . cut face . . . hands . . . knees . . .'

'Can you get a foothold?'

'Yes . . . Hold on a sec . . . Take the strain now, Bill . . . Pull . . . Got it . . . let out . . . I'm on a good stance . . . Pheeew!'

'Come on up, when you're ready.'

She looked up at him, and he saw the scratches on her face. She said, 'Don't you think we'd better give up for today, Bill? I'm not going well at all.'

She's nervous, he thought, because of the fall. But she'll never regain her confidence if she doesn't overcome that lack of self-confidence now. It was a tricky climb, but not a suicidal one. He said, 'I think we should go on up, if you can.'

'I can,' she said shortly. 'Ready?'

'Wait till I check the belay . . . ready!'

'Climbing!'

She came up, faster this time, making no mistake and with no hesitation, moving to the left of the place where the rock had given way before. When she was beside him, Bill called, 'Ready, Roger?'

Roger looked up and Bill cried, 'You're bleeding! What happened?'

'That piece of rock that dislodged under Lesley fell on my face. I think my nose is broken. It's bleeding like blazes.'

Lesley said, 'We should go down, Bill, He's really hurt.'

Bill called, 'Can you climb, Roger? Test your hands and feet . . . make sure nothing's broken.'

Roger called, 'I'm all right, Dad. Ready above?'

Bill cried, 'See that your hands don't get slippery with blood . . . nor the rock. Ready here.'

'Climbing!'

Twenty minutes later they crawled out over the upper lip of the rock onto deep grass. Lesley at once began working on Roger's face with her handkerchief. Then she called down to Brenda, 'We're walking down round the edge, Brenda. Roger's got to have his face seen to.' She turned to Roger. 'Your nose is definitely broken.'

'I know . . . but we did it!'

'We did,' Lesley said. 'Now come on, and we'll find a doctor. I don't think there's any other serious damage, though your face is going to look a bit messed up in an hour or two's time.'

They were sitting in the saloon bar of the Foley Arms, a pleasant Claygate pub, near one o'clock. A good part of Roger's face was covered with bandages and what was visible was largely yellow-stained with iodine, but X-rays at a local doctor's had shown that no other bones were broken except the nose. There the doctor had elevated the nose and packed it with lint impregnated with ointment to prevent it sticking to the bloody tissue when it had to be removed. The boy was in considerable discomfort, his eyes half closed from the puffing up of the cheeks below, but he was managing to drink a pint of bitter, muttering, 'This is better, Dad. Two or three more of these and I won't feel any pain.'

Bill said, 'Two or three more of those and you'll be sick in the gutter. Twenty generations of British soldiers have proved that bitter makes you sick before it makes you drunk . . . It's time I called Morgan. Order some bread and cheese, onion and a pickle for me, please, darling.'

He went out to the telephone in its little booth in the hall and dialled Morgan Lloyd's number at the War Office, where he had said he would be working until at least four in the afternoon.

Morgan came on the line. 'General Lloyd . . . Ah, Bill. You're in Claygate, I presume, at the Foley Arms?'

'Yes, sir.'

'Finish your lunch and come on up at once. The German Army's on the move, in both directions, but mainly towards Poland. We're issuing the final mobilization order as soon as the chief has persuaded the Prime Minister to allow it.'

'All right, sir. I'll be with you in about three quarters of an hour unless the traffic gets bad.'

He hung up and returned to the little corner table where Lesley, Brenda and Roger sat. 'Food's on its way, Dad,' Roger said. 'You look serious.'

'The balloon has gone up,' Bill said. 'The final mobilization order will go out any moment. Drink up, and we'll take the food with us, to eat in the car.'

'Ugh, what a lot of crumbs,' Lesley said disdainfully. 'I'm going to have another gin and tonic, if we're going to war.'

'And another pint for me, Dad,' Roger pleaded.

'And a big lemonade for me,' Brenda said.

Bill hesitated. But what the hell, this was going to last a long time. What difference would five minutes make? Finally, 'All right,' he said. 'Another pint for me too . . . Miss!'

They were on the Kingston bypass, heading towards London at a good speed in light traffic. Roger, munching on a huge slice of bread and an almost equally thick slab of cheddar cheese, said, 'I'm going to join up, Dad.'

Brenda said, 'Me too, in the FANYs.'

Bill, at the wheel, stiffened. 'No, you're not, neither of you!' he snapped over his shoulder. 'You're barely seventeen, Roger, and, Brenda, you're only fifteen. They won't take either of you, and anyway I forbid you to try.'

Roger said seriously, speaking indistinctly because of his blocked nose, 'Look, Dad, it'll be over in a few weeks, and I want to be there. *You* joined up when you were sixteen.'

'I know, but it was a damned silly thing to do, and I only did it because I didn't want to go to grammar school or work in Dad's shop. You're at a good school, you're doing well, you have another year to go, and then you'll be able to go to university, or Sandhurst, if you prefer.'

'I don't want to go to university,' Roger said. 'I don't know what I want to do, except get out of school now, and . . .'

'Out of the house?' Lesley cut in. 'There's a bit of that, too, isn't there?'

'Yes,' Roger said grudgingly. 'It's not much fun living with Mummy and Paul, you know.'

Bill said unhappily, 'Roger, if you join up, it'll have to be as a private soldier, giving a false age. Your education, your background will be wasted. If you wait till you are eighteen or nineteen, you can go in as an officer, in the Wessex. You will serve the country much better, and not waste your education.'

'Two thousand pounds of education, drops to an old jezail,' Brenda quoted. 'Isn't there anything I can do, Daddy? I hate it at home, too.'

'You've got school to finish, too,' Bill said. 'And you're going to try for a scholarship to Girton, in maths. You'll get it, and go to Cambridge, and God knows what you might do there . . . Invent something that'll help win the war, perhaps. We're going to need brains as much as blood . . . and it's not going to be a short war . . . If you really want to, you can put off going to Girton, after you've got your scholarship, and spend some time in a women's service . . . Now, let's not talk any more about it. War is a serious business, not something to help you escape from a home that you're not quite happy in.'

After a long silence, as they were approaching Putney bridge, Roger said, 'I wonder how long it will be before I can play rugger again.'

'About four weeks,' Lesley said.

'I'll get out at the War House,' Bill said. 'You take them on home. Call your mother, Roger, and tell her what's happened.'

He came home near half past eleven, still dressed in climbing clothes, except that before leaving Claygate he had changed from his nailed climbing boots to ordinary walking shoes.

Lesley kissed him as he came in, then turned away, saying, 'Roger's gone to bed here with a couple of aspirins. He didn't want to eat anything but he drank a lot of tea. I hope he isn't worse than we or that doctor think.'

'Shock,' Bill said. 'He'll be all right in the morning. If he isn't,

220

we'll take him to hospital. They have better facilities for diagnosis. Is Brenda here, too?'

'No, I sent her back to Pauline. She didn't want to go, but I know that Pauline will feel very lonely in that flat with all this talk of war on the radio. Paul's off somewhere again, apparently.' She poured Bill a whisky and soda, then said, remaining standing as Bill sank into a chair, 'You were pretty military this morning, weren't you, in the quarry? Almost Nazi.'

'What do you mean?' Bill said defensively, but he knew what she meant, for he added at once, 'I didn't want to turn back. I wasn't in the mood.'

'I was, though . . . and poor Roger might have been in such a state that he'd fall and kill himself. Is that what you wanted?'

Bill took a big gulp of the whisky. 'Of course not . . . I can't explain it properly, Lesley, but there it is . . . I'm keyed up for war now. Have been for days, as it has become more and more inevitable. That quarry was like an enemy – a German quarry, to be beaten . . . I know that's not the right attitude for a climber, but today that *was* my attitude. I thought you needed to get your confidence back . . . Roger – I looked at him, and saw a strong young man with a minor wound, nothing even to go back to an RAP for.'

'He's your son,' she said, but more gently.

'So is every man I command,' he said vehemently, 'but I still have to send them to their deaths. Please, darling . . . don't talk about it any more. It won't happen again. I'll be in the real thing soon enough, not taking it out on my wife and son in a Surrey quarry.'

'I understand . . . Anything special happen at the office? It must be a madhouse there.'

'Sort of . . . Morgan is planning to make me a GSO1 – lieutenant colonel – at once. And he's thinking of sending me down to Aldershot to help the general there with mobilization. If I go, I'd be able to visit the actual battalions and regiments and see for myself exactly what snags and delays were developing. It's easier and quicker because I can just ring my G2 at the office, or talk to Morgan, instead of the units having to write letters up through channels.'

'You'd like that, of course,' Lesley said.

'Yes,' Bill said, adding quickly, 'Because it's the best way to do my

221

job. But I wouldn't be happy leaving you here to face the bombing . . . and there will be bombing.'

'I can take it,' she said briefly.

'Why don't you go down to Pennel Crecy? My mother can find a place for you to live, and you'll be safe there. It's a lovely part of the country.'

'I know. But I'll stay here. When will you go to Aldershot?'

He stood up and walked away from her down the long studio room, turning at the end to face her. 'I don't want to go to Aldershot . . . or stay in my office. I want to leave the job altogether . . . Morgan's been my mentor and guide all my military life, Lesley. I trust him and believe in his wisdom. Now he wants me to stay in those great rooms, pacing those marble halls, cerebrating, thinking, climbing the ladder in comfort . . . the time in Aldershot would only be a week or two, and wouldn't alter the basic fact that I would stay what I now am, a headquarters staff officer, a brass hat . . . living in comfort here with my wife, toddling home every evening to a nice whisky and soda . . .'

'And some bombs, you said.'

He ignored her interruption, and went on, 'Morgan's plan for me is very flattering, and very tempting, but . . . I can't accept it . . . because this time, for me, his plan is fundamentally wrong. I *can* do the work at the War Office, but it's not what I *should* be doing, not what I can do best. It isn't what I went to Spain for. It would be wrong. I'm a regular officer. I have twenty-two years of commissioned service, mostly with troops. Intelligent civilians can make high-level plans. They can learn the technical side of the business quickly – feed the right facts and probabilities into any first-class brain and it will give you solutions . . . but commanding troops in action is something else. The men who have been conscripted, and the millions more who will be, are brave enough, but bravery isn't sufficient. *We* have to know when to drive our men, and when to lead them . . . when to press on and when to pull back . . . when to spend them and when to conserve them . . . We have to keep guns, armour, infantry, aircraft, engineers, supplies, all in balance, like an expert juggler, in constantly changing situations. We have to train, and inspire, and protect . . . The best plans in the world won't work unless the troops carry them out . . . When war became inevitable, I felt some exhilaration. At last, I thought, after all the evasions and lies, the insults and the browbeating, we are facing up to what has to be done: fight evil, and beat it, for our own sakes, and for the world's. Then, when Morgan was talking to me, all that exhilaration drained away, evaporated. After all, I would sit at a desk, shuffling papers, noting what had gone wrong last time, suggesting what should be done next time . . . *thinking*, not doing. I felt utterly flat and miserable. Then I thought, I don't have to accept what Morgan is offering. I thought, I want to go back to the regiment, in whatever job they have for me. And at once, as soon as that thought had come to me and I'd spoken it to myself, exhilaration started to return. I felt my body becoming stronger and more supple, ready to face challenges, my mind working faster, more sharply.'

'My man of war,' she said. 'My war horse . . . He saith among the trumpets Ha ha; and he smelleth the battle afar off, the thunder of the captains, and the shouting.'

Bill said at last, 'It's true. I have made myself a soldier, but I think I was born a particular sort of soldier, or leader. I work best, and reach my best, in battle . . . I shall tell Morgan tomorrow that I want to be posted to a battalion of the regiment that's going to France . . . at once.'

'He'll understand . . . So shall I, when I stop feeling so miserable about it.'

He sat down beside her, put his arm round her and held her silently, while a tear ran down her cheek.

Lieutenant Colonel Richard Merton, Commanding Officer, 1st Battalion Queen's Own Wessex Rifles, kept him standing stiffly at attention after he had formally reported his arrival at the battalion's orderly room in Aldershot. 'Major Miller, reporting for duty as second-in-command, sir.'

Merton leaned back in his chair. 'I didn't ask for you, you know, Miller. I was happy with Tom Bagshaw, but then he was suddenly posted to a territorial battalion, presumably to make room for you. That was Morgan Lloyd's doing, eh?'

'I don't know, sir.'

'You didn't apply for posting here?'

'I asked General Lloyd to have me posted to any battalion of the regiment that was due to go on active service soon.'

Merton said, 'You made a mistake there. If you'd stayed at the War Office, you'd have been a full colonel in a year . . . There'd be no stopping you, with Morgan backing you as his blue-eyed boy.'

Bill said nothing. Merton sat forward again. 'You'll take over the funds, of course, as president of the Regimental Institutes. Otherwise I have nothing special for you.'

Bill said, 'Very good, sir,' saluted, turned, marched out and walked the short distance to his own office, as second-in-command, beyond the adjutant's. Merton meant to cut him out of doing effective work in the battalion, but he probably wouldn't be able to; there was simply too much to do, and it would need every man's hands and head, working all out, to be ready to go overseas by the target date of 18 September. The Prime Minister had declared on the 3rd, at noon, that Britain was already at war; and that day, before the speech on the radio was over, they'd heard the air-raid sirens wailing over London. Now here he was, with the 1st Battalion: he'd had a hard time persuading Morgan to let him go, and he must not allow Merton to negate all his efforts by not letting him do anything useful.

He drew a piece of paper towards him and began to make notes in pencil:

1. Find PRI clerk; check and take over accounts.
2. Get list of officers, warrant officers and sergeants with their dates of promotion and present jobs.
3. Make ways to see all the above at their jobs, and make estimates of their capacities and possibilities.
4. Read the mobilization plan and check on progress daily.

He paused, pencil poised. Merton would come a cropper if he tried to work without a second-in-command . . . well, wasn't that what he hoped for? In his heart of hearts, yes, damn it, he had to admit it; but Merton was his CO and a brother officer of the regiment. He must find ways to take the strain off him, for the sake of the men, if for no other reason.

There was a knock on the outer door and a small sharp-faced soldier with lance corporal's stripes on his sleeve came in, halted and saluted. 'Lance Corporal Gibson, sir,' he said. 'PRI's clerk.'

224

'Ah,' Bill said, 'just the man I was going to send fo . . . How much service do you have?'

'Six years, sir, all with the 1st Battalion.'

'What were you before you joined up? You look about thirty . . . must have had some sort of a job.'

'Bookkeeper in a bootlace factory, down Deptford way, sir.'

'Good,' Bill said. 'Accounts are not my strong suit. Are the books in order?'

'Yes, sir. Major Bagshaw was very particular about them.'

That's probably true, Bill thought. He hadn't served with old Baggie for donkey's years, but he'd always been a very careful and conscientious officer, with no imagination whatever, and no tactical skill. Aloud, he said, 'All right, bring them along and we'll go through them, count the cash, check out the bank books, everything.'

'Very good, sir.'

Gibson slipped out, returning in five minutes with a pile of heavy tomes, which he carefully set down on the side table. They began to work, and an hour later Bill signed the formal papers that he had inspected, balanced the books, counted the cash, confirmed the bank balances, found all in order, and was from this time and date officially taking over the duties of PRI.

Corporal Gibson left, staggering under the books, and another knock came at the door. 'Come!' Bill called.

A familiar figure marched in, web belt perfectly green-blancoed, boots shining black like polished ebony – Bogey Harris, wearing on his right sleeve the embroidered crown of a warrant officer class II, a company sergeant major. He saluted punctiliously as Bill jumped up and came round the table to shake his hand.

'By God, I'm glad to see you, Bogey!' Bill exclaimed. 'I knew you were on the 1st Battalion's strength, but I thought you might have been sent off to the territorials, or command headquarters, or the small-arms school, or somewhere.'

'Came home from the Shiny in '37, sir,' Harris said. 'Done my time overseas, and more, by then . . . the wife was fed up with it, and it was about time the kids learned that everyone in the world wasn't going to call 'em "sahib".'

'What are you now?'

'CSM, B Company, sir. And you're the second-in-command, the *bat* is.'

'Quite right. I feel a bit lost. It's a long time since I served with the 1st Battalion, and practically everyone I knew has left.'

'Mind if I make a suggestion, sir?'

'Of course not, Bogey. Go ahead.'

'You know the Black Boy pub, in Frimley?'

'Barely, but I know where it is.'

'They have a private upstairs room. Suppose we meet there at eight tonight, sir, after we've eaten our suppers . . . Go in the back way and straight upstairs, and it's the door on your left marked "Private". I'll call the owner – it's a free house and he's a good man, knows how to keep his mouth shut . . . was RSM in the 60th.'

'I'll be there.'

They sat in the little room facing each other across a narrow table under an electric light hanging in an olde-worlde iron cage, pint glasses of beer beside them. Harris said, 'I know this isn't regimental, sir, a warrant officer talking about other officers to the second-in-command, but there's things you need to know, and I reckon Colonel Merton isn't going to tell you.'

'I reckon the same thing,' Bill said grimly. 'Go ahead.'

Harris produced some sheets of paper and put them on the table. He said, 'This is a list of officers, warrant officers and sergeants now with the battalion. Someone gets to be hauled off for ERE every day, so I can't guarantee that everyone on the list will always be here . . . but there they are, with their jobs.'

He started to go down the list. 'Colonel Merton, I don't need to say anything about him.'

'No,' Bill said.

'A Company's got Major Hodge as company commander, Captain Tunning as second-in-command. The platoon commanders are Lieutenant Barnett, Lieutenant Harrington, Second Lieutenant Larson and PSM Davies; the CSM is Goddard, the CQMS is Roberts; and the platoon sergeants are Mabey, Young, Templeman and O'Donnell. Major Hodge is . . .'

'I know him. He was in the 2nd Battalion in Lucknow back in '29 and '30.'

'Yes, sir. Captain Tunning's a good officer, but lazy. If he can pass any job on to the CSM or CQMS, he does. He isn't popular with the men, either – I don't know why. I think they feel that he doesn't really know them or care about them . . . Mr Barnett's a very conscientious officer, and very strict. He was going to take the Staff College exam next year, but I doubt if he'll pass it . . . Mr Harrington is over thirty but he's not married and the men think he's a pouf . . . walks a bit effeminate, waves his hand about. He may be brave enough when the bullets begin to fly, but he'll have to prove it. The men call him the Puffball . . . Mr Larson's the best in the company, very good at football, keen, cares about the men, raises a stink if there's anything wrong with their food in the cookhouses, never puts a man on a charge if he can help it, but gives him hell privately. His platoon's the best in the battalion . . . PSM Davies, well, he's an ex-sergeant from the Oxf and Bucks and he's doing an officer's job, but he's not a real officer. The men don't like these platoon sergeant majors, though they've nothing against Davies. Of course he's an older man, married with two kids . . . Goddard is . . .'

'I know him. He was in my platoon in France, and later in Aldershot and Dover.'

'Yes, sir, of course. CQMS Roberts is a good CQMS, but that's about all. He'll never make CSM let alone anything higher. He's fat and out of training and just wants a cushy berth till he retires . . . Mabey's young and good . . . Young isn't – he's old and careful . . . he was with us at Dalzai and he was very careful of his own skin then, and I don't suppose he's changed . . . Templeman's a flyer, only about four years' service and thinks he's going to be a PSM and next a field marshal . . . might be right, too . . . O'Donnell's a twenty-year man, joined us just after the war, and has only just been made sergeant to fill vacancies created by all the men we've had to send off to ERE . . .'

Bill, who had been assiduously making notes, took a deep swig of his beer and said, 'This is very helpful to me, Bogey. I could eventually find it all out for myself, if there's time. But there may not be . . . probably won't be.'

'No, sir. All right, B Company now . . . Captain Stokes, Lieutenant Graham, Lieutenant Gooley, Second Lieutenant Blake, PSM Saul, PSM Quinn; the CSM is me, CQMS is Pruett; platoon sergeants –

227

Parker, Morrow, Lynn, Enloe . . . Captain Stokes is a bitter man. He thinks he ought to have got a brevet majority five years ago and he didn't. He thinks he ought to have been nominated to the Staff College but he wasn't. He thinks he could have married better than he did, socially speaking, that is, sir . . . He needs prodding all the time, or he'll dig in his toes and obstruct as much as he can. He's careful not to do anything actually insubordinate, though. I have a hard time with him, I can tell you. He won't be a good company commander in the field, in my opinion. Mr Graham is . . .'

The evening wore on, past closing time.

Merton was a harassed man, and in a bad temper. The daily mobilization-progress conference had just ended and all the other officers and warrant officer attending had left, except Bill and Merton himself. Merton said, 'These deficiencies are intolerable! The bloody War Office knew what Aldershot Command consists of, they knew the divisions here would be top priority for going overseas, so what the hell is the excuse for not having the 3-inch mortars to make us up to War Establishment? Or the carriers? The greatcoats for reservists, even?'

Bill said nothing. Merton glowered at him. 'You've been in the War Office. You fellows didn't do a very good job, from Morgan Lloyd on down . . . I've got a job for you. There is apparently no hope of getting the 15-hundredweight trucks we were entitled to. They've been given to the Nigerian Army, or the Burma Police, or something. Anyway, they aren't here and they aren't going to be. A commandeering expedition has been authorized, and GHQ have ordered us to find an officer of field rank to lead it. I'm choosing you. You'll have an Ordnance Corps warrant officer, and two RASC officers to help you, but you're in command and responsible. They'll give you your orders at GHQ as soon as you can get there, but I can tell you that in essence you have to find and commandeer, anywhere in England, four light vehicles for every battalion in the BEF . . . about two hundred small trucks, vans, anything that can be made to do the job. That's all.'

Outside, Bill drew a deep breath . . . sounded like a pirate expedition to him. Better make sure that the documents authorizing him to seize the vehicles were in order . . . and better take an ex-second-hand-car dealer along, to tell him what vehicles were duds, and what others were fairly worth, so that no one was robbed, neither the owners nor the government.

Three weeks later, it was raining in Brest as the 1st Battalion of the Queen's Own Wessex Rifles disembarked onto French soil. Guides had come aboard as soon as the gangways were down, to tell the OC Troops where each unit was going, and to lead it there, the men marching, the vehicles going only with what was already loaded in them. Standing near one of the bollards round which the mooring ropes were looped, his Burberry well buttoned up, his collar turned up against the rain, Bill thought, *see the conquering heroes come* . . . Half a dozen French dock workers were sheltering behind a shed, smoking Caporals. The battalion was forming up without its band, which had been put in another ship at the last moment. Colonel Merton shouted a command, followed by the company commanders. RSM Barrow strutted up and down, his pace stick under his arm, his steel helmet gleaming wet but set just so on his head.

The battalion moved off at a brisk pace. Near the dock gates the little column of vehicles began to pass them. Two military 15-hundredweight trucks led, followed by two 3-tonners, correctly green-painted. Then came a small van, marked PENGUIN LAUNDRY, 41 Archway, Southampton; behind that another van, black-painted and chastely lettered in gold LUNLEY & FEARSTONE, Undertakers, 228 Barton Road, Birmingham; there followed a butcher's van from Coventry, a small passenger bus from an old people's home in Oxford, a Ford estate wagon from DUNEMORE ESTATES, Carlisle. Bill knew every one of them, and at what cost in blood and sweat, tears and money it had taken to wring them from their owners. They were his contribution to the mobilization of the British Expeditionary Force, and he was proud of them, but . . .

A French navvy near the gate, watching the convoy pass, muttered, '*Mon Dieu!*' and spat accurately into the gutter. I agree with you, Bill thought, but . . . when the time comes we'll fight. You'll see.

16

October 1939: France

The commander-in-chief of the British Expeditionary Force, General the Viscount Gort, VC, was inspecting the battalion in its billets in the village of Escobecques, just south-west of the great industrial city of Lille. The soldiers liked Escobecques, for their billets were comfortable, often in quite modern houses – or, if not, then in large tightly roofed barns, still redolent with the smell of cows. Only a couple of miles to the north-west was Armentières; and the men seemed to keep themselves happy singing, over and over again, various scurrilous verses of '*Mademoiselle from Armentières*', as if they'd actually found such a lady – which few did.

The C-in-C's GHQ, when warning the battalion of the inspection, had said that the general didn't want to see any spit and polish, just the men in field-service marching order, by companies. Later, he might direct some simple manoeuvres to be carried out, but they would not be tactical – that would come after there had been more time for individual training in the fundamentals. It was mid-October, and for a marvel not raining. Autumn colours painted the woods south of Escobecques soft umber and russet; and the pall of smoke that always hung over Lille seemed to have taken on a little of the same colours.

Bill walked at the general's side as he inspected, for Richard Merton was in bed with flu, furious to miss this opportunity of letting the C-in-C at least know who he was. Gort walked slowly, his peaked general's cap slightly tilted, his steel helmet hooked to his right shoulder by the chin strap having been passed through the epaulettes bearing the bronzed badges of his rank: a crown above a star above a crossed sword and baton.

Gort turned now to Captain Stokes, the company commander of the troops he was inspecting, walking at his other side, and said, 'These men are carrying their steel helmets on their left shoulders. Why?'

'Battalion standing orders for inspection, sir,' Stokes answered.

'Why is that better than the right shoulder?'

'I don't know, sir,' Stokes said.

Bill cut in, 'The ceremonial position for the rifle, when marching, sir, is the trail, in the right hand. It would make a man look and feel rather overbalanced to the right side if his steel helmet was on that shoulder.'

'Of course . . . you're a rifle regiment,' Gort said. 'We carry the steel helmet on the right shoulder in the Guards . . . ah, because the ceremonial slope arms position is on the left shoulder, eh?'

'I suppose so, sir.'

Gort continued his inspection, soon stopping in front of a large rifleman a little farther down the front rank of B Company. 'Take off your pack,' he said, 'and let's have a look at the contents.'

The soldier addressed slipped out of his heavy pack, put it on the ground, knelt, opened it, and began to spread out the contents. The commander-in-chief enumerated each item aloud as it came to light: 'Spare shirt . . . spare socks, one pair . . . spare socks, second pair . . . housewife. Open it up, and let's see what you have inside . . . needle, khaki thread, thimble, cloth patches, buttons . . . eight, but none of those buttons will fit your battle-dress blouse. What will you do if you lose one of those, eh?'

The soldier said nothing, overawed by the red hat and the rows of bright medal ribbons. The C-in-C turned to Stokes. 'Eh, what *does* he do?'

Stokes said, 'He should have two or three blouse buttons, sir.'

Bill said, 'The buttons are often allotted among a section, sir, so that one man has more fly buttons and another more blouse buttons; then they can share out when necessary.'

'I see,' Gort said. 'But what if the men of the section are separated?'

Bill said nothing, thinking, the men of a section should never be separated and if they are an isolated man can live without a bloody blouse button for an hour or two.

The inspection wore on. Lord Gort looked at waterbottles and pack straps, and counted hobnails under soldiers' boots; he took half a dozen rifles from soldiers' hands, extracted the bolts and inspected the barrels. He counted the rounds in Bren gun magazines and tested the batteries of signal lamps. After inspecting two companies and ordering some simple arms drill he headed for his waiting staff car, Bill at his side, while Gort's ADC, following a few steps behind, talked to the adjutant of the battalion. At the car Gort turned, his hand out. 'A good inspection, Miller . . . Where did you get your DSO?'

'North-west Frontier of India, sir . . . 1932.'

'Ah . . . I remember reading about it . . . A few things need tightening up, but I'm pleased with what I saw. It's the little details that matter in battle, Miller.'

'Yes, sir.' The general didn't seem to be in any hurry and Bill steeled himself. 'Sir, our tactical training is being hampered because we don't know what our first tasks are going to be. Can you tell us anything about that?'

'Plans keep changing,' Gort said. 'We're under the French, as you know. General Gamelin makes the plans for us, and we carry them out . . . unless I think the BEF is being endangered.'

'Yes, sir . . . It would help us enormously – give a purpose to our training – if we could know whether we are going to move forward to attack Germany or hold a defensive line. We'd like to rehearse the first move – at least.'

'Can't do that . . . spies everywhere. They'd see what you were doing and that would give the game away. They'd know what we were going to do when the balloon goes up.'

'About that, sir . . . Is there any reason we can give to the men as to why we aren't attacking now, while the Germans are still occupied in Poland? Though their main forces are already coming back westward to our front, the intelligence reports say.'

'It's up to the French, Miller,' Gort said, at last showing some testiness. 'We don't have a separate BEF plan, we're part of the overall plan . . . And don't you worry your head about things like that. See that every little detail works, and then when the orders come, you can go forward or back, or stay and dig, or whatever is ordered, without a hitch.' He stepped back and into his car, followed by his ADC, as Bill and the Wessex adjutant saluted, holding the position until the green staff car flying the Union Jack from the radiator cap had gone twenty yards down the road.

Bill lowered his arm, followed by the adjutant, Lieutenant Tom Slater, a tall immaculate young man of eight years' service, a most eligible bachelor wearing the most beautiful pair of field boots in the BEF. Slater said, smiling, 'I'm glad he didn't inspect Rifleman

232

Burdock's pack, in C Company, sir.'

'Why?'

'He always has a pair of white mice who live in his pack when he's in field-service marching order. He never leaves them in his barrack room or billet.'

'We ought to be attacking the bloody Germans,' Bill said, fiercely. 'We ought to have *been* attacking them since 1 September . . . now we've lost six weeks, and they've wiped out a dangerous threat to their rear. I don't understand it, I just don't understand it . . . Tell the company commanders to stand down, the rest of the day free for all ranks, but usual restriction as to movement. I have to tell the CO how it went.'

Slater saluted smartly as Bill headed for Merton's billet in the mayor's house. He found Merton sitting up in bed, a book beside him, staring out of the window. He looked up as Bill entered. 'How did it go?'

'Very well, sir. I gave the C-in-C your apologies and he agreed that it wasn't worth your while risking pneumonia just to make an appearance, or his to risk getting flu from you. We'll have real work on our hands soon, and we must be fit for it, he said. But I couldn't get any inkling from him of what the work is going to be.'

'You asked him about the plans?' Merton said sharply.

'Yes, sir. I told him we could make our tactical exercises much more realistic, and more valuable, if we knew what we were going to be called on to do. He said in effect that he didn't know, that the French were making the plans.'

'You'd have done better using what time he could spare to remind him that we want to make a sports field here,' Merton said, 'and we need money to do it.'

Bill said, 'I thought it was more important to get at least enough information so that we can practise specific moves . . . but he didn't give me any real answers. I asked him why we hadn't attacked while the Huns were busy in Poland. He didn't give me an answer.'

Merton said, 'Our concern is the battalion, Miller. These matters of high strategy that you are poking your nose into are the concerns of the Prime Minister and the French high command.'

Bill said, 'Yes, sir,' saluted and left.

* * *

A week later Merton was addressing all the officers, warrant officers and sergeants in the battalion, an assemblage of about eighty men, gathered in the Escobecques school on a Sunday morning late in October. He started genially, 'I'm sorry to disturb your Sunday morning kip, but we can't use the school on weekdays because it's full of children, and so . . . The commander-in-chief knows war. His 1914-18 war record is almost unequalled in the army. I'm stressing this because some of us are apt to feel that senior officers are too old and out of touch to know anything. We talk, or at least think in our hearts, that their experience was in the Crimea –' There was some tittering in the room, which Merton had obviously expected, since he paused a moment, then continued: 'But Lord Gort is not that old, and he has recent experience of the last major war, at the front. When he speaks we must listen carefully, not only because he is the commander-in-chief, but because he speaks with the authority of experience. And Lord Gort has stressed, personally and in general orders, that the key to victory is individual training . . . Until next February – if nothing happens by then – we shall do one tactical exercise a week, at company level. The rest of the time we shall devote to individual training. Every man will fire a small-arms course, and companies will repeat the course until we achieve eighty per cent first-class shots and marksmen, combined. A rifle range is being constructed five miles back down the road. It will only be four hundred yards, but I don't think we'll do much shooting beyond that range. In the last war, once we settled into the trenches, we were shooting mostly at about eighty yards . . . We shall throw grenades, every man in the battalion, of whatever rank and whatever position, until he can land eighty per cent inside a five-foot-radius circle from twenty yards. Officers will carry out pistol practice to the same standards as the men. Bren gunners will concentrate on fleeting targets during their range practices, and also on achieving a first-class rating for every man of the team. If not, company commanders will change the teams. I also want every man of the Bren teams to be able to take the gun down and put it together again, in darkness, in thirty seconds – and change barrels in five seconds. There must be intensive practice of clearing stoppages of all kinds, with every member of the team, and practice in loading Bren magazines in the dark . . . All rifles will be inspected by the armourer sergeant within the next two weeks, and we will then get rid of any rifles that are cord-worn or corroded. After *that*, any man who develops corrosion or cord wear in his rifle will be put on a charge . . . We will get fit . . . running every morning, by platoons or companies, starting with a mile in seven minutes, building up to ten miles, once a week, in eighty minutes . . . Vehicles and drivers: intensive practice in repairing flat tyres and dealing with every kind of mechanical failure. The carriers are not to be run more than five miles a week, to conserve tread mileage, but they are to be kept in perfect mechanical condition . . . Everyone I haven't mentioned specifically – signallers, clerks, armourers, medical, 3-inch and 2-inch mortar crews, are to make themselves, as individuals, thoroughly efficient and proficient in their jobs. Then, when the time comes that we have to act, everything will automatically function perfectly. Any question?'

The commander of the headquarters company, Captain Griffin, stood up. 'Sir, are these morning runs to be done in PT dress?'

'No,' Merton said. 'We don't fight in PT dress, so we won't train in it, and in a week or two it would be too cold, too. Fighting order, with weapons, of course.'

'Thank you, sir,' Griffin said, and sat down.

Bill had a host of questions, but this public auditorium was not the place to ask them. Here it was his job to support Merton.

Merton said, 'Church parade is in . . . half an hour, in the market-place, remember. Let's hope, when the balloon goes up, that the padre has done *his* individual training, too.' Amid a roar of laughter he said, 'Dismiss!' and walked out.

Bill followed him and fell in step beside him, saying, 'I think the daily runs are a great idea, sir. I'll see that no one escapes, however important he thinks it is that he be doing something else at that time . . . and there will be plenty of that opinion.'

'But you don't agree with the rest of the programme?' Merton said.

Bill said, 'I think that individual training is vital, sir, every part of it . . . weapons proficiency, vehicle maintenance, everything. But I suggest that after a month or so of basic training you might consider putting in more, and large-scale, tactical exercises. I'd like to see the battalion, and later the whole division, practise a move to start at, say, 4 a.m. with RASC vehicles provided, and the orders not reaching us until, say, 2.00 a.m. . . . There'd be chaos, I think, because however well the drivers actually drive it takes practice organizing them into big convoys, by night.'

'Too much chaos,' Merton said. 'We'd learn nothing.'

'I think we would, sir . . . and then we'd do another, and another, learning more each time, until we could do it perfectly.'

'We have been forbidden to practise specific moves,' Merton said, 'owing to the danger of giving away our plan.'

'But there isn't a real plan yet, sir, as far as I know, so how can we give it away?'

'There's a plan,' Merton said shortly. 'I've been told and I was told to tell you. I've been waiting, as the fewer people know the better, in my opinion, but I'll tell you now. The BEF will make no move, nor will the French, until the Germans attack, and invade Belgium or Holland. Then we, the BEF, move forward into Belgium. Our division's allotted task is to hold the Dyle east of Brussels, at Baardewijk. The Belgians won't permit any sort of reconnaissance in Belgium.'

Bill said heatedly, 'So we're letting the Germans attack in their own good time, and meantime we must refrain from any action that might upset Mr Hitler. It's a . . . it's a damned disgrace!'

'Perhaps,' Merton said, 'but those are the orders. They're called Plan F and sooner or later we'll all get them, in full detail, in writing.'

It took Bill a week of agonizing to decide that he must disobey the orders and make a personal reconnaissance of the area in which the division, and the battalion as part of it, was going to have to fight. As a first step, he applied for, and obtained, five days' leave to cover the Christmas period. Then he set to work on the other necessary preparations. On various visits to Lille he amassed a sufficient amount of Belgian currency, mostly in small denominations. He also bought some second-hand clothing, sturdy, well used but not decrepit enough for the wearer to be instantly labelled a tramp. It had taken longer to acquire and conceal a bicycle in Béthune, a few miles to the west, but it had been done; and by diligent work in the evenings, he also acquired enough basic French to be able to order food, drink or lodging, and to ask his way, though he intended to do that as little as possible, as it invited attention to himself. He acquired Michelin road maps of the part of Belgium which interested him, but did not intend to take them with him, instead studying the maps close and long, until he knew the general lie of the land, and the names of at least all small towns by heart. He would carry no notebook or pencil, make no notes and draw no sketches, but commit everything to memory. He felt that it was worth taking the obvious risks in order to see the ground and bring back a comprehensive picture of it; it was not worth the much greater risk of carrying anything that would link him with the military of any country.

One item he tried to but could not obtain was a Belgian identity card. British intelligence would have provided him with an expertly forged one if he could have asked them for it – but he could not. He had toyed with the idea of buying one through the underworld of Lille, which probably would not have been difficult, once he had penetrated that underworld; but the dangers were too great, and in the end he had decided, with Nelson, that 'something must be left to chance'. So, having set out on leave early on 21 December – to visit his family in England, but liable to recall at a moment's notice – he actually left by train for Béthune, picked up his bicycle, changed his clothing, leaving his British uniform in a small suitcase at the pawnshop where he had bought the bike, and next day crossed the frontier into Belgium on a deserted country lane, by then muddy with the winter rains, near Clachorre, east of Dunkirk, and pedalled steadily eastwards, intending to pass to the north of Brussels and so to the river Dyle and Baardewijk.

This day, he decided to get an identity card. As far as accommodation for the night went, he could sleep out in barns and root clamps; but if he was seen the farmer might call the police; also, it would be extremely cold and damp; and it would make him look progressively more villainous in appearance. But to get accommodation in a house or inn he'd have to show an ID. So, from about eleven o'clock in the morning he began to examine each tavern he passed, looking for signs of pre-Christmas merriment and the presence of a large number of parked bicycles, which would show that the tavern was full of people celebrating in the usual manner . . . drinking . . . and getting drunk.

Close to noon, he found what he was looking for – a large brick-built tavern, its concrete yard filled to overflowing with parked and stacked bicycles. He rode in, dismounted, parked his own at the end of the row near the side entrance to the tavern, and went in.

It was full, the air dense blue with tobacco smoke, and loud with the voices of the seventy or eighty men, and a few women, all drinking beer and schnapps. They seemed to be speaking both of Belgium's main languages, French and Flemish; and they were, as far as he could see, again almost equally divided between farmers and farm labourers and factory workers; for the little town, with its mean main street now darkening under steady sleet, stood on the divide between city and country – the green northern fields full of black and white cows, to the south factory chimneys and the pall of smoke that blanketed Brussels.

Bill edged to the bar through the dense crowd, and signalled by pointing to a beer engine and with his hands indicating a large glass. The blowsy overworked barmaid hardly looked at him as she drew the beer, meanwhile continuing her conversation with another man, and held out her hand for his money. He paid, pocketed the change, withdrew to a bench near the middle of the room, and buried his face in the beer. No one took any notice of him, the stranger; they were all busy telling stories, recounting local gossip, smacking each other on the back in the recalling of old jokes, of other occasions such as this.

There was a drunk, leaning on the end of the bar, but he was very small, almost a dwarf, and quite bald . . . his ID wouldn't do . . . There was another, sagging by the side door . . . he'd do . . . damn it, he had staggered out, and over the noise inside Bill heard the retching and groaning as the man vomited just outside the door . . . Too late . . . There was another . . . about the right height, clean-shaven, nondescript sort of face, build near enough . . . he was almost falling off the bench on which he sat, against the wall by the rear door. Signs there in French and Flemish indicated that the door led to the toilet. Bill waited, ready to move. The man he was watching staggered to the bar, replenished his huge tankard and staggered back, spilling nearly a quarter of the beer on the floor. Bill drank more slowly, but half an hour later he felt he must refill, so went to the bar and repeated his order.

When he turned to come back, the man had gone. A momentary panic took possession of Bill. Where the hell had he gone? To inform the police?

He got a grip on himself. The man had gone to the toilet. He must act at once or it would be too late. He put down his glass on the table where he had been sitting and walked through the back door, his collar turned up, his head down, moving a little unsteadily.

The only light in the toilet was a naked 25-watt bulb hanging from the low ceiling. To the left, a bare wall with a gutter below was the men's pissoir. On the right, two raised porcelain footrests and a hole marked the squatter sort of WC with which Bill had first become familiar in France over twenty years earlier. His quarry was leaning against the left wall, presumably pissing, but there was no sound . . . Christ, he was too drunk to undo his flies, and was pissing in his trousers. He had to move fast. He went up to the man and shook his shoulder. The man turned, still pissing, and mumbled, 'Eh? Wa . . .?' Bill hit him hard on the point of the jaw, and he fell sideways, sliding at last to the floor with his head just out of the gutter. Bill dragged him back a pace, then started on his pockets . . . nothing in the jacket left, jacket right . . . jacket inside . . . here it was! He held it up to the light: Belgian identity card . . . name of man Pieter Welloudt . . . so, Flemish. He put the card in his pocket and walked out, through the bar, out of the side door, and mounted his bicycle. As far as he knew, no one had observed him leave. The sleet changed to wet snow as he pedalled east.

The grubby little town was called Ramderzeel. There was a factory, several taverns, a mine, and some slummy back streets behind the main road through the middle which led on to Baardewijk and the Dyle, five miles ahead. In those back slums, as Bill had hoped, he found a meanlooking house with a sign in a lower window, CHAMBRE, and, with no more than a perfunctory showing of his identity card, he had taken the room for three nights. The owner looked more afraid that Bill would ask him embarrassing questions than the other way round, and in any case was only interested in the money. So Bill wheeled his bicycle into the tiny back yard, went to his room and napped for an hour. Then he went out, found another crowded tavern, and, waiting till he saw someone order a plate of sausage, pointed to it and mumbled, '*Même chose . . . et bière.*' He ought to be speaking Flemish with a name like Welloudt, but no one was going to ask him his name, and if the worst came to the worst he was prepared to act dumb. He did not intend that anyone should ever find out that he was a British officer.

In the night it snowed a little more, then rain washed most of it away by morning, when Bill got up, had bread and coffee in a café and, mounting his bicycle, set out for the Dyle. By now he was right in the middle of Belgium, far from the frontiers and so less likely to be stopped by random roadblocks or roving police. Soldiers were about, falling in for parade behind tall iron railings on a large parade ground . . . infantry, they were . . . with some field guns parked at the farther end of the parade ground, and what looked like four mobile heavy anti-aircraft guns. He could not be sure, for the guns were covered by green tarpaulins, but they definitely had long barrels and were too big for any anti-tank gun that he knew of, though these could probably be used in both roles, like the German 88 mm he had read a lot about . . .

At last he came to the lip of the valley in which flowed the Dyle, at a small village called Woesten, two miles north of Baardewijk. The land sloped gently down to the river a mile ahead, but there was no equally high ground to right or left. Woesten was at the high point. He made a mental note that it offered excellent artillery observation over the Dyle valley to the north, and also over Baardewijk to the south and beyond. Woesten must be strongly held.

He looked up and down, saw no one, dismounted and wheeled his bike into a field and behind a hedge. Then, sitting at the foot of the hedge, and so out of sight from the road a few yards off, he began to make a systematic study of the valley.

Close to his left the road – wide, two-lane, tarmac – ran down to a bridge over the Dyle . . . probably 30-ton capacity, so usable by tanks. The Dyle itself, about thirty yards wide, might be fordable in very dry weather in some spots – not now, though, or for some time to come. It was conceivable that a hard frost would make ice thick enough for a crossing by infantry certainly, and perhaps guns and tanks. The tank treads spread their weight over a large area and a tank could cross ice which would not support a field gun of much less weight . . . Then, going south, there was a country lane, and another, smaller bridge for it over the Dyle a mile down, halfway to Baardewijk. The tall buildings of the town hid whatever other bridges might be there, but that would be a separate problem, because the fighting would be at close range, from house to house, and the Germans could move bridging material up very close and make a sudden assault by night or under cover of smoke, from just over the river; whereas any bridging attack would have to start from at least a mile back. Baardewijk, therefore, was important not only for itself but because it would be the easiest place for the Germans to attempt to establish a major bridgehead over the Dyle.

A railway line ran along the near bank of the Dyle, mostly level, but very steep-sided at one place in a deepish cutting, and in another on an embankment as it climbed, past Baardewijk, out of the valley up onto this western escarpment. Tanks would avoid both the cutting and the embankment. Baardewijk itself was a defile, but the Germans probably would not try to avoid it, if only for its bridges . . . Reverse slope positions . . . none here. Farther south it looked as though there was a rise of land close to the river, soon dropping again. He'd look at that tomorrow. The town itself – now . . . Something on the near side of the Dyle caught his eye and he stayed motionless, hard to see in his grey-brown clothes, his hat pulled down over his forehead, sitting against the grey-brown hedge. Down there, a man was walking in the meadow beyond the railway line. He was wearing a raincoat and a grey felt hat. He was looking at . . . Bill couldn't see what he was looking at, but he wasn't just striding along, going from one place to another. Perhaps he was looking at the soil . . . or at fish . . . or at the river to see – what? Whether the banks would support an assault bridge? Whether the water was deep enough for pontoons? Bill couldn't tell. But he thought he was looking at another spy. Whose?

He did not move until the man in the raincoat had vanished among the houses of Baardewijk, then stood up, took his bicycle and pedalled into the town. What he needed to know he could see from the saddle, so he set off, cycling slowly across one bridge, south behind the riverfront buildings, back over the next bridge, south again on the first street he came to; back over the next bridge . . .

By three in the afternoon he had a very clear picture of Baardewijk in his head. It contained five bridges over the Dyle, of which two were footbridges and would not take any vehicle larger than a motor-bike. One was old and made of wood and would not take tanks or heavy lorries; the other two were strong, steel, modern, probably

241

class 40, so would take any existing tank or other vehicle. There was also a railway bridge, for a single line . . . that could be planked and used by trucks and tanks.

So much he had learned; but twice he had run into the man in the raincoat – once on a bridge, once at a café where he was eating stewed beef near one o'clock. The man had glanced at him, the second time, then away, bending over his plate, but for a moment their eyes had met and locked. Bill was certain now that the man was a spy, a German. And he was certain that the other knew that *he* was a spy, but probably not that he was British.

Bill did not allow himself to try to sleep until after one in the morning, sitting in his room in the dark, running over and over in his mind everything that he had seen, everything that he had deduced, now placing them in mnemonic order, so that each word or phrase would lead on to the next when the time came for him to pass on the results of his reconnaissance.

In the morning, Christmas Eve, he was up before seven, to more snow, and did not know whether to curse or be glad, for, while the snow would protect him in his comings and goings, it would also shorten his views and limit his perspectives. Today he intended to concentrate on the back areas of the division, looking for suitable sites for gun areas, supply points, ammunition points, headquarters, perhaps a casualty clearing station, but that would most likely be sited farther to the rear, beyond the reach of enemy artillery. Then tomorrow, with a thorough picture in his mind of Baardewijk and the Dyle valley over an area some ten miles wide by ten miles deep, he would make a careful check of the Dyle itself, examining its advantages and disadvantages as a defensive work, as a bridging task, as an obstacle or defile.

Light snow continued all day, but the temperature stayed close above freezing so that it did not lie where there was any surface heat or heat from the hidden sun, as on tarmac roads; and there was no more than four inches in the fields by the time he returned to the rooming house in Ramderzeel in the early dark of four o'clock. He had eaten in Baardewijk, but he had not seen the man in the raincoat.

Now again he sat late in his room, till midnight, adding the new information to the old, correlating it all in his mind: fields of fire for machine-guns, good mortar sites, tank approaches, anti-tank minefield sites, observation posts . . .

On Christmas Day, again he was up by seven, and on his way by eight, on a day of dull low clouds, sunless, snow threatening but not falling, yesterday's snow now dirtied by the passage of boots and hooves and tyres and the fall of soot and ash from factory and train and household fireplace.

At the Dyle, he hid his bicycle under the road bridge and walked back on footpaths and narrow lanes, some gravelled for bicycle traffic, towards Baardewijk, all the time carefully examining this left bank of the river. That took two hours; then he went through the town at a brisk pace and on two hours more to the south, then crossed over in the next village and came back down the west, right, bank, past Baardewijk (which occupied both banks). There he ate and drank, and spent another hour in the tavern collecting his thoughts. Then out again into the cold snow flurries, mixed with sleet, and northwards on the west bank. At half past three, dark was setting in because of the low clouds and the sleet. Bill was wet through and shivering with cold, his head huddled down as far as possible into his jacket collar, trying to avoid the pitiless sleet. For that reason, and through his general fatigue, he did not see the figure in a raincoat, coming towards him a hundred yards away, before the other had seen him and stepped quickly into the thick hedge. A minute later, Bill passed, his mind focused on the shape of the riverbank, its width, the surface of a lane leading up to it at that point – when the man in the raincoat jumped out at him from two yards' distance.

Bill caught the flash of steel first and, with a sudden burst of fury, thought, the swine's got a knife. The dagger stabbed downward – Bill thought, he doesn't know how to use it properly; if he was a Wazir, I'd be dead . . . He felt the slash of pain high on his left shoulder, punched hard for the other's face and closed in, driving his knee into the man's crotch. The man staggered under the punch, the knife dropping from his hand, and Bill jumped, bearing him down. Bill's hands groped for the throat. He found it, and gripped, his teeth bared. Got you, you Hun swine, I'll never let go . . . never . . . bulldog . . . England . . . After a long time the man stopped struggling and squirming and kicking, to become a body. Bill dragged it back into the hedge and went through its pockets: a marked map, writing on it in German . . . nothing else – no notebook, just a pencil, to mark the map, nothing more. This man had been on the same mission as Bill, and had taken the same precautions, except for the one map.

Bill folded the map into his pocket and continued north, crossing the Woesten bridge. He found his bike in the darkness, pedalled back to the rooming house in Ramderzeel and went up to his room. There he undressed and saw that his shirt and jacket were stained red from the left shoulder to the waist, the blood coming from a knife slash that began near the top of the shoulder and extended to the middle of the shoulder blade. Only a surface wound, he thought, thank God, though his left arm would probably be hard to move soon.

He re-dressed and sat down to study the German's map, the curtains drawn in the nightly blackout against German or British aircraft mistaking neutral Belgium for enemy territory. The map had been marked with unfamiliar signs, but they were easy enough to understand . . . figures written in at the river – 3.4 – 2.7 – probably metres of water, estimated . . . scribbles on the bank . . . these he couldn't understand; nothing about troops, no marks showing guns or armour, no headquarters flags . . . The man had been told to reconnoitre and then report back on possibilities. Like Bill, he had memorized the best places for gun areas and river crossings, all from the German point of view – that is, for an army coming from the east.

But there was something else. He had killed this man, his fellow spy . . . his brother, each spying for his country. For a moment, the man's gaping mouth and bulging eyes returned to him, as they had looked when he was staring down at them, throttling the life out of them, for ever. 'I'm sorry,' he whispered aloud, at last. 'It's the war.'

There was an empty fireplace in the room and Bill carefully burned the map, crunching up the ashes under his boot; then he lit a cigarette and thought . . . better get to bed, he was dog-tired and hadn't eaten . . . Then better go out and eat, if he could find a place on Christmas night . . . but what about the blood? . . . It was a dark stain, and his coat was dark . . . he should have taken the German's raincoat . . . but it wouldn't have gone with his other clothes; the German's disguise was that of a man of a higher class than Pieter Welloudt.

244

He heard voices downstairs and opened the door a crack. Looking through the bannisters, he saw the owner talking to two men in uniform. He closed the door silently, opened the window and lowered himself to the back yard, falling the last five feet from the windowsill. His bicycle was there and he wheeled it out of the back gate, as he had done every morning, and, mounting it, pedalled rapidly into the darkness, heading westwards.

He crossed the border near Clachorre, where he had crossed eastbound four days ago, near dawn, thirty-six hours after he had fled from the rooming house. He did not know who the men in uniform had been or why they had come. Perhaps it was to check on the identity of Pieter Welloudt; perhaps it was to investigate the death of a man in a raincoat, found by the Dyle. Perhaps they had come to collect graft. He had had to act at once, without waiting to find out, and it had worked. The night was wet but not snowy, and he had found his way, almost on his own tracks, until day dawned, a good sunny day, thank God. He found a barn full of hay and slept in it and no one disturbed him. At dusk he started out again, and soon saw lights ahead in the road, so stopped and hid his bicycle. Then he walked down a side alley – it was in the middle of a small town – and came cautiously from that side until he could see what was happening: four policemen, their bicycles stacked against a wall, a makeshift barrier across the road; they were checking drivers' licences and IDs of every motor vehicle that passed. A few bicycles came from each direction and these they allowed to pass without examination. Bill returned to his own machine, mounted, and with his heart in his mouth pedalled round the barrier, raising one hand in salute to the police as he passed, his head buried in his collar against the wind. He worked slowly westwards through the night, found the lane he had used before, and again crossed the frontier without incident. Now he had to pedal hard for several hours to reach Béthune, where his suitcase and uniform were. The pawnbroker raised his eyebrows as he came in, but said nothing. Bill took his suitcase, went to the railway station, changed in the men's room, and by five o'clock was reporting at the orderly room, having come out by taxi from the main railway station at Lille.

The adjutant, Slater, greeted him with a serious face. 'We've been trying to contact you for days, sir,' he said.

'Why?' Bill said, easing his shoulders. The left one burned like the open wound it was. He must get to the RMO and pretend he'd been stabbed in a bar brawl . . .

Slater said, 'There was a false alarm of a German attack the morning after you left, and we telephoned your London address. Mrs Miller claimed not to know anything about your coming home on leave. The flap was called off later the same day, but . . . the CO would like to see you.'

'I have to see him,' Bill said. 'I've got a lot to tell him.'

'Well, good luck, sir,' Slater said.

Merton had a strange expression on his face when Bill reached him in his large comfortable billet. Bill, trying to read it, decided that it was composed in part of anger that Bill should have done something wrong, partly of bafflement as to exactly what the wrong-doing had been, and partly of triumph at having caught him out in it, whatever it was.

Merton said coldly, after acknowledging Bill's salute, 'When you were granted leave, you were told that you must go directly to, and stay at, the address you gave in your leave application, so that we could contact you. We tried to, but you weren't there. What do you have to say?'

'I didn't go home to Lesley, sir,' Bill said, and at once noticed Merton's expression lighten. God, he thought, Merton thinks he's caught me out in a sordid liaison; he thinks I was with another woman all these days.

Merton said, 'You'd better tell me the truth, Miller. I didn't have to report that we couldn't contact you, because the alarm was cancelled so soon, so it's a matter that I can deal with myself.'

He'd let me off any serious punishment, Bill thought, for the sake of hearing that my marriage is finished; that I don't love Lesley but go chasing after French whores. And that would be my punishment – that he would see that Lesley got to hear of it.

He said, 'I didn't go to England at all, sir. I went into Belgium, in disguise, and reconnoitred the Baardewijk area. The Germans are doing the same. I killed one of their spies.'

Merton sprang out of his chair. 'What! You went into Belgium, a British officer, and murdered someone?'

Bill said, 'No one found out that I was a British officer. I made a full recce, from the divisional commander's point of view, and can tell him most of the things he will need to know when the balloon goes up on Plan F.'

Merton sat down. 'I think you'll have to go to court-martial, Miller.'

Bill said, 'I am speaking to you privately, and personally. I shall deny everything, if court-martialled. There is no evidence whatever. But, please, sir, listen . . . I've done it, and come back safe and sound, more or less . . . let me tell the general everything I know, and then he can decide what to do with me.'

'Did you take and mark maps?'

'Nothing. It's all in my head.'

Merton swung back and forth in indecision. He muttered, half to himself, 'You've broken a strict army order. You've broken battalion standing orders for leave. You've murdered someone. You've . . . my God, what *haven't* you done? . . . I'll make an appointment to see the general, and you'll come with me.'

The general stood by the window in his big room on the second floor of the chateau, looking out over the formal gardens. 'You have been guilty of gross insubordination, Major Miller. The consequences if you had been discovered would have been disastrous . . . especially if you were now being held on a charge of murdering this German . . . I shall severely reprimand you, and that award will go into your record of service. Also, when you leave here, go to your RMO and have him treat whatever's causing you to bleed through the left shoulder of your tunic. Tell him from me he's not to ask any questions about it . . . Now, here's a map of the whole Baardewijk area, down to Louvain and beyond. Show me everything. Fortunately the information will not be of any use to any other formation, so I won't have to pass it on or explain how I came by it. But . . . thank God you did it. Now at least I'll have some eyes, instead of rushing into Belgium like a blind man . . .'

17

April 1940: France

It was April, and raining. The French earth was heavy with the rain and with the seasonal burgeoning of life under its heart. The trees glowed with the fresh green of young buds, the woods were full of bluebells and primroses, the sunken lanes were lined with the vivid green of the hazel leaves. Bill Miller walked eastward with his batman along one of those lanes leading out of the village of St Germain-en-Bois, towards a slight curved rise in the land. The 1st Battalion of the Queen's Own Wessex Rifles was working on that rise, preparing a defensive position, as part of field exercises recently ordered by the brigade commander. The battalion's commanding officer, Lieutenant Colonel Richard Merton, was attending a conference at divisional headquarters, so Bill, his second-in-command, was conducting the exercise.

The rain dripped off the rim of his steel helmet onto the shoulders of his Burberry. It was not warm, but nor was it cold, and he felt comfortable and reasonably well protected against the elements . . . How far from here had he been when the last war dragged to its end? Not more than a dozen miles, if that . . . somewhere over there, and it had been raining and cold, and he'd been hungry and tired, and frightened, not really knowing what was going on, except that the Germans were near breaking, and it would only take one more push, one more day perhaps, and . . . he'd been a second lieutenant, nineteen years old. Now he was a major, and close to forty-one.

Why wasn't he driving up to the battalion now? There was a road, and he had a car. Well, he needed some exercise . . . and when he arrived he wanted to look the same as the men, who'd already been digging for three hours in the rain, not step out of the closed car, obviously dry and well fed . . . and he wanted to see what was happening in the rear areas. Orders had been to dig a defensive system back there too; and he'd sited it and had it taped starting at dawn this morning. Now, where . . .?

Ah, here they were, the men of the headquarters company and the reserve company – it was C today – digging and wiring. He began to examine the trench in detail, as wet earth and watery mud from the bottom were thrown out by the soldiers. They weren't making much noise, not much banter. That showed they were not in a good mood. British soldiers would normally have been swearing, joking, grumbling. He moved on, found a place where he could jump across the half-dug trench and approached a 2-pounder anti-tank gun post. The man in charge was a sergeant of Royal Artillery. Bill looked at the gun position – the gun itself was outside, its muzzle tarpaulin covered – and said, 'Sergeant, where do you expect the enemy to come from, in this exercise?'

The sergeant pointed east. 'That way, sir. Us and the No. 2 gun of the section are here to try to turn them south – so the rest of the battery can get good targets from the flank.'

'I know that,' Bill said impatiently; it was he who had worked out the siting and interaction of the 2-pounders, the battalion's .5-inch anti-tank rifles, and the defensive fire of field guns, to turn and then break up any armoured attack from the east. He said, 'What will you do if enemy tanks come from the west, having broken through somewhere up or down the line and circled round behind us?'

The sergeant scratched his head. 'Wheel the gun round and let 'em have it when they show themselves,' he said.

'Quite,' Bill said. 'So make sure that you *can* swing the gun, in a full circle, three hundred and sixty degrees, and that there's no immediate obstacle to your fire.' He turned and looked west.

The sergeant followed his gaze, and after a few seconds, said, 'Ah, like that old wurzel clamp, sir?'

'Exactly,' Bill said. 'Flatten it. Use the bricks to strengthen the walls of the gunpit here.'

'But, sir . . .'

'I know we're not allowed to touch French property without permission of the local French authorities, or until the Germans actually attack, but that clamp is ruined already. If anyone asks, tell 'em I told you to tidy up the field.'

'Very good, sir.'

Bill walked on. The orders were to dig the trenches no more than four feet deep, for this was only an exercise, and later the trenches would have to be filled in. The digging was going on well enough, for the men had had plenty of practice at it. They'd dug a lot of trenches since they'd come over to France in such a hurry last September . . . and filled them in . . . and dug some more. In such training as this, the trench system was not as important as the communications system. He'd sited battalion headquarters round an isolated farm just behind the crest of the rise. He'd better go up there, talk to the signal officer, check out the field telephone lines, the radio links and the gunner network. The battery commander should be up there now. The guns themselves were digging in a couple of miles back – he'd passed them on his way up.

At the farm he looked around, surveying what had been done. They'd dug a good though shallow command post and an alternative, plus three or four defensive positions, linked by trenches, in fallow land out to the west of the farm buildings. The farmer himself was sowing wheat in newly ploughed land across the slope. Two small female children stood under the high roof of a hay barn, staring at the British soldiers digging in their fallow land.

The regimental sergeant major, Barrow, marched up to Bill, saluting fiercely. 'Good afternoon, sir. Everything shipshape and Bristol fashion here.'

Bill said, 'Thank you, Mr Barrow. Where's the artillery command post?'

'Just round the corner, sir. You said they were to make it as close to ours as they could.'

'Quite right.'

The RSM jumped down into a trench and Bill followed, walking a few yards round a corner to a deep dugout, equipped with a corrugated-iron roof, heavily sandbagged walls and entrance and a gas curtain. Two radio aerials projected from the top, and telephone cables led in under the roof at one side.

Bill stooped and stepped carefully down and in. Candles were burning in empty bottles, and a map was spread on a makeshift table. There was Hill, the field battery commander, sitting on an ammunition box, smoking a pipe. Again Bill's memory leaped back more than twenty years. How often had he come down steps like this, into just this stage set, just this fug of damp wool, tobacco smoke, guttering candles?

He took off his helmet and said, 'You gunners always do yourselves well.'

'Superior training and intelligence, old boy,' the artillery major said. 'How's the digging going?'

'Pretty well. We ought to be able to inspect it all in another couple of hours.'

'And then tell the men to fill it all in again?'

Bill nodded.

The major sang softly:

'Oh, the noble Duke of York,
He had ten thousand men
He marched them up a bloody great hill
And he marched them down again
And when they were up they were up,
And when they were down they were down
And when they were only halfway up they were neither up nor down.
Oh, the noble Duke of York . . .'

'We have to do the exercise,' Bill cut in impatiently.

'I know, I know . . . How much longer, though, before the real thing?'

There were two artillery signallers in the dugout, headsets on their heads. Radio signals had been buzzing and murmuring in a subdued way, but now, as Major Hill spoke, everything fell quiet. The signallers eased the headsets off their ears.

Bill said, 'I don't know. But not long, in my opinion.'

The RSM came in, saying, 'General Lloyd here, sir.'

Morgan Lloyd, his field boots spattered with mud, came in as the two officers rose and saluted, still stooped. Morgan said, 'Ah . . . Bill, I'm over in France for a couple of days and found I had a few hours to spare, so thought I'd come up and have a cup of tea with the regiment.'

'Just behind the farmhouse, sir,' the RSM said. 'And if you'd like a spot of something stronger in it . . .?'

'Good, good. Where's Colonel Merton?'

Bill said, 'At a conference at division, sir.' He had a suspicion, from something in Morgan's tone, that the general had known that all along – which meant that he had come up to talk to him, Bill, alone.

He said, 'Want to look around for a bit, sir?'

'Yes, indeed. We'll be back for your tea in, say, an hour, Mr Barrow.'

'Very good, sir.'

The general climbed out of the dugout into the trench, Bill at his heels, and as soon as there was a break, out of the trench and up into the open. The rain was less, but it was still falling, a dewy essence of spring. Morgan said, 'How's everything?'

'All right,' Bill answered cautiously. Morgan Lloyd was his friend and mentor, but he was also a major general, on the Imperial General Staff at the War Office. Bill needed to know what particular matter interested him, and would guide his answers accordingly. Morgan knew nothing of Bill's Christmas expedition into Belgium.

Lloyd said, 'How are you getting along with Merton? And vice versa?'

'So far, so good,' Bill said. 'Our relations are not cordial, but they're correct. A bit more than that, perhaps, though I often have a feeling that he's lying in wait for me to slip up . . . But we've been through a lot together, and whatever he has against me he is dedicated to the regiment. Things are better than I thought they'd be when I joined the battalion in Aldershot last September.'

Lloyd said, 'Good. How's Barrow doing as RSM?'

'He was appointed last July, just before I joined,' Bill said. 'I never really served with him before, but he seems all right.'

'He was one of my platoon sergeants when I had A Company early in the last war,' Lloyd said. 'A little shifty was my opinion . . . clever, though. Merton always had a very high opinion of him – and that's as it should be, as he's Merton's RSM . . . How are the men bearing up under this phoney war – that's what the Americans are calling it.'

'Pretty well, considering,' Bill said. 'But there's a feeling that we're leaving the initiative to the Germans. And BEF general orders are far from inspiring. They seem to deal mostly with whether soldiers should carry matches in their pockets or haversacks – things like that. The CO and I are the only people in the battalion who know anything about Plan F, and I must say I don't like what I do know.'

'We're in the lap of the French,' Lloyd said. 'And they're in the lap of 1914–18. You talk of war to them and they immediately get nightmares of huge losses, like 1914 and 1917, when they mutinied.

They're the reason we didn't attack as soon as war broke out. They wouldn't do it.'

'Have you visited them, sir?'

Lloyd said, 'Yes.' He dropped his voice, though there was no one within a hundred yards as they walked on through the light rain. 'The French are in a bad way. Brookie thinks they won't fight at all. I agree with him.'

'So do I,' Bill said. 'We do spells in the Maginot Line, as you know, in turns. I was down there in February, and the impressions I got were very bad. They're sullen . . . unready . . . unwilling . . . And that's whom we have to rely on for aggressive leadership!'

Lloyd said, 'The French politicians – and generals – are still hoping that Germany will be satisfied after swallowing Poland and will offer terms.'

'Christ!' Bill exploded.

Three days after the defensive exercise by St Germain-en-Bois there was a knock at the door of Bill's room in Escobecques. It was in a house which had been emptied by the men going to war and the women moving away to live with relatives in the south. The battalion had taken it over completely; Bill and two other officers shared the upper floor as living quarters; the downstairs was occupied by Bill's office as second-in-command and president of the Regimental Institute, responsible for managing much of the battalion's private funds; and by the battalion's intelligence room, which was also the office of the intelligence officer.

'Come in,' Bill called.

It was Company Sergeant Major Bogey Harris of B Company, bearing a file of papers. 'Morning, sir,' he said. 'I looked in at your office downstairs and Gibson said you were working in your room.'

'I am, after a fashion,' Bill said. 'But it's not important. What can I do for you?'

'The arrangements for the athletic meeting, sir. I've laid out a track, and there's a slope for spectators, but it's going to take some money to level the ground a bit more . . . not much.'

'How much?'

'I think you'd better come and take a look, sir,' Harris said. 'P'raps you'll want to alter my layout a bit . . . save a bit . . . or, if we're flush, flatten it out some more, make it really good.'

'All right,' Bill said. 'I'm fed up with sitting here, anyway.' He reached for his gasmask and steel helmet, then followed Harris down the stairs and out of the house. He noticed Lance Corporal Gibson, his PRI clerk, glance up as they went past the door.

Out in the street, Harris said busily, 'This way, sir. It's behind the school . . . thought there'd be a playground we could start with, but the Frogs don't have playgrounds, even nowadays . . . Sir, Sergeant Hodder of D is running a brothel in town here, and the RSM knows about it. He's keeping the regimental police off.'

There had been no change in Harris's tone, and after an instinctive sudden jerk Bill walked on as though he had not been shocked. He said, 'Go on.'

'The girls are from Lille, smuggled out here, living in the back of the house, where no one sees 'em . . . or knows they're there. Six. They're clean.'

'Who inspects them? Surely not the RMO?'

'No, sir. A trained nurse from Lille – she comes out once a week.'

'Are you sure of this?'

'Quite, sir. It took me near a couple of months to check it all out. They've all been very careful, very smart. No one's talked. Didn't want to lose it, I s'pose.'

'Where's the place?'

'See that house down the road, beyond the church, sir – the one with two gables? That's it.'

'Who's supposed to live in it?'

'An old bloke retired from a bank and his wife. They do, too. But the back rooms aren't empty and boarded up the way they look. And there's a way in at the back, off the little lane that goes along by the stream.'

'All right. Thanks.'

They returned to the business at hand. Bill made his decision about the sports field, returned to his billet and sat down to think. The battalion's VD rate was very low, one of the lowest in the BEF. Facilities had always been given for the men to take short leave to Lille, which was full of clean, well-run, frequently inspected civilian brothels. But all commanding officers of the BEF had been faced with the same fact: that the soldiers didn't like the long trip, or the antiseptic surroundings, or the 'official' atmosphere; so the girls and women of the villages

254

and towns where troops were billeted had gone into business on their own, either in their houses or among the cabbages and roots in the fields. These women were not inspected. Some of them already had VD, others soon contracted it; and the army's rate went up . . . but not in the Queen's Own Wessex, and here was the reason.

The question was, did Merton know about it? Had he authorized it? If he had, he'd be for the high jump – as the army's political overlords had stressed, many times, that they could not afford to risk any outcry from mothers and wives at home against such practices being actually organized by the army. But if Merton had not authorized it, RSM Barrow was deceiving him and putting his career in great peril, while probably making a good bit of money for himself on the side.

So, what should he do? Bogey had obviously told him in the hope that he'd do something about it . . . bare the whole business . . . which could lead to Merton being sacked, and himself taking over as CO . . . Bogey was a good friend. But this should not be looked at in such a way. What was *right*?

It was against British military policy for the army itself to run brothels, though the existence of brothels run by civilians or local authorities was winked at. This was hypocritical, but there it was. But suppose it turned out to be hard, or impossible, to link Barrow or even Sergeant Hodder with the brothel? Then it would just be private enterprise on the part of some French citizens. Perhaps he should try to plant some marked money on men whom he knew were attending the brothel . . . but how could he find that out? And how, later, find the money in Barrow's or Hodder's possession?

He stood up with a jerk. He could not act alone in this. The only proper course was to tell Merton what Bogey Harris had told him, and after that let the cards fall where they might.

It was early May 1940, and the divisional commander was holding a top-secret conference of all field officers of his division. The officers, to the number of about a hundred and fifty, were seated in a suburban church in the southern outskirts of Lille. It was a huge building and the officers occupied less than a third of it, though the suburb had long since lost its importance and most of its population. The contingent from the Wessex sat together, Colonel Merton in the middle, flanked by Bill on his right and Majors Hodge and Mainwaring, commanding

A and D Companies, on his left. Their hands were empty, for they had been ordered to bring no maps and make no notes.

The general said, 'The situation's hotting up. From many sources our intelligence is receiving information that can lead to only one conclusion: the Germans are going to attack soon, perhaps within forty-eight hours, perhaps not for ten days. My purpose in bringing you here is to tell you that our GHQ Plan, Plan F, is to advance, as soon as the enemy has violated the Belgian frontier, to the line of the Dyle, in conjunction with the French. What we don't know, and will not know until it happens, is whether the enemy intend also to violate Dutch neutrality. They did not in 1914, but this is 1940 . . . and Hitler is not the Kaiser. This time they might, which would alter our situation on the Dyle. It would affect the French corps on our left even more seriously, of course. Now . . .' He turned to the huge map displayed on the wall behind him. 'As you leave here, all COs will receive a copy of Divisional Operation Instruction No. 4. That instruction becomes effective on receipt of the code word TANQUERAY from this headquarters. As soon as possible after that, I will issue an operation order, dealing mainly with changes to be made if the Germans are moving through or into Holland. The operation order will be as brief as we can make it, and will first be sent out in cipher radio messages to those most concerned. It will be confirmed in writing to everyone, of course. Now, my G1 will run through the operation instruction on the map. Take over, Willie.'

He sat down on one of the folding chairs that had been set up near the altar. The G1 stepped forward and said, 'Now is the time to ask questions, so don't hesitate to interrupt me – or the A/Q, who will go through the administrative sections – or Colonel Preece, who will explain the signal diagram, which is under this map. Now . . .'

Bill listened, his mind concentrated. He had found that it was nearly always more important to listen carefully than to make voluminous notes, and he was glad that no notes were allowed today. After an hour, the A/Q took over, and Bill tried to keep his attention level high. Positioning of supply points and casualty clearing stations was not as exciting as working out an artillery plan, but they were just as important, especially for him, because in battle much of the administrative supervision of the battalion was the responsibility of the second-in-command.

The A/Q sat down and the commander Royal Signals took his place, explaining the communications plan, from the various command radio nets to the use of dispatch riders and field telephones.

At last it was over and the general stood up again. 'Any final questions?'

One of the infantry brigadiers stood up in his pew. 'Sir, is the ban on forward reconnaissance still in force?'

'Very much so,' the general said, 'The Belgians won't allow it. So all your recces will have to be done off the maps and the aerial photographs which will be issued with the operation instruction. Any more? . . . Dismiss, please, gentlemen.'

Back at the battalion, after lunch in the officers' mess, Merton called Bill into his office and said, 'COs have been told privately that they must be ready to move at two hours' notice. That means we can't go very far from our billet area, for any reason at all. So, no more route marches, no trench digging and siting. About all we can do is arms drill and PT.'

Bill said, 'We can do some individual and section training with tanks and artillery, right here.'

'What do you mean?'

'We've done a little training on cooperation with tanks, but I think we can do more. The 3rd Tanks are only two miles up the road. I'd like to run a sort of continuous exercise with, say, three of their tanks and a platoon of ours at a time, over the same ground . . . another platoon and some anti-tank guns acting as enemy . . . and with a gunner FOO with our platoon. We can use smoke candles, and make it quite realistic, and still be only twenty minutes away from billets, if we use that common land off the road to Villeveine.'

Merton considered a while and then said, 'All right. Go ahead and arrange it. But make sure that everyone can get back here in a hurry if the balloon goes up.'

'Very good, sir.'

Outside, Bill walked quickly down the street to his own office, thinking, Merton was definitely mellowing towards him. The affair of the brothel had been settled quickly and efficaciously, though not in the way Bill himself would have done it; for almost Merton's first remark, when Bill told him what was going on, was: 'We'll never implicate Barrow. He's too smart a man, and anyway I'm sure he's been doing it for the good of the battalion and without implicating me.'

Bill said nothing; but he had thought, you *would* be implicated, whether you wanted it or not, if this had been discovered by an outside agency. A CO *is* responsible, whether he knows of such things or not.

Merton had continued, 'I'm going to recommend Barrow for a commission. He'll go home and get his pip, and within a month he'll be quartermaster for another battalion. He'll be an excellent quartermaster. We've been ordered to send a sergeant to GHQ for sanitary duties, and I'll send Hodder. That'll get rid of him for the duration. And I'll see that the police keep a closer eye on old Monsieur and Madame Fleuret.'

Bill had been about to ask whom Merton proposed to promote to RSM in Barrow's place, but decided to say nothing. The obvious choice was Bogey Harris; but it was Bogey who would indirectly cause the removal of Barrow, and Merton knew of the boyhood friendship between himself and Bogey. He'd best keep his mouth shut.

But, before ending the interview, Merton said, 'I propose to make Harris RSM. I think he's the best of our CSMs. Any comments?'

'No, sir, I agree,' Bill said.

And so it had all worked out. The RSM suddenly disappeared; the brothel was closed; Sergeant Hodder drove away in a ration truck; and Monsieur and Madame Fleuret re-closed their back rooms and stored away under the floorboards the considerable number of francs they had made from the British soldiers and/or the French women who had been using the rooms for the past few months. The affair was over.

On the morning of 8 May, the battalion stick orderly appeared at Bill's office, saluted, and said, 'Commanding officer's compliments, sir, and he'd like to see you in his office.'

Bill got up and followed the orderly to battalion headquarters. Merton was leaning back in his chair when Bill went in and acknowledged his salute with a brief nod. Bill stayed at attention. Merton said, 'I have reason to believe that your books as PRI are being cooked, that some regimental funds have been embezzled. The books are being seized at this moment by the RSM, on my orders, and Corporal Gibson, your PRI clerk, is being placed under arrest. Consider yourself, also, under open arrest.'

He paused, waiting. Bill said, 'Yes, sir.' He felt cold in the pit of his stomach, but was able to control his muscles and voice.

Merton said, 'Return to your office, perform your duties as usual. A court of inquiry will convene in this matter tomorrow morning. I don't want to waste any time getting to the truth. That's all.'

Bill saluted, swung round, and marched out. In his office he found the RSM, Bogey Harris, and the intelligence clerk from across the hall. There was no sign of Gibson, his own PRI clerk. As he walked in, Harris said briskly, 'Run along to the orderly room, Simonds, and get me the file of battalion orders for the past two months, plus the ammunition returns since 1 January.'

The rifleman clerk got up and went out. Harris turned to Bill. 'That'll keep him busy for twenty minutes at least . . . It was Barrow's doing, sir.'

'How?'

'Barrow learned that Gibson was cooking the books – not much – making a quid a week extra for himself. He had to give Barrow five bob out of it.'

Bill groaned. 'And this is the man we've made an officer!'

'Yes, sir. When you told the colonel about the brothel, Barrow made up his mind to get even with you, even though the colonel was going to recommend him for a commission, and save him from any other trouble. So he told the colonel about it, that there was something wrong with your books – and Gibson, who's in the guard room now, is not going to be able to get back at Barrow because there's no proof that Barrow was taking a rakeoff.'

Bill sat down. 'Well, thanks, Bogey. But I deserve whatever's coming to me. Barrow couldn't have done me any harm if I'd kept a proper check on Gibson and the books. General Lloyd must have told me a dozen times never to trip up over small things because my eyes were on big ones.'

'You were too busy training for war, and teaching us how to,' Harris said. 'Those tank and infantry exercises are great stuff.'

'Thanks . . . Well, they probably won't cashier me, because they won't be able to find that any money's stuck to my fingers. But there'll be a severe reprimand, at the least.'

'The colonel will send you back home, sir, if you ask me.'

Bill jumped to his feet. 'With the Germans just about to attack! The moment I've been training for, waiting for, for the last twenty years? . . . What a bloody careless fool I've been!'

'It's a matter of time, sir. Depends on when the balloon goes up, doesn't it?'

'I suppose so. Thanks again, Bogey.'

'It's nothing . . . and good luck, Dusty. We need you.'

He saluted with an RSM's authority and vigour and marched out. Bill sat dejectedly at his desk, his head in his hands. What a damned fool . . . damned fool . . . idiot . . . bloody idiot . . . he had slipped up . . . you couldn't afford to forget or ignore *anything* . . . and that was as it should be. A general in command, in battle, must know everything, ignore nothing, read the meaning of everything. Morgan Lloyd had told him that General Montgomery, commanding the 3rd Division, had damned nearly lost his command over issuing a rather matey order on VD which the chaplains hadn't liked. Only Brooke, the corps commander, had been able to save him, at the cost of a royal rocket. And if Monty, reputed the most GS general in the army, could be sacked over a thing like that, how much more could he, a bloody little major, be dispensed with over something that was inherently worse: permitting embezzlement?

The CO sent for him again at noon on 9 May, half an hour after the court of inquiry had completed its work and delivered its findings. Merton wasted no time. 'Miller, these findings prove that you've been lax and careless as PRI. You have lost about twenty pounds of our regimental funds to embezzlement by Lance Corporal Gibson. You have not yourself embezzled anything, so I am not going to have you court-martialled. But I am going to send you back to the depot with a recommendation that you spend the next year on administrative work. You've never been keen on it, and this is the result. The quartermaster will give you a travel warrant tomorrow morning. Leave immediately after that.'

'Yes, sir.'

Bill detected a gleam of triumph in Merton's eye as he saluted and turned away.

18

May 1940: Flanders

At six o'clock in the morning of 10 May 1940, Bill was gloomily packing his uniforms and belongings into two suitcases, one of them the battered cardboard object he'd bought in preparation for his secret reconnaissance into Belgium. What a bloody fool I have been, he thought, as he folded away a pair of khaki whipcord slacks, what a blithering idiot! After so many years of struggling and striving for the top, for the chance to command in battle, to be tripped up and sent reeling back by the petty venality of a lance corporal, ex-bookkeeper. That ought to have alerted him, or at least triggered a warning bell in his mind: this fellow had been a bookkeeper – that is, he knows how to keep books . . . *ergo* he also knows how to cook them. At the very least he should have made spot inspections without warning; better yet, he should have taken a correspondence course in accounting and made himself expert enough to detect what was going on under his nose.

The door of his room swung open, simultaneously with a knock on it, and Bogey Harris burst in. 'Balloon's going up, sir,' he said, crashing to a halt just inside the door, slapping his swagger cane under his left armpit and saluting.

Bill turned. 'What do you mean? Have we had orders from brigade to put Plan F into effect? What is H-hour?'

Harris came down from the salute. 'Nothing official yet, sir, but we have a French cook in the sergeants' mess . . .'

'I know.'

'He's been listening to the wireless, the Belgian wireless, talking in French . . . and it's been saying that the Germans invaded Belgium over an hour ago. There are a lot of rumours. Jerries are reported everywhere, at the same time . . . but, according to Alphonse, there's no doubt it's started. Just thought I'd come and tell you, so you'd have some advance warning.'

'Well thanks, Bogey, but I'm due to go back on the ration lorry. Blighty for me. You know that.'

'Yes, sir, but this'll alter things. You've got jobs to do in Plan F, and the colonel can't replace you without pulling out a company commander, which would be even worse. I think that, if you go to Colonel Merton now, he'll cancel his order. He'll have to.'

'It's worth trying,' Bill said, 'because I'm bloody well not going back anyway . . . Look, you go first and tell him the news. Don't tell him you came here first. I'll follow in ten minutes, saying that my batman told me, and he heard it from some sergeant.'

'Very good, sir.'

Harris saluted again, and crashed out, his hobnail boots clumping sharply down the stairs and out into the street.

Bill waited, standing at his window, looking out over the village. He expected to hear bugles blowing, calling officers to battalion headquarters; but Merton was doing nothing yet. Here came Harris, marching smartly back down the street, not looking up. Bill put on his Sam Browne, set his service-dress cap straight on his head and picked up his swagger cane, thinking he wouldn't be needing any of those items for some time, if Harris's news was correct. Then he went downstairs and along the street to Merton's billet.

Inside the door he said, 'I have come to ask you to reconsider your orders sending me back to the depot, sir. If the news is correct . . .'

'What news, what have you heard, who from?' Merton snapped. He was half dressed, his battle-dress trousers and shirt on, but not the blouse. His black boots, beautifully polished, were still outside his door where his batman had put them the night before.

Bill said, 'My batman told me that he'd heard from a sergeant that the Germans have invaded Belgium.'

'That's what Harris has just told me,' Merton muttered. 'Nothing about Holland, though. Have you heard anything about Holland?'

'No, sir.'

Merton stood in front of his dressing table, brushing his hair, talking to himself. 'You *ought* to go back . . . your administration is weak, and administration's all important for a second-in-command . . . saved by the gun, God damn it . . . I can't do without you now . . . not till I get another good company commander . . . and how can I ask for one while you're here?'

He turned round and Bill saw that his face was sheened with

sweat, though it was a fresh morning, and his hands shaking. 'You can stay, damn you!'

Bill's post for the move was at the very back of the battalion, riding in his 15-hundredweight truck, accompanied by the regimental provost corporal and three regimental police on motorcycles. The battalion was the last in the brigade, all using the same road forward. Immediately in front of the Wessex was a regiment of field artillery and in front of them the other two battalions of the brigade, the 2nd Oxford Fusiliers and the 6th Cardiff Regiment. The move began from Escobecques at 1.00 p.m., and the leading troops of the division passed into Belgium at H-hour, 2.30 p.m. Bill crossed two and a half hours later, at 5.00 p.m., still in broadest daylight at this time of year.

The vehicles were jammed together on the road ahead, far more than eighty to the mile, which was the ordered spacing for the move – and even eighty v.t.m. was dangerously close-packed when the enemy had air superiority . . . but only a few German aircraft came, and they dropped no bombs. Twice in the afternoon Bill saw high-flying twin-engined bombers pass overhead; but no bombs had been dropped. Why? Here was this long, packed column, moving forward to its battle positions; there were other columns to east and west, as all the divisions of the British Expeditionary Force moved up in accordance with Plan F. Surely the Germans would try to prevent or hinder the move? And according to all intelligence reports Bill had ever seen, they had the strength to do it. So . . .? Was it a trap? Time alone would tell.

Darkness fell at last, at about ten o'clock, and at once conditions worsened. Now the Belgian people filled the roads, all heading in the opposite direction, fleeing from the Hun terror, their belongings on their backs, or pushed in wheelbarrows, or loaded into farm carts, the patient horses plodding west and south. There were few motor vehicles, because there was no gasoline for them. More and more often the column halted, and each time Bill sent an MP forward to report on the cause of the stoppage. Time and again the report was: 'Refugees blocking the road, sir . . . Haycart broken down in the middle of the road, sir. The gunners are towing it into a field with one of their quads . . .'

Bill's eyes ached from peering into the dark, at the tiny shaded glow from the tail lamp of the big 3-tonner in front of him, loaded with B Echelon supplies for the battalion.

The column stopped again. Again Bill sent a motorcycle MP forward. He returned in ten minutes. 'Bridge blocked, sir, halfway up the battalion. We've got C and D Companies and B Echelon on our side, the rest are in front, but no one knows how far. They just kept going.'

'How is the bridge blocked? What by?'

'It's quite a narrow bridge, sir, and there's a stream of people coming back over it, with their carts and horses and all . . . some cars, too. Soon's they're over the bridge, they turn off on a side road; that's why we haven't seen any coming back past here.'

Bill jumped down and climbed on the back of the MP's bike. 'Take me forward . . . Careful, man, I don't want my bloody leg broken before the war's really started.'

'Sorry, sir. Skidded a bit on me.'

They worked their way forward past and between and round the halted carriers, trucks and lorries, and came at last to the bridge, a seething antheap sensed in the starlight.

A figure loomed up close and Bill, peering, said, 'Captain Griffin?'

'Yes, sir.'

'Debus your leading platoon, with all their weapons, of course. No packs . . . Hurry, man!'

'Yes, sir.'

The men appeared in a few minutes and Bill, peering, said, 'Who's this?'

'Lieutenant Vance, sir, with Sergeant Wilkinson and No. 10 Platoon.'

'All right. Give me a couple of hefty fellows with rifles to lead the way . . . don't fix bayonets, use your butts and boots as much as you like. Follow me, with all your men.'

He edged into the stream of refugees, at the extreme left side, and began working forward against the current of it. Heavy bodies pressed him against the low wall of the bridge and cart wheels ground ever closer. The soldiers in front of him struggled valiantly, swearing and shoving and ramming their rifle butts down on refugees' feet. They came to one man who would not or perhaps could not budge, from the force of the crowd pressing him forward and at

264

the same time up against the wall. 'Over the wall with him!' Bill yelled. The two burly soldiers forced the man's body over and back till he lost his balance and fell, dropping six feet with a loud splash and shout.

After that, movement was easier and in another five minutes the thirty men of the platoon were on the far side, gathered on the left verge of the road.

'Now,' Bill shouted to Vance, 'make a wedge and move across. Don't let anyone through. Form a wall across the road . . . Divert the people into the river. The water's shallow . . . Ready? Go!'

The soldiers edged out, rifles raised menacingly, butts forward. They cut through slowly, and as they inched forward Sergeant Wilkinson grabbed a carthorse's head and led it off to the right, toward the sloping grass bank that led into the water. 'This way, *jaldi*!' the sergeant yelled.

A car came on, pushing through the crowd, running over people. Women were screaming, men cursing. Bill snapped to the soldier nearest to him, 'Put a bullet close over the driver's head.'

With difficulty the rifleman got his rifle into the aim, and fired. The car came on at the soldiers, and by the starlight Bill saw that the driver seemed to be crazed, half standing in his seat, screaming in French.

'Kill him,' he said to the rifleman.

The soldier fired again and the driver fell over backward into the tonneau of his car.

The platoon was across the road, facing the refugees. Slowly, led by Sergeant Wilkinson, the Belgians began to move down toward the water on the right. Behind Bill, the bridge was clear. 'Push that car into the ditch,' he said briefly. 'Stay here, Vance, till your trucks come.'

He walked back over the bridge and said to Captain Griffin, 'Start up, get moving . . . Put two men on the bridge with orders to shoot any civilian who tries to use it. I'll pick them up and bring them along when I pass . . . where's my MP?'

'Here, sir.'

'Wait here, with me. No point in riding back.' He walked a little away, hearing the roar of the engines, the grind of gears close behind him. The column was on the move again. Griffin was weak. He could have forced the refugees off the bridge long since if he'd used his man-power. He returned to the roadside. The MP said, 'I went over to look at the bloke that got shot. He's got two suitcases full of money with him – nothing else.'

'Belgian money?'

'I suppose so, sir. I left it as it was.'

'Good.'

Poor bastard, he thought, mad to escape with his money. Now he didn't even have life.

Soon the tail of the battalion's column came along and Bill climbed back into his truck, picking up the two bridge sentries. The refugees were still coming, but they were now leaving the road before the bridge, fording the stream, and then turning off onto the side road. The advance continued. Half an hour later, it stopped again; and again, after waiting five minutes, Bill went forward on the back of an MP's motorcycle. This time he found Captain Griffin halted at a cross-roads, studying a map in the cab of his truck, under a shaded light.

Bill was brusque. 'What's the matter? Are you lost?'

Griffin said, 'The crossroads is not marked, sir. I think it's this one, on the map' – he pointed – 'but the route we're supposed to follow isn't marked. There ought to be a green light and a guide here.'

'Well, there isn't . . . Here, you get on the bike behind Rifleman Cree, and I'll take over your cab. I need to be able to look at the map. Follow close . . . Ready, driver? Take the right road. Keep up speed.'

Someone had forgotten to leave the guide and the light. Or the guide had been murdered by refugees, or by German agents, and the light removed. It would have to be looked into, but meantime he knew the route to be followed and had marked it on his map. Baardewijk wasn't more than ten miles ahead now and he couldn't go far wrong.

Half an hour later, at another crossroads, there was a shaded green light, and an officer in a steel helmet waving them to a stop. The officer peered up. 'Who's there?'

'C and D Companies of the 1st Wessex. We got separated from the rest of the battalion a few miles back.'

'Good. Turn left here. The battalion's half a mile down the road, debussed. All second-line vehicles will come back as soon as you've rejoined and debussed.'

Merton was waiting outside a house that looked like a tavern and greeted Bill sharply. 'Where the hell have you been?'

'Our column got split at a bridge a few miles back. We spent some time making the refugees give way for us, and after that there were no markers or guides.'

Merton growled something and said, 'Into this tavern. The other officers are waiting . . . have been for an hour.'

Inside, the big room was redolent of stale beer and tobacco smoke. The curtains were drawn tight, the lights shining brilliant white. Merton said, 'We're in Melverdem, two miles behind Woesten. We are to hold the crest line of the slope leading down to the Dyle, from Woesten southwards towards Baardewijk. I'm going now with the adjutant and intelligence officer to brigade headquarters, and will send back detailed orders by runner as soon as I have received them. Meanwhile, the men are to rest, and a hot meal is to be cooked immediately. I want that to be in the men's bellies before the battalion moves forward from here. You understand, Major Miller?'

'Yes, sir.'

'I don't think we'll be starting our move forward until at least 4.00 a.m. It's dark until 4.30, and I don't imagine we'll occupy our positions in the dark, especially as we haven't had a chance to see the ground.'

I have, Bill thought, with a touch of smugness, I know exactly what the view is like from Woesten.

Merton said, 'That's all,' and the meeting broke up, the officers going carefully out into the warm night and fumbling their ways to their companies and platoons.

The RSM fell in beside Bill. 'Had a rough trip, sir?'

'Had to shoot a crazy refugee . . . I can't understand why we didn't have any German air attacks. We were sitting ducks, jammed on those roads all afternoon.'

'I can understand, sir, but I don't like to think about it.'

'A trap, eh? Well, we'll give them a bloody nose before they get the trap shut, if it is one . . .'

Harris lowered his voice. 'The CO's acting queer, sir . . . giving orders, and then cancelling them, all the way up . . . won't eat anything . . . won't drink either . . . can't stop his hands trembling . . . doesn't seem to hear you sometimes, when you're speaking to him, as though he's miles away.'

Bill stopped and said, 'Look, you know he and I don't get on, but we've got to support him, as far as we can.'

'But if I can't, sir, if he does something that's going to send the whole battalion down the drain . . . will you be near?'

'I'll be where I'm supposed to be. Right now, with the cooks.'

'Very good, sir.'

It didn't take long for the battalion cooks to open a few hundred cans of bully beef and empty them into the cookers, mixed with tomatoes, cabbage and potatoes, and so prepare one of the soldiers' favourite dishes, bully stew. Two hours later all officers and men had eaten, and were lying in fields and barns wrapped in their greatcoats, sleeping off the last of the night. Bill tried to sleep, but could only catnap, as he waited anxiously for orders from Merton . . . At 6.00 a.m. they came, in a written message which the duty officer brought to him:

> Move battalion up to western outskirts of Woesten. Belgians are still holding their positions in and forward of Woesten but are expected to vacate soon. 2 i/c report at Woesten railway station on arrival.

Bill called the officers in, and half an hour later the battalion was on the move, swinging down the road eastwards, the morning sun in their faces, marching by platoons, each at fifty yards' interval from the one in front. Bill marched in front, the RSM on one side and the CO of HQ company, Captain Cowling, on the other. The men in the ranks began to sing, at first almost every platoon singing a different song, as they were separated. Then, as they realized the opportunities, each platoon sang one verse of a popular ditty, the platoon behind singing the second verse and so on down the long column.

They reached the outskirts of Woesten at half past seven, and Bill ordered the companies to scatter into the fields on either side, trying not to get mixed up with the Belgian soldiers who seemed to be everywhere, in the houses, streets and fields – some in defensive posts or trenches, others lolling against the houses or wandering up the street. Then Bill went forward with his batman on foot to the railway station. Merton was already there, with the brigadier, Latour, an artillery colonel, and the other two battalion commanders. As Bill arrived, so did the other two battalion second-in-commands. The brigadier had a reddish face at the best of times, now it was almost purple with fury and frustration, and his powerful hands kept opening and closing as though he were crushing an invisible object between them. His brigade major said to him, 'Everyone here now, sir.'

The brigadier said abruptly, 'The bloody Belgians won't move. Their general – he's about seventy and has a long white moustache – says his King gave him this sector to hold with his division and he's going to hold it.'

The gunner colonel said, 'Didn't anyone send him a copy of Plan F, sir?'

'I don't know and it doesn't matter,' the brigadier snapped. 'He's here, with his men, where we are supposed to be. The GOC is arguing with him now, but meantime . . . keep your anti-aircraft defences on alert, particularly you –' He nodded at the artillery officer.

The outer door of the waiting room swung open and the general commanding the division strode in. 'Thought I'd come and tell you the news in person, Harry.' He faced the assembled officers. 'As you've been told, the Belgians won't move. We obviously can't attack them, and they swear they'll never retreat. As to that, we'll see, but . . . the corps commander has ordered us to take positions behind them, not too close, covering the same lateral frontage. So your brigade will occupy the Melverdem line where most of you bivouacked last night. It's not a long walk back, and it'll do the men good, after sitting cooped up in the vehicles all yesterday. Any questions?'

'Some of their gun areas will be in our infantry areas, sir,' the CO of the Cardiffs said. 'We had two howitzer batteries in among us last night.'

The general said, 'Perhaps. Ignore them. And, Harry, you're obviously never going to have to defend these positions, because, if the Belgians hold, you'll be in reserve for counterattacks . . . and if they don't, you'll move up and take over their positions. Where we are supposed to be anyway. So prepare for that . . . Got to see the other brigades. This is too damned complicated to explain by messages. Besides, who'd believe it?'

He nodded and went out. The brigadier said, 'You heard that, gentlemen . . . Our junction point with the flank brigade on the right will be the hamlet at 098342, inclusive to us. That'll be in your area.

Twitchell. Our left junction point, with the French 7th Army, will be the road and rail bridge at 087409, inclusive to them. That'll be in your area, Merton. Arrange battalion junction points among yourselves . . . My headquarters will be at Hafenzeele 078365, probably in the school or *mairie*, but we'll have another set up outside in case of heavy German shelling or bombing. We'll be open there from' – he glanced at his watch – '1000. Meantime, I'll stay here. That's all.'

Back in Melverdem, at six o'clock that night, having checked up on all the defensive positions of the battalion headquarters area, and set up his own bivouac close to an isolated small farmhouse, Bill went to battalion headquarters for the evening meeting, which was always called 'evening prayers' – just as, if the battalion wasn't in close action, another meeting held at 8.00 a.m. was referred to as 'morning prayers'. The purpose of each meeting was to disseminate information that had been gleaned during the past twelve hours, explain what our own forces were proposing to do, tell what was known about enemy infiltration, and pass on other messages, tactical and administrative.

Here, in the back room of the estaminet, Lieutenant Wade, the battalion intelligence officer, had pinned a large-scale map on the wall of the room, and half a dozen officers were sitting around on bar benches, the CO in a chair with a back to it. Wade expounded, 'As far as solid information goes, sir, we have very little certain knowledge of Germany's early movements. There are unconfirmed reports that they took Eben Emael fortress with paratroops, and broke through there quite easily. There are no reports from French GQG about any attack on the Maginot Line. Holland has definitely been invaded, but we don't know just where. There is no enemy within thirty-five miles of us here, and none is expected to arrive on the Dyle within the next forty-eight hours.'

'Is that certain, Bill?' Merton asked. 'We're safe for forty-eight hours?'

'According to GHQ, sir, yes.'

'Do the Belgians know that?'

'I don't know, sir. They should.'

'I'll send someone up to make sure they do, when we finish here. Go on.'

Wade continued his review of the situation; from which it

appeared, in Bill's eyes, that the Germans were heading in force for the junction between the BEF and the French armies to the south. But in fact, to the south of the BEF there were very few troops, for there lay the mountainous and heavily wooded Ardennes, with few roads and many obstacles to movement. The Germans would surely not throw their panzers through there? But what if they did? When would we know? That was a question which should be asked of the intelligence branch at General Gort's HQ, not of poor Bill Wade here.

At the end of 'prayers', Merton said briefly to Bill, 'Take a motorbike and go back up to the Belgians in Woesten, Miller, and tell them the Germans are still thirty-five miles away. See what they've done to add to their defences and let me know when you come back.'

Bill set off a few minutes later on a motorcycle borrowed from the signal platoon, and rode slowly eastwards along the same road he had traversed so often nearly six months ago. He slowed the big Norton down to little more than a crawl, savouring the scents of late spring, the blossom in the hedgerow, the riot of wildflower colour in the fields and little gardens. Last Christmas he had bicycled up and down here, freezing cold, wet, fearful of every face that even glanced at him. Now, peace . . . a young couple walking out in the bright evening, his arm round her waist, her head on his shoulder. Love and . . .

Machine-gun bullets clattered over his head; he swung the bike round to a skidding stop and dived for the ditch. Who the hell was shooting at him? Why? The young lovers, two hundred yards behind him, had vanished. Up ahead, less than a quarter of a mile away, were the first houses of Woesten. He saw movement there and made out the shapes of Belgian steel helmets. Christ, it had been a Belgian machine-gun that had fired at him . . . one facing to the rear, at that. He found his handkerchief in his pocket and waved it in the air. Faintly he heard shouts from ahead, but could not make out what was being said. Carefully he stood up, still waving the handkerchief. Half a dozen Belgian soldiers stood in plain view, waving their hands in gestures which Bill hoped meant 'Come on.' He remounted the Norton, kick-started it, and again headed towards Woesten.

At the entrance to the town he dismounted, as Belgians surrounded him, gesticulating and gabbling in French and Flemish. He said carefully, '*Je suis un officier anglais. Pourquoi avez-vous tiré sur moi?*'

An older man appeared, walking briskly, his left breast bright with medal ribbons. Bill recognized the badges of a full colonel and saluted, saying, '*Ces soldats tiraient sur moi . . .*'

The colonel raised a well-manicured hand. 'Don't bother to mangle the French language any more, my dear boy. I'm an Old Etonian . . . I heard the firing, and can only rejoice that you were not hurt.' He turned and spat a few violent phrases at the soldiers, who cringed and returned to the shelter of their sandbagged post. The colonel turned back to Bill, saying, 'But let's hope they make better shooting against the Germans than they do against a British major. By the way, what did you come up here for?'

Bill said, 'My CO, Colonel Merton, wanted me to make sure that whoever's in command here knows that the Germans are at least thirty-five miles away and that no contact can be expected for forty-eight hours.'

The colonel said, 'Our general has read that intelligence report. Unfortunately, he does not believe it. He believes that we are being surrounded by two German armoured divisions.'

'That's . . . nonsense, sir!' Bill cried. 'How can it be true?'

'It isn't,' the colonel said suavely, 'but it's what our general believes to be true. He is quite old.'

'We want to be sure that you will hold your positions here overlooking the Dyle, sir,' Bill said. 'We're behind you, as you know, because your general refused to let us take over, as we are supposed to do under Plan F.'

'Ah. yes,' the colonel said. 'The general had personal orders from His Majesty to hold this position . . . but that was a long, long time ago and plans have been changed. But not in his head . . . Now, this German attack developing against us . . .' He cocked his head as Bill recognized the thudding of field artillery pieces being fired from two or three miles to the rear. As they waited, shells screamed overhead, passing east. The colonel said, 'We will defend the position to the last man. They shall not get this Woesten ridge, nor Baardewijk, without a struggle. That is some of our artillery firing a defensive task.'

'But there's no one there!' Bill almost shouted.

'True, true,' the colonel said. 'Now go back to your Colonel Merton, dear boy, and tell him to be prepared for anything . . . *anything*, you understand? As for me, I must return to divisional headquarters and assure my general that the left flank of his position is holding firm . . . so far, at least. *Au revoir, mon ami.*'

He moved away. Bill saluted the retreating figure, climbed on his machine and hurried back to rejoin the Wessex. At battalion headquarters he found Merton sitting alone in a small chair in the gathering dusk, facing a table covered with maps. Bill went up to him at once. 'Sir, the Belgians in Woesten . . . along the whole Baardewijk sector . . . are convinced that they are being surrounded by two German armoured divisions. At least their general is, and they have to believe him. One of their outposts shot at me . . . You heard their artillery firing twenty minutes ago.'

'I thought they were ranging,' Merton said.

'No, sir. It was defensive fire. Falling on absolutely empty ground. There are no Germans anywhere near. The colonel I met told me to warn you to be prepared for anything tonight.'

'What did he mean?' Merton said. His hands were flat on the table, trembling slightly on the pinned-down maps. His eyes were duller in the dull light.

Bill said, 'Sir, the way they are now, I believe they may pull out in the middle of the night. Then they'd come back through our positions. Unless we're careful we'll slaughter them. In any case they'll cause chaos and hinder our move forward. May I warn all company commanders to that effect, sir?'

'Wait a minute,' Merton said. 'If they leave their positions, aren't we supposed to take them over? Someone's got to hold the line of the Dyle.'

'Yes, sir, but I suggest we move forward at first light . . . assuming that the Belgians do retreat. They may not.'

'How the hell do we *know* that the Germans haven't advanced those thirty-five miles during the day? We never knew they'd advanced up to the Dutch and Belgian frontiers the day before yesterday . . . All right. Warn all company commanders.'

Bill slipped off, and found the headquarters company commander Cowling sharing cups of cookhouse tea with the RSM. He said, 'I've been up to Woesten and the Belgians are jumpy as hell. The CO has

273

ordered me to warn all companies that they – the Belgians – may retreat through us during the night, and to be ready for them. That means every man must be warned not to open fire unless he is absolutely damned sure he's not shooting at Belgians. They don't look anything like Germans so there shouldn't be any trouble as long as everyone knows what might happen, and does not panic. See that everyone in headquarters and headquarters company knows. All right?'

'Yes, sir,' the two chorused, and Bill went on to pass the message in person to the commanders of the rifle companies. It was eleven o'clock and very dark when he returned to headquarters, found his straw bed in a small toolshed, and lay down to rest, his batman a few feet away.

Bill fell asleep at once, but thought he had slept barely five minutes, when, three hours later, near two in the morning, the sound of heavy artillery fire awakened him. The Belgian guns, he thought – there were batteries of them all round. Now, under them, he heard the muted distant rattle of machine-guns, and the clack of bullets high overhead. He got up, pulled his bootlaces tight, fastened his equipment, awakened his snoring batman Rifleman Driver, and walked the few yards over to the battalion headquarters command truck. Merton was there, peering at him in the dark. 'Miller? Do you hear the guns?'

'Yes, sir,' Bill said, thinking, how could anyone not hear them?

'They must be engaging enemy targets along the line of the Dyle,' Merton said.

It was Bill's turn to peer and wish he could see Merton's face clearly. Merton continued, 'Look, the Belgians are sending up star shell.'

'They're firing at nothing, sir,' Bill said. 'We know the Germans aren't close. It probably started by an outpost firing at a fellow staggering back late from a tavern. Their general had them worked up to a panic yesterday morning, and now they're worse.'

Merton began to pace up and down. A tiny chink of light shone diagonally out from the rear canopy of the command truck, and every time Merton passed it the light shone on his face and touched up the highlights in his steel helmet, even through the camouflage netting covering it.

From the shadows by the truck Bogey Harris spoke quietly. 'Here come some of 'em, sir.'

Merton swung round, 'Where? Where?'

'Right down the lane. I'll grab a couple . . . Here, come with me.'

He darted forward with three or four riflemen at his heels, and came back five minutes later, his revolver in the back of one Belgian soldier while he held another by the nape of the neck. The other British soldiers stood around with rifles and fixed bayonets thrust menacingly forward.

Merton asked the Belgians in French why they were retreating.

One of the Belgians gabbled in Flemish and Merton snapped, '*En français!*'

The Belgian said, '*Allemands . . . chars allemands . . . beaucoup d'artillerie!*'

'*Combien des allemands, combien des chars?*'

'*Mille . . . cent . . .*'

'*Vous avez vu, vous-même? Vous avez reçu les ordres pour retraiter?*'

'*Oui, oui, oui, monsieur!*'

Merton made a gesture of dismissal and Harris let the men go. They dropped back into the lane, and broke into a run, heading west.

Merton said, 'They saw a thousand Germans and a hundred tanks – they, personally.'

Bill said, 'But they can't have, sir! There's nothing there. The Germans are miles away.'

Merton turned away again. The lane beside them was full of Belgians now, and on the road a hundred yards to the north trucks and guns and motorcycles passed westwards in a rapidly increasing flood.

A Belgian officer appeared and spoke in broken English. 'We almost surrounded . . . just got away . . . me and six men . . . everyone else, *kaput* . . . They shell us now, *hein*?' He moved an arm, gesturing at the sounds of nearby explosions in the night, and the continual clattering of rifle and machine-gun bullets overhead.

'How many Germans did *you* see?' Bill cut in. 'Where?'

'Impossible see,' the officer said. 'My company wipe out . . . only me and these six men save . . . get through.'

He hurried on rearward. Bill said, 'This is like the March retreat in 1918, sir. Don't you remember how often one would find men . . . officers too . . . who swore they were the sole survivor of a company, a battalion, even a brigade . . . and when the dust settled you'd find that there were only two men missing and one killed, and he'd been shot by mistake by our own sentries. It was the same even in the retreat from Mons, when all our men were regulars, the old stiffs told me.'

Merton said nothing for a while, then abruptly: 'We're being fired at . . .'

'Belgian mortars, sir!'

'Machine-guns . . .'

'Belgian, sir, from Woesten or even closer now.'

'GHQ told us the Germans were thirty-five miles away, but they aren't always right . . . We've lost all contact with the flank battalion and the French.'

'The Belgians are flooding back, sir, breaking cables, our runners can't get through . . .'

'This is my battalion,' Merton snarled, 'and I'm not going to have it put in the bag by two German panzer divisions outnumbering us twenty to one . . . Tom, get out an order to the battalion – prepare to move, on my signal.' To Bill he said, 'I'm going to work out positions we can retreat to.' He climbed up the rear steps of the command truck and disappeared inside.

Bogey Harris muttered to Bill, 'He's in a bad way, sir.'

'It's . . . it's panic,' Bill said. 'The same thing that hit him in Bois des Loups in 1918. But what the hell am I going to do?'

'It'll take a little time to work out the orders, sir. Could we send a message for the brigadier to come here – urgently?'

'We could, but I don't know if we'd reach him in time . . . Let me speak to him again, first.'

He climbed up the steps and into the big truck, closing the blackout curtain fully behind him. Merton was working at a small side table, a map spread out before him. Two clerks were huddled in a corner and a signal operator was taking down a message coming in through his headset.

Bill said, 'Sir . . . colonel . . .'

Merton didn't look up but said, 'Yes, what is it?'

'We must not retreat from this position. Instead, we should be preparing to move forward, to take over the old Belgian positions at first light.'

'They'll have been overrun long before then,' Merton said. 'The Germans are in them now. If we don't move in a hurry, we'll be cut off or wiped out in our turn.'

Bill said desperately, 'It's not true, sir. We haven't seen a single

276

German. Nothing but overs and stray Belgian mortar bombs have come our way. There's been no artillery fire on the retreating Belgians or on their gun areas and reserve positions. Germans would have been plastering them.'

Merton went on writing. What now? Bill thought. He had his revolver. What if he drew it and stuck it into Merton's neck? Merton would yell for help. The soldiers in the truck were armed; and they were well disciplined. They probably wouldn't shoot him, but . . . He tried again. 'Sir, you'll be cashiered if you order a retreat now. The regiment will be disgraced and so will you personally. Let me go out with a patrol . . . let me take the carriers forward and I guarantee that within an hour or two at the most we will have reported back from the Dyle that there are no Germans there.'

The rear curtain swung open and a voice boomed, 'Of course there are no Germans anywhere near. Bloody Belgians panicking, that's all, led by their damned old fool of a general.' It was the brigadier, Harry Latour, in a jovially choleric mood as usual. 'What're you doing there, Merton?'

Merton said, 'I . . . I . . .'

Bill cut in, 'The CO was preparing the orders for us to move forward at first light and take over the positions the Belgians have vacated.'

'Good man,' the brigadier said. 'But you don't need written orders for that, just take your O Group forward now, and move the battalion up at first light.'

Bill stole a look at Merton, who was on his feet now, white and trembling. The brigadier did not seem to notice, but said, 'As soon as you get up there, make contact with the French 7th Army. When the Belgians cut loose, we lost all contact . . . Any other problems?'

'No, sir,' Bill said. The brigadier went out, and a moment later Bill heard his staff car staring up.

RSM Harris came in. 'Like a nice cup of hot tea, sir?' he said to Merton. 'Laced with a dram of ration rum, too. We'll be moving forward at first light then, sir?'

'Yes,' Bill said.

Merton sat down suddenly. Bill said, 'Leave the CO that tea, Mr Harris. I'll find Mr Slater and we'll get started on the preparations for the move.'

19

May 1940: Flanders

Intelligence reports from GHQ reported the steady and rapid advance of German forces, but the Queen's Own Wessex Rifles made no contact until midnight of 14/15 May. Then, at the command truck, a message arrived from B Company:

Enemy patrols approaching Dyle bridge stop am engaging.

Bill checked again the large-scale map showing the dispositions of the battalion. The battalion was disposed in a square, facing east. B Company was forward left, holding the road bridge over the Dyle beyond Woesten, where he had hidden his bicycle the last day of his reconnaissance in December. In the company's position was a section, two guns, of the brigade's 2-pounder anti-tank guns, well dug in. Two Vickers guns of the divisional machine-gun battalion, the 2nd Royal Mercia, were actually placed in C Company's area, behind B, but their task was to cover the flanks of B Company.

Merton came over to look at the map, and Bill, making way for him, left the truck and stood outside in the starlight. A few years ago, before Spain, he would have been dying for a cigarette; but now he felt no craving, and was the better off for it, because no smoking was allowed except under cover. As the distant stutter of Bren-gun fire was borne up from the Dyle and through the little town, he thought of Lesley and his children. He wished they could be together – it would somehow make it easier for him to conjure them up into reality in his mind if he knew they were together, standing perhaps by the big north window of the studio, their arms round each other, looking out over the darkened roofs of London. But then poor Pauline would be more lonely and miserable than ever, and she was the kids' mother.

He heard a 25-pounder battery open fire from the rear, the shells smashing low overhead, and returned to the truck. Tom Slater, the adjutant, standing beside Merton, said briefly, 'B Company have called down one of the SOS tasks, sir. No. Able 8.'

Bill looked at the map again, then went over to the artillery map on the opposite wall of the truck. SOS target Able 8 was a hundred yards east of the bridge, astride the main road. So the Germans, or some of them, were coming straight down the road, heading for the bridge.

He turned to the artillery major sitting by the artillery map. 'Any reports of tanks or action against them yet, George?'

George Millington had been on the same course with him at the Staff College, Quetta, and now commanded 107 Battery of 25-pounder gun-hows in 46 Field Regiment, which usually supported 21 Brigade.

Millington shook his head. 'Nothing. B Company haven't reported any tanks, nor has my FOO with them. And the anti-tank-gun section specifically reported a few minutes ago that they hadn't heard any tank engines or tracks.'

Bill thought, it's not likely that the Germans will use tanks so far forward, at night. They would be wary of running into mines, hidden anti-tank guns, dug-in tanks, even . . . anything.

Slater said, 'Another message from B, sir: "*Enemy retreated stop no firing last five minutes stop our casualties one wounded.*" '

Bill looked again at the infantry map. There was a little plank bridge over the Dyle about half a mile south of the road bridge which B was defending. It had been almost opposite the place where he had strangled the German spy. The bridge itself was easy to cover with fire, but the Germans might attempt to wade the river in the area, where the water was only four foot deep. Still, four feet, with a muddy, slippery bottom and a strong current, was a lot for heavily laden infantry. All the same, the Germans, having been stopped by B, would probe right and left along the river line, and find the plank bridge, even if they didn't know how comparatively shallow the water was there. The bridge was in D Company's area. He ought to warn Mainwaring . . . but D would have heard the firing on their left and would be on their toes. Mainwaring would see to that. He'd won a very good DSO with the regiment at Cambrai, in 1918, as a second lieutenant and, though not a brainy sort, he was a good and thoroughly efficient regimental officer. Leave him alone to do his job.

The night wore on, with further reports of enemy probing from B Company at the road bridge, and later also from D at the plank bridge. At 4.00 a.m. D reported that about twenty enemy had swum the Dyle between them and B, and might be expected to run into the rear companies' defences soon; but nothing had happened – the Germans apparently vanished.

Bill forced himself to sleep in snatches. These encounter skirmishes were nothing to do with him. Merton and the company commanders were responsible. His own responsibilities were B Echelon and second-line transport, if any; and they were in the right place, ready for any eventuality. So he lay down, told Slater to see that he was awakened only if the CO went forward or urgent news came in necessitating new orders . . . then tried to sleep; but the sporadic sounds of battle kept interrupting him, and eagerness to know, to take some part in this first battle of the war, weakened his resolve, and three times in the night he got up, went to the command truck, had a cup of tea, watched and listened for ten minutes, then returned to his straw bed.

At five past five in the morning of 15 May a message came in from B Company:

> Engagements reported during the night were against men of Belgian 14 Div fleeing from German advance farther east. 4 Belgian dead and 12 wounded on road east of bridge, most caused by our artillery.

Merton was furious. 'Damned idiots!' he stormed. 'Why the hell didn't Stokes find out they were Belgians? If they couldn't *see* them, why were they firing?'

'They must have seen movement, sir,' Bill said.

'Of course they did, but it might have been anyone, civilian refugees, even.'

Bill thought, now we've made asses of ourselves, just as the other Belgians did three days ago. It doesn't do to be too cocky in war, or fate and change will conspire to give you a fall.

'Send a signal to brigade,' Merton snapped to the adjutant. 'Tell the RAP to send a truck forward and bring back the wounded . . . Those twenty men who swam the river and vanished must have been Belgians too.'

Bill waited a few minutes for the air to clear, then said, 'Why don't you lie down for a bit, sir? You've been up all night, and . . .'

'I'm staying here,' Merton said, turning his back.

The signaller on duty at the brigade set said, 'Signal coming in about German activity, sir . . . 22 Brigade report German infantry supported by tanks reconnoitring the Baardewijk bridges . . . and have been engaged . . . two tanks burned out, casualties inflicted on infantry.'

They were pretty close on the fleeing Belgians' heels, Bill thought. Perhaps they thought there'd be no stiffer opposition than that put up by the Belgians, and came charging on, to bloody their noses against 22 Brigade. Now they'd pull back a bit and reconnoitre properly, all along the front. That meant that soon B and D Companies, which had been up all night fighting Belgians, would be put to a much more severe testing.

He turned to Merton and said, 'May I go down and spend the day with B and D, sir? I think they're liable to have a roughish time.'

'And you don't think Stokes and Mainwaring are capable of doing whatever has to be done? Or are you just looking for another DSO, perhaps?'

'No, sir,' Bill said patiently. 'I just want to see what's going on. There's nothing for me to do here unless we get new orders, and if we do I'll come back as fast as I can.'

'All right, then,' Merton said after a while. 'But don't interfere with the company commanders. *I* command them, you don't.'

Bill saluted and turned away. Merton was wearing himself to a frazzle. He was reasonably fit physically, but not mentally. In war, one needed mental stamina. Merton knew that, but . . . well, Bogey Harris would keep an eye on Merton and get a message to him if there was any sign of a real breakdown. Meanwhile, how to get forward? Merton wouldn't let him take a carrier, and quite right too. He'd walk. It wouldn't take him much more than twenty minutes.

He called his batman to him, and they set off eastwards through the neat houses of Woesten, now almost unoccupied, but undamaged, many doors and windows open, white lace curtains fluttering in the breeze, British soldiers leaning over the sill or busy sandbagging a doorway for a Bren-gun position. At the eastern edge of town, at the top of the slope down to the Dyle and the road bridge, he found C Company headquarters and said to Captain Griffin, 'Tell B that Corporal Driver and I are going up to them, straight along the road, and not to shoot. We're not Germans . . . or Belgians.'

He waited till the message had been passed, in the simple voice code that was used for such communications in the front line, then walked forward on the left side of the road, Driver level with him on the right.

It felt naked out there, in spite of the chirping birds, fluttering butterflies and flying insects. The air was heavy with the drowsiness of summer, but somewhere over there, up the slope beyond the Dyle, among the trees, barns and scattered houses, he knew that he was focused in a pair of Zeiss binoculars – German binoculars. The range would be long for small arms – must be about two thousand yards now, though lessening as they went forward; but some Hun might think it a good joke to snipe at them with a 105 mm field gun, or one of the 88 mm anti-aircraft guns which were also fitted out with armour-piercing ammunition and sights for use in an anti-tank role. Two thousand yards wasn't at all long range for them; in fact, it was almost point-blank.

The Germans were saving their ammunition, he decided as he passed a dug-down, wired and sandbagged post and entered B Company's defensive position. The road bridge over the Dyle was the core of it, and the bridge had been prepared for demolition. At the company headquarters, in the corner of a field fifty yards back from the bridge, he found Captain Stokes and his CSM, three runners, a gunner second lieutenant, a signal set-up and a corporal of Royal Engineers. Stokes was busy talking to the artilleryman, a forward observation officer, or FOO, so Bill turned to the sapper. 'What's your job here, corporal?'

'Make sure the bridge gets blown up, sir.'

Bill thought back to the most recent operation order – who was responsible for issuing the order to blow the Dyle bridges, this one and the others in Baardewijk? To the corporal he said, 'Our CO has to give you the order direct, doesn't he?'

'Yes, sir, on the radio, by code. This bridge is Dago 11. But if we are about to be overrun here, I can blow it on my own authority.'

Bill nodded and stood aside, waiting for Stokes to finish with the young gunner. Blowing bridges was a tricky business. Stokes had a platoon on the far side of the river, covering the approaches to the bridge, and they'd be in a fix if they were still there when Merton gave the order to blow. From another aspect the danger was quite a different one. The company commander on the spot – Stokes here – might realize that the Germans were about to gain possession of the bridge intact, but he had no authority to order it to be blown.

The gunner turned away and went over to his artillery radio and signallers, crouched under a hedge a few yards off. Stokes turned on Bill, saluting, and started to speak before Bill could open his mouth. 'We couldn't know they were Belgians, sir. They were coming down the road, through the fields . . . It was pitch dark . . . They were getting past us, on the right, up to the riverbank, and . . .'

'Didn't anyone fire any Very lights?' Bill asked.

'Yes. We saw men with rifles and steel helmets, but not close . . .'

'They can't have looked like German helmets,' Bill cut in.

' . . . who began firing at us as soon as the lights went up. It wasn't our fault. The bloody Belgians were in a panic, and . . .'

'Calm down, Mort,' Bill said. 'The CO wasn't pleased when we got your message this morning, but he's got over it . . . Do you still have a platoon across the river?'

'Yes, sir. And at nightfall I'm going to send out two listening posts, about three hundred yards – right and left along the river, on the far bank. They'll be two men each, with a field telephone and wire back to here.'

A runner came in, crouched low, knelt, tapped his rifle sling and said, 'From PSM Quinn, sir . . . He can see enemy vehicles at eight hundred yards, moving across our front in the front edge of a wood.'

Bill raised his own binoculars and gazed ahead . . . yes, there they were, grey-green half-tracks, moving slowly northwards, just in cover. He turned to Stokes, but Stokes was already calling to the artillery FOO . . . 'There, Tanner, see? Give 'em hell.'

The gunner sat down by his radio set and reeled off a fire order. A minute later the first salvo of 25-pounder high-explosive shells burst among the crawling vehicles . . . then another . . . another . . . A battery of 5.5-inch gun-hows joined in, with their much heavier projectiles. Earth and shattered branches flew into the air, and smoke and dust partially obscured the view.

'Good work!' Bill exulted. 'That'll teach the bastards to motor into battle in their bloody charabancs . . . The men are tumbling out as fast as they can, spreading out . . . heading this way, about two platoons . . . forty or so.'

283

Hold your fire, he wanted to tell Stokes, but Stokes had trained his men well, in spite of his sour disposition; and no one in B Company fired, though a minute later the two Vickers machine-guns from C Company's position, behind on the Woesten hill, opened fire over B at the advancing Germans.

The Boches are well trained, even if they are over confident, Bill thought, watching the field grey-green figures advance from hedge to hedge, from one fold in the ground to another, always moving. And now they were firing too, light machine-guns from the flank of the advance. It was nothing like the Somme, of course, but it was beginning to get a little dangerous to be standing about in full view. He saw a German fall – that was the machine-guns' work . . . then another was down . . . still they came on. Now their artillery came into action, 105 mm shells bursting at short intervals on and around the bridge, and some, far back, close to the Vickers gun position on the outskirts of Woesten. Ranging, Bill thought, but if their infantry think they can take the bridge, they won't wait for the artillery support to be properly organized – they'll just come straight on . . . and if B Company of the Wessex stood firm, they'd get a bloody nose.

In the next three hours, it came to pass. German infantry came skirmishing on, not fast but inexorably, like a wide stream of water flowing across sand. Their artillery fired short heavy salvoes on targets obviously passed to them by the infantry as they advanced; but no damage had been done to B Company's positions when the Germans made an assault on PSM Quinn's No. 8 Platoon on the east bank of the river. It was preceded by a ten-minute concentration of high explosive on the bridge and on 8 Platoon, and accompanied by two tanks which motored out of the woods and straight down the road at the last minute before the infantry attacked, firing their heavy guns. But the company's Bren guns, firing at short range across the river, cut the German infantry to pieces, and the dug-in anti-tank guns set one of the German tanks on fire and blew the tracks off the other. The Germans started to retreat, in the same manner that they had come forward, the British artillery harassing them until at last they disappeared into the shelter of the woods.

Bill turned to Stokes. 'They've gone, Mort . . . but not all of them. They'll have left a few out there. I don't think you'll be able to send out your listening posts without a battle.'

'I'll clear the area,' Stokes said. 'I don't want them too close. It'll only take a platoon – my reserve platoon . . . and some artillery, once we've pinpointed where they are. Eh, Tanner?'

Bill said, 'Well, I'll leave you to it. I'm going over to see how D are getting on. Is there any lateral route I can follow? I don't want to have to go all the way back up to Woesten, along the ridge, then down again.'

Stokes looked dubious. 'There's no real road or even lane, but there's a narrow track that seems to have been used mainly by bicycles. It's not more than a hundred yards in from the riverbank most of the way, so you'll be pretty close to any Germans across the river, but' – he shrugged – 'it'll save you half an hour.'

'I'll take it, then. Tell me when you've warned D that we are coming – Driver and I.'

A few moments later Stokes reported that the message had been acknowledged, and Bill set out along the narrow path, Driver at his heels with rifle at the ready, a round in the chamber and the safety catch off. Bill had felt naked and exposed walking down the road towards B Company in the morning, expecting to be sniped at by German 88s, but this was worse, for the river ran so close to their left – and across it, somewhere in those meadows and reeds and scattered trees, or behind those straggling hedges, were Germans.

But no shot was fired at them and they reached D Company without incident, to be greeted by Major Mainwaring, pipe in mouth, in his headquarters set up in a grove of willows two hundred yards back from the riverbank.

'Morning, Bill,' he said cheerfully. 'Sounded as if you were having quite a scrap over with B.'

'It was quite hot while it lasted. They knocked out two Mark IV tanks – brewed up one. Judging by the half-tracks we saw and shelled earlier, and the Mark IVs, it must be an armoured division we've got facing us.'

'It is,' Mainwaring said. 'The 13th Panzer Division.'

'H 7 on earth do you know that?' Bill asked.

'I sent a patrol over the plank bridge just before dawn and they ambushed a couple of German scouts – killed one, brought the other back. He was quite happy to tell us what division and regiment he belonged to. It'll all be over in a few days, so what's the difference, he said, the cheeky swine.'

'Any other action here?'

'A little. They've sent patrols up to the riverbank and shot at us . . . machine-guns, rifles, mortars . . . hoping we'd give away our positions. We didn't . . . but there was a light plane hovering around, too – one of theirs – long-legged sort of thing, going very slowly, and the passenger peering down at us through binoculars.'

'I saw it,' Bill said. 'It was a Fieseler Storch. They can land on a handkerchief, and every armoured division commander has one, according to intelligence. You've been thoroughly reconnoitred, perhaps by General von Fart in person.'

'We threw a lot of stuff up at him, whoever he was, but didn't get him. But those things must be sitting ducks for light ack-ack . . . of which we have none here.'

'Quite . . . Look, I don't think the Boche will do much more till nightfall. He's realized, here and in Baardewijk, that we're on the Dyle line and that we mean to hold it. So now he'll organize a proper attack. It'll start tonight, is my guess. The German high command is obviously in a hurry. I'm going back up to battalion headquarters. Any messages?'

'Nothing, Bill. Just tell the CO we're in good shape and that I don't think any Germans are going to cross the Dyle in my area. The danger is that they can take one of the bridges, or use their own assault bridging, and get in behind us.'

'You seem to be well organized for all-round defence.'

'We are, but it's not easy to actually fight facing three ways at once.'

Bill nodded and set off westwards, this time in a lane partly sunken below the level of the ground, up to A Company on the ridge behind, and thence back to battalion headquarters in the eastern outskirts of Woesten.

After reading the signals that had been sent and received since he left early in the morning, he said to Merton, 'It looks as though the Boche is getting ready for a major attack tonight or tomorrow.'

'With two armoured and one infantry division,' Merton said. 'We've had positive identifications of 13 and 16 Panzer and 108 Infantry . . . three divisions against one. About forty thousand men against us.'

'We have the Dyle,' Bill said. 'It's worth at least a division . . . Sir, I think that B and D Companies should be ordered to re-site their anti-tank guns in their areas, after dark. We should probably do the same for all our anti-tank guns, and the Vickers too. The Boches have been reconnoitring us from the ground and from the air . . . and the anti-tank guns with B actually opened fire. I think that the Germans will give them all hell from artillery as part of their preparations for the attack.'

Merton said, 'All right, all right . . . though it won't make much difference. Tom, get the order out.'

He looked haggard and worn and the trembling of his hands was even more noticeable than before. Bill said, 'I'll go and get a little sleep, sir. We may be kept up most of the night.' He saluted and went towards his bivouac.

Bogey Harris appeared at his side, saying, 'Afternoon, sir . . . From the report it looks as though B Company had a good scrap this morning.'

'They did . . . Has the CO had any sleep yet?'

'A few minutes, sir, in his chair. Hardly eaten anything, either. He'll keel over any minute. No one could go on like this much longer. And do you know what's keeping him going?'

Bill shook his head, and Harris said, 'He's afraid that if he does doze off something'll happen to give you a chance to shine. He daren't sleep in case that happens.'

'Christ! Keep an eye on him. I'm going to kip.'

He was awakened in the dusk at about half past eight in the evening by the sound of small arms, artillery and mortar fire from the southeast. He got up, pulled on his boots and equipment and went to the command truck. Merton was there, seated, staring at a map on the wall. At another table, Tom Slater was eating a bully-beef sandwich and washing it down with a big mug of tea. The radio operator was taking down a message and the two clerks were enciphering another.

To Slater, Bill said, 'What's happening, Tom?'

'A lot of activity against 22 Brigade in Baardewijk, sir. The Huns seem to be throwing a lot of infantry, with mortar support, at the bridges.'

'No tanks?'

'Some were reported earlier, to the east of Baardewijk, but they don't seem to have engaged in the fighting yet.'

'Casualties?'

'Light, so far . . . All our anti-tank gunners are ready to start digging their new positions. Machine-gunners, too.'

Bill nodded. 'Good, but they mustn't actually start until it's a little darker than this, or the move will be spotted and pinpointed.'

The RSM came in bearing a mug of tea and handed it to Bill. 'Saw you come up, sir . . . Everything in order here, sir. And I've got a couple of carriers ready loaded to take more small arms and 2-pounder ammunition down to B if they need it.'

They waited. The hours ticked away. The messages kept coming in. Enemy infantry were again attacking B Company, concentrating on 8 Platoon across the river. A fire fight was developing between D Company and Germans facing them across the Dyle. Heavy artillery fire from German 105s and the long-barrelled 150 mms was hitting the central part of the Baardewijk defences, causing houses to collapse and fill the streets with rubble. When Bill went out for fresh air and to see and hear what he could, a red glare filled the sky over Baardewijk, painting the undersides of the drifting clouds lurid pink and orange. He stayed for a moment, thinking of the Western Front . . . it had looked like this there, too, but that was just from the bursting of the myriad shells. There had been no houses to burn on the Somme or Passchendaele. Then he thought of Lesley. This could be her view, at night, too – of a burning city – if the Germans started bombing London in earnest.

Back in the command truck, a message had come in that B Company was being attacked from the south, on the west bank of the river. 8 Platoon was still holding firm on the east bank.

Bill, looking at the map, wondered whether the Germans had swum the river between D and B or used assault boats. If the latter, they'd have supporting weapons with them, such as mortars and heavy machine-guns; otherwise, not.

Merton muttered, 'They're across the Dyle!'

Bill glanced at a message just in from B Company:

Enemy attack from south repelled, heavy enemy casualties.

He handed it to Merton, saying, 'B seem able to look after themselves.'

Shelling continued relentlessly on Baardewijk, now concentrated on the northern part of 22 Brigade's area – that is, just south of the Wessex D Company's position. 22 Brigade reported that enemy infantry had seized the railway bridge in that area before it could be blown. A message came in from GHQ ordering immediate destruction of all bridges on the Dyle.

That includes Dago 11, which B Company is guarding, Bill thought. He said to Merton, 'Sir, you have to give the sapper corporal the order, personally, to blow Dago 11. But B Company have one platoon the other side. Shall I tell Stokes to get it back at once, if he can?'

'Yes . . . No . . . How long can we wait?'

'The GHQ order says immediately, sir, but I'm sure we can give the B Company five minutes. The platoon's only fifty yards forward of the bridge, but they may be heavily engaged.'

'All right.'

Bill took the radio telephone, got Stokes on the other end, and spoke in clear terms: 'Mort, your sapper corporal's got to do his job now. Get Quinn's lot back at once . . . *at once*. Cover them with all the artillery that Tanner can give you. Over.'

'Wilco. Out.'

They waited, Bill looking at his watch. British artillery shells started screaming overhead in noisy flocks. Five minutes passed. Stokes came on the blower. 'Got Quinn's lot back, less ten wounded, four killed – had to leave 'em . . . Here's Corporal Brougham.'

Merton took the set and, reading aloud from the slip of paper Slater had handed him, said, 'Dago 11, confirm.'

'Happy 11, confirm.'

'Happy 11 . . . X-ray Dog Fox . . . repeat, X-ray Dog Fox.'

'Happy 11 – Wilco. Over.'

Merton said, 'Get your No. 9 back on the blower.' Bill, listening from a few feet away, heard a tiny voice on the other end of the radio telephone, and knew that Merton was talking to Captain Stokes; he could make out the substance of what Stokes was saying.

Merton said, 'Are you all right?'

'Yes, sir. I reported some time ago that enemy had crossed the river and were attacking us from the south. They swam it, and we had no trouble wiping them out, and then I put my reserve platoon in to clean up. There were only about twenty of them.'

'Are they still attacking frontally?'

'They were . . . there goes the bridge . . . you might be able to hear the bang up there. We're all right.'

Merton gave the handset back to the signaller and returned to staring at the map. Bill said, 'They can't get at him with anything heavy now.'

'Not from ahead,' Merton said, 'but they're across the river in Baardewijk and can spread out from there.'

'We'll clear them out at daylight,' Bill said. The general has 23 Brigade and the whole of 14 Royal Tanks in reserve.'

Merton relapsed into silence. Messages kept coming in. Fighting had become very heavy in the northern part of Baardewijk. A counterattack had retaken the railway bridge from the Germans, and blown it up. 22 Brigade was suffering casualties from artillery and small arms at close quarters, but was holding its positions. No enemy tanks or guns of any kind had yet crossed the Dyle, only infantry. Now all the bridges, including the railway bridge, had been blown; whatever forces had crossed were cut off from support until the Germans succeeded in putting assault bridging across the river; there was no sign of that yet.

Bill rubbed his hands happily. He didn't know how many German infantry had got across the river; and of course they could be reinforced by men swimming or crossing in small assault boats, but, however many it was, 23 Brigade, with the Matilda tanks allotted to it, should have no difficulty in wiping out the lodgement. Then there would be work to do . . . rewire, re-sandbag, change positions of anti-tank weapons again, have the RAF locate the enemy mobile bridging equipment, restock forward areas with ammunition . . . Was it possible to contemplate counterattacking the Germans across the river? Probably not, with all the bridges blown; but it might pay General Drew, or even the corps commander, to let the Germans get a lot of troops, guns and tanks into his bridgehead, *then* wipe it all out. A blow like that would make the Germans reel. The possibility of it must certainly be under examination at this moment, by the corps and divisional general staffs. It might even be possible to . . .

Slater said, 'Sir, message from B Company – they're under heavy attack from the north.'

'The north!' Merton exclaimed. 'But that's impossible!'

'I'm afraid not, sir,' Bill said. 'The French 7th Army haven't told us much, as far as I can see from the messages, but the Germans could have crossed the Dyle in their area and now be fanning out from them southwards . . . Listen!' Everyone in the truck heard the rattle of rifle and machine-gun fire, this time from close. Bullets whistled and slapped overhead, and a few passed through the truck itself.

'That's from C Company area,' Bill said. 'Get C on the blower.' Captain Griffin came on at once, and Bill said, 'What's happening, Griff?'

'We're being attacked. I can hear tank tracks on the cobblestones, somewhere down the road behind us, but can't see anything, even with the Very lights we're putting up. But we've got a fair number of German infantry coming at us.'

Bill handed the microphone back. Now A Company, in reserve at the right rear of the battalion's position, was the only one not in contact with the enemy. The road to the rear might be cut too, if Griffin was right about hearing tanks behind him. Time to look into that in the morning – meantime, hang on here, and prepare to bring up A Company to wipe out any lodgement that the Boches might have made in C Company's area. It was important, too, to find out the situation of the French 7th Army. Had a portion of their right flank been overrun, allowing the Germans to sweep through like this? Or had the Germans infiltrated a comparatively small party across the Dyle, perhaps between the French and B Company? If that was the case, and the French still held their main positions, the situation here could be rectified fairly easily, perhaps at the same time as 23 Brigade was clearing the enemy out of Baardewijk with the tanks . . . Tanks . . . perhaps those tanks which Griffin had heard were British. 14 Royal Tanks were in reserve a mile or two back westwards along the road, and the wind was from the west.

The RSM burst in. 'Jerries in the battalion headquarters area, sir. I'm collecting all spare signallers and clerks to push 'em out . . . there aren't many.' He disappeared and they heard his voice shouting orders outside, mingled with the crackle of rifle fire, the roar of bursting grenades and the unmistakable rapid burping of a German Schmeisser machine pistol.

To Merton, Bill said, 'We'd better get A Company up to clear C Company's position, sir. Shall I give them the order? They reconnoitred it all, the day we took up these positions.'

Merton stood up suddenly, knocking over his chair behind him. 'We've got to get out,' he said, hoarsely. 'The battalion is surrounded. The road behind us is going to be cut soon if it hasn't been already. We must pull back.'

Bill's mind raced. Merton had broken, again. This time he could not expect the brigadier to appear as a *deus ex machina* and solve his dilemma for him. If he let Merton order a retreat now, the brigadier would react soon enough, either by a signal or in person. But by then it might be too late. The forward positions the battalion held now would not be easy to retake once they had been abandoned. But if at this instant he prevented Merton from giving the disastrous order, he would have no leg to stand on if Merton later denied that he had intended to retreat.

He made up his mind and said, 'Sir, I don't think we can do that without an express order from the brigadier.'

'Of course we can,' Merton said, his face ashen and grey and sheened with sweat. 'Any officer is entitled to do what he thinks best if his superior is not present and aware of the changed circumstances.'

'We can tell him, sir . . . call up brigade headquarters on the blower, and explain what's happening and what you propose to do.'

Merton half turned to the signal operator, who said stolidly, 'Can't get brigade, sir. 'Aven't been able to raise them for the last half-hour.'

'Try again. Keep trying,' Bill said, 'or – wait – can you cut into the div net? We could pass a message through them, or speak to the GOC direct, sir.'

'I'll 'ave a try, sir,' the signaller said. Merton turned back to the maps, then back again, his face working.

RSM Harris came tumbling into the truck. 'You, you,' he barked, pointing at the two clerks. 'Go and join CSM Tydings at the cookhouse . . . take your rifles and bayonets, you useless men! . . . We've killed a dozen Jerries, sir, but there are still some about . . . a couple were under this truck . . . we did for 'em with the bayonet, so's not to disturb you.' He laughed excitedly and made to leave.

'Stay, Mr Harris!' Bill snapped. Harris looked up, met Bill's eyes, and seemed to understand at once. Bill turned to the adjutant. 'Go

292

and take over command of the mopping-up operations from CSM Tydings, Tom.'

Slater hesitated, then in response to Bill's urgent jerk of the head he went out. Bill drew his revolver and said to Merton, 'Sir, order up A Company to counterattack and stabilize C Company's position. That's the only place where we're in any trouble.'

'We've got to retire before it's too late,' Merton said. 'Put that revolver away, the Germans aren't in here.'

Bill said, 'Give the orders for the counterattack, sir. Nothing else. No order for any part of the battalion to retire will go out until you have spoken to the brigadier or the GOC. I'll shoot you first.'

Merton staggered back. 'You too, Harris?' he gasped, and Bill saw that Harris too had drawn his revolver.

'Keep trying, Johnson,' Harris said to the signaller.

Merton cried, 'Mutiny! . . . By God, I've got you at last, Miller – blatant, open mutiny . . . you and your boyhood friend, Harris . . . you'll finish up in front of a firing squad, both of you!'

The signaller said, 'I've raised div HQ, sir.'

Bill said, 'Tell them we want to speak to No. 9 most immediate.'

'Very good, sir.' The signaller gave the proper call signs and in a moment said, 'He's on the line, sir.'

Bill took the microphone and said, 'Major Miller here, sir. You know what battalion. Our CO proposes to order a retreat. I have told him I will not allow any such orders to go out without your approval. Over.'

'Put him on.'

Bill gave the handset to Merton. Merton listened for a few moments, then said, 'The enemy have wiped out our C Company, sir. They've broken through the French somewhere north and are now behind us. Major Miller is threatening me with a pistol – the RSM, too; it's open mutiny. I can save the battalion if we act fast . . . over.'

He listened, his face draining of what little colour it possessed, then slowly handed the set to Bill. The GOC's voice was harsh. 'I have relieved him of command. You take over. Send him back to UK at once. How long has this been developing?'

'Three or four days, sir. Over.'

'You should have reported it sooner, however difficult . . . understand? Over.'

'Yes, sir. Over.'

'The army's not a damned prep school. Loyalty to him was disloyalty to me and to your men. Understand? I shall keep an eye on you. Out.'

Bill turned to Merton. 'I'm sorry, but it had to be done. You've brought this on yourself by not eating or sleeping properly. Anyone would break down.'

'I couldn't . . . You've won. You've got rid of me.'

'Take the ration truck back first thing. Now, you'd better have a stiff drink and try to get some sleep. You're no longer responsible . . . Good luck.'

He held out his hand, but Merton ignored it and staggered out and away. Harris breathed out a long deep sigh and put away his revolver. 'Sorry to scare you, Johnson, but it had to be done, and don't you dare say a word about what you heard in here, ever – got it?'

'Yes, Mr Harris.'

Harris turned to Bill. 'Congratulations on getting command, sir. I can tell you on behalf of all the other ranks that we're delighted. Now, if you'll excuse me, I'll see how Mr Slater's getting on with tidying up this headquarters area. Can't have dead Jerries lying around to trip up over.'

Bill said, 'Thanks, Bogey . . . I'm going to order A Company up right away to restore C. Send Major Millington here at once, please. We'll want artillery support.'

20

May 1940: Flanders

By eight o'clock in the morning of 16 May, the situation was back to normal with the 1st Battalion Queen's Own Wessex Rifles: D Company, forward right on the Dyle, was still holding its defences, though the Germans had pushed some infantry across the river between D Company and 22 Brigade in Baardewijk. B Company, left front, also held its positions, except that No. 8 Platoon, which had been on the east bank, was now in company reserve – what was left of it, for it had suffered the brunt of the German attacks during the day before and in the night. The road bridge was blown. C Company, left rear, had been partially overrun by German infantry and panzer pioneers during the night, but had held fast to what remained; and in the hour between dark and dawn A Company, from their reserve location in the right rear area, had come forward and wiped out the German lodgement with artillery and mortar support, and had also cleaned up the battalion-headquarters area. Patrols back westward along the main road had found no trace of Germans, neither tanks nor infantry; but they had made contact with 14 Royal Tanks, still waiting to take part in a counterattack to throw the Germans out of Baardewijk. In all these operations the Wessex had suffered twenty men killed and fifty wounded, of which ten were still with their companies. Seventy-eight German bodies had been counted in and close to the areas where there had been fighting, and more must have been killed by heavy shelling of reserve and rear areas.

In the command truck, looking at the map, with Tom Slater beside him, Bill said, 'First, have we stocked B and D up with ammunition?'

'Yes, sir. They reported complete twenty minutes ago.'

'Are the carriers stocked up and full of petrol?'

'Yes, sir. Collier reports one carrier hit by German shell fire and u/s. It didn't blow up, but it's had it.'

'All right. Try and get a replacement, though it's probably hopeless. Mortar platoon?'

'All filled up . . . they fired off a lot of bombs.'

'They always will in close-quarter work, like we had with C Company, and they were supporting D too . . . Any news from the rest of the division?'

'23 Brigade is due to counterattack in Baardewijk, with 14 Royal Tanks, sir, at 1000 hours . . . with all the divisional and most of the corps artillery in support. The Germans have the best part of one infantry regiment across the river, but no panzer units. Their bridging equipment is moving up close, though, and div intelligence think they may try to push a bridge across while we're busy counter-attacking.'

'Hm . . . they'll launch the bridge into the bridgehead they already hold, of course. 23 Brigade's counterattack might be too late . . . Tom, I'm going to go round the battalion. I'll take Wade with me, plus both our batmen. I'll go first to C, then B, then D, then A and back here. I'll clock in on the R/T at every company and check if there have been any messages.'

'Yes, sir. Who will be acting as 2nd-in-command?'

'Major Hodge, from A Company – permanently. Send for him now. Roland Tunning will take over A, but he'll have to function without a second-in-command. I'm going to have a bite to eat, then we'll be off. Tell me as soon as Major Hodge arrives.'

'Very good, sir. One thing . . .' Slater fished in his trouser pocket and held out his hand. In the palm lay two black stars, by themselves the rank badges of a second lieutenant, worn one on each shoulder, but when worn below the crowns that Bill was already wearing, as a major, they turned him into a lieutenant colonel. 'The quartermaster scrounged them from somewhere, sir.'

'Well, thanks,' Bill said, feeling himself blushing. He would get Driver to pin the stars on while he was getting some bread and jam and perhaps a sausage, at the HQ company cooker. Merton was gone. Bill had not seen him off, but had watched, unseen behind a house, while he climbed into a ration truck, solicitously escorted by old Fairey, the quartermaster, and the truck had started up and headed for the rear, followed in convoy by other lorries carrying many of the battalion's lightly wounded, some battlefield salvage and a few German prisoners. When they were out of sight, Bill had come out from his concealment, feeling, at last, that he was really free, and in command.

*　　*　　*

In B Company Stokes had reverted to his normal crustiness and, as soon as Bill arrived, started complaining about everything from the non-delivery of mail, through the quality of the rations, to the slow evacuation of the wounded, and the fact that many British artillery shells had landed in his area, fortunately without causing any casualties. He finished: 'And if they didn't hurt us, what reason do we have to think they hurt the Germans?'

Bill said, 'The gunners did us proud last night, Mort, and you know it. They enabled you to pull 8 Platoon back across the river without any serious trouble, and I think you would do well to tell your young FOO how much you appreciate his efforts, even if a few shells did fall short – it certainly wasn't his fault.'

'It was only two, I think,' Stokes said. 'And I suppose we really can't be sure even of that. The Boche was firing 105s at us at the same time. By the way, keep your head down while you're with us, sir. There aren't many Boche opposite now, and none of them are within five hundred yards of the river as far as I know, but they have left a few snipers up there in the edge of the woods. I've had a sergeant nicked in the shoulder – Enloe, Quinn's platoon sergeant in 8. He won't let himself be evacuated.'

'Good man. I want to speak to that platoon before I leave. Do you plan to put Quinn in for a DCM or an MM?'

'I hadn't thought of it,' Stokes said, 'but if you want . . .'

'I wasn't here,' Bill said, thinking, Stokes doesn't have any gongs himself and resents the idea of having to recommend younger men for them. He went on, 'And I don't want the regiment to get a reputation for cheap medals, but think about it. It seems to me that Quinn did admirably and should probably get an MM. If you find you can't phrase the recommendation for it, it means I'm wrong. And . . .' He fished in his pocket, as Slater had, and pulled out a pair of black crowns that he had taken out of his spare tunic. He held them out. 'Here, you're a major from now on.'

Stokes's long dour face brightened, and his pale blue eyes shone. 'Well, thank you, sir . . . I appreciate it . . . I won't let you down.'

'I know that. You've done damned well so far, you and your company. Keep it up . . . I'm going across to D. Tell them at battalion, and warn D.'

'All right, sir. But move faster than you did yesterday . . . I think you should send for a carrier.'

'Can't spare one just for taxi service . . . We'll be off.'

Today, the trip to D Company through the water meadows was made at a fast jog trot, the speed varying, with three halts in cover to break the enemy snipers' concentration. But they seemed to realize that it was a senior officer making his rounds, for a dozen shots were fired at the little group, well dispersed though they moved, and two came close, one plucking at the sleeve of Corporal Driver's tunic, and the other taking a little snip out of the rim of Bill's steel helmet, with a loud clang. Then they were in shelter, in a trench, partially waterlogged, with Major Mainwaring. Mainwaring handed him a message form, saying, 'GHQ intelligence summary, sir . . . doesn't look good.'

Bill read, and at the end murmured, 'The understatement of the year, Greg . . . the Germans across the Meuse at Sedan. We're well outflanked by that lot already.'

'Wonder what they'll do next,' Mainwaring said, puffing at his pipe. 'Head for Paris, I suppose, same as 1914.'

'Perhaps. Let's hope they do. But if they sweep round north-wards, more or less along the line of the Somme . . .'

'Behind us? Cut us off from the sea?' Mainwaring said.

'It's a possibility. Don't tell the men . . . no, that's not the way I want the battalion to be. Tell them the facts as we know them, but don't speculate on the future. Our job now is to hold the Dyle line and we're holding it.'

The sound of shelling increased and Mainwaring lifted a hand. 'Wait a mo', sir . . . hear that? That's the supporting fire for 23 Brigade's counterattack in Baardewijk . . . The shells are falling less than a quarter of a mile from us.' He jerked his head southward, downriver towards the plainly visible houses and chimneys of the city.

Bill listened a minute and said, 'I can hear the tank 2-pounders in action . . . There's been no report of the Boches getting a bridge across, so Baardewijk should be cleaned up soon.'

'Meanwhile, a whole German Army thrusts in deeper behind all of us, French 7th Army, Belgians, BEF – the lot,' Mainwaring said. 'Well, we'll just have to fight our way out. The French can't be doing much.'

'As much as the Belgians,' Bill said bitterly, 'and this is their own bloody country. I'm going up to A.'

At A Company, Captain Roland Tunning greeted him with an urgent message from Slater, the adjutant, to return to battalion HQ as soon as possible. He said to Tunning, 'Sorry. I'll have to go. Any problems?'

'No, sir.'

'Can Sergeant Young take over Harrington's platoon?'

'I believe so. He's inexperienced, but enthusiastic.'

'Good, I'll write to Harrington's mother as soon as I get a chance. It was a Schmeisser burst in the head, wasn't it, during the counter-attack on C's position?'

'Yes, sir. Cut his face into shreds.'

'That I don't have to tell his mother. Good luck and make the men rest – you, too.'

At battalion HQ, Slater said, 'We've just finished deciphering an order from brigade, sir. The whole BEF is pulling back to the line of the Dendre, to be in our new positions by 0700 tomorrow. 21 Brigade is to break contact at 2300 tonight – an hour after last light – and pass back through 23 Brigade, which will move back to an intermediate position as soon as it can disentangle itself from Baardewijk.'

'I hope it's going to be allowed to finish wiping out the Boche lodgement on this bank first,' Bill said, 'otherwise breaking contact isn't going to be so damned easy, especially for us and 22 Brigade.'

'I don't know, sir . . . The brigadier's coming up to discuss your plan for disengagement in' – he looked at his watch – 'about two hours.'

'We're the only battalion of the brigade in contact,' Bill said. 'And 23's action in Baardewijk should be over soon, so . . . guns, guns. We'll ask for lots of guns.' He turned to the battery commander sitting nearby on the front bumper of an artillery truck. 'George, come and help me make an artillery plan.'

'Do you think I'll get to shoot the whole divisional artillery? And the corps artillery?'

'Most of them, I hope.'

'Goody goody! I shall signal General Gort that we don't need a commander Royal Artillery here . . . or even a commander Corps Royal Artillery.'

Bill led to a folding table set up in the open under an apple tree and, with Major Millington at his side, began to work out how to extract B and D Companies from their forward positions, both in contact with the enemy, making a clean break so that the two companies could get away without being followed at close range by enemy troops.

'They can pass back through C and A when they reach the Woesten ridge line,' Bill said, 'but the moment of crisis will be before that – when they want to get out of their trenches and sneak off quietly. I feel that they'll never do it without heavy artillery support, but before we plan that let's think a moment . . . The more gun fire we put down, the more the Boches opposite will smell a rat – unless they're attacking at that precise moment, which would be a strange coincidence. So, suppose we put down no supporting fire – our companies just disappear.'

Millington said, 'I think they'll have to thin out that way, sir, starting at dark . . . a process that might last, say, half an hour. So it should begin at 2230, with no artillery fire. But when the final break is made, at 2300, H-hour, we have to discourage any sudden enemy rush or follow-up. I suggest that at H-hour we put down heavy concentrations, for about fifteen minutes, on three sides of B and D . . . while they run like hell. Where are they picking up transport?'

'A mile west of Woesten – we all are. But we don't go far in the trucks – fifteen miles, to 23 Brigade's intermediate position, debus, send the trucks back to Woesten to pick up the rear elements, while we march to the Dendre . . . So, OK, let's plan it that way, and hope the brigadier can get us the artillery we think we need. You can work that out?'

Millington said, 'Yes. Where are you going to be?'

'On the ridge crest, with C . . . plus my advanced headquarters radio sets. I'm not going to move back, or let C or A move, until B and D are safely back through them . . . and if the Germans do get on B and D's heels, we'll have to hold the ridge until we have scraped them off.'

'Then someone'll have to come back and scrape them off you.'

'Perhaps, but I'm not going to leave B and D until they're clear.

300

They'd never fight well again if they felt they'd been left in the lurch. Now, anti-tank defence . . . I think we'll get ample warning if the Germans succeed in getting tanks across the Dyle anywhere on our div front . . . but it's a different matter if they break through the French, and come down on us from that direction. We've got to be ready for anything, while we're static *and* while we're on the move.'

They worked on, until at one in the afternoon the brigadier, Latour, arrived. He listened to Bill's plan for withdrawing his battalion, and at the end said, 'Good . . . That's a good plan, but you must realize that 22 is withdrawing – *must* withdraw – at the same time, and it will want artillery support, too . . . more than you do, because 23 haven't been able to clear all the Germans out of Baardewijk. There are still about a hundred infantry left, with anti-tank guns, and the GOC has decided he can't afford to spend any more time or effort on them, as 23 has to go back to the intermediate position, and dig in there. So 22 have to break, while at least one of their battalions will be in very close contact with the Germans on this bank – ten to fifteen yards, to be exact. So all we have been allotted is one field regiment; the other two, plus all the corps artillery, will be in support of 22. Our field regiment – 46, of course – will revert to divisional control as soon as you have embussed and started back. Any questions?'

'No, sir.'

'Well . . . I'd like to speak to you alone for a moment, Miller.'

The brigadier stood up from the table and walked off under the apple trees, Bill at his side. In a far corner of the orchard, the brigadier turned and looked Bill in the eye. 'I heard some months ago, from a friend who knew your regiment, that you and Merton had been having a running feud for a number of years? Is that true?'

'Yes, sir.'

'Circumstances forced you to go direct to the GOC last night, and I don't blame you at all . . . something had to be done at once and you couldn't reach me, but . . . I would like to be assured that you and your RSM, and perhaps the adjutant, didn't frame Merton, as the Americans say.'

'No, sir,' Bill said steadily. 'He was on the edge of a breakdown, as he'd been before . . . when you came into our command truck a couple of nights ago, he was on the point of ordering a retreat then, of having us run from what turned out to be Belgians . . . Last night I felt I had to act. And now it looks as though we might just as well have retreated when Merton wanted to.'

The brigadier growled, 'There's a big difference between running in panic and making an orderly withdrawal to fight again another day.'

'Yes, sir.'

At 10.45 p.m. Bill waited tensely outside his command truck, which he had moved, together with skeleton personnel for advanced battalion headquarters, into C Company's area on the eastern outskirts of Woesten. The first men had slipped away from B Company on the river and were now trudging past the forward sentry posts of C. The sky was bright with the reflection of artillery fire on Baardewijk, but no guns were firing on or close to the two Wessex forward companies.

'The gunners are having a bit of a field day, aren't they, sir?' Tom Slater said to Bill.

Bill said, 'They had ammunition stacked up for a long battle on this line, and now not enough transport to move it all, so they're getting rid of it on the Germans . . . but they wouldn't have to be firing so heavily in support of 22 in Baardewijk if 23 had been able to clear the Boches off this bank. 22's having a hard time breaking contact, that's why there's so much artillery fire down there.'

He relapsed into silence, thinking, the Germans must smell a rat by now . . . but perhaps they were thinking that all the fury in Baardewijk was another final effort to wipe out the German bridgehead on the west bank.

He went to the door of the command truck and said, 'Anything from B or D?'

'Just an OK from both of them, two minutes ago, sir . . .'

Bill peered at the luminous dial of his watch, holding it up to the sky so that it could catch and reflect the glare up there. One minute to H-hour . . . thirty seconds . . . fifteen . . . time!

Shells from 46 Field Regiment's twenty-four guns started screaming overhead on their way to form a box of high explosive and flying steel fragments round the two forward Wessex companies. From inside the truck, the signaller called, 'Greenhouse from D, sir . . . and from B.'

Greenhouse was the code word agreed on to mean 'closing down

302

and moving'. The rear parties of the two forward companies were on the move. Bill waited, listening for anything that would tell him all was going well. To Captain Griffin, at his side, he said, 'They ought to be coming up the hill any minute now, Griff. . . Go to your front area and make sure there aren't any Germans following close.'

Griffin vanished into the ragged darkness. Bill waited, walking impatiently two paces towards the command truck, then two paces away. By his own radio truck George Millington sat back, headphones on his head, listening to the relaying of fire orders from the gun positions in the rear.

The minutes crawled by. Suddenly Griffin appeared, Mort Stokes beside him, both grinning in the eerie flickering light. 'All clear and a clean break, sir,' Stokes said.

'The Boches didn't suspect that you were going?'

'No, sir,' Griffin said.

Bill thought, perhaps not, or perhaps they're under orders not to press us too hard. The longer we hold fast up here in Belgium, the deeper the other German armies penetrate behind us.

To Stokes he said, 'Well done. Go on back to the transport now. You have the rendezvous?'

'Yes, sir.'

'We're planning to move and march in convoy, but things are apt to go wrong at night.'

'Or at any other time,' Stokes said. He saluted and moved on, followed by his company.

Slater said, 'D ought to be in soon, sir.'

'They have a longer way to go . . . back up to the ridge top and then along, but . . .'

'Here they are, sir.'

Coming down a side road that led from upper Baardewijk, D Company came out of the darkness, marching in open column. Mainwaring took the pipe from his mouth, saluted and said, 'D Company present and correct, sir. No casualties . . . thanks to the gunners.'

'Move on back then. You know the rendezvous?'

'Yes, sir.'

'Good luck, then. I'll be about ten minutes behind you.'

He turned to George Millington, now standing up beside his radio truck, and put out his hand. 'Thanks, George.'

'Don't mention it. *Quo fas et gloria ducunt*, and all that, don't you know?'

'Are you going to leave an FOO with C now?'

Millington nodded. 'Tanner – I took him away from B as he passed just now. He's got all his communications with him and I don't have anyone else up here.'

'All right . . . Griff, start moving back in ten minutes and, when you go, clear out quickly, no dawdling, no straggling, just get to the transport. As soon as you and A are embussed, I'll give the order to move, because we're supposed to be first into position on the Dendre. You know the rendezvous?'

'Yes, sir.'

'Prepare to move in five minutes,' Bill said to Slater.

'We're all ready when you give the word, sir.'

'Where's the RSM?'

'Here, sir –' Harris stepped out of the farther dark.

'Ride with me, Mr Harris,' Bill said. 'I want to talk to you about the mortar platoon – they were damned slow getting into action last night – and about ways of setting up ammunition points and letting everyone know where they are. I have a feeling we'll be doing some more of these sudden moves, and you have to be free to set up the AP in the best place to get the ammunition to, *and* the companies have to know early where it is.'

'Very good, sir.'

Bill thought, did he have time to write to Mrs Harrington? Three minutes . . . it wasn't enough. He'd have to find time tomorrow.

Time. 'Let's go,' he said, and climbed up into the front seat of the command truck. The driver started it up, slipped into gear and moved off slowly across the bumpy field, onto the cobblestones, and westwards towards Brussels, and beyond it the river Dendre, or Dender.

The distance from Woesten to Grosart on the Dendre was thirty-eight kilometres, or twenty-three miles, of which the troops did fifteen miles in the 3-ton motor transport, and marched the remaining eight in the last of the night. But, in Grosart, when Bill had put out outposts and ordered the remaining men to rest where they could, he found that the move had not gone at all as planned. Instead of an orderly formation of 21 Brigade, the troops now with him included bits and pieces of units from all over the place. He had his own battalion, complete; in addition, scattered now all round Grosart, was 46 Field Regiment, Royal Artillery; 282 Anti-Tank Battery, of sixteen 2-pounder guns, from another division; two companies of 14 Royal Tanks, with Matilda tanks; two companies of 6th South Yorks, a territorial infantry battalion; B Company of 2 Macdonald Highlanders, an Army Troops Medium Machine Gun Battalion; and 49 Field Company, Royal Engineers, also Army Troops.

Slater, who had been with him on his rounds while he was trying to find out where 21 Brigade headquarters was and who all the troops were, said, 'What a mixed bag, sir . . . Where on earth have they all come from?'

'All over, as you can see,' Bill said grimly. 'I don't like to see saboteurs and spies where there aren't any, but this really looks as though there was a Boche fifth column operating during the night, knocking out guides on crossroads and replacing them with their own men . . . changing signs and lights . . . Is there any touch with brigade . . . *our* brigade?'

'Not yet, sir. They were supposed to be here in Grosart before us.'

'I know. Keep trying.'

He moved away, sat down on a bench outside the door of a deserted and half-ruined house, and brought out his message pad.

Dear Mrs Harrington . . .

He stopped, and called over to Slater, 'Are you sure that Harrington's father is dead?'

'Yes, sir. I was correcting the officers' next-of-kin rolls the day before the balloon went up.'

Bill began again:

Dear Mrs Harrington,

    As you may have been officially notified by now, your son Edward was killed in action with us on the night of 15/16 May, in Belgium. He was a good young officer, and good friend, and always a cheerful soul in Mess. We shall miss him. He died instantly, and without suffering. [God knows whether he did or

305

not, but I can't say anything else.] Please accept the deepest sympathy of his brother officers.

He signed it *William Miller, Lieutenant Colonel*, and then the full unabbreviated title of the battalion: *1st Battalion the Queen's Own Wessex Rifles*.

He folded it up and called to Slater, 'Put that in an envelope and see that it gets out with our first mail. Censor it first.'

'Right, sir. There's a message coming in from brigade. It's not long.'

Bill waited, looking at the wooded slope falling down to the Dendre from the east. Would the GOC plan to place the forward defended localities east or west of the river? In other words, was he planning to use the river to defend the troops or the troops to defend the river . . . probably the latter, as it was not a good idea to let the enemy – any enemy – come right up to an obstacle – any obstacle. An undefended obstacle is no obstacle, as the saying was. The Dendre seemed a little deeper than the Dyle, definitely not fordable any-where . . . open banks away from the village, here and there cluttered with farm buildings and barns.

Slater came up beside him, message form in hand. He gave it to Bill, who read:

From 21 Brigade to all units – Orders to concentrate at GROSART cancelled repeat cancelled stop concentrate immedi-ately at BRUYERES 482619.

Bill looked at his map, properly folded in its talc-covered case . . . 482 619 . . . there it was, another small town or village like Grosart, but ten miles farther north on the Dendre. Obviously there had been another change of plan in the night, and someone else was going to come here to Grosart while his own division was moved north. Damned nuisance, and more delay.

He turned to Slater. 'Warn all our people we'll move north in twenty minutes from now. Order of march same as last night. Start line: the church here in Grosart. Head of column will pass start line at . . . 0730.'

'Right ho, sir.'

The lieutenant colonel commanding 46 Field Regiment Royal

Artillery was here, with a major from the South Yorks, the captain commanding the Macdonalds, a tank corps major, another gunner major from the anti-tank battery, and a sapper major commanding the Engineer Field Company. The lieutenant colonel spoke first. 'Miller, have you had any new orders? We can't all sit around here. There's obviously been a cock-up.'

'All units of 21 Brigade have orders to go north to Bruyères,' Bill said. 'But I don't know about anyone else. You might as well come with us. At least, *you're* in the same division.'

'I will. I can lift some of your men, too. We'll move in fifteen minutes.'

'Thanks . . . I honestly don't know what the rest of you should do, but if you don't have communication with your own formations, I suggest you come along too, and we'll get it all sorted out in Bruyères. Someone else must be supposed to come here.'

'Very well,' and 'All right,' the majors and captains said, and Bill turned to his second-in-command, Major Hodge. 'Peter, work out an order of march with them. And Tom, detail a company to go with 46 Field.'

'I hear an aeroplane,' the Highland major said sharply.

Then Bill heard it, growing louder, and others heard, and all round whistles began to blow the air-raid alarm. The aircraft came into sight, a single-engined monoplane, with a long canopy behind the engine. Behind the canopy Bill saw two heads and under the wings the roundels of the Royal Air Force . . . but someone was already shooting. Bren guns set up on their anti-aircraft mountings were blazing away. Bill recognized the machine as a Fairey Battle, a British fighter-bomber of very moderate performance in either role. It was coming down towards the open plaza at the end of the Dendre bridge, where they stood. The man in the back of the cockpit was struggling to open the canopy . . . were they going to try to land . . . or parachute . . . from that height, of barely three hundred feet?

The fire being sent up at the aircraft began to die down as more of the firers saw and recognized the RAF roundels. The machine came lower and as it passed over the plaza something flew out of the opened back-half of the cockpit and fluttered down to land a hundred feet away from Bill. It was one of the old-style message streamers the RAF used to employ on the North-west Frontier of India, and which he'd seen in training exercises and actually used in the campaign of '34. A soldier had to run to pick it up, as the Battle climbed away, waggled its wings once and disappeared north-westward. Bill called, 'Let me have that.'

The soldier gave him the streamer; he opened the lead-weighted message pouch in the tail and took out a folded signal form. It read:

> 30 German tanks, 60 half tracks, 20 guns, five miles due east of GROSART heading west at 0715 hrs.

It was now 0722. Bill leaped across to his command truck, shouting, 'Get brigade on the blower – the brigadier, immediately!'

In and around the town all the drivers were starting their engines. The Royal Artillery quads were backing down onto the 25-pounders. Troops who had been stretching their legs, smoking, urinating in the hedges and alleys, were climbing back into their vehicles. The Wessex and South Yorks, who now had no vehicles except tactical ones, were falling in ready to march north.

The signaller at the set said, 'Can't raise 'em, sir.'

Slater said, 'Perhaps they're moving again.'

'Why the hell can't he stay in one place?' Bill exploded.

He jumped to the ground and stared eastwards . . . The Germans would arrive any minute and whoever was supposed to be here to defend the Dendre line at this point – wasn't. If the Germans weren't stopped, the new British position farther north would be tactically outflanked even before any troops had settled into it. He made up his mind.

He said, 'Tom . . . send out DRs at once to get the anti-tank battery commander here, *with his guns*, at once. Also, all our company commanders, except . . . Griff!' He raised his voice, bellowing at the commander of C Company, who was falling in his men fifty yards away. Griffin ran towards him. Bill caught him by the lapel. 'Griff, Germans coming down from the east, that road, take your company and *double* out to meet them . . . one mile, no more. You'll get the anti-tank battery right behind you. Set up a defensive position with them astride the road. I'll be along in a few minutes with the rest of the battalion . . . George!'

'Yes, sir.'

'Go forward with the anti-tank guns, as FOO, until I come up.

Tell your 46 CO – Marshall, isn't it? – that I'm taking his regiment under command . . . tell him to get trails down at once, targets to the east.'

'Right-ho.'

C Company was already running past them, heavy packs bouncing on their backs. Christ, he should have told them to leave those behind. Too late now . . . and perhaps they'd need them soon. A runner passed and Bill grabbed him. 'Where are you going, Thompson?'

'B Company, sir.'

'Don't! Go to the carriers, and tell Mr Collier to bring them all here, full speed.'

He turned to another truck, to see the moon face of Second Lieutenant Vail, the mortar-platoon commander, who was in the front seat. He yelled, 'Get into action there, across the bridge, *now*, facing east!'

The carriers came, deafening him with the grind of their tracks on the cobbles and the roar of their open exhausts. Bill grabbed Lieutenant Collier by the shoulder. 'Up the road, fast. Support C Company when they take up position . . . Here come the anti-tank guns! Follow them! Watch the flanks.'

He ran over to the leading vehicle of the anti-tank battery and leaned in to the major commanding, seated in the front. 'German armour coming down that road. One of my companies is on its way into position – follow and work out defences with them. We're all following . . . Go!'

He returned to his command truck. 'Tom, bring the whole battalion up the road after me. Peter . . . stay here by the bridge. Keep the second signal truck and try to raise brigade or division to tell them what's happening – most immediate . . . Put the Macdonalds and one company South Yorks into a defensive position by the bridge there, far side . . . the other company South Yorks to be ready to come up to me, in reserve.'

The Royal Tank Regiment major appeared, saying, 'Heard there was a flap. Anything for me to do?'

'You're in command of the two companies?'

'I'm the senior officer, so I suppose I am – Major Hammond, at your service.'

309

'I'm taking you under command. We have German armour coming straight at us, and nothing between us and them. You don't have any other orders?'

The tank major looked dubious, scratching his head through his black beret. 'Well, sir, we've just been told to wait in Grosart for further orders.'

'Well, I'm telling you you're about to be attacked by German armour and panzer infantry. We have to defend ourselves . . . and I'm in command.'

'All right, sir, what do you want us to do?'

'Good man . . . Make sure you're on my command radio net and bring your tanks up the road until you find my headquarters. There, I'll give you one of my companies for close support, to go wherever you go.'

The major's face brightened. 'Will do, sir.' He saluted and hurried back to his grumbling rumbling tanks.

Bill stood a moment, mentally checking: his own battalion – dealt with; the two companies of South Yorks – dealt with; anti-tank guns – dealt with; artillery – dealt with; tanks – dealt with; machine-gunners – dealt with; administration – would look after it; ah, engineers.

He said, 'Where's the field company commander?'

'Here, sir –' The engineer major came forward.

Bill said, 'Leave men here to prepare this bridge for demolition. Bring the rest of your men forward to make anti-tank obstacles with whatever mines you have . . . The order to blow this bridge is to be given by me only, understood?'

'Yes, sir,' the sapper said coolly.

Ten minutes later Bill had set up his headquarters behind two isolated labourers' cottages at a crossroads half a mile east of Grosart. C Company was in position astride the road, digging hard, half a mile forward; A was moving out right, D left, where anti-tank-gun crews were already preparing their positions. B had just arrived, panting, at headquarters. A few yards away Millington was speaking into his radio set and here now came the first shell from the 25-pounders behind Grosart, ranging on the road ahead. So far, no sign of the Germans. Bill thought their column must have stopped for a routine rest or brew-up.

Now, preceded by the rumble and roar of engines and steel tracks, came twenty-five Matilda tanks of 14 Royal Tank Regiment.

The leading tank stopped near Bill and the major leaned out of his turret. 'All present and correct, sir. What orders?'

Bill went close and cupped his hands. 'Here's my B Company commander, Major Stokes. He and you will be my reserve . . . take positions somewhere close, where you can fire to either flank. I want you to let the Germans come to you, if they do . . . they'll certainly try to work round us here. I don't want you to charge at them . . . let them come . . . so be hidden, then give them hell from close . . . Can you get on the gunner net?'

'Yes, sir. And I can give artillery-fire directions.'

'Good. Mort, climb up on the tank and go and find a good position. Quickly!'

He returned to his command truck. Slater met him. 'A Company reports contact with enemy, sir . . . three armoured cars and some half-tracks. They knocked out two of the armoured cars; the men in the half-tracks have dismounted and are spreading out.'

'Just in time,' Bill said. 'Has Griffin asked for artillery support, George?'

'Yes . . . He's got young Tanner . . . they're calling down fire on more half-tracks and some tanks . . .' He listened on his own headset for a moment. 'Tanner says the tanks are Mark IIs.'

Bill rubbed his hands. 'The Matildas will eat *them* up for breakfast if they get that far . . . Just in time, just in bloody time!'

He felt alert and cool and, yes, happy, thoroughly happy. The first German shell rumbled over, to burst a hundred yards from the crossroads. Good! 'Let battle commence!' as Stanley Holloway said in his famous recitation.

At four o'clock in the afternoon there was a lull in the fighting. The battalion had held fast. The anti-tank guns dug in with the rifle companies had turned attacking German panzers, forcing them to go wide and then sweep in, expecting to catch the British defences in rear. Instead, they themselves were caught by the concealed and partly dug-down Matildas, whose high-velocity 2-pounders and thick armour were too much for the smaller and lighter Mark II panzers. Nine charred or shattered German tanks stood in the fields between the crossroads and the Dendre, and forty corpses lay with them, scattered in the crops, or inside the hulls. Ten prisoners were in a barbed-wire enclosure set up close to Bill's headquarters, guarded by a couple of sentries.

The duty signaller called to Slater, 'Message from BEF coming in, sir.'

Bill climbed up into the truck. One felt very exposed in here when German 105s were shelling the area – and with reason, for shell splinters had riddled the woodwork, scored a long gash in the hood and ripped open a tyre. His force had suffered more than material damage, too, for close on fifty men had been killed or wounded, the casualties spread evenly among all arms. There had been three messages from 21 Brigade: the first peremptorily ordered Bill to take his force to Bruyères – to which Bill had answered that he was in action against what appeared to be a German panzer division one mile east of Grosart and could not disengage before dark without help.

The second message, an hour later, congratulated him on his initiative and told him to hang on at least until dark, when he should retire across the Dendre and endeavour to move north to rejoin the rest of the division round Bruyères. The third message, half an hour ago, advised him that the 1st Wessex and certain other troops now with him were being detached from their parent formations, formed into an independent force, and placed directly under command of GHQ, as Army Troops; orders would follow shortly. The message now coming in obviously contained the new orders.

George Millington came over to him and said, 'Pretty good cockup all round, don't you think?'

Bill said, 'It looks like it. They've changed orders twice already, and now . . . how are we going to function, directly under BEF? Where the hell are we going to get rations and ammunition from? How are we going to evacuate our wounded?'

Millington said, 'God knows. Perhaps they'll deign to tell us soon . . . I've found out who's commanding the panzers opposite us.'

'Who?'

'Someone nicknamed *Der Henker*. That's old German for "the hangman" . . . I understand German and two of the prisoners were saying they wouldn't have been sent piecemeal into battle against our Matildas if the Hangman had been up in time. Later it appeared that the Hangman was a major general, and commanded 13 Panzer –

the same people who were bumping us on the Dyle.'

Bill said, 'Well, they've moved pretty fast . . . someone else must have taken over from them on the Dyle to release them to hurry down here to try to turn our flank . . . again. The Hangman, eh . . .' His mind went back to the sun-drenched dusty mountains of Teruel, the olive grove in front of Villalba. Aloud he said, 'The Hangman is Major General Stefan von Krug . . . you could call him an old friend of mine.'

Slater came out with a message form. 'Here it is, sir.'

Bill read:

> To 1 WESSEX for Lt Col MILLER Tps now with you are constituted as GADFORCE which you will command until arrival of Colonel K.B. GADNEY from HQ 4 CORPS as commander stop GADFORCE will protect southern flank of BEF between line of DENDRE and ESCAUT from incl GROSART while moving to reach BANDIER not later than 1200 MAY 20 in conformity with movement of BEF to ESCAUT line stop.

Then followed administrative details, radio channels to be used, forecast movements of BEF Advanced HQ, finishing with the plea *Signal immediately details of all units now with you* and ending with the usual curt admonition ACK meaning 'Acknowledge receipt'.

'We've ack'd, sir,' Slater said, 'and I'm starting to work on the message telling them who we have here . . . Do you think I could forget to tell them about 14 Royal Tanks? I'm sure they'll take them away once they realize where they are.'

'Wish we could,' Bill said. 'But tanks ought to be used en masse. They *should* take them away – or send us the rest of the regiment . . . some hope! . . . Do you realize that this message means that the BEF is not going to hold the Dendre line at all? They're pulling back to the Escaut at once . . . and we're being detached as a sort of moving flankguard. Why didn't they just tell the right flank div of the corps to protect the southern flank, and give it some tanks to do it with? Then the flankguard would be able to call on a whole div and corps artillery if they needed it. Now we'll be swanning around by ourselves, out in the blue with just 46 Field Regiment – twenty-four 25-pounders. I hope to God they have plenty of ammunition, George . . . and gunners who can do without sleep.'

He withdrew a little from the others. Here was Bandier . . . How far, how long would it take to get back there? How many bridges were there between Grosart and Bandier which would have to be protected? Should Gadforce get back across the Dendre now and retreat down the far bank . . . or should it stay on this bank? With the enemy strength unknown, it would be quite reasonable to use the Dendre as an obstacle . . . for the British main line of defence was now about to move back to the Escaut.

When was this Colonel Gadney coming? He'd never heard of him but apparently he was being hauled out of some staff job at 4 Corps HQ. Well, as soon as he arrived, he'd have to make some important decisions. Should Gadforce break contact at dark? Should the tanks be got out before there was any chance of the Grosart bridge being blown behind them? Might it be feasible to counterattack the Germans just before dark, in another couple of hours? They had obviously been rather unnerved and thrown off balance by the severe mauling they had received in the late morning. Keep your eye on the objective, he repeated to himself . . . *protect the southern flank of the BEF*, but . . . wouldn't it be doing just that to give 13 Panzer a really bloody nose?

Well, it wouldn't be in his hands much longer. Where in *hell* was Colonel Bloody Gadney, coming to supercede him just when he was beginning to enjoy himself?

314

21

May 1940: Flanders

Wade, the intelligence officer, was tall and sandy-haired, in his early
thirties and not a regular, having been posted to the 1st Battalion
from a territorial battalion soon after the outbreak of war. In peacetime he was a broker at Lloyds. He was speaking now to Bill, near
five o'clock of the summer evening, as both sat on the edge of Bill's
command HQ slit trench, their legs dangling down inside. Wade
said, 'It's very hard to make an accurate estimate, sir. We know from
the prisoners that we are facing elements of 13 Panzer, but it's not
clear just how many elements. From what that prisoner said whom
Major Millington overheard, the divisional commander was not up
at the start of the battle. Therefore it's reasonable to assume that his
whole division wasn't either . . . that we, this morning, were facing
perhaps two battalions of the division's rifle regiment and one of its
panzer regiments. I feel personally that they have been reinforced by
now – that the whole of the division is up – but without aerial
reconnaissance, I can't prove it.'

'This might help, sir,' said Tom Slater, who had walked up and
stood by, listening, a few moments earlier. He handed Bill a signal
form.

Bill read:

> From BEF to GADFORCE – air recce and other intelligence
> sources identify enemy with whom you are in contact as 13
> Panzer Div with one regiment from 108 Inf Div under command
> stop latter is NOT repeat NOT mechanized and was last reported
> fifteen miles east of HQ 13 Panzer.

Bill scrambled to his feet, handing back the signal, and walked aside,
thinking. When that extra infantry regiment arrived on the battlefield it would alter the balance of numbers decisively. Also, he
believed that Wade was right in thinking that by now the whole of 13
Panzer's armour would be up, plus the rest of its mechanized infantry. That would make some ten thousand troops and a hundred tanks

against his two-thousand-odd men and twenty-five Matildas – no, only twenty-three, for two had been put out of action in the morning's engagement.

Where the hell was Gadney?

To retreat or not to retreat? That was a question to be answered by the official commander, and he wasn't here. But it was also a problem which would solve itself, perhaps disastrously, if someone didn't give the right answer soon. The definition of his task rang in his ears: to protect the southern flank of the British Expeditionary Force from the Dendre at Grosart to the Escaut at Bandier.

He returned to his slit trench and said briefly, 'Wade, take over at the command truck. Tom, come and help me work out some orders. We're going to get back behind the Dendre before von Krug has a chance to swallow us whole.'

Seated in an empty front room of one of the labourers' cottages, plaster all over the floor and on the deal table, Bill said, 'Take notes, Tom . . . We'll start thinning out at dark . . . first, the sappers and all the tanks, with our B Company still attached to them. I want all that lot out before midnight . . . There'll be an artillery plan to cover the withdrawal as a whole but I hope we don't have to use artillery that early . . . which way's the wind blowing?'

'From the east, sir.'

'Good. Let's hope it stays like that, then the Germans may not hear the tanks moving . . . Major Hodge is to organize units into the defence of the bridgehead at Grosart as they come in – all defences to be on the east bank of the Dendre . . . the road bridge should already be prepared for demolition . . . Now, our anti-tank guns are mechanized, the infantry are not. The guns must go first, starting at say, 0200 hours . . . and the infantry soon after, say 0215 . . . all back to the Grosart bridgehead . . . Warn Major Hodge that I'll order the Grosart bridge to be blown as soon as the last of our people are over, and he's to tell me when that is. He'll know because he is to be there at the bridge, checking them all across . . . Start working out the detailed timings on that basis, while I make an artillery plan with Major Millington.'

The light began to fade finally from the sky at half past ten, and in the rear areas the men made ready to move. The engineers loaded their unused stores and mines into their big vehicles; 14 Royal Tanks made sure that the tanks were in perfect order, and marked out the routes by which they would leave their tactical, dug-in positions for the withdrawal; B Company, under the tank major's command, split up into twos and threes ready to climb up onto the tanks allotted to them as their somewhat exposed and uncomfortable transportation. At 2330 hours the leading tanks of 14 Royal Tanks moved rearward past the start point on the road, followed by the Field Company Royal Engineers. RSM Harris, who had been at the start point to oversee traffic control, returned to Bill at headquarters. 'Got that lot off all right, sir,' he said. 'Seemed to me they were making enough noise to wake the dead, but p'raps not.'

Bill said, 'Thanks, Mr Harris . . . you got our reserve ammunition off with them?'

'Yes, sir, and I only hope we don't need it before it's our turn to get back.'

Bill heard, quite clearly, the rattle of machine-gun fire from the west, behind him, from the direction of Grosart. My God, he thought, have I been too late already? Has von Krug passed a regiment round me and gone for the bridge, which is at the moment my jugular?

He heard shells bursting back down there . . . were they landing a bit farther north, right as he looked back, rather than due west? Perhaps the Boche had made a right hook . . . but the shells could be British, too . . . Very lights went up and hovered in the warm night before fluttering, like wounded moths, back into the darkness of earth.

From the command truck close behind him Slater said, 'Major Hodge reports enemy infantry attacking the Grosart bridge from the north-east, sir . . . our leading tanks crossing now.'

'Thank God for that!' Bill said aloud. They'd be under small-arms fire, but that wouldn't bother them. The sappers following on the tanks' tail would have to hope for the best; but at least the bridge had not been seized or blown up.

But the Germans, back there at the bridge, would have seen the Matildas crossing, rearward. They would report it. Any enemy commander in his right mind would deduce that the rest of the British force on the east bank would be following soon. He couldn't afford to wait till 0215 to start the final withdrawal. It must begin at once, now!

He said to Tom, 'Get a message out to everyone – withdrawal H-hour is changed to 1245 . . . acknowledge . . . Got it?'

'Yes, sir.'

'George? . . . there you are! Tell your CO to stand by to fire SOS tasks on all our front, any moment now. Remember, we'll cover C with our own mortar platoon. That'll free some of your guns for other tasks. Who's leading the withdrawal?'

'D, sir.'

'I must go and talk to Mainwaring now. We'll go by carrier this time. Ready, Driver? Carrier ready? Hop in. Go!'

The little tracked vehicle careened off into the darkness across a beet field, and in a few minutes arrived at the headquarters of D Company. Bill knew he was in the right place, from the marshmallow smell of Mainwaring's pipe tobacco. He jumped down from the crowded carrier and said, 'Greg, have you had the message about putting H-hour ahead to 1245 yet?'

'No, sir.'

'Well, you will, any minute. We've got to get out fast . . . you're leading on the road back to Grosart. When you get close, remember that you may run into German infantry who've been attacking the bridge for the past half-hour. You'll hit them from the rear, so they will be taken by surprise. But make sure your fellows aren't surprised, too, so that they take advantage of the situation . . . think in terms of clearing the Boche out of your way with the bayonet.'

Mainwaring sucked on his pipe and said, 'I hope those bloody Highlanders behind the Vickers guns will know we're coming.'

'They will,' Bill said. 'All right otherwise?'

'The men are getting a bit tired, that's all.'

'Who isn't? I'll be getting back. See you on the road, at the start point.'

'Right-ho, sir.'

At 0530 hours in the morning of 18 May Bill was shaving in a bowl of hot water provided from the headquarters-company cooker. He was established in an old house, barely damaged, in the middle of Grosart, the whole of Gadforce settled in around him. The two South Yorks companies, plus two of his own, half the anti-tank guns and all the Macdonald machine-guns were guarding the line of the

318

Dendre. The tanks and his own remaining two companies were in reserve. The engineers were blowing another bridge two miles farther upstream – the main Grosart bridge had gone up at near 0130 hours, when the last of C Company had doubled back across it, pursued by desultory fire from German light machine-guns.

As he shaved, Bill glanced at the map spread out on the windowsill in the early sunlight. Here he was, on this bank, and there von Krug was, on the other bank . . . though not actually in sight or in contact, for the enemy had withdrawn all forward troops before first light, so that, though Bill was sure the Germans were watching him and making their plans, he could not see any. The map showed that there were twelve bridges over the Dendre between Grosart and Bandier. 13 Panzer could obviously get assault bridging equipment up in a hurry if they wanted it; but they probably didn't have any now. So, as he withdrew south-west along the Dendre, von Krug would either have to beat him to one of those bridges, get across in front of him and block his withdrawal . . . or he'd have to cross behind Gadforce on temporary bridging or pontoons, and then follow him up the west bank – a long rearguard action for Bill, a long stern chase for von Krug.

He put down his razor, washed and dried his face and made a note:

Inquire BEF if may blow all bridges to BANDIER.

It would be a good idea, if permission was given, for it would force von Krug to choose a crossing site where assault bridging could be used – and that would take time. He wrote out the message, and yelled, 'Driver! Take that to the adjutant please, for immediate dispatch.'

He continued staring at the map, and thinking. Blowing the bridges would ensure that, as he withdrew, he'd have von Krug on his tail, looking for an opportunity to cut him off. So he should be looking for an opportunity to give Panzer 13 another bloody nose. One good way of doing that would be to stand and fight, in some place in which von Krug could not bypass him but would have to come at him more or less head-on . . . Well, put in its simplest terms, he should look for a place where he could force battle on von Krug on terms favourable to himself, or at least reasonably so.

He made another note:

Warn RE to prepare to blow all Dendre brs to excl BANDIER.

Where the hell was Gadney? It was infuriating to think that, as soon as the man arrived, all his planning and thinking might well be thrown out of the window.

He sat down, took a signal pad and began to write:

Dearest Roger and Brenda,

One letter will have to do for both of you as I am rather busy. I can't tell you more except that it is exciting, and the men have behaved marvellously. I am very proud to be commanding them. How is the cricket coming along, Roger? Though I suppose your term has hardly started yet? And Brenda, try not to worry about the war too much, or even Mummy's problems, as I know you do, because it is really important that you get eight credits in your School Cert exam. You have the capacity for it, I know, but capacity is not much use without concentration. I shall be writing to Lesley in a few minutes, if I am not interrupted by the Boches, but in case I am, call her on the phone and tell her you have heard from me, and I am fit and well, though I have rings under my eyes from oversleeping, ha ha! At least I am washed and shaved and do not smell too much. It is . . .

He looked up as he heard a knock on the door. 'Come!'

The RSM marched in, saluted and said, 'May I have a word with you, sir?'

'Of course. Fire away.'

'The men are getting a little jumpy, sir. They don't show it much, but it's there. This walking backwards has upset them, particularly when they have never *had* to go back. They've been ordered to, after they've beaten all the Jerries that's come at them.'

'I know,' Bill said, 'but it can't be helped. Our glorious Allies are either actually running, or at least not fighting, and we're nowhere near strong enough to stand up to the whole German Army by ourselves.'

'The men know it, sir. But they understand that, in a way, the better they fight now the less chance there'll be of them ever getting out. How *are* we going to get out, sir, if the French and Belgians are collapsing all round us?'

'I don't know,' Bill said. 'I don't know. But I do know that we have to do our job as we see it, from day to day.'

'Can you tell the blokes that, sir? They'll listen to you. They're very proud of you . . . and they're all here in Grosart.'

'Good idea,' Bill said. 'I will . . . I haven't had time to work out the withdrawal plan yet, but we'll probably move at 0800. I'll issue orders at 0645, and go round the companies right after that. Will that do?'

'Yes, sir. Thank you, sir.' Harris saluted and went out.

Bill finished his note to his children, folded it away and sat a moment, head in his hands.

He sat up straight. Time to think . . . order of march . . . who would recce the new positions, and on what line . . . where was a good place to face von Krug . . . time would be needed to dig in and prepare, so it shouldn't be too close – about fifteen miles back would be fine . . . here. He put his hand on the map – somewhere about here, according to the ground, Gadforce would turn and fight . . . if Colonel Gadney permitted it.

Slater came in with a message. 'Colonel Gadney was killed in a car accident last night, sir, trying to get to us from 4 Corps. GHQ says they will be sending another commander as soon as possible. Meanwhile you are to continue in command.'

'Don't sound so damned happy,' Bill snarled. 'Colonel Gadney was probably a good fellow and a good officer, and now he's dead.'

'Sorry, sir,' Slater said, but he didn't sound it, Bill thought, and I'm not either. Poor Gadney. Now how long would it be before the next colonel or brigadier would actually arrive to supersede him?

To Slater he said, 'Now, ready to take notes? All right: *withdrawal will continue at 0800 hrs towards BANDIER.* How many roads can we use, as far as this place . . . Turnhoudt?'

'Two, sir, as far as I can see . . . here and here.'

'All right. Put all our infantry and anti-tank guns on this one, nearest the Dendre – it runs practically along the riverbank in spots; put what soft stuff we have, the field regiment, the tanks or transporters, the Macdonalds, on the other. Let the sappers go on their own, with an escort of one company South Yorks . . . they'll be busy blowing bridges . . . forward RV . . . start line . . . start time . . . I'm leaving in ten minutes with Wade, Major Millington and the tank major to recce the next position I propose to take up, near Turnhoudt.'

'Major Hodge will be in command of the move then?'

'No. Colonel Marshall of 46 Field . . . unless he wants to come with me to make the artillery plan – but he's been quite happy to let me make it with George Millington, so far.'

'Colonel Marshal is not p.s.c., sir,' Slater said. 'I think he has an inferiority complex.'

'First gunner who ever did, if he has,' Bill said. 'Anyway, send him a polite message asking him to lend us the honour of his company for a few minutes, etc.'

Slater went out and the RSM reappeared. 'Sorry you won't be able to speak to the men, sir.'

'I can't help it, Bogey, I really can't. I've *got* to have time to reconnoitre our next position. Look, go round the companies and tell the company commanders, as from me, that I want them to speak to the men, all together as far as that's possible, about the necessity of us all, men of the Queen's Own Wessex Rifles, doing what we have to do, without looking over our shoulders. That leads to panic. You know our rifle order "Stand to your front!" Tell the company commanders to make sure that every man under his command understands that he must continue to stand to his front!'

'Right-ho, sir. May I tell the South Yorks and Macdonald officers the same?'

'Of course. And the gunners – everyone. They won't understand what "stand to your front" means, but they'll get the idea. And, you know, I think it's actually better that the company commanders speak to them, rather than me. If we get hit by some crisis, the company commander will be there, on the spot, with them. I won't.'

When he was awakened, an hour before dawn, the following day, 19 May 1940, he had had five hours sleep and felt thoroughly refreshed and renewed. Gadforce had moved back from Grosart to Turnhoudt in five hours, arriving early in the afternoon. Some of the men had been able to travel on tanks or in engineer or heavy artillery vehicles, but the others had had to march. On arrival at Turnhoudt, Bill knew that they needed a rest, but he did not give them one until they had dug their trenches, put out the small quantity of barbed wire available, laid telephone lines and anti-tank mines, and in all other aspects completed what preparations were possible for the defensive battle he had planned for this site. By dark they were ready, and then everyone had slept, half of each unit and sub-unit at a time, waiting. By then they knew that 13 Panzer was coming, for at 1600 hours a signal from BEF had informed them that the Germans had thrown an assault bridge across the Dendre at Grosart, and were crossing in large numbers and heading south-west, on roads to the west of the river. At the time, Bill had calculated that they would reach the Turnhoudt area at about last light, would blunder into his outposts and then withdraw a bit to wait for light. If they came on more cautiously, and did not contact his outposts, the result would be the same: no major contact before first light tomorrow.

He sat up on the bed in his billet, yawning and stretching. Corporal Driver was holding out a plate of soya link sausages and mashed dehydrated potatoes. A candle burned in a bottle . . . for a moment he smelled again the dankness of the trenches of 1917 . . . how many times had he eaten sausages then, by the light of a candle, his equipment hanging on nails in the wall, his steel helmet on his head? But then there'd always been, outside, the world of war, the whine and crash of shells, the occasional menacing silences, the smells of death. Now . . .

Slater came in and said, 'The South Yorks report enemy-patrol activity on their front. They think they've killed a couple of Jerries, but they're lying doggo and not using any Very lights.'

Bill finished his sausage and tea and said, 'I'm going to take a look at the RAP. Anyone in there?'

'I don't think so, sir . . . except the five men who were wounded in front of Grosart and won't be evacuated.'

Bill shrugged into his equipment, checked that his revolver was loaded and went off down the stairs, out of the house and down the street towards the village school, where the regimental aid post had been set up. He found Captain Dunfee, the regimental medical officer, working by the light of old-fashioned oil lanterns behind heavy black curtains on a soldier of the battalion. The man was sitting on the edge of a table, his face white, while Dunfee examined his right index finger, the end of which was missing.

'Shot m'self, sir,' the man mumbled.

323

'Rifleman Bodman, D Company,' Bill said. 'How did that happen?' His tone was grim.

Bodman stammered, 'I swear I didn't mean to do it, sir . . . I was loading my rifle, r-ready for stand-to . . . and it went off.'

'With your trigger finger over the muzzle? I don't believe you. You'll be for court-martial later, Bodman. It's an army order . . . Meantime, patch him up, doc, and send him back to his company. We need every man now. He can at least run messages, or dig.'

'It hurts, sir . . .'

'I'm sure it does.'

He turned his back and walked over to a corner of the big room where five men were struggling to put on their equipment. All wore khaki bandages somewhere about them. One said, as Bill came close, 'Another scrap today, sir?'

'I hope so. The South Yorks are in contact.'

'And then, sir? Is it true that the Jerries is surrounding us? I mean all of us, the whole British Army?'

'Up to a point, yes. But we're not in any bag yet, and we don't intend to be put in one. Stand to your front . . . and look after yourselves.'

Bill returned to his headquarters. As soon as he saw the burly figure of the Rev. James Gardner, the regimental padre, waiting for him, he felt a twinge of guilt. He had hardly seen or spoken to Gardner since the war began. Merton had liked him and brought him into discussions which, Bill thought, had nothing to do with the church or the men's spiritual well-being. He was about thirty-five with a bluff manner and the shoulders of a rugby forward, which he had been, having earned caps for Oxford and England.

Bill said heartily, 'Well, padre, what can I do for you?'

Gardner said, 'I came to ask if there was time to have a communion service, sir.'

'All the battalion together? I'm afraid not.'

Gardner looked downcast. 'I was hoping to be able to tell the men that they are fighting for a most worthy cause. Hitler is a fiend in human shape, you know, sir. They are being asked to die for their beliefs, and I thought that I could confirm . . .'

Bill cut in briskly, 'Why don't you go round the companies, as best you can . . . speak to the men in the trenches, just where they are? They'll appreciate that.'

'If that's the best that can be done now,' Gardner said. 'Well, thank you, sir. I'll take my communion bag with me, in case . . .' He saluted and went out.

Bill climbed to the top storey of the house, then out through a large hole onto the roof. From here he had a good view towards the north-east. With his binoculars, he scanned the countryside: there was the Dendre, on the right; there was the road running close to it, two hamlets strung along it, and open rolling fields of beet and root crops between the road and the river; there on the left was wooded, broken-up country rising to the Mont de Verclours, barely a hundred feet high but by far the most prominent feature of the landscape. The Mont and the country behind and to the left of it were heavily wooded. Here was his chosen battlefield. Of the German forces he could see nothing, neither their tanks nor guns nor infantry nor trucks – all hidden, except a burned-out truck in the road half a mile beyond his own forward defended localities.

'Come on, Stefan,' he murmured. 'What are you waiting for?'

He was eager for the battle to be joined in earnest, for he believed he would give von Krug a bloody nose, and force on him the pause which the BEF needed if it was to continue its retreat in an orderly manner. The Mont de Verclours was the dominant feature in the landscape, and it dominated the left half of the terrain more than the right half. Von Krug would certainly seize it for an artillery observation and, for von Krug, 'artillery observation' not 'good tank country' would decide the route of attack. Therefore, here, he would attack down the left side, in spite of the broken ground and woods, streams and small quarries, for the Mont did not give a good view over the right half, east of the hamlets. The only question was whether von Krug would make a feint towards the right, to force him to move his reserves to that flank . . . Let him feint; the reserves would stay where they were.

By half past ten there had been fighting all along the arched British front, from right to left, and even round the refused flanks. One enemy probe of about two platoons had worked its way between positions to the south of Turnhoudt and come within two hundred yards of Bill's main headquarters in the central *place*. Bill was growing impatient, for there had been no real German move yet, just this continuous probing, feeling, advancing, retreating. It had cost the Germans a good many men already, and Gadforce very few, but . . . what did it mean? He needed a call on aircraft for reconnaissance. A single sortie would tell him where the majority of the German tanks was, and that . . .

Slater handed him a message:

South Yorks report enemy tanks seen at 478362.

Bill quickly checked his map. Ah, that was against the river, at the far end of the right-hand sector. The expected feint was taking shape. Now there'd be artillery fire on his right FDLs, and some tanks would advance. No need to give any orders; everyone knew what to do.

Slater said, 'South Yorks report twenty enemy tanks advancing against their position, with some infantry, sir . . . They are being shelled by smoke.'

Now, from his vantage point, Bill saw puffs of white smoke sprouting all over the view: by the hamlets on the road, where his A Company was; out to the left this side of the Mont de Verclours, where D Company was . . . (both companies had four anti-tank guns); smoke too on the northern outskirts of Turnhoudt itself, where C Company and the Macdonalds held the edge of town, nominally in reserve, but the enemy probes had made contact with them too. Von Krug was smoking all his FDLs, forward defended localities . . . why?

Now he heard a low drumming sound, and after a moment thought, aircraft . . . another Fairey Battle? But the sound had a different calibre to that of the Battle a few days ago. This was denser, thicker, heavier . . . It was growing steadily louder, from the east, wavering now, up, down. Bill stared through his binoculars, and made out a speckling of black dots that seemed to pockmark the whole sky towards Grosart and the north-east. He shouted to Slater, 'Air-raid alarm!'

'Already gone out, sir,' Slater called back.

Down in the *place* below, Bill saw the men of headquarters set up their two Bren guns on the anti-aircraft mounting and take position in the middle of the *place*. Every Bren in the battalion should be doing the same . . . why, oh why, hadn't he asked, *demanded*, a light anti-aircraft battery to complete the balance of his force? How many

Jerries were coming? He tried to count . . . twenty . . . thirty . . . about forty . . . in stepped-up waves, from ten thousand to fifteen thousand feet above him, in the hazy blue sky.

He became conscious of a distant whistling, such as he had been hearing the last few minutes as the air-raid whistles were blown all round Turnhoudt, but this was a wavering, shriller note in a minor key, and it came from the sky, as though the advancing planes were mewing eagles or whistling falcons. He made out their shape clearly now: they were all stiff-legged Junkers Ju 87s, Stuka dive-bombers.

The leading wing of Stukas peeled slowly over on their sides one after the other, and slid down the sky, one by one, aimed at the smoke markers their artillery had laid down for them, and at the *place* in the centre of Turnhoudt. The whistling increased to a shrieking. The planes screamed down ever faster; the bombs fell in shining clusters from under their bellies, and now the bombs too were screaming in the sky, an unearthly banshee wailing and moaning. The hair on the back of Bill's neck stood on end and he felt an emptiness in the pit of his stomach. He had never heard or seen or experienced anything so terrifying . . . and now the bombs were bursting, clouds of smoke and dust rising in the town, earth erupting skywards out there by the river, the church steeple toppling over, bells clanging as it fell . . . The Stukas were attacking all his FDLs, and the town itself, his headquarters. And he had no Bofors guns to ward them off. He was helpless.

No, by God, he wasn't! How many Brens did he have in the force? It must be nearly a hundred, all told. These Stukas were not releasing their bombs until they were down to a thousand feet, well within small-arms range. But he did not hear the clatter of the guns. Why?

Because the men were cowered in their trenches, stunned, shocked, on the verge of breaking. No one was now manning the two Brens out there in the *place* directly below him. He forced his legs to move, stumbled down the stairs, and ran to the nearest Bren. Aiming it up, he began to fire long bursts at the Stukas. 'Loader, loader!' he yelled, and found RSM Harris at his side. Then two more men ran out of the houses to the other gun – Slater and his own batman, Driver. The Stukas kept coming, sliding straight down in long screaming dives, releasing their bombs, swooping up, climbing away, rejoining the flock of their brethren circling above, peeling down again, sometimes now without bombs . . .

Here was one coming straight at him, its front gun blinking orange fire. He heard the bullets clatter around him, coughed, jerked, and was smashed to the ground by the impact of a bullet that passed clear through the fleshy part of his left thigh. He crawled and was pulled to his feet by Bogey Harris and staggered back to the gun. That Stuka had gone, here was another . . . the houses all round seemed to be crumbling. He held the sights steady on the Stuka's nose and kept the trigger pressed. This magazine had been specially loaded for anti-aircraft work, one round in every four was tracer, and he saw the points of light curve away from the muzzle and up towards the cowling of the Stuka . . . smoke suddenly poured out, the windscreen ceased to glitter in the sun, the nose lifted. He emptied the last of the magazine into its belly, but it was already gone, turning sideways, its angle of descent steepening. It crashed into the houses a hundred yards away, and a great sheet of yellow flame and black smoke roared skyward.

From all around Bill heard a ragged cheer, and then the shouting: 'We got one . . . we got one . . .' and he was pulled away from the gun by its regular crew. 'We'll take over now, sir . . . We got one!'

Harris said, 'You're hit, sir. You can hardly stand.'

He nodded. 'Bleeding like a pig, too, but I can't feel a thing . . . nothing to be done.'

At last, far and near, he heard the chatter of Bren guns as the gunners took heart from the fall of their terrifying enemy. Bill had shown that the fiends were after all mortal. Very few in Gadforce had seen him at the gun or knew who had shot down the Stuka, but everyone had seen its crash, and in that instant the battle was saved, and won. For the men came out of their slit trenches and foxholes and returned to their duty, firing at the enemy tanks – which had advanced considerably, without opposition, while the Stukas were attacking – and manning the anti-tank guns and the mortars and Bren guns and Vickers.

Within a minute, another Stuka stumbled and fell in flames close to A Company's hamlets, and soon a third, badly hit, sank lower and lower and crawled off eastward behind the Mont de Verclours, trailing smoke. A few minutes later, the whole flock climbed up, reformed waves, and flew away.

By then, the entry and exit wounds of Bill's bullet had been covered with first field dressings, and he was sitting trouserless in his command truck, a trickle of blood congealing on his bare thigh below the front dressing. There was no blood at the back, where the exit wound was a couple of inches from the thigh bone. Both legs ached and throbbed and he felt that he was floating a foot above the ground, but that was all.

He said to Slater, 'What's the latest from the South Yorks and C and A Companies, out there?'

'The FOO with C reports he is engaging forty tanks below the Mont de Verclours hill. They got close during the dive-bombing.'

Bill stumbled to a chair opposite the radio set and sat down. The 25-pounder shells from 46 Field Regiment were whistling overhead in great numbers now, and they were going just where Bill had expected the enemy attack to come, into the broken ground below the Mont. The German artillery seemed to be giving C Company, on that flank, a pasting, but C were well dug in and well sited.

Slater said, 'C Company reports about thirty tanks have got by them, to the east, between them and the hamlets. Infantry was with them, but . . . hold on a minute, sir . . . most of them have dropped off.'

A moment later Slater said, 'A Company reports tanks passing them to the east, between them and the Mont . . . no infantry with them . . . the tanks are Mark IIIs and IVs.'

'That's the same lot,' Bill said. Now where would Stefan launch the rest of his armour?

'C Company reports a whole lot of tanks emerging from the woods and heading in their direction, with infantry. Artillery fire is increasing on their positions.'

Bill turned to Major Millington. 'George, tell your CO that this is it . . . Give SOS calls from C Company all priority, and don't worry about using up ammunition. *This* is where we have to stop them . . . Can you get the tanks on the radio?'

'Yes, sir . . . Sir, there's a brigadier here to see you.'

'Tell him –' Bill began furiously.

Then he stood up, for a man in the battle-dress uniform of a brigadier was already in the truck. He was thin, with big horn-rimmed glasses, looking not unlike Morgan Lloyd, but without

Morgan's stern demeanour or rows of medal ribbons. This brigadier wore only four ribbons on his battle-dress blouse: Mutt and Jeff from the Great War, and the Coronation and Jubilee medals. He said now, 'Sorry to disturb you. I'm Heatheringford, from GHQ . . . I've been sent to take command of this force.'

Bill said, 'Glad you've come, sir . . . but would you mind waiting a minute to actually take over? We're rather busy, and . . . I don't have time to explain what's happening or where everyone is.'

'I quite understand. Carry on, Miller, carry on. I'll just watch and try to help.'

Bill turned to the radio and picked up the microphone. 'Glowworm, this is No. 9. Carry out preliminary move for Operation Codfish. Over.'

'Wilco. Out.'

That order launched the Matildas from their harbour to prepared positions on the northern outskirts of Turnhoudt, where the German armoured assault must come if it continued on its present line.

Bill turned to Slater. 'Get reports on ammunition in hand from 46 Field and 282 Anti-tank.'

'I'll see to that,' Brigadier Heatheringford said. 'That was my job at GHQ.' He started talking into another radio set on a different wavelength. Bill looked at the situation map, which Slater was marking up. The main panzer attack was coming down the left side of the road, supported by artillery fire controlled from the Mont de Verclours. C Company had already been bypassed, and A soon would be; but the tanks were coming on with less and less infantry in close support, as the machine-guns of the Macdonald Highlanders and the fierce high-explosive concentrations of the 25-pounders separated the infantry from the tanks, killing or wounding the footsoldiers, or sending them to cover, while the tanks rumbled on. Now the anti-tank guns up there did not have to fear attack from determined infantry; they would give the panzers a very hard time, and the Matildas would deal with any remnants that reached the line of FDLs here . . . and when the panzers started back, they'd have to run the gauntlet all over again, as long as C and A and the anti-tank guns dug in with them all held fast.

To Millington, Bill said, 'George, the panzers are milling about right in front of Turnhoudt – there, look! Let 'em have it! They're

330

barely four hundred yards away . . . I think the Matildas are engaging them, too . . . Tom, what news from C?'

'They report surrounded, sir, but not by very many Germans.'

'We'll clear that up when the main tank battle is over. What from A?'

'Same thing. They're surrounded but they're doing big slaughter of German infantry out in the fields round them – the ones that were scraped off the panzers as they went by. There are a lot of them, but they seem pretty disorganized. By the way, sir, A reported none killed, one wounded in the dive-bombing; C had one and two, B had none, D had two wounded, and there were three in the headquarters area, one and two – not counting you.'

'So the whole Stuka attack cost us only two killed and six wounded, but it damn nearly broke us . . . See that those figures are known to every man in the force. Though I don't think anyone who was here today is likely to let Stukas panic him again.'

Brigadier Heatheringford said, 'I've got the information you wanted, Miller. And I've arranged for more 25-pounder and 2-pounder ammunition to be sent to you as a top priority.'

'Can you get us a light anti-aircraft battery too, sir? There was a big Stuka attack just before you got here, and it nearly cooked our goose. It was our first and the men were very shaky.'

'I was in the fringes of it. I'll try to get some LAA for you, but don't count on it. They're very short, and becoming much in demand as the Germans begin to divert more of their air force from the Sedan front.'

'Any idea what's going to happen next?' Bill asked.

'The BEF is withdrawing to the Canal line . . . Look, here, these canals stretch from Arras to Dunkirk . . . but, between you and me, some of us think that the only hope of saving the BEF is for everyone to head for Dunkirk and get out that way.'

Bill's surprised whistle was interrupted by Slater. '14 Royal Tanks in action, sir, on Codfish. They've got forty Mark IIIs and IVs boxed in between themselves and the anti-tank guns with A . . . They report that they've brewed up eight Mark IIIs so far – lost two themselves. Your trap is working beautifully, sir . . . perfect!'

'It wouldn't have been so perfect if von Krug had known that I was in command here,' Bill said grimly. 'He has just as good a memory as I have . . . though he never had the benefit of talks on psychology with Dr Israel Steinberg . . . and he wouldn't have listened if he had, I suppose, being a good Nazi.'

He turned to bend over a large-scale map. Von Krug still had great numerical superiority. Also, the Germans always counterattacked: that was the clearest lesson from 1914–18. So . . . he'd better get A and C out before they were overrun. How to do it, in daylight? Using the Matildas, perhaps? That would depend on the outcome of the battle now raging in front of Turnhoudt, and how far Hammond of the tanks thought it was safe to go forward. Those Matildas would be needed tomorrow and tomorrow and tomorrow. They must not now be allowed to drive into a trap, as von Krug's had been.

To Slater he said, 'Find out in code how much farther forward Glowworm think they can go. Can they reach C? A? With artillery support, of course . . . but without risk of undue loss.'

'Wilco, sir.' Slater started to scribble notes on a pad.

Bill leaned back, yawning. Brigadier Heatheringford said, 'With your permission, colonel, I'm going to advise GHQ that you are fully in control of the situation here, and I recommend that you be left in command of Gadforce, with the temporary rank of full colonel . . . I am a Q staff officer, colonel. I'm very good at it, but I've worked all my life in large headquarters. The biggest force I've commanded is a company, some fifteen years ago. Lord Gort doesn't know me, and made a terrible mistake in accepting someone's suggestion that I be sent to replace you, who are considered too junior for this command. But you will do much better than I ever could – you already have – and, besides, I am sure that by now they are badly missing me in GHQ. They'll agree to my suggestion.'

'Well, thank you, sir. Will you tell General Gort that I intend to break contact right away, and start back for Bandier on the Escaut by about midnight. I hope GHQ will have new orders waiting for me when I make contact from there at first light.'

'I'll see to that, Miller. And I can tell you that the orders will be to continue protecting the southern flank as the BEF falls back to the Canal line . . . unless some other unforeseen disaster strikes us, and yet another finger has to be stuffed in some new hole in some other crumbling dyke.'

With a wave of his hand, Heatheringford left. Bill sank back into a chair and slowly felt all strength draining out of him, through his wounded leg, until, half a minute later, he slid off the chair onto the floor, as Tom Slater ran to him, crying, 'Sir . . . sir . . . are you all right?'

22

May 1940: Flanders

He came to twenty minutes later, to find himself lying on a chintz-covered sofa in a ground-floor room of the house which had been his billet. Captain Dunfee was standing a few feet away, talking to someone Bill did not at first recognize; then he did, and croaked, 'Marshall . . .'

Marshall and the doctor turned and came to him. Dunfee said, 'So you've come round.'

'The wound hasn't played up or anything, has it?' Bill asked. He tried to sit up, but Dunfee's hand firmly restrained him. He lay back again. 'My thigh aches like hell, but . . . I feel fine. What happened?'

Tom Slater, from a corner, said, 'You passed out, sir.'

'And no wonder,' Dunfee said with some asperity. 'You've had a bullet clear through the thigh and, though by a miracle it doesn't seem to have hit a bone, it's a severe shock. And you haven't even rested since.'

Bill turned his head to Marshall. 'Marshall – Joe, isn't it? – I've got to start pulling the forward troops back or they'll be over-whelmed. You're the next senior officer in Gadforce and I'd like you to stay by me in case I pass out again . . . to take command.'

The artillery colonel said, 'I hope to God that doesn't happen, but I'll stay close and keep in the overall picture. George can keep on firing the regiment, as he has been.'

'Thanks . . . Look, doc, don't try to send me back because I'm not going. And I don't need any pills. Get back to the RAP and prepare yourselves to move at dusk . . . Tom, get 14 Royal Tanks on the blower and find out just where they are.'

'Their CO was on just before you came round, sir, and reported he was advancing to A Company's hamlet, with the German tanks retreating in front of him. He said it might be a trap, but he would go on as long as he was still inflicting casualties on them, which he was.'

Bill supported himself on one elbow. 'Tell him to cover the withdrawal of C and A Companies, and also, as far as he can, of the South Yorks companies from the right flank. Tell all of the companies to start their withdrawal, by bounds within sub-units, at once.'

He lay back, momentarily exhausted, and stared at the ceiling. He'd take the force back to Bandier now, in one continuous move, starting at dusk . . . make sure to have the south and east ends of Turnhoudt strongly held for as long as possible in case von Krug kept coming on, pressing him.

Marshall said, 'The South Yorks are calling for covering fire, sir . . . George is giving it to them now, two batteries . . . the third battery is firing defensive tasks in front of C, who are . . .'

Tom Slater interrupted, 'C are starting to move, closing station . . . 14 Royal Tanks in position east of A Company hamlet, and can see C withdrawing . . . A are withdrawing now.'

'The tanks have still got B with them as escort, haven't they?' Bill asked anxiously.

'Yes, sir.'

'Send for Major Hodge, please.'

'He's just outside, sir.'

Bill lay back, and slowly the world went from bright to drab to dull to dark. His head flopped sideways. Slater, bending over him, cried, 'Sir . . . sir . . . are you all right?'

Bill came round again, but to a different world, a world of half-light and immense weariness. He was lost in a sea of swirling, drifting fog. His body did not hurt, because it had little or no substance, except for heavy bandages on his left leg. He could not grasp things or ideas. There were people here, but who were they? He broke out in a cold sweat and cried, miserably, 'Where am I? What's happening? What do I have to do?'

A face appeared through the fog and he peered at it, wondering, till suddenly he recognized it and croaked, 'Bogey . . . where am I? I know I have to do something, but I can't . . . I can't!'

Harris's hand was on his, firm and warm. Harris's handkerchief was out, mopping and carefully wiping his brow. 'There, Bill,' he muttered. 'Thee bisn't gone crazy, boy . . . thee's, well . . . tired, a 'course . . . Lie back now, lie back.'

There were other men in the room, a frieze of them at a distance, making dark patterns behind the fog.

Bill muttered, 'I can't do it, Bob. There's too much to think of, and I . . . I can't.'

'You can,' Harris said softly. 'You was always able to. Remember when our Alfie fell in the canal in December and none of us could stand to stay in more than a few seconds, looking for him? But you went back and back and dived and dived, and pulled the little bugger out alive . . . you did it! You can do it now.'

He turned his head and Bill muttered anxiously, 'Don't go, Bob.'

'I bean't going nowhere. I was just asking the adjutant to get us cups of hot tea . . . and he's doing that . . . Here now, sit up a bit . . .' Bill felt Harris's arms round his shoulder, pulling slowly up to a sitting position. 'Here, here's the char. It's hot and sweet, just like Mary's kisses used to be, eh? No, no, man, I doan't know how her kisses were, she never kissed me, only you.'

The fog lifted inch by inch, until, five minutes later, Bill was looking at a row of familiar figures: Marshall, Slater, Millington, Hodge, Dunfee; and, sitting beside him, his boyhood friend, RSM Harris.

He said, 'I'm back . . . I don't know where I was, but . . . I'm back.'

'Thank God!' Marshall said forcibly.

Dunfee said, 'Really, sir, you can't pretend that . . .'

'I can and must and will,' Bill said fiercely. 'Thank you, Mr Harris.'

'You'd have done the same for me, sir, I'm sure,' Harris said cheerfully, standing up and away.

Bill lay back, thinking. He had sent for Hodge . . . ah, the withdrawal. Marshall was here, too – good. He said, 'Joe, Peter, listen . . . we're bringing the forward troops back to Turnhoudt – that's under way now. Then until dusk, say 2200 hours, we sit tight here.

335

At 2200 we start thinning out, from the back, to withdraw to Bandier on the Escaut. The last positions here are to be vacated by 2400 hours, midnight . . . look at the map and find some suitable report lines, say three . . . order of march, which means order of evacuation of the positions here . . . movement of artillery . . . I'm going to nap for half an hour, then we'll work out the withdrawal plan in detail.'

The force reached Bandier before daylight the next day, 20 May. It stayed in Bandier in defensive positions all that day without seeing any enemy except some high-flying bombers. Near noon on 21 May a peremptory signal arrived from GHQ of the British Expeditionary Force. It read, in toto:

GADFORCE will move BILLAN soonest possible and is placed under orders of Maj Gen MACARTNEY GOC 55 DIV on arrival BILLAN ACK.

Bill got up and limped to the map. The nearest reported enemy were well to the east. When Gadforce got close to Billan the Germans would be only five or six miles off. Some might be closer, but it wasn't likely. Besides, if he was to move in a hurry, he couldn't afford to move tactically. He sent for Colonel Marshall and said, 'We have to move to Billan – the whole force. I'm going there right away with my advanced headquarters. Bring the rest along as fast as you can. I'll have guides out at the entrance to Billan by the time you get there . . . and perhaps by then I'll be able to tell you what's going on and what we're supposed to do . . . though that would be asking a lot.'

Half an hour later, having seen that all preparations for the move were in train, he drove westward out of Bandier in his 15-hundred-weight truck, accompanied by another Royal Signals truck, two truckloads of escort and two motorcyclists. At the entrance to the small market town of Billan he found a red-armbanded military policeman and asked him where General Macartney's headquarters were.

'Colonel Miller? We've been waiting for you, sir,' the MP said. 'Go right on through town and half a mile beyond. There's a big chateau on the left. That's 55 Div HQ.'

Bill said, 'Thanks,' and drove on, thinking, General Macartney runs a taut ship. It was getting unusual in the BEF for anyone to know where anyone else was, or what he was supposed to be doing.

It was chiming three o'clock by an antique grandfather clock in the hall when he entered General Macartney's main operations room on the ground floor of the chateau. The general was short and square, his reddish hair tinged with grey. He wore no moustache. He was bent over a big map when Bill entered but looked up at once and said, 'Ha! Colonel Miller, the Gadfly of Gadforce . . . why aren't you wearing the proper badges and red tabs?'

'I haven't received any notice of promotion, sir.'

'Well, you have been. Nigel, see that Colonel Miller gets another two pips and a red hat, and gorget patches, at once . . . Come here. Look.' His red-haired hand slapped down on the map. 'Here is the BEF, here . . . and, to the north of us, the Belgians and some French. Pushing against us from the east are a lot of Germans – their Army Group A, to be exact. Here' – the hand moved to the bottom of the map – 'is the rest of the French Army . . . and here, sweeping through between the BEF and the French Army, is the German Army Group B. They have forced through a corridor, about twenty miles wide, between us here at Billan and the French at Mezecour – and the head of that Army Group B is now turning north behind us, going down the line of the Somme and heading for Boulogne. That was the situation as of noon. God knows what it will be by tomorrow noon. I have been ordered to cut through that corridor . . . cut off that German arm, if you like, through which is pouring all the men and material sustaining the German advance. We shall do it tomorrow at dawn, from here.'

'Your division, sir?'

'One brigade of it,' the general growled. 'The rest have been split off into force this and force that, or got mislaid, or cut off . . . but I have also been alloted your Gadforce, under command, and a good number of tanks. We're going to start from just south of Billan, on this line, in two parallel columns, one on this road, one on this . . . one battalion of infantry and one regiment of tanks on each road . . . with artillery support, of course. Our objective is the railway line here, from where the east road crosses it at Darant to where the west road crosses it at St Vith-les-Fosses. H-hour for leading troops to cross the start line is 0430 hours tomorrow, 22 May. You'll get detailed orders within an hour, but meantime any questions?'

Bill had been thinking as he studied the map and listened to the general. He said, 'How many Germans can we expect to encounter, sir?'

'In the whole corridor there are some fourteen armoured and motorized divisions. On our objective, or short of it, GHQ intelligence believes there are two – the 7th Armoured, under a fellow called Rommel, and the 13th, under von Krug.'

'We were fighting him at Turnhoudt the day before yesterday!' Bill exclaimed.

The general said, 'Perhaps. Well, he moved down fast, while you were moving to Bandier. Anything else?'

'Will I be taking the east or west road, sir? And am I to get any more tanks than the two companies of 14 RTR that I have now?'

'You'll be on the east road, aimed at Darant . . . and you'll get the whole of 14 RTR – I have the rest of it here, in Billan now. Their CO is a fellow called Smythe, and sometimes needs pushing. He keeps telling me such and such isn't "good tank country". I tell him the filthy Boche has chosen to fight in it with *his* tanks and his precious black-beret boys will have to do the same. By the way, I'm commanding the west column myself.'

'Do we have a reserve, sir?' Bill asked cautiously.

'The other two infantry battalions of my one brigade,' the general said, 'but no tanks. I propose to switch what we have from flank to flank, according to who gets on best. That's all.' He turned his back and Bill left, his mind racing.

He stood facing his assembled junior commanders in the school house, as the sun sank lower in the west. There were a lot of people present: all his own company commanders from the Wessex; the anti-tank battery commander; Colonel Marshall and Major Millington of the Field Artillery; the engineer Field Company commander; Colonel Smythe, commanding 14 Royal Tanks; and a Royal Artillery major commanding a newly arrived battery of light anti-aircraft artillery.

Bill said, 'Well, those are the detailed orders for getting us on the move without falling over each other on the start line. Now I want to talk a little about the sort of battle I envisage . . . 14 Royal Tanks will be at the point, as we know – moving astride the road. 49 Field Company, Royal Engineers, will be on the road, clearing mines and other obstacles, level with the leading tanks . . . the tanks' close escort will be my B and D Companies . . . A and C and the anti-tank guns will be with me about four hundred yards behind the tanks, moving on the road but ready for instant dispersal to either or both flanks. Now, sooner or later the tanks are going to run into opposition, probably infantry and anti-tank guns. I want the tanks to call down artillery fire at once, and the close support infantry to go in at once. If the German anti-tank guns can be silenced or masked, let the tanks go on to get behind the enemy – but not more than four hundred yards or so without their close support infantry . . .'

He went on slowly, foreseeing the battle in his mind's eye, trying to make all these men see it as he did, clearly enough to be able to transmit that vision to their junior subalterns and sergeants when they left the school house; and, more importantly, still be able to see the shape of it when the German tanks loomed out of the morning mist, when German guns and machine-guns began to speak, and earth and bodies flew and fell, and tanks and trucks caught fire, and the world was full of hostile noise.

He finished. 'Any questions?'

The tank corps colonel, Smythe, said, 'You said we have two armoured divisions against us, sir?'

'That is the intelligence estimate.'

'With their 88s?'

'Yes.'

'Then . . . sir, I think we must expect heavy casualties, in the tanks at least.'

Bill said grimly, 'The BEF can expect more than heavy casualties if we don't make this counterattack. It can expect annihilation . . . and we as part of it.' He addressed the whole group, as the tank colonel sat down. 'The 88 is a damned good gun. It's effective in anti-aircraft, anti-tank, and even anti-personnel roles. And, as we know, the Germans have brought up all three kinds of ammunition for it. But it's not a death ray. It can be knocked out by artillery fire, by determined infantry attacking it, by tanks coming in from a masked direction or out of smoke . . . The Germans are not dangerous because they have the 88, but because they coordinate all arms . . . and so must we tomorrow. Then we will attain our objective . . . which will force the German high command to look to its defences . . . which will give the BEF a respite and a chance. That's all, gentlemen.'

Fifteen minutes later Bogey Harris came to him where he sat alone on a folding camp chair outside the command truck, saluted, and said, 'Could I have a word with you in private, sir?'

'Certainly.' Bill got up heavily and limped away into the field, beyond where the headquarters trucks were parked, where the men were even now eating their evening meal.

When they were out of earshot from anyone else, Harris said, 'Sir, the men know what they're going to be up against tomorrow. They don't like it. Nor do some of the officers. The blokes are muttering that it's suicide . . . just two battalions and about ninety tanks going up against two Jerry divisions.'

'What do you think, Bogey?' Bill asked quietly.

'It doesn't seem much of a good idea to me, to tell the truth . . . Don't get me wrong, sir. We can have a go, but with the blokes thinking the way they are, once they run into real opposition, they'll likely pack in, because they know we don't have a hope of cutting right through this German corridor. Why, there must be seven hundred tanks and near a quarter of a million Huns in there!'

Bill collected his thoughts, then said, 'It may be a suicide mission, in the way that every attack, every defence, is a suicide for *someone* . . . only he doesn't know it until he cops it . . . What matters here is the price the enemy has to pay. We *must* make the German high command think of their flanks, of defending themselves, instead of being able to concentrate on isolating us in the north here. The harder we hit, the more they'll pause, the more defensive actions they will take. We have to attack now, to the hilt, for our own sakes. If we don't make the Germans stop somehow, Bogey, we're done for – the whole BEF. Don't tell the men that . . . just go back to the old motto: *Stand to your front!* We've got a job to do, and we're bloody well going to do it . . . How do you know that some officers are unhappy?'

'Captain Tunning was talking to young Mr Larson, just now, sir, on their way back to A Company. He was saying that we didn't have a hope, and there'll be a terrible slaughter tomorrow.'

'Thank you.'

Bill walked back towards the command truck, raising his voice. 'Tom!'

'Sir?'

'Give Captain Tunning my compliments, please.'

Harris saluted and walked briskly away. Bill waited for Tunning to appear, which he did within five minutes. Bill, standing, said, 'Did you tell Larson, and perhaps others, that we didn't have a hope tomorrow, or words to that effect?'

Tunning's eyes shifted, coming to rest at last on Bill's. 'Yes, sir,' he said. 'I think it's true.'

'Perhaps, but that doesn't alter the fact that we're going to do it. Without you, though. I am relieving you of command of A Company. Take the first returning ration truck out. Tell Larson I want to see him at once.'

Tunning had turned pale, and his hands trembled as he said, 'Sir . . . I'll do my best . . . I'm not afraid. I'll . . .'

'It's too late for that,' Bill said. 'And I know Larson is junior to Barnett, but I'm going to give him the company, because he has a fire in his belly. You don't.' He nodded, turning away. Feeling a pang of guilt he turned back at once. 'Listen, Tunning, don't take it too hard. Not everyone is suited for battle. You're a very good trainer and administrator, so go home and do that. Goodbye, and good luck.'

At half past three in the morning, with a heavy ground mist lying low over the fields and among the scattered houses and farms, a message was received from 55 Div postponing H-hour by two hours, from 0430 to 0630. Slater brought the slip to Bill to read by the shaded light in his billet. Bill read, swore, scrunched it up and threw it on the floor. 'What the hell are they doing this for?' he demanded angrily. 'At half past six the sun will be beginning to clear the mist . . . the mist has disadvantages for the tanks, but it would have been a great help for the infantry. They could have got right up to Boche anti-tank guns and, if we get far enough, even to field artillery. Now . . .!' He swore again, thinking, there is also a chance that the Germans will send over air reconnaissance and spot the attacking columns forming up on the roads. Well, nothing to be done about it . . . time to serve the men another hot meal? No, they were eating

341

now, and they wouldn't be hungry. He ought to sleep some more, but he couldn't. Nothing to do but wait ... watch the creeping hands of his watch, watch the light grow, stare into the damp, low mist, watch it change texture, begin to glow with colour as the sun rose ... the mist had not all gone, visibility was barely four hundred yards; that was all right.

'H-hour, sir,' Tom Slater said.

Outside, he heard the rumble and clatter of the tank engines, and the heavy steel tracks passing. He went out and stood by the road-side, watching, as B and D Companies shook out into the fields, going steadily and fast across country close behind the tanks. 'Get ready to move,' he said, and climbed up into the front seat of the big Royal Signals truck, keeping his attention concentrated on the tanks and his two companies spread out to right and left of the road in front. The driver engaged gear and the headquarters trucks took their places, followed by anti-tank guns, low-slung light ack-ack guns and marching infantry.

A mile done, twenty minutes ... two miles, forty-five minutes: time – 0715 ... The tanks were keeping their pace down, but so far they had met no obstacles, the ground was almost flat and they were outdistancing their infantry. Smythe had realized it, and his leading wave had halted, taking up positions half hidden behind a long hedge and in a farm road that had been sunk down six feet by centuries of use. The second wave of tanks passed through the first and in its turn halted. B and D Companies caught in, passed through and then ... bang, bang, bang ... Bill distinctly heard the whiplike crack of the British 2-pounders. The anti-tank battery was on the road just behind him, so it couldn't be their 2-pounders in action; it must be the tanks'. The column of vehicles stopped moving and he anxiously scanned forward through his binoculars. He could see the British Matildas clearly enough, three hundred yards ahead; then, disappearing into the mist, the men of his own B and D Companies; beyond that, just the wall of mist ... but obviously the Matildas could see something, for against the mist there flashed daggers of yellow flame from their turrets. Behind him the anti-tank and anti-aircraft batteries were leaving the road, spreading out in the fields, taking up action stations.

Through the little window behind him, Slater, inside the truck, called, 'Sir, 14 Royal Tanks report enemy armour coming up the road in single column . . . they've got them in flank and are giving them what for.'

Now, Bill prayed, let the mist lift, let's see! And in answer to his prayer the mist did dissolve upwards into the sun, the lower part of it rising first to give a clear, long view underneath it. Now Bill saw the German tanks, halted on a curved stretch of the road half a mile ahead. Two were on fire, others were struggling out into the fields. There were anti-tank guns at the rear of the German tank column, coming into action now: he could make out the camouflage-painted barrels of the 88s . . . and hear the rattle of machine-gun fire . . . ah, B and D getting at the German soft vehicles and the 88s, while the tanks were suffering severely from the fire of the halted and half-concealed Matildas.

The Matildas began to advance, one wave staying in position, engaging the German tanks, the next lurching forward, going straight at the Germans, presenting only their thickest frontal armour as a target. The road up there was a shambles . . . British field artillery fire falling heavily on the German column . . . at least eight enemy tanks in ruins, three of them in flames, or already no more than blackened hulks . . . the rest retreating fast, on the run. This was not a full-scale German attack that they had run into, but a move . . . of the whole German force perhaps, this being no more than its vanguard, which had certainly not expected to run into this powerful British column coming at them from the opposite direction. The British were supposed to be in full retreat.

A huge ordnance crane vehicle was coming up the road, demanding right of way. Bill's driver pulled the truck over. Ahead, two Matildas had reached the road and were pushing an immobilized German tank off it. Another was still burning . . . with men in it, Bill thought, for the wind was from the south, and he could smell the distinctive odour of roasting meat. The crane would have to clear that.

He climbed down, hobbled round and up into the truck body behind, picked up the radio microphone tuned to the tank net and said, 'Longhorn, Marigold No. 9 here, well done . . . How many enemy put out of action?'

'I make it nine altogether. We've lost two, both to 88s. Their

343

tank-gun fire is gouging chunks out of our armour but not penetrating. Over.'

'Keep moving, then! Keep on their tails, don't let them regroup . . . suggest you put my chaps on your vehicles until you run into something.'

'Wilco.'

Bill handed the mike back, thinking, that Smythe fellow is not so sticky in battle as he is before it – much better that than the other way round.

He returned to the truck cab and waited. Ten minutes later the advance continued. Now a section of four tanks led the advance, on the road itself. The orders were that tanks should not lead the column on the road, but Bill understood why Smythe was disobeying it. German armour had just come up this same road, so there could not have been any anti-tank mines laid before that, and the retreating Germans did not have time to lay any now.

The British anti-tank battery and light ack-ack guns were back on the road, in column. They had not had to fire a shot, as far as he knew. His own leading infantry, of B and D Companies, were riding the tanks ahead, and the pace of the advance was quickening. A and C were being left farther behind . . . better watch that. The mortars were up, also the carriers. The field regiment had two batteries with trails down, one moving forward. The regiment had fired about eight rounds a gun during the recent engagement, concentrating on the German 88s, and knocking out at least two – he had just passed them, overturned beside the road, the mangled corpses of dead crewmen surrounding them.

The advance continued . . . three miles . . . four miles . . . five . . . they were getting close to Darant now. Surely the Germans were holding it? Ah – the rattle of the tanks' co-axial machine-guns ahead . . . from behind him Tom Slater's voice: 'Sir . . . Colonel Miller . . . the tank FOO is calling for HE concentrations on enemy infantry, not dug in, defending Darant, half a mile ahead of them.'

'Good . . . Any news of how General Macartney's column is getting on? Get on the div command net and find out.'

He turned back to his front, binoculars to his eyes. He could see the rear wave of the Matildas, to the right of the road, and could make out his Wessex soldiers sliding and scrambling down from the tanks' chassis and turrets, and shaking out into attacking formation. The anti-tank guns were moving up the road, fast, the light ack-ack was spreading out and taking up positions. 25-pounder field artillery shells were beginning to scream overhead, to burst among the nearest houses of Darant, which nestled under a long, low rise of green fields with woods to the left.

From behind him Slater called, 'The general's column is level with us, sir, near St Vith-les-Fosses. They met enemy armour advancing, too, and drove them back, half an hour ago. I thought I had heard firing from the west about then.'

Bill waited a few more minutes. The battle ouside Darant seemed to have come to a standstill. The tanks were not moving, nor were the infantry, as far as he could see. There might be some movement on the left, in the woods, but he could not see it. He made up his mind and called back, 'Get me the tank net. I'm coming round.'

A few moments later he was speaking to Colonel Smythe. 'Longhorn, Marigold No. 9 here, what's the situation?'

'We've run into enemy infantry supported by artillery in Darant – about a battalion reinforced, with plenty of 88s. We're pinned down right and centre.'

'What about left? Do you have anyone in the woods on that flank?'

'One company of ours and most of your D are in there. I haven't heard from them for ten minutes and can't get my company commander on the blower.'

George Millington had run forward from his artillery command truck immediately behind. Bill turned to him. 'Have you still got two batteries in action?'

'No – one down, two moving. They'll all be in action in fifteen minutes, about two miles behind us.'

'Good.'

Bill sat motionless, thinking hard. His column was now engaged with a strong enemy force in and around Darant. Half of 14 Royal Tanks were up there, pinned down: but by the same token, they were pinning down the enemy. B Company was with them; and they were being supported by one field battery, eight 25-pounders. As far as he knew, there were no enemy tanks close, but there must be plenty not very far off, if this was indeed 13 or 7 Panzer Division which he was fighting . . . The woods to the left were not very thick, and, more important, they were not very old. The trees in them were young and thin; they presented no obstacle to Matildas. Unless he heard something new in the next few minutes, or the situation changed drastically, he'd take the remaining company of 14 Royal Tanks, plus his own two reserve companies, and all his carriers and mortars, and go round the left of Darant, through the woods.

'Forward, Haggard,' he said. 'Look out for potholes ... and shellholes.'

The column of vehicles moved slowly up the road, German shells bursting at intervals around and among them. When a truck was damaged, the one behind it, or the men who had been in it, pushed it out of the way, and the advance continued.

Now he was close, as close as it was wise to go in the trucks. Here was a company of tanks, twelve tanks, with Major Hammond leaning out of his turret – Hammond had been with him since the formation of Gadforce; here was Mainwaring of the Wessex D, Griffin of C, young Larson of A, Collier of the carriers, and Vail of the mortars. He gathered them round him in the shelter of a woodcutter's shack, and said, 'We'll continue the advance on the left – here ... tanks leading with our D still as close support. Got that, Greg?'

'Yes, sir.'

'When you hit opposition, A will pass through or round, to either flank, as seems best. Understand, Larson?'

'Yes, sir.'

'You'll have to act as your own anti-tank protection – I'm keeping the anti-tank battery here by the road to protect the rest of the column ... artillery support, two batteries, from H-hour, which will be ... 0900. Griff, you keep close to me, to be ready to exploit with your company any holes that the tanks and A can make, or find ... George, are all three batteries' trails down now?'

'Yes, sir.'

Griffin said, 'Are you coming with us yourself, sir? In the signal truck?'

'Yes, as far as it will go ... or until an 88 spots us. There are usually forest tracks and so on in these woods ... All right, chaps, that's all. Press on. Support each other ... The German Army may be knocking hell out of the French, but we've got these particular Jerries on the run.'

He stood beside his truck until H-hour, waiting, thinking, watching. The fire fight continued over on the right flank. German artillery continued to shell the road, but mostly farther to the rear, as though to prevent British reinforcements coming up. He thought he heard the grumble of tank engines and tracks borne up on the south wind, from beyond Darant, but could not be sure. Whether he heard them now or not he certainly had to be prepared to meet them, at any moment.

The twelve Matildas rumbled into position . . . nine o'clock – off they went, wide spread, the men of his D Company spaced between them . . . There was Mainwaring in the lead, right beside Hammond's tank – good man! Here was Larson, holding A back until D and the tanks had got far enough ahead so that he wouldn't be pinned down in their battle.

He climbed up into the signal truck and said, 'Forward.' The driver took the big vehicle carefully across a field, then along the edge of the wood . . . ah, here was a track, wide, grassy, probably impassable in wet weather, but dry and hard-packed now. The trees stretched ahead and to each side in moving geometrical rows, himself always at the focus of the pattern. It was a plantation, and the Matildas, where they did not have room between the trees, took them head on and easily pushed them over.

Gun fire ahead – the hysterical burping of a Schmeisser, the shorter, heavier bark of Brens. The mortar platoon was in action, its bombs arching up, whistling, out of the woods . . . There was the target: grey-clad figures, ahead, two hundred yards' range, the tanks heading for them . . . They were running, stumbling, scores of them, running away. He saw them flinging down their arms in order to be able to run faster. He stood up in his seat, yelling at the top of his lungs, 'Get 'em! Get 'em!'

The tanks burst out of the wood and there, directly overhead, was a Fieseler Storch, the German spotting and communication aircraft. It swooped low into a storm of Bren-gun fire, but climbed up again unscathed. It had come so close that Bill had clearly seen the man in the passenger seat, with a gold-braided cord strap round his cap, sun goggles covering his eyes, the clear-cut cold outline of nose, chin and mouth below . . . The Matildas' guns were cracking now, and the Storch was landing, no more than five hundred yards away.

Through his binoculars Bill saw the passenger jump down and start running; then he saw the long barrels of 105 mm field guns close by, and the Storch passenger running to them. The Matildas kept advancing. A few 88s began firing at them from Darant and there, farther off, half hidden among the houses, were German tanks, Mark IIIs and a few Mark IVs, about thirty in all, waiting on the right flank of the Matildas.

From directly ahead the 105 mm field guns opened fire over open sights. The lone figure who had been the passenger in the Storch was running from that battery to another. The heavy shells were crashing overhead, bursting among the trees. The Matildas were now being engaged from two directions simultaneously, by the 105s in front and by Mark IIIs and 88s to their right. D Company was pinned down with the Matildas. A Company was breaking away to the left and going straight for the 88s. Hammond had called for maximum artillery fire on the 105s; the German tanks were partially masked by the houses and were not so dangerous at the moment. By God, A were going in like demons – he could hear the continuous clatter of their Brens and the roar of bursting grenades. The 88s fell suddenly silent; the thunder of the 105s became less as the heavy 25-pounder fire knocked out two guns and killed the crew of a third.

Bill scrambled down to find Captain Griffin beside his truck. 'Griff,' he cried, 'take the carriers and go past A, on their left. Get into Darant. George, switch fire support to C as soon as they pass A.'

He climbed back into his truck, even as C Company ran out into open formation and began to advance, the twelve carriers on their left. Bill said, 'Get me Longhorn . . . Longhorn, how are things your side? Over.'

'Resistance slackening.'

'Push on then, into Darant. There are about thirty Mark IIIs and IVs at the far end of the village. Try and force them out, so that we have the whole village. Out.'

He took stock, considering. No tanks yet built could withstand field artillery firing at them from under six hundred yards. So the 105s would have to be put out of action or forced to pull back . . . ah, they were going now, the half-tracks coming up through the steady bursting of British shells to pull the guns out of their exposed position, outflanked by the advance of A and C Companies. Hammond ought to be able to take his Matildas into Darant now, and join up with Smythe, so that together they'd be strong enough to push the German tanks right out and away. Meantime, he himself had no reserve – better pull D and the carriers out of action and take them into Darant – call the anti-tank battery up, too . . . tell A to take over as close support infantry for Hammond's tanks . . . get George to range the 25-pounders onto the Mark IIIs . . .

Slater called to him, 'Sir, message from General Macartney. His column is held up in front of St Vith but has inflicted and is inflicting heavy damage and casualties on enemy. Both columns will withdraw to Billan by the same routes as they came out, starting from present positions at 1200 hours . . . I've acknowledged, sir.'

Bill nodded absently. Out there one Matilda was on fire, its turret askew, the 2-pounder gun and co-axial machine-gun pointing to the ground. That would jam the exit and the poor devils of crew would not be able to get out. The other Matildas were moving into Darant, through the gap where the 88s had been. The Mark IIIs were firing steadily, but slowly, holding their positions. Bill wondered if he was justified in pushing on to secure the whole of Darant. He'd take more casualties in doing it, and the order to retire had already been given . . . Damn it, he would go on. His task was to frighten the wits out of the German high command, and the more stick he gave these troops facing him the more he would have succeeded. He thought back to the German infantry running out of the wood. You didn't often see that. They must have been second-line troops – funny to find them with a crack armoured division; but in any case, they *had* run, and German armour *had* been defeated in open battle. It had been well worth while.

Slater came to him, saying, 'Message from A, sir. Larson was killed leading the assault on Darant . . . an 88 shell to himself.'

Bill turned away, feeling sick. A moment later he braced himself and turned back. 'Tell Captain Cowling to come up and take over command of A. Turlett to command headquarters company as well as being signal officer. He has a good signal sergeant.'

That evening he sat in General Macartney's small private room in the chateau outside Billan, a bottle of whisky on the table between them, and glasses of whisky and water in their hands. The general

349

was saying, 'You've got to release those two companies of 14 Royal Tanks you've had in Gadforce, Miller – GHQ was insistent . . . and the two companies of South Yorks . . . and the company of Macdonalds . . . and the light ack-ack battery.'

'Are they all going back to their parent units, sir?'

'Not a chance. GHQ's still playing patch, patch, patch. They're going to some newly organized force. I've forgotten it's name already, but command of all of them passes from you to the new force at midnight tonight . . . at 2359 hours, to be precise.' He took a healthy drink of his whisky. 'You did damn well, Miller . . . better than I did on the west, to tell the truth. My infantry were sticky at St Vith, and wouldn't keep up with the tanks . . . I'll see that you get something for your part in this . . . gallant counterattack, shall we call it? Or forlorn hope?'

'I think we did what General Gort expected of us, sir,' Bill said.

'We lost twenty-four tanks altogether, by the time we'd disengaged . . . and fifty-six men killed, two hundred and twenty wounded . . . quite a lot of soft transport knocked out – for what?'

'You said our object was to give the Germans a fright, sir, and we did. If that fellow – I'm sure it was the divisional commander – hadn't personally come do vn from his Storch and given his artillery-fire orders, I'm sure we could have gone on another mile or two, and overrun a lot of their gun and administrative areas.'

'That was the 7th Panzer Div you were up against – Rommel's their commander, so that was probably him in the Storch. I was fighting your friend von Krug . . . crafty bugger, craftier than Rommel, but not as aggressive . . . Yes, we did our job, Miller. We did what we were ordered to, but . . . was it a good order? Between you and me, I think that by now General Gort is a slave to events. He doesn't act, he reacts, as best he can.'

'Our counterstroke was an original action, sir,' Bill said obstinately, 'and I feel that it was worth it, even though I lost some good officers and men. We expected it to be much worse. We beat the Germans, man for man, and none of us will forget it.'

'You may be right,' General Macartney said. 'I hope so . . . Is your force organized for the defence of your sector of Billan by now?'

'Yes, sir. We were pretty well dug in by dark. The men are tired, though. Let's hope we get a rest soon. They've been moving and

350

fighting practically without a break since 10 May.'

'Whether we get a rest or not will depend on how the Germans see our counterstroke of today. Good night.'

At 0715 hours the following day, 23 May, as Bill was being served breakfast at the headquarters-company cook truck, Slater came to him with a message: 'Intelligence report from GHQ, sir.' Bill read:

> All forward movement of German Army Group B has halted in area ARRAS – BOULOGNE stop some German armour reported withdrawing from SEDAN front towards BILLAN.

Bill flung the message in the air. 'Do we still have that bottle of champagne anywhere, Tom?'

'Yes, sir. It's pretty warm, but . . .'

'Bring it out, and a mug, and my spare bottle of whisky. We did it. Gort was right, and we did it . . .! We'll go round the companies to drink the men's health and tell them that they're going to get a rest because of what they did yesterday. They forced the Germans to halt their advance!'

'Yes, sir . . . The post corporal gave me this, sir.' He held out his hand, containing a pale blue envelope addressed to Gunnar Larson, Esq., 1st Batt. Queen's Own Wessex Rifles. 'It's from his fiancée, sir.'

Bill said harshly, 'I'll send it back unopened, when I write . . . to her, and to his parents, later today. Not now, not now!'

'Very good, sir.'

23

May 1940: Flanders

It was late in the morning of 27 May, and Bill was sitting in the front room of an estaminet in Estevelles, on the canal de la Haute Deulle. The new, weaker Gadforce had been operating as a semi-independent flank guard since the counterstroke at Billan, moving position only once, for the German forward movement had not started again until yesterday. The great counterattack had made them stop for five days, five vital days in which Lord Gort had been able to regain control over the BEF and, more important, take stock of his true strategic situation.

At 11.00 p.m. on 27 May Gadforce had been placed under command of III Corps, Lieutenant General Haines, who had signalled two hours later that he would visit Gadforce this day, before noon.

Bill waited, studying a Michelin map spread out on the wine-stained wooden table before him. GHQ had not issued any proper topographical maps for the past three days, so Bill had ordered the seizure of all Michelin road maps of the area from a bookstore in Douai, where Gadforce had been on the 25th. Here in Estevelles they were a few miles north of Douai, facing west across the Deulle. Other British forces stretched away along the line of the same canal, then continued north-westward along the canal d'Aire, the canal Neufossée, and the canal d'Aa to reach the English Channel between Calais and Dunkirk. All these British troops along the so-called Canal line, were facing west, warding off the now renewed threats of the German Army Group B towards Calais. A few miles behind them, other troops of the BEF were facing east, against the German Army Group A. North of Ypres that line was held by French and Belgians, to reach the Channel near Nieuport, about twenty miles east of Dunkirk.

So here we are, Bill thought gloomily, the whole BEF, some French, and all that remained of the Belgian Army, shut into a wedge, its point down near Douai, the east flank reaching the sea at Nieuport, the west flank – this Canal line – between Calais and

Dunkirk; and the whole wedge under attack from both east and west by greatly superior forces. So what was to be done? Think offensively! German Army Group B was certainly sweeping on towards Dunkirk, but that meant that they had their backs towards the main French armies to the south-west. The French should mount an all-out counterstroke aimed at cutting off that armoured head of Army Group B. If that could not be done, General Gort would have to attempt to do something of the same sort himself. If nothing was done, the answer would be . . . the defeat and surrender of the whole BEF, over a quarter of a million men and all their guns, vehicles, tanks and stores. Suppose the BEF struck east, against Army Group A, heading up towards Holland, perhaps to recapture Antwerp? From there the navy could re-embark them, take them round to France's west-coast ports, and land them to fight again. But that would take the BEF farther away from the French, and there could be no real hope of success unless the two armies cooperated in a single stroke.

From the doorway Slater said, 'The corps commander's here, sir.'

Bill put on his steel helmet and went out. General Haines climbed out of his staff car, and touched his short leatherbound swagger cane to the peak of his cap as Bill saluted.

'Miller? Glad to meet you.' Bill led him inside. The general glanced at the map and said, 'Michelin road map . . . we're using them, too. How the hell the gunners manage to do predicted fire off them I don't know, but they do . . . Sit down.' He sat down himself, opposite. 'What were you doing with the map?'

'Trying to work out what is the best way to attack the Germans, sir.'

The general was small and wiry and wore big horn-rimmed glasses. His eyes were pale blue behind them, his hair dark and his upper lip long. Bill thought, there's a lot of Celtic blood in there. The general said, 'The French should attack from the west, and we should attack towards them, to cut off Army Group B's head, then we'd rejoin the main French battle front . . . but it won't happen. The C-in-C told me so this morning. Instead, he is thinking of ordering us – the whole BEF – to fight our way south from this general line . . . cut our way through the middle of the German Army Group B. The code name for the operation is Dragon.'

353

'And then roll them up towards the sea, sir?' Bill said eagerly, 'I[f] the French would put six or seven divisions into it, all their armour[ ] and all their air force, we could really smash Army Group B, befor[e] Army Group A could influence the battle.'

'We could, *if* . . .' the general said grimly, 'but the purpose o[f] Dragon is not offensive. It is to get ourselves out of this trap . . . an[d] there is no chance of French cooperation or support.'

'But . . . that corridor is still twenty miles wide,' Bill said. 'It stil[l] must have ten to twelve armoured and motorized divisions in it, an[d] we're only . . . six divisions with the equivalent of one armoure[d] division in the way of tanks. I don't think it's feasible, especially i[f] our motive is escape. To have the faintest chance, the men's motive [–] and motivation – must be to destroy Germans.'

'I agree,' the general said, 'I'm trying to get all the tanks I can[,] because if Lord Gort orders Dragon, my corps will be leading, wit[h] you under command. I shall give you most of the tanks, and you wi[ll] be the spearhead. I like what I have heard about your work in th[e] counterstroke from Billan.'

'Thank you, sir, but . . .'

'Don't but me, Miller . . . those will be your orders. The breakou[t] may begin tomorrow at dawn, so prepare to move down to Doua[i] after dark. You'll meet your tanks there – about a hundred, probabl[y] in three regiments, including some light tanks . . . Then be prepare[d] to kick off the attack heading southward from Douai astride this roa[d] – N43 – heading for Cambrai.'

'I was there in '18!' Bill exclaimed.

'So was I . . . waiting with my cavalry regiment for the grea[t] breakthrough . . . a bit different from this breakout . . . I'm goin[g] round my divisions. Good luck, and . . . whatever the orders sa[y] about breaking out, you make your men understand that there wi[ll] be no breakout until all the Germans in the way have been killed. S[o] . . . it's not a breakout, it's an attack!'

'Yes, sir.'

When the general had gone, Bill returned to his map, calling fo[r] his batman to bring him a beer from the cellars of the estaminet. Bee[r] glass in hand, he thought, this breakout is lunacy. This really will b[e] a forlorn hope. How am I to get the men . . . and the officers . . . t[o] go into such an affair with the dash and determination they mus[t] show to have any chance of success? The best way, in the past, fighting, say, Attila or Genghis Khan, would be to make everyone understand that there was no such thing as honourable surrender; that the enemy would give no quarter, so you might as well take some of them with you as die garrotted like a criminal. But with the enemy being twentieth-century Germans, no one would believe him, though in fact the Germans had committed one atrocity, murdering about eighty prisoners of the Royal Warwicks a few days ago. He might stress that, but . . . it wouldn't wash. So, back to basic principles. Stand to your front! One day, long ago, Morgan Lloyd had told him he would have to grow out of 'the regiment' before he could be a good higher commander; but it seemed to him that without 'the regiment' a general would have nothing to command, no men willing to follow him and obey his orders. He would be building on dust if he had not steeped himself and his men in the best traditions of his regiment, of all regiments: comradeship, self-sacrifice, self-respect, one for all and all for one . . . the things that were drummed into you from the day you joined, on parade grounds and football fields, and fields of manoeuvre, and finally, all over the world, in battle.

He had no other recourse. He would tell the men the truth, and tell them what he expected of them, company by company, today before dark.

By five o'clock no confirmatory orders had been received about Operation Dragon and Bill decided he must go round his companies. He made ready to leave the estaminet, brief speaking notes in the breast pocket of his battle-dress blouse, accompanied by Slater, who was carrying copies of a written warning order for the move and operation next day. As they left the estaminet, Lieutenant Turlett, the signal officer, stuck his head out of the back of the signals truck, calling, 'Message has come in from BEF, sir . . . we're deciphering it now. It'll be ready in about five minutes.'

Bill stepped back into the shelter of the estaminet, for it was raining, and waited. For a moment he had thought of ignoring the message and continuing with his plan to speak to the companies, but he had at once dismissed the thought. GHQ's messages were usually either unnecessary or vitally important: he had to know which, in this case.

Turlett came running in, rain dripping from his helmet, and produced a signal form from under his cape. Bill read:

From GHQ to GADFORCE operation DRAGON cancelled stop GADFORCE will move immediately to area WEST of DIXMUDE on YSER on arrival GADFORCE will come under command 6 DIV stop GERMAN attack from EAST believed imminent this area stop 34 coy RASC is placed under command GADFORCE in ESTEVELLES immediately ACK.

'Christ!' Bill exploded. 'Get corps on the blower and tell them we've been ordered out of their command. GHQ may not have bothered to tell them.'

'The signal was repeated to III Corps, sir,' Turlett said.

'So I see, but that doesn't mean they've actually had it. Make sure that they have.'

'Very good, sir.'

Bill said to Slater, 'Send out a warning order to all units: prepare for immediate move northward, detailed orders will follow . . . Find out how many vehicles that RASC company has, and what size . . . probably 3-tonners, but we must be sure . . . And send my compliments to Colonel Marshall.'

He sat down in front of the map. There was Dixmude up near the top-right corner . . . about sixty kilometres, or thirty-seven miles almost due north. The best road there would be through Ypres . . . but had he not seen in an intelligence report that one of the BEF divisions was heavily engaged just east of Ypres? If they'd fallen back even a mile or two, the road through Ypres would be blocked, and in any case it might be jammed with transport and guns . . . better find out.

He scribbled a note on a message pad and called, 'Driver, take this to the signals truck at once, please.'

Now, this could not be a tactical move, though some common sense care would have to be taken to keep units together. In view of the generally unstable conditions of the fronts to both east and west he must break the force up into sub-units and make sure that each sub-unit commander realized where he had to go and how to get there if his sub-unit was separated from others. The gunners had plenty of men and vehicles, so it might be a good idea to put Marshall in charge of the move, with orders to leave guides at every single junction and crossroads . . . that would mean having more gunners

356

trucks come along at the very tail to pick up the guides . . . Speed – 15 m.i.h. would be safe, in this rain and poor visibility, with the certainty of running into unexpected obstacles . . . He didn't have enough Michelin maps to issue them down to company and battery commanders. Was there time to have diagrammatic copies of the route made? The battalion clerks could do it, starting at once; but first he must choose the route and mark it on a master map for them to copy; and that depended on hearing from GHQ about Ypres. He sat back, feeling that he was on a treadmill that had begun to quicken its pace, and would continue to go faster and faster, until he must run like a madman merely to stay in the same place.

Turlett came back into the room and Bill said, 'I can't wait for an answer to that message about Ypres. Get on the corps command net and ask permission to speak direct to the division in Ypres . . . and ask their GOC or G1 the question. I want an answer in five minutes.'

Lieutenant Colonel Marshall of the artillery came in and Bill said, 'Sit down, Joe . . . Gadforce has been ordered to go to Dixmude. I am going to make you responsible for traffic control. There's nothing more important . . . We won't get into action until we get there, but we *won't* get there at all without really perfect traffic control. It's a matter of nuts and bolts. Get George to help you work it out. We were in the same syndicate for a big movement exercise at the Staff College, and he's wizard at it. Use as many men as you need . . . use lights, guides in pairs at least, armed . . . have officers ready to answer questions who know what the answers are . . .'

'Yes, sir,' Marshall said, looking dubious. 'What is the route . . . and the order of march . . . the start time . . . starting line?'

'All in good time,' Bill said.

Turlett came back in. 'I got through right away, sir. It's 6 Div, sir, whom we come under command of. Their G1 told me that we can safely pass through Ypres unless something unexpected happens in the night. There may be some German shelling on the road, as they – 6 Div – are using it for their nightly supply and ammunition columns. He wants to know when you expect to pass through, and he wants someone to make contact to receive his GOC's orders.'

'Tell him I'll tell him in an hour . . . and I'll send off a liaison officer at about the same time, who can get the orders and coordinate our passage through Ypres with 6 Div's traffic staff.'

357

He paused, considering, then spoke. 'Is Major Hodge here? Good.
You'll go, Pete, as the liaison officer, with the RSM. You'll make a
strong team. Now, we'll have a conference to plan the move, here, in
ten minutes.'

Ten minutes later, with Hodge, Harris, Marshall, Millington and
Slater standing round the table, Bill began, 'The move is from here
to the west bank of the Yser opposite Dixmude. We shall be crossing
the lines of communication of most of the BEF, by night, in pouring
rain. *Every* junction, where anyone could possibly go wrong, must
be marked, without possibility of the mark being moved or stolen or
obliterated. Use guides wherever possible . . . Now, let's agree on
the route we will take. I'm going to pencil my ideas in on this map,
watch carefully and speak up if you have any comments or suggestions for choosing some other route – give your reasons, one, two,
three, don't waffle, we don't have any time to waste. No changes
after the conference, because as soon as we have agreed on the route
and I have marked it on this map in red ink, I am going to have my
headquarters clerks make copies of it for company and battery commanders. Now, here's Estevelles . . .'

At 5.45 a.m. in cold daylight, Bill eased himself carefully down from
his command truck at the road junction half a mile west of Ysertoren,
on the west bank of the Yser, facing Dixmude across the canalized
river. 46 Field Regiment had dropped off into fields two miles back
south-west down the road behind him, and was now ready to fire at
any targets in range. The anti-tank battery commander was at his
side, the trucks towing the 2-pounders in line behind. Most of his
battalion was in trucks pulled off the road behind or close in front.
There was no anti-aircraft protection except the Bren guns, but the
skies were lowering and promised more of the rain which had fallen
continuously through the night, stopping only an hour ago. Bill
turned to Slater. 'Tom, tell Captain Cowling to take A Company and
hold the bridge at Ysertoren – this side of the river. One troop of
2-pounders to go with him.'

He leaned back against the hood of the truck as the bustle of
movement and the grind of engines began again round him. That
had gone on all night, in the nightmare passage from Estevelles. In
some spots the route markers had been wrongly placed and he had to

358

decide whether to follow the route now marked or take the rest of the convoy, behind him, by the correct but different route. In every case he had decided to follow the markings as they had been set out. Marshall and his gunners would not make any gross mistakes, and they all knew what the destination was. So, as long as the column stuck together, they would all arrive opposite Dixmude, perhaps a little late, but together and ready to fight.

The matter of the route markers was nothing like the worst of the night's passage. As he had suspected, in its sudden move Gadforce had to cross the lines of communication of all that part of the BEF which was facing east, down the east side of the wedge into which the German attacks had forced it. At every crossroads there had been halts to allow columns of ammunition lorries to go east, or columns of ambulance cars to go west. Sometimes the road had been blocked by the vehicles of a mobile workshop, heading north, or a casualty clearing station, heading south.

The worst problem, however, was the Belgian refugees, mixed now with Dutch, all pouring down from the north-east. With the various army units, Bill had been always able to sort out the muddle, or clear the blocked road, by the magic of his red gorget patches and the red band painted round his steel helmet. He had often thanked God that General Macartney had been such a stickler in insisting that he get and wear them. Every time they came to an obstruction, he had jumped down and gone forward, with Slater on one side and Corporal Driver on the other, flashlight in hand. Driver then shone the flashlight on Bill's torso and head with the imposing red bands round the helmet, while Bill stopped a truck to ask who was in charge. Then, a few minutes later, Bill had been able to say, 'I have priority of movement here, major, and you must halt your column until mine has passed over this crossroads,' and so it had always happened. Each time Bill had given thanks not only to General Macartney but to the training and discipline of the British soldier, who seemed to take an almost sensual pleasure in obeying the orders of his superior officer, even in such a damned mess as this campaign was becoming. But the civilian refugees, and the thousands of Belgian deserters among them – there was no stopping *them*, except by main force. The trucks and lorries and the big artillery quads towing the 25-pounders had simply ground forward, here and there running over a foot or crushing a body against a wall. Twice Bill had ordered his men to fire to clear a crossroads, in each case leaving a few men and women dead or writhing and screaming in the dark rain.

The strain on Bill had been great, wondering whether Marshall's men would indeed lead the column to Dixmude . . . passing through Ypres at two in the morning, under desultory shelling from German 105s and 150s . . . passing a burning lorry full of mortar ammunition in a narrow street, the bombs bursting every few seconds . . . ducking instinctively but pointlessly as his own truck edged past . . . then on into the flat lands of northern Flanders, mostly polder. In winter this would be flooded and impassable off the raised and metalled main roads; but now the land was basically dry, under a slimy, slippery surface caused by recent rain. The bridges over the Yser–Commines canal to the east funnelled the refugees into intermittent floods of humanity across Gadforce's path. But by then the light was coming, and Bill left Slater to deal with the refugees, while, hunched over the map, he decided how he should dispose of his force until orders came, and what steps he could take to find out where the Germans were and what they were doing.

Slater said, 'A Company and the anti-tank troop have disappeared into Ysertoren, sir . . . no sounds of shooting.'

Bill yawned, stretched, and said, 'Now, where are Peter and the RSM? They're supposed to meet us here to tell us what 6 Div want us to do.'

Slater said, 'Major Hodge was on the blower just now, sir. He's two miles back down the road, on his way.'

Bill nodded, saying nothing. The sea was about fifteen miles away, north-west at Nieuport, due north at Ostend. The main road on which he was now standing led west by Furnes and behind La Panne and Bray Dunes to Dunkirk, nearly twenty-five miles due west of his present position. The only obstacles to tank movement were the Yser, the Furnes canal and another nameless canal that ran along parallel with the sea coast a couple of miles inland to Dunkirk. He must think about . . . He stifled another yawn and leaned his head against the still-warm bonnet of the truck.

A voice was murmuring, 'Sir . . . colonel, Major Hodge and the RSM are here.'

Bill stood up and away from the truck with a start . . . He'd been asleep standing up, like a ruddy horse. Well, a man could do almost anything, if the necessity was great enough. Hodge and the RSM were saluting. Bill said wearily, 'What orders for us, Pete?'

Hodge came up and looked at the map spread out on the truck bonnet. 'Sir . . . the GOC 6 Div told us he was under increasingly fierce attack in Ypres itself, and he believes that the Germans will try to out-flank him to the north, that is, between Ypres and here. Another division is supposed to be coming in on his left, this side, any moment now – I believe it's 3 Div – but he wants us to hold the sector from Steenstraat, here, to Dixmude, both inclusive, until this other div arrives, if it ever does. He's sent some sappers with me, with explosives, to prepare bridges for demolition.'

Bill said, 'Hm . . . about ten kilometres of front . . . the Yser in the north half, the Ypres–Commines canal in the south . . . four bridges . . . Christ, I wish we still had those two companies of South Yorks . . . All right. I'll put force headquarters in Nieuwkapelle, here, close to the guns. A Company's already in Ysertoren. D will defend the bridge and village of Steenstraat with another troop of anti-tank guns. B will defend the bridges at Merkem and Knokke-brug, with a troop of anti-tank guns. C will be in battalion reserve east of Nieuwkapelle, with the carriers and the fourth anti-tank troop. Artillery FOOs, sapper parties and a mortar section to each forward company. All companies are to patrol the canals in their sector to make sure the Germans don't sneak some infantry over in rubber boats, between the bridges. Tom, you work out and notify everyone of dividing lines . . . I've got to talk to Colonel Marshall about the artillery plan and make quite sure that *all* his guns can put down defensive fire in support of *all* our positions. Then I'll issue the defensive and counterattack plans.'

He hobbled a little distance away down the road, westward, leaving the group of officers with their heads together over the bonnet of the command truck. He'd given the main orders, let them work out the minor details while he thought – what next? And after that? And after that? The treadmill was picking up speed again.

Slater came to him. 'I've given out the preliminary orders, sir. Shall we start moving back to Nieuwkapelle?'

Bill said, 'Right away. Did you tell 6 Div that my HQ would be there?'

'Yes, sir.'

Bill climbed up and settled back in his seat. He must keep awake. He must eat something, for he was ravenously hungry. But if he ate would he not feel even more sleepy? What about some coffee? There was no coffee; they'd run out of it in the headquarters mess four days ago. Strong tea, then . . . His head fell back and he began to snore.

Bill returned to his headquarters in a little cottage on the eastern outskirts of Nieuwkapelle at 11.15 a.m., after visiting each of his forward companies and seeing how they were getting on in the digging of their defences, siting their anti-tank guns and preparing the bridge or bridges for which they were responsible for demolition. The bed in the back room, visible through the open inner door, looked wonderfully inviting, but he sat down in the chair at the table and thought, what now, what must be done before I can rest?

Slater came in. 'Message from 6 Div, sir. 3 Div is passing through Ypres now and will be taking over our positions as far north as Knokke-brug, inclusive, as soon as possible, probably within two hours.'

Bill said, 'Good. I'll just have time to write some letters to next of kin . . . and our companies will just have time to finish digging their trenches, for someone else to use. Just once I'd like to occupy a set of trenches that someone else has dug . . . Any news of Germans? D were expecting some action when I left them, oh, an hour ago.'

'Yes, sir. D have now reported enemy patrols working up to the canal opposite them – that was ten minutes ago . . . they saw tanks in the distance. The 2-pounders took a couple of shots, but didn't do any damage.'

'They shouldn't have fired,' Bill said crossly. 'They've just given away their position for nothing.'

'Major Mainwaring says they weren't in their final positions yet when they fired, sir.'

'All right. Pass the information on to 6 Div . . . and find out whether I am now just to hold the Dixmude crossing, with all my force.'

Alone, he carefully wrote two letters to next of kin, then, taking another signal form, began a third letter:

Darling Lesley,
I'm so tired I can hardly see straight, but overall we are in good shape. The men are as tired as I am, in a different way – more

physically than mentally exhausted – but they are bearing up marvellously, as usual. I have a feeling that I may reach you before this letter does, so will say no more, except – I love you.

Turlett, the signal officer, entered. 'Sir, a most immediate and top-secret message from GHQ is coming in. It's short.'

Bill thought, but pithy, perhaps? Move back to Estevelles? Attack German Army Group A and roll it up south-west from Dixmude to the Ardennes? He laughed and said, 'Get me a big mug of tea, Turl, there's a good fellow.'

'Of course, sir.'

A signal clerk came in. 'Here's the message, sir, deciphered.'

It was from GHQ, BEF, to Gadforce:

> Belgian King is surrendering whole Belgian Army today GADFORCE will hold line of YSER from incl YSERTOREN to incl NIEUPORT.

Bill swore and sat down. Here was that unpleasant sensation again, of the ground sliding under his feet, of a movement he could not control but must somehow keep pace with or be swept away. Must get a grip on himself . . . 3 Div would be taking over the southern half of his present responsibilities, including the three southernmost bridges, in one to two hours. That left him only one, the Ysertoren bridge leading over the Yser to Dixmude . . . so he could leave A Company there. But could he wait for 3 Div to arrive before abandoning the others? No, he could not; north of Ysertoren there was now *nothing* to stop the Germans. He must get some troops up there at once.

Turlett came back with a pot of tea, followed by Slater and Major Hodge. Bill said, 'Warning order at once: prepare to move – all except A Company and attached troops, which will hold present position stop Gadforce HQ moving to Furnes, at east entry to town, on route N302. 46 Field to move guns to same general area . . . speak to Colonel Marshall on the blower and confirm that that's OK before you send it out. Blow canal bridges at Steenstraat, Merkem and Knokke-brug forthwith . . . that's all for now.'

He thought, we can move inside half an hour – but how? The RASC lorry park was here, behind Nieuwkapelle, so he could embus

C and send it plus the reserve anti-tank troop off at once to the farthest north point – Nieuport. Now, how many bridges in his new sector? God damn it, fifteen miles was too much for a battalion to cover . . . can't be helped; have to do the best he could . . . there was a road bridge over the Yser at Schoorbekke, about six miles north of Ysertoren . . . another at Hoogland, north-east of Furnes . . . better put B to hold both these, with its anti-tank troop, then C and A in reserve near Furnes. Furnes was rather far back for him to take immediate action if he had to, but it seemed the best available. If he put his reserves any farther forward he was in danger of not being able to move laterally, for in this flat country all movement would be under scrutiny of any Germans who came up to the east bank of the Yser – not to mention their flying observers.

Slater came back. 'D Company reports ready to move as soon as ordered, sir . . . but there are Germans watching them across the canal. They have blown up their bridge. B report they'll be blowing their bridges in less than five minutes. I've sent out the 3-tonners, sir.'

'C Company embus at once, then – RV for Gadforce less A Company is the T-junction on route 302 one mile west of Ysertoren . . . Warn 3 Div we must move and there may be some Germans this side of the canal and river by the time they arrive.'

'I'll try to get them to hurry, sir . . . We've had another message from GHQ, confirming that the whole BEF will be evacuated through Dunkirk and beaches to the east of it, in cooperation with the navy from Dover.'

'Who's holding the line west of Dunkirk?' Bill asked quickly.

'I Corps, sir.'

'Hm. Well, they'd better hold firm . . . meantime, let's get moving. I want this headquarters in full operation from Furnes within an hour from now, at the most.'

During the night the remains of the Belgian Army passed through, flooding back over the Yser bridges, trudging westward in thick, disorganized masses, just as the civil population and many deserters had done the previous two nights. If any Germans had infiltrated the mobs of Belgian soldiers, it would have been impossible for the British troops guarding the Yser line to prevent them crossing without mowing down thousands of Belgians, too . . . but, as far as Bill knew and as far as his companies reported to him, no Germans came. He thought, perhaps they don't realize yet what utter demoralization and chaos is before them, to take advantage of as they wish.

The next day, 29 May, the weather changed, from cloudy and wet to clear and sunny; and the Stukas came. By now the high command of German Army Group A had learned that the Yser was held all the way to the sea, and they set about demoralizing the defenders while they moved up armour and infantry to break through towards Dunkirk, thus sealing the fate of the BEF. Without any light Bofors or heavy 3.7-inch ack-ack guns, the Brens of the Wessex did little damage, causing no certain kills and claiming only two winged; but nor did the men panic or leave their positions, as they had that first time so few days ago. Late in the day, German infantry and armour attacked, in coordination with the dive-bombers, against three of the bridges which Gadforce was holding; they did not succeed in seizing any of them, and Bill then ordered them all destroyed. German action was reduced to artillery harassing while they prepared assault bridging for a more formal attack to get across the Yser. Twenty-five miles to the west, beyond Dunkirk, the French and British lines were holding fast against the attacks of German Army Group B. So far the BEF wedge had held firm, though it was shrinking towards the north.

This situation could not last for long, Bill thought. The enemy was methodically piling up against him, and now they knew just how strong – or rather weak – he was. Tomorrow, before noon at the latest, they would come on in strength, along his whole front from Ysertoren to the sea. He must give them a bloody nose, make them pause, even . . . but how?

He had not solved that problem when, shortly after dark, Slater came to him with two messages from GHQ. The first ordered Gadforce to hand over its positions to Adamforce at 2100 hours. Adamforce, Bill knew, contained tanks and anti-aircraft artillery, so perhaps it would be able to hold the Yser line for another twenty-four or forty-eight hours. After that, the message continued, Gadforce would retreat through Furnes to Bray dunes, abandoning all its vehicles and guns in Furnes . . . and in the dunes it would await orders for evacuation by sea to England.

The second message decreed that henceforth Gadforce would be known as Millforce.

'Congratulations, sir,' Slater said, laughing. 'Someone at GHQ has at last noticed that you are in command.'

Bill was in no mood for humour. 'Christ!' he exploded. 'We're just going to sneak out with our tails between our legs . . . leaving all our guns, our trucks, our radios . . . This battalion will not leave its rifles or Bren guns, by God! . . . but we'll leave everything else, including our self-respect!'

'That's too hard on all of us, sir,' another voice said, and Bill saw the RSM had come in. Harris continued, 'The French let us down, and the Belgians ran away. We've done our bit . . . the men have done everything you've asked of them, and more.'

'I don't care,' Bill almost shouted. 'Two thousand of us have fought forty thousand of these swine to a standstill wherever and whenever we've met them, for two weeks, and I'm not going to give up like this . . . We'll attack! The bridge at Nieuport is still intact. I'll concentrate the whole force up there, and go for them when they're least expecting it, when they think they're going to sweep us up like rotten apples.'

Harris said, 'We'll lose a lot of men for nothing if you do that, sir. We have no tanks . . . and, without them, you yourself have said . . .'

'I'll take the tanks out of Adamforce,' Bill said. 'Forge an order that they are to come into Gadforce . . .'

He stood in the middle of the room, fists clenched, jaws working. After a long pause Harris said, 'It won't work, sir.'

After another long pause, Bill said, 'You're right, Bogey . . . Get out a warning order at once, Tom. Mr Harris, make some notes, please. We won't abandon our provost or signal motorcycles, so make sure they are all full of petrol, and that extra rations are taken on the carriers . . . manhandle the mortars and six rounds per mortar as far as the top of Bray dunes . . . every man except Bren No. 1s to have full pouches plus a bandolier of fifty rounds. You and all the battalion clerks and MPs to stay with me – they'll be the only communications I have with the rest of the force . . . Tom, any communication with Adamforce yet?'

'Yes, sir. Major General Adam is here now.'

366

In the next hour, Bill oversaw the takeover by Adamforce of all his defensive positions and outposts; while his second-in-command, Major Hodge, gave out detailed orders for the withdrawal of Gadforce to Bray dunes, and the disposal of its guns, vehicles and heavy weapons. The field artillery stepped up its fire, to cover the takeover by Adamforce, and to use up, against German bodies, ammunition which it would otherwise have to abandon in fields outside Furnes.

The final retreat began. The forward Wessex companies did the first few miles from their positions on the Yser in their RASC lorries, then had to get out, as the lorries were abandoned and their engines smashed, and begin to march the four miles to Bray dunes. There they lay down in the cold sand and counted the hours till dawn. As the light spread, they mounted their Bren guns on the anti-aircraft tripod mounts and waited for the Stukas. Out to sea, trails of black smoke marked the passage of British destroyers in and out of Dunkirk. Close at hand, others were edging in close to the beach and sending ashore their few boats.

Bogey Harris, beside Bill in a slit trench in the sand, said, 'It'll take them a long time to get us all off this way, sir.'

Bill said, 'If ever! They'll have to use the piers at Dunkirk port . . . but, look, they're making causeways out of vehicles, running them out to sea and the men are climbing over them, out to the destroyers . . .'

The sun rose, but the sky darkened with smoke towering up in black columns from the city of Dunkirk, from ships burning in the narrow harbour. Out to sea, the destroyers came and went, came and went. Out of the blue sky the Stukas dived, and the bombs made fountains of sand on land and plumes of water in the sea. Hurricanes and Spitfires from England plunged in among the Stukas, machine-guns ripping, and half a dozen Stukas never lifted their noses out of their dives, but went straight on down into the shallow sea.

The sun sank. The men had been without water or food under the Stukas and shelling from inland for nearly sixteen hours, and still they waited. In the twilight a lone figure came down the beach, threading its way through the men, who crouched thick as fleas on a blanket on the yellow sand. The figure saw Bill's red-banded helmet and came towards him. When he was close, Bill saw that it was Richard Merton.

Bill stood up. 'Hullo, Richard. What are you doing here?'

Merton stared at him as though he had never seen him before. 'Miller . . . are you in command here?'

'Of my own force, yes.'

'March them to Dunkirk port, east mole. You should get away before dawn . . . you're only wearing a colonel's badges.'

'Yes. That's what I am.'

'No. You were made a brigadier the day before yesterday. It was in general orders.'

Bill laughed, without humour. Merton continued, 'I'm in Q Movements at the War Office. They sent me over three days ago to help organize evacuation. But there's nothing to organize.'

He seemed more than a little distrait, and Bill said, 'The battalion did marvels. You trained them well, Richard . . . Would you like a tot of rum? We've got a little left.'

Merton shook his head. 'No thanks. I don't want anything from you, Miller . . . or you, Harris . . . not now, or ever.'

He walked away down the darkening beach, his gas mask high on his chest in its haversack, his steel helmet flat on his head.

Bogey Harris said at last, 'I have a funny feeling that that's the last anyone will ever see of Colonel Merton. He may have thought of getting himself killed before – but meeting you settled it. I could read his mind . . . He tried to do you in and, instead, he did himself in. You won, you're going to the top, and he can't face it. You're a brigadier, and on your way.'

'There's a price,' Bill said. 'And it isn't I who have had to pay it.'

'It can't be helped, sir. It's our job. We all know you were ready to pay. It's war, the way war is. We're all proud of you, the ones who are here and know what you did, and . . . the others.'

Bill was silent for a long time, thinking of the absent dead. At last: 'Let's get the men moving,' he said brusquely.

The destroyer pulled away from the east mole in Dunkirk at dawn, and eased out into the channel, away from the straggling narrow catwalk along which thousands of soldiers had reached the ships. Six Stukas were diving out of the eastern light and a flight of Spitfires circling up from the north-west, the sun glinting on their wings. From his place jammed into a corner of the bridge, Bill thought there must be nearly a thousand soldiers on board the destroyer in addition to its crew of over a hundred. Dunkirk had been burning all night, and now, as the wind veered into the south, acrid black smoke swept out to sea in deep curtains, blanketing the destroyer's deck and making everyone on board choke and cough.

Ten minutes from the pier, two Stukas dived on the destroyer out of the sun, one behind the other. The first's big bomb fell on the crowded foredeck, and splinters of steel swept parts of the deck clear as though a giant broom had brushed everyone overboard, leaving only pools of blood and chunks of flesh and clothing. On the bridge the captain was on his knees, falling forward, coughing blood. Beside him lay a young sub-lieutenant, staring at the morning sky through dead eyes, the top of his head sheared off by a shard of steel. Bogey Harris was calling, 'Are you all right, sir?' but, before Bill could feel any emotion or respond to the question, the second Stuka's bomb struck the destroyer's flank at the starboard waterline, tearing a huge hole in the thin plates. Water rushed in. The vessel heeled more and more rapidly. Soon clean seawater was washing the foredeck clear of all the blood and bones and pieces of human flesh that had been littering it. The corpses of the captain and the sub-lieutenant slid down the bridge until they came up against the starboard rail, then the ship keeled over and Bill found himself in the sea. For a moment he thought of giving up, letting himself go under, for his bandaged leg still throbbed and he could not use it to swim. Then he heard Bogey's voice. 'Dusty, is thee all right? Not wounded? Thank God! Hold on to me . . . we must get a bit away afore she goes down.'

Bill felt strong arms under his shoulders and turned on his back, tilting his head back, floating as best he could. All round them the sea was dotted with heads. Life rafts were floating away from the sinking destroyer and men were heading for them. Soon they'd be desperately overcrowded – no room for such as he. He called weakly over his shoulder, 'Bogey, get to a raft. Save yourself. I'm done for.'

'Like hell!' the RSM answered succinctly. 'We'll both stay away from them. They're already overcrowded and the sea's full of other ships. Someone will pick us up soon enough.'

The rafts floated away to the north under the influence of wind and current. A huge patch of glistening oil marked the grave of the destroyer and the soldiers and sailors who had gone down in her. The sea was empty for a time, except for they two. Then Bogey said, 'Sail ahead, coming straight for us, sir.'

Bill thought, we'll be rescued. Perhaps, after all, the world will learn what the Queen's Own Wessex Rifles had done in the last three weeks. Perhaps he'd even get a bar to his DSO. He chuckled weakly, swallowed water and coughed.

'Take it easy,' Bogey said. 'They're not here yet.'

What of his battalion? How many had been lost in the destroyer, in the Stuka bombing and then the sinking? He knew he'd reached the Dunkirk mole with just under four hundred men of all ranks, for Bogey had given him the figures – about half the battalion's original strength; and that was something to be proud of, considering what they had done and been through. But when they reached England they'd have to be reorganized and re-equipped, for now they had nothing but the clothes they were wearing. Then they, and millions more, would have to be retrained, not to fight this Dunkirk battle over again, but to fight and win the sort of campaigns that would develop when the lessons of Dunkirk had been digested and the new weapons, the new tanks, the new communications, the new ideas, had come into service. They'd lost a campaign, with a vengeance, driven like rats back into the sea from which they had come. But they'd return; and he'd be leading them. He'd earned that right now, with the help of such as Bogey and the sacrifice of unnamed, unknown scores of others. He must not fail them.

Bogey said, 'Here they are, sir!' He raised his voice. 'Ship ahoy!'

Arms were lifting Bill up, strange voices calling. Someone was leaning over him; and through fading eyes Bill recognized his friend from long ago Dover days, Perry Hillman, the drunken poet of the Lord Nelson pub. He hadn't changed, for there was a bottle of whisky beside him at the wheel now. 'Have a drop, laddie,' he said. 'You look as though you need it. Especially as you'll have to face Dunkirk and the pier again. I can't go back to Dover with just two bods, however important . . . and by God you *are* somebody now! Look at those red patches! You've made yourself a real general!'

'At a price,' Bill whispered, but no one heard him.

Bogey came with a blanket and wrapped it round him. For a few moments more Bill felt fully conscious, awake, himself; then gradually everything began to slip away. He would go to London and see

Morgan Lloyd, of course, first thing; and find out what was being done about reorganizing the battalion. As he was a brigadier now, Morgan would probably take him to see the CIGS, and they'd talk of what was most urgently needed to recreate the British Army . . . Lesley would be waiting for him. The children would come as soon as they knew he was home. All these things ought to matter, but they didn't now. What mattered *now* was that he had fought and lost . . . and won. Victory lay far ahead, but it was within his new grasp. Slowly consciousness left him.

By the Green of the Spring

JOHN MASTERS

1918 dawns desolate over the fields of Flanders. Decimated by the worst war the world has ever seen, neither British nor German troops can break the deadlock of the trenches. After four years of murderous stalemate, peace seems buried for ever. But finally, one by one, the guns fall silent . . .

BY THE GREEN OF THE SPRING
relives the last terrible months of the Great War and the uneasy, exhausted peace which followed it.

BY THE GREEN OF THE SPRING
from the North-West Frontier to the war in France and the civil war in Ireland, John Masters follows the fortunes of four Kent families – the Cates, the Rowlands, the Strattons and the Gorses – through the cataclysm that ended the golden Edwardian dream for ever.

BY THE GREEN OF THE SPRING
is the third, self-contained volume of the **LOSS OF EDEN** trilogy, a magnificent conclusion to an enthralling epic of war and peace by a major contemporary novelist.

GENERAL FICTION   0 7221 0468 5   £2.50

Heart of War

by John Masters

January 1 1916: Europe is bleeding to death as the corpses rot from Poland to Gallipoli in the cruel grip of the Great War . . .

HEART OF WAR

- follows the fate and fortunes of the Rowland family and those people bound up in their lives, the Cate squirearchy, the Strattons who manage the Rowland-owned factory, and the humble, multi-talented Gorse family.

HEART OF WAR

- during the years 1916 and 1917, the appalling slaughter of the Somme and Passchendaele cuts deep into the hearts of the British people as military conscription looms over Britain for the first time in a thousand years.

HEART OF WAR

- is the second self-contained volume in a trilogy entitled LOSS OF EDEN. It is probably the crowning achievement in the long and distinguished career of one of our leading contemporary novelists.

GENERAL FICTION   0 7221 0467 7   £1.95

And, also by John Masters in Sphere Books:
NOW, GOD BE THANKED
NIGHTRUNNERS OF BENGAL
THE FIELD-MARSHAL'S MEMOIRS
FANDANGO ROCK
THE HIMALAYAN CONCERTO

THE MAGNIFICENT NOVEL
OF A NATION AT WAR

THE SIRENS OF AUTUMN

TOM BARLING

Set in the year 1940, THE SIRENS OF
AUTUMN is a vivid and compelling portrait of
men and women in wartime – and of two very
different families, the Coopers and the
Lutyens, who are brought together by fate to
share the hardships of that terrible year.

Rich in the detail of the period and crowded
with memorable characters, THE SIRENS OF
AUTUMN brilliantly evokes Britain's darkest
hour. For some, it will stir memories. For all
who read it, it will bring the past unforgettably
to life.

GENERAL FICTION   0 7221 1435 4   £1.95